Arthur Robert Pennington

The counter-reformation in Europe

Arthur Robert Pennington

The counter-reformation in Europe

ISBN/EAN: 9783741193576

Manufactured in Europe, USA, Canada, Australia, Japa

Cover: Foto ©Andreas Hilbeck / pixelio.de

Manufactured and distributed by brebook publishing software
(www.brebook.com)

Arthur Robert Pennington

The counter-reformation in Europe

THE
COUNTER-REFORMATION
IN EUROPE.

BY

REV. ARTHUR ROBERT PENNINGTON, M.A.,

Canon Non-Residentiary of Lincoln;

AND

Rector of Utterby, Lincolnshire;

AUTHOR OF 'THE LIFE OF ERASMUS,' 'THE LIFE OF WICLIF,' 'EPOCHS OF THE
PAPACY,' 'HISTORY OF THE CHURCH IN ITALY,' 'RECOLLECTIONS
OF PERSONS AND EVENTS,' ETC.

LONDON:

ELLIOT STOCK, 62, PATERNOSTER ROW, E.C.

1899.

PREFACE.

THE Counter-Reformation in Europe was the great subject of Ranke's 'Ecclesiastical and Political History of the Popes,' published about sixty years ago. His object was to give information on a period of history which had escaped the notice of ecclesiastical historians. The important matter before him was to give the reasons for the failure of the Lutheran Reformation to conquer Europe. With this view he sought for information in the archives at Vienna, Berlin and Venice.

Lord Macaulay, in his essay on Ranke's work, gives a history of four periods in which the Church of Rome, having suffered loss, afterwards regained its ascendancy. A few pages, however, in the *Edinburgh Review* on one of those periods, the Counter-Reformation, do not give room for an exhaustive treatment of this important subject. Besides, errors and serious omissions are to be found in it. He states that 'the history of the Order of Jesus is the history of the great Catholic reaction. That Order possessed itself at once of all the strongholds which command the public mind, of the pulpit, of the press, of the confessional, of the academies.' He then proceeds to show that when the Jesuits came to the succour of the

Papacy they found it in a very critical condition, but that afterwards, mainly through them, the tide of conquest was arrested in its course. He states that Protestantism, which during twenty-five years had overcome all resistance, was driven back through their instrumentality from the foot of the Alps to the borders of the Baltic.

Lord Macaulay has attached too much importance to the Order of the Jesuits. Protestantism in Italy, Spain and the Netherlands was not suppressed by them, but by the Roman and Spanish Inquisition, by the Pope, by Philip II. of Spain, and by the Dominicans. We shall see that in France, during the sixteenth century, the Jesuits have not exercised much influence, and that Germany has been the only country in which they at first made any progress. I have shown (pp. 55, 56) that they acted an important, but only a subordinate, part in this great drama.

In fact, after, as before, 1550, Protestantism continued to advance in Germany, in Poland, in Hungary, in the Scandinavian kingdoms, and in Austria. The principal agents in arresting its progress were, as we shall see, in addition to Philip II., Ferdinand of Austria and the Council of Trent. But the only reference to Philip II. is the following : 'Philip II. was a Papist in a very different sense from that in which Elizabeth was a Protestant.' Lord Macaulay does not bring forward the intense zeal with which Philip, and Ferdinand II. about thirty years after the death of Philip, laboured for the advancement of Romanism, but states incorrectly, as we shall see, that ' the Thirty Years' War was less a contest for the reformed doctrines than for national independence.' He does not make the least reference to the decrees of the Council of Trent in connection with the work of the Jesuits. But without them the Jesuits would have been unable to stay the advance of the Reformation.

Again he writes: 'The Catholic reaction went on at full speed in spite of the destruction of the Armada.' But this is a very serious misstatement. It will appear that the destruction of the Spanish Armada was a most important episode in the reign of Elizabeth, and in the general history of the Counter - Reformation, both in England and on the Continent. It was the means of saving Europe, as we shall see, from subjection to the Church of Rome. I have endeavoured to give prominence to this result. It has as yet been scarcely brought before readers of history. In fact, the bearing of the Counter-Reformation in England on the general struggle on the Continent has been omitted by writers of ecclesiastical history.

We have much information of late years as to the general history of this period from State Papers, letters, and other documents which have hitherto been buried in family or State archives in England or in foreign countries. We are only now in a position, through materials which have come before us, to understand that part of the history which is connected with this country, including the aims and schemes of the opponents of Elizabeth. No more important contribution has been made to the history of this time than the publication of the diaries of the English College at Douai and the letters of Cardinal Allen, which will be fully described. I have also obtained new and important information as to the spy system, and as to the training and work of Allen's seminary priests, as well as to the commencement of the work of the Jesuits in England. The papers brought before us in the course of the last few

years enable us to see in a way not seen before that Allen
was the leader of the Counter-Reformation in England,
and that if, separating his religious from his political
work, he had not stimulated the decaying zeal of Philip,
the Armada would never have been sent against England.
He thus, as we shall see, indirectly prevented the complete triumph of the Counter-Reformation not only in
England, but throughout the continent of Europe.

I add these errors to those which have been discovered
in Macaulay's essays and history in regard to Bacon,
Strafford, Laud, Hampden, Clive, Warren Hastings, and
others. We know that in many cases prejudices and
prepossessions led him to distort the truth, and to give
an incorrect view of these and other historical characters.
Notwithstanding these errors, he still has a hold upon the
admiration of his fellow-countrymen. His history is read
everywhere. It has been translated into several languages
of Europe. We believe that his style has been a cause
of the success of this work, and that it has served
to blind his admirers to the errors in his essays
and history. Professor Saintsbury pronounces a just
judgment on his style when he says that ' it is the
clearest style in English that does not, like those of Swift
and Cobbett, deliberately or scornfully eschew historical
ornament. What Macaulay means you can never, being
any degree short of an idiot, fail to understand.' I hold
that truthfulness and good faith are most important
qualities in everyone who undertakes to pronounce a
judgment on the events of history, and on those who have
acted an important part on the world's high stage. We
observe that these qualities are conspicuous in Bishop
Creighton's history of the Popes during the Reformation.
The following work gives the history of the period required

for the completion, of that work, beginning from the sack of Rome, the last event described by him in the time of Clement VII. He has stated that, on account of his numerous engagements, there is no probability that he will be able to complete his work. Thus we should be left without a description of a most important period of ecclesiastical history. My object is not only to correct the errors to which reference has been made, but also to give in a popular form a history of the Counter-Reformation from about 1558 to the Peace of Westphalia in 1648. I have placed at the beginning a list of works and of papers which I have found useful in writing this history. The foreign works particularly will be found to add very much to the information at the disposal of Ranke when his work was first published. As Lord Acton writes in his admirable lecture on the study of history : ' When Hallam wrote his chapter on James II. France was the only Power whose reports were available ; Rome followed and the Hague ; and then came the stores of the Italian States, and at last the Prussian and the Austrian papers, and partly those of Spain. The topics indeed are few on which the resources have been so employed that we can be content with the work done for us, and never wish it to be done over again. . . . I would not even venture to claim for Ranke, the real originator of the heroic study of the records, and the most prompt and fortunate of European pathfinders, that there is one of his seventy volumes that has not been overtaken, and in part surpassed. . . . It was his mission to preserve, not to undermine, and to set up masters in their proper sphere whom he could obey. The many excellent dissertations in which he displayed this art, though his successors in the next generation matched his skill and did still more thorough work, are the best introduction from which we can learn the technical process by which, within living memory, the story of modern history has been renewed.'

The conclusion to which Lord Acton wishes to bring us is that we must follow Ranke's example if we hope to be successful. He tells us, in fact, that we must never shrink from the labour of searching for materials, now examining a long-forgotten record, now a large mass of State Papers recently brought to light, now a field of battle ; that we must bring the subject before our readers in a style which will rivet their attention and give them a distinct idea of the scenes which pass before them. I trust that I have acted in the spirit and adopted the method here recommended, and that the new information obtained from the sources indicated has been made available for a most important period in the history of Europe.

LIST OF WORKS CONSULTED.

Allen, Cardinal, Life of, by Dr. Bellesheim.
—— Letters and Memorials of.
Baird, History of the Rise of the Huguenots.
Botta, Storia d' Italia.
Brompton, Letters of the Fathers of the Oratory of.
Butler, History of the English Catholics.
Butler, Tracts of.
Campian, Life of, by Simpson.
Cantu, Cæsare, Gli Eretici d' Italia.
Clarendon Papers, The, Vol. I.
Conclaves, The Papal, Trollope and Canon Pennington.
Dejob, De l'Influence du Concilo de Trente, Paris, 1884.
Dodd, History of the English Catholics.
Douai, Diaries of the College of.
Froude's British Seamen.
—— Lectures on the Council of Trent.
—— History of England, Vol. XI.
Gardner, S. R., History of England from the Accession of James I.
    to the Outbreak of the Civil War.
—— History of the Thirty Years' War.
Green, History of the English People.
Gustavus Adolphus, Life of, by Fletcher and Chapman.
Hallam, History of England.
Hübner, Count von, Monograph on Sixtus V.
Inquisition, Records of the.
Jessopp, One Generation of a Norfolk House.
Llorente, Histoire Critique de l'Inquisition d'Espagne.

McCrie, History of the Reformation in Italy.

Martin Phillippson, Contre-Revolution Religieuse.

Maurenbrecher, Geschichte der Katholiscen Reformation.

Moritz Brosch, Geschichte des Kirchenstaates.

Motley, United Netherlands.

Mutenelli, Storia Arcana d' Italia.

Pallavicini, Storia del Concilio Tridentino.

Panzani, Memoirs of, by Berrington.

Ranke, History of the Popes, Vols. I., II., III., translated by Sarah Austin.

—— History of France.

—— History of England.

Sarpi, Life of, by A. G. Campbell.

Sismondi, History of the Italian Republics.

State Papers, Domestic Series, A.D. 1581-1590.

Symonds, The Catholic Reaction.

Tracts for the Times: Catena Patrum (81); Deus, Natura, et Gratia (90).

Trent, History of the Council of, by Fra Paolo Sarpi, published in London in 1619 under the assumed name of Pietro Soave Polano, translated by Nathaniel Brent.

—— History of, by Rev. Dr. Littledale.

—— Martin Phillippson on.

—— Canons and Decrees of, translated by Rev. J. Waterworth.

ERRATA.

Page 22, line 20, *for* 'the' *read* 'her.'
Page 25, line 2, *for* 'pursuasion' *read* 'persuasion.
Page 35, line 5 from foot, *for* 'in' *read* 'by.'
Page 37, line 16, *for* 'Misaccio' *read* 'Masaccio.'
Page 42, line 3, *for* 'allegiance' *read* 'submission.'
Page 44, line 18, *for* 'this' *read* 'thus.'
Page 44, line 19, *for* 'Guistiani' *read* 'Giustiani.'
Page 44, line 20, *for* 'Adrian VII.' *read* 'Adrian VI.'
Page 47, line 19, *omit* 'not.'
Page 69, line 17 from foot, *for* 'Pius' *read* 'Paul.'
Page 130, line 20 from foot, *for* 'chiefly' *read* 'partly.'

CONTENTS.

CHAPTER I.

INTRODUCTORY.

CHAPTER II.

THE EARLY CAUSES OF THE COUNTER-REFORMATION.

CHAPTER III.

THE JESUITS.

CHAPTER IV.

THE INQUISITION.

CHAPTER VII.

THE COUNTER-REFORMATION IN ENGLAND.

CHAPTER VIII.

THE CONTINUATION OF THE STRUGGLE.

CHAPTER IX.

THE THIRTY YEARS' WAR AND THE END OF THE STRUGGLE.

CHAPTER I.

INTRODUCTORY.

Importance of considering the causes of any great event—The
Reformation in the sixteenth century one of those events—The
alienation of the laity from the clergy on account of their wealth
and luxury, one of the preludes to it—The corrupt state of the
monasteries another of the grievances of Christendom—Their failure
to fulfil the end designed by their establishment explained—The
abuses of the Papacy, including the despotic authority of the Popes,
and their interference with Church patronage, causes of the decline
of their power—Other complaints against them—The wealth, luxury,
ostentatious style of living, and extortions of the Popes during their
residence at Avignon, and their absence from Rome, causes of the
decline of the Papacy—Petrarch's description of the Papal Court—
The Papal schism a cause of the decline of the Papacy—The
Councils of Constance and Basel, and their failure to apply a
remedy to the evils of Christendom—Proof of the corrupt state
of the Church—The evil lives of the Popes, and the humanism
encouraged by them, causes of the decline of the Papacy—Failure
of Adrian VI. to apply a remedy to the evils of Christendom—The
vices and irreligion which prevailed, causes of the rapid progress
of the Reformation—Description of the progress—The doctrines
preached by the Reformers.

IN considering any great crisis of the world's history,
we must look not only at the immediate causes of it,
or the prominent actors in it, but we must trace also
the preparations for it which have been made through the
ages. These antecedents often elude the cursory attention given to them by a large proportion of the readers of
history. They admire the grandeur of the thunder-storm,
but they do not consider the manner of the gradual
formation of the store of electric forces which have caused
it suddenly to roll down the valleys and to awaken the

I

echoes of the mountains. Thus certain historians fix
their attention on the Reformation under Luther in the
sixteenth century, which is the object of their admiration,
while they overlook the four or five centuries preceding it,
which they call, contemptuously, dark ages. They should,
however, remember that the one period is necessary to
the production of the other.

The wealth, the luxury, and the ostentatious style of
living adopted by the clergy served more than any other
causes to alienate the affection of the laity from them,
and to prepare the way for the Reformation. Superstitious
men commonly supposed that the best mode of evincing
their gratitude to the priests for the benefits which they
were supposed to have conferred was to invest them with
temporal authority, and to bestow wealth upon them. In
Germany the clergy owed much of their opulence, and
much of their temporal distinction, to the disputes between
the Emperors and the clergy with which the country was
for a long time distracted. Ranging themselves beneath
the banner of the Popes in the civil warfare which
followed, they gradually availed themselves of the opportunity thus afforded them of usurping the royal prerogatives in their respective dioceses, and of wresting from
the Emperor some of the largest and most important
domains in the empire.

Another circumstance also contributed to swell the
revenues of the clergy. As the property of the latter was
considered sacred when the surrounding country was laid
waste, many of the laity made over their lands to the
clergy, and consented to become their vassals until the
storm of war had exhausted its fury. Thus the clergy
very often obtained absolute possession of the lands
entrusted to them for a limited period. Much property
also, which, if the law of celibacy had not been imposed
on the clergy, would have been distributed among their
families, was appropriated to the sole use of the Church

The wealth and temporal authority thus acquired proved very injurious to Romanism. Men were convinced that a reformation was wanted when they saw the rulers of the Church indulging in all those vices which often follow in the train of wealth and rank, adopting an ostentatious style of living, issuing from their feudal castle on the gaily caparisoned palfrey, or exhibiting the same marks of grandeur as the highest and mightiest potentates.

Another cause of the excessive unpopularity of the clergy was their immunity from civil jurisdiction. An idea prevailed very extensively in those dark ages, that if the clergy had been guilty of crimes which rendered them justly obnoxious to punishment, the laity ought not to lay their hands upon their sacred persons, but that they ought to be arraigned before a spiritual tribunal. The clergy, who had always been indebted to the superstitions of the laity for the opportunity of extending their jurisdiction, at length claimed as an absolute right that they should take exclusive cognizance of offences committed by their own body. Afterwards they obtained absolution on very easy terms. A pecuniary payment, proportioned to the rank of the offender, at once freed them from the punishment inflicted by the civil tribunal.

This practice of compounding for crimes—originally commenced in a rude and turbulent age, when the law found a difficulty in vindicating its majesty—was retained by the Church long after it had been abolished by the civil jurisdiction from a conviction of the disastrous effects which it produced. The result was that the clergy were emboldened to plunge without scruple and remorse into the practice of every vice and the perpetration of every crime. While malefactors among the laity were brought before the ordinary tribunal, and suffered the condign punishment which they had fully merited, clerical offenders dared to stand before the altar, and to perform the most sacred rites of their religion, even after they had been guilty of the greatest enormities.

The monks also had gradually become as corrupt as the remainder of the clerical body.   Originally certain advantages flowed from monastic institutions.   The individual who was pursued by the savage violence of a foe rejoiced when, on arriving at the brow of some hill, he saw the gray walls of the monastery rising in the valley before him ; for he was well aware that, if he could only succeed in crossing the threshold, the hand of violence would be unable to assail him.   The monasteries were also the home of all the learning of the age.   To the monks we owe the preservation of the works of those illustrious men of ancient times who still mould the taste and genius of mankind.

Their services, too, as chroniclers have been invaluable. If the monks had not preserved a record of contemporary events, the probability is that the memory of them would have altogether perished.   To them also we are indebted for the preservation and multiplication by transcription of ancient copies of the inspired writings, and of commentaries upon them during a stormy and turbulent era. Within those walls, too, the study of church architecture was successfully prosecuted ; so that it is to the monks that we owe the idea of those time-honoured structures which astonish and delight us by the harmony of their proportions, and by the chaste beauty of their architecture.   In addition they ministered to the wants of the distressed and the perishing, and poured the oil and wine of heavenly consolation into the wounded spirit.

While, however, we make these admissions, we must not forget that the monastic system was the fruitful parent of all those vices which disgrace human nature, and reduce man to the level of the brute creation.   Many of the monks were lazy and ignorant.   The compulsory celibacy of the inmates of those institutions was a source of incalculable evil. Moreover, we find that in the absence of the check imposed by a regular episcopal visitation, from which they had obtained exemption, they systematically disregarded the high ends for which they were established.

The surplus wealth originally intended to be applied to the maintenance of learning, and to the relief of the aged and the helpless, was spent in keeping large retinues of servants to do the work which ought to have been done by the monks themselves, and in enriching men who were forbidden by the laws of their founder to possess any private property. Meanwhile fraud and simony prevailed in these institutions; and the large majority of their inmates lived in the habitual practice of all those vices which bring the greatest disgrace on human nature. We need not wonder, therefore, to hear that the unanimous voice of the public had denounced them. The clouds overhanging them had been gathering blackness from age to age. A storm might at any time be expected to break forth which would lay low many of them and spread desolation around them.

We observe, too, that there were deeply-seated abuses and corruptions in the Papal system itself. No doubt they were to some extent the cause of its descent from its proud elevation. We cannot fix the exact time when the Papal empire over mankind began to be shaken. We have the same difficulty in settling when old age creeping on a man robs him of his strength. Slowly this power had been decaying through numerous generations. The strongly-built walls and the stately columns seem to rise before us with the same imposing grandeur during the thirteenth century. But a close examination will serve to show us that they were exhibiting symptoms of decay before the accession of Boniface VIII. in 1294, and will prepare us to see the causes of the fissures which appear in them, the symptoms of the coming of a time when they should be upheaved from their firm foundation.

The causes of the decline of the Papacy are to be sought in the history of the preceding age. The Pope, in the prosecution of his design of reigning supreme over the monarchs as well as over the Churches of Christendom, had appropriated to himself not only the rights and institutions of the Church, but the power formerly exercised by the Emperors and Frankish Kings in ecclesiastical matters. The Bishops were first placed in absolute subjection to the See of Rome. In the ninth century the French prelates presented a firm front to the Pope, and they even threatened to excommunicate Gregory IV. because he had come into France, and had, under the pretext of mediating between the contending parties, espoused the cause of the sons of Louis the Meek who had rebelled against their father. The title of Universal Bishop was admitted only as implying a power of general oversight, not as entitling the Popes to exercise their functions in every diocese. But at length, convinced that a persuasion of the Pope's omnipotence was fixed in the minds of the laity, the weapons which they had hitherto wielded successfully fell from their hands, and they were no longer able to resist this spiritual autocrat.

National Churches now found themselves subject to an irresistible despotism. But the hand of arbitrary power must be seen and felt in order that it may be obeyed. Accordingly, with the view of subverting the ancient constitution of the Church, Legates were appointed to represent the majesty of the Pope in territories far remote from the central seat of the Government. The ensigns of sovereignty with which they were invested struck terror even into assemblies consisting of the highest and mightiest of this world's potentates. Assuming unlimited authority over national Churches, and determined to extort money which they might pour into the Papal coffers, these Legates lived in splendour at the expense of the victims of their tyranny, deposing Bishops, holding synods, promulgating Canons, and pronouncing the sentence of excommunication against those who had dared to resist some arbitrary decree which they had issued from their council chamber.

Again, when the freedom of episcopal elections was restored by the concordat at Worms, the Popes came to be considered as the judges in all cases of appeal. The litigants were required to carry their cause to Rome, where, in consequence of the minute formalities required by the canon law, the Popes found no difficulty in setting aside the election, and in conferring the bishopric on their own candidate. They also supplied the want of election or the unfitness of the election by a nomination of their own.

But these were not the only instances of interference with Church patronage. The Popes began by asking that a particular living might be conferred on someone whom they strongly recommended. These recommendatory letters were called mandates. But examples produce custom. The doubtful precedent of one generation became the established rule of the next ; so that at length they obtained a large share of the patronage in most of the countries of Europe. Through the imbecility of Henry III., who offered no opposition to Papal encroachments, the Pope had obtained the presentation to some of the best benefices in England. Then he claimed the presentation to the preferment held by all clerks who died at Rome. As from various causes the number of them was considerable, he had obtained by this means a large share of ecclesiastical patronage. Thus, then, he wrested benefices in various ways from their lawful patrons, which enabled those who held them to live in ignoble ease in their palaces on the banks of the Tiber. The Popes, too, extorted large sums of money from the Churches of Europe, at first for the purpose of promoting a Crusade for the recovery of the Holy Sepulchre, but afterwards that they might be able to conduct to a' successful issue some scheme which had for its object their aggrandizement as temporal Princes. The Papal legates continued by their extortions and assumptions to excite the indignation of those to whom they were sent. Innocent IV., in whose pontificate (1243-1254) the tyranny of Rome, if we consider her temporal and spiritual pretensions, seems to have been greater than it ever was before, directed the English prelates to furnish at their own expense a certain number of men-at-arms for the defence of the Church. This extortion and appropriation of benefices were causes of the loss of the prodigious influence which the Popes exercised over the secular clergy and the hierarchy. The laity also were justly indignant on account of their venality when they found them openly selling bishoprics and benefices at Rome to the highest bidder, especially when they found that the wealth thus poured into their treasury was appropriated to the purposes of swelling the pomp and augmenting the retinue of the pretended successor of the fisherman of Galilee.

There were other causes of complaint against the Papacy. The long contest between the Popes and the Empire had left in the minds of the vanquished party an animosity which sought its gratification in vituperative language against the Papacy by which it had been deprived of its pre-eminence among the nations. Interdicts had the effect of exasperating the minds of men against a power which deprived men of the ordinances of religion, because their monarchs had disobeyed an edict which had gone forth from the council chamber of the Lateran. Many of the best friends of the Papacy, without intending to do so, shook the Papal power to its foundation. St. Bernard, in the twelfth century, and other distinguished ecclesiastics, seem to have forgotten that, when they were denouncing the avarice, the luxury, and corruption of the Pope and the hierarchy, they were doing their utmost to bring Rome into contempt, and to impair the might and majesty for which they were anxious that she should be conspicuous among the nations. Others aided them in their assault upon the Papacy. Songs in which the venality and the avarice of the Pope, Legates, and Cardinals were made the subject of satire, were sung at the boards of the monks or in the banqueting-hall of the feudal castle.

We have other proofs of the widespread reaction among the laity against Papal predominance. The period of seventy years which began in 1305 was not unfitly termed the ' Babylonish Captivity,' because it was passed by the Popes beneath the sceptre of a foreign monarch, and because they also were slaves like the Jews during their exile from the city of their fathers. A struggle for the Papacy had been carried on between rival factions. At length the friends of Boniface agreed to accept a proposal made to them by the French party, that the former should nominate three prelates, from whom the French faction should choose a Pope within forty days. One of those so nominated was the Archbishop of Bordeaux. The French party at once saw their advantage. The Papacy was in their gift. The Archbishop had hitherto identified himself with the party which had supported Boniface in opposition to Philip. He was a man who could easily be bribed to make common cause with themselves. The King was therefore recommended to make terms with him. In an interview which he had with him in the depths of a forest belonging to the monastery of St. Jean d'Angely, Philip agreed to make the Archbishop Pope on six conditions, one of which was that he should condemn the memory of Boniface. The compact was sealed, and the Archbishop was unanimously elected to the Papacy. Having assumed the title of Clement V., he was compelled by Philip, who wished to have him near him, in order that he might insure an exact obedience, to reside first at Lyons, afterwards at Bordeaux, and finally at Avignon.

Clement has left a character stained with sensuality and rapacity; and he will be for ever memorable for having reduced the Papacy to a state of vassalage to the King of France, from which it is wonderful that it ever rose to its former independent position among the nations. He and his successor, John XXII., died shamefully rich. The latter bequeathed to his nephew 300,000 golden florins, under pretext of succour to the Holy Land. The lord of a castle where he had deposited his wealth, consisting of gold and silver vessels, precious stones and other ornaments, seized and appropriated it to his own use. John endeavoured to compel restitution under pain of excommunication, but he was unable to do so. The demand amounted to 1,774,800 florins of gold. John had amassed wealth to the amount of 18,000,000 of gold florins in specie, and 7,000,000 in plate and jewels, the produce of exactions levied under the pretext of a Crusade, of annates, or the first year's income of all ecclesiastical dignities, which he was the first to invent, and of a skilful promotion of each Bishop to a richer bishopric, whereby, as on each vacancy the annates were paid, six or more fines would accrue to the Papal treasury. He also compelled pluralists to give up all but one benefice each, reserving to himself the disposal of the rest, and adopted other devices deserving of the strongest condemnation.

This extortion had, in fact, become necessary in consequence of the continued residence of the Popes at Avignon. The Barons in the Papal territory, whom they had found a difficulty in coercing into submission, even during their residence at Rome, availed themselves of the opportunity afforded by their absence of wresting from them one province after another, with its revenues. They were then obliged, in the manner above described, to supply their deficiencies. This extortion was, however, greatly prejudicial to the Papacy. The clergy were alienated from the Popes when they found them laying their hands on their treasures. They would, indeed, have taken patiently the spoiling of their goods, if the Popes had been satisfied with supplying their immediate and pressing wants, or even with maintaining the pomp and ceremonial befitting their high dignity. But their indignation knew no bounds when they saw themselves robbed of their treasures, that their spiritual lords might not only live in luxury, and exhibit in their Courts the mimic splendour of Oriental magnificence, but that they might even hoard up the massive bars of gold and silver in their treasure-vaults.

The minds of men had been dazzled by the glory which seemed to surround the Popes when they planted their feet on the necks of the prostrate monarchs of Christendom, and seemed to be aiming at dominion that they might give liberty to the captives and break in pieces the chains of the oppressor. They did not see that the Popes were only aiming at aggrandizement, and that the polity which they sought to establish was bad enough when considered as an ideal of a kingdom of this world, but unseemly in the extreme in connection with the kingdom, not of this world, which it was the great object of the mission of their Divine Master to establish. But the spell was broken, the charm was dissolved, when they saw the pretended successor of St. Peter bowing down before the golden idol, and soiling his hands like Mammon, 'the least erected spirit that fell from heaven,' by ransacking the bowels of the earth in search of perishing earthly treasure.

The terrible licentiousness, luxury, and worldly pomp of the Court at Avignon, especially during the pontificate of Clement VI. (1342-1352), were also causes of the decline of the Papacy. The illustrious Petrarch, the ' Italian songster of Laura and of love,' who was for a time residing at Avignon, has given us the following description of it in his letters called ' The Mysteries ': ' All that they say of Assyrian and Egyptian Babylon, of the four labyrinths, of the Avernian and Tartarean lakes, is nothing in comparison of this hell. All that is vile and execrable is assembled in this place. Gold is the only means of escaping from this labyrinth. . . . Here reign the successors of poor fishermen who have forgotten their origin. They march covered with gold and purple, proud of the spoils of Princes and of people. Instead of those little boats in which they gained their living in the Lake of Gennesaret, they inhabit superb palaces. . . . To the most simple repasts have succeeded the most sumptuous feasts ; and where the Apostles went on foot, covered only with sandals, are now to be seen insolent satraps, mounted on horses ornamented with gold, and champing golden bits.' He has elsewhere expressed the greatest horror of the abominations which filled the ' New Babylon of the West,' and speaks of her in his Sonetto 107 as ' Babylon faithless and wicked,' and as a ' hell upon earth.'

His accuracy is confirmed by all contemporary writers. Vice in the persons of Clement V., John XXII., and Clement VI., sat enthroned in the high places of Christendom. The plague called the Black Death, which at this time came as a judgment from God on the nations of Europe, converting Avignon and many of the cities into one vast sepulchre, did indeed startle into seriousness the debauchees of the Papal Court ; but no sooner had the visitation passed away than they plunged madly into the vortex of pleasure and dissipation, and became more the children of hell than before. We cannot wonder to hear that the world had lost all reverence for the

Papacy when we find that the Pope and his Cardinals only too closely answered to the description here given by Petrarch.

This was a state of things which everyone could understand. The errors and superstitions introduced into the Church did not inflict the first blow on the Papal system. Christendom must be placed above the Church in intellectual and religious development, in order that it may see whether the Church had corrupted and mutilated the faith once delivered unto the saints. But there was an order of things quite level to the comprehension of the meanest intellect, when men saw the Ambassadors of the Prince of Peace making use of secular weapons for the defence of their spiritual interests; when they saw that the offerings which the tribes of Christendom poured into the treasury of the Church became the means of pampering a luxurious Court, and of enabling the Papacy to send forth soldiers to ravage and to destroy. Then immediately the Church became powerless for good because the men of the world could say that she had sunk to the same level as those whom she ought to have taught both by precept and example to look with contempt on the pomps and pleasures of a passing world, and to become candidates for the incorruptible crown.

The residence at Avignon had been in another way injurious to the Papacy. The Pope was indeed surrounded there, as at Rome, with the pomp and ceremonial of a Court. The world, however, lost its awe of him because he was only nominally seated on the throne of St. Peter, in a cathedral unhallowed by the ancient and sacred associations connected with that great shrine which rises in stately grandeur above the supposed tomb of the chief of the Apostles. He was no longer, besides, an independent Sovereign, reigning in the territory which Constantine and Charlemagne were supposed to have conferred on the Church, but a subordinate Prince in an obscure city, in a narrow territory not his own, where he was surrounded on all sides by the kingdom of France. He was thus completely under the influence of a monarch, Philip the Fair. The Pope's ecclesiastical censures were generally disregarded, and the Papal claims sounded ridiculous when made by a captive. Notwithstanding his anathemas, Louis of Bavaria continued in possession of the imperial dignity, and the rebellious lords refused to surrender the territories which they had wrested from him in Central Italy.

The schism of the anti-Popes, which followed the death of Gregory XI., with whom ended the 'Babylonian Captivity,' was still more disastrous to the Papacy than the residence at Avignon. While the Cardinals were engaged in deliberating as to his successor, the Roman mob surrounded the conclave with loud shouts, and demanded the election of a Pope who should be a Roman or an Italian. The Cardinals, terrified by their shouts, elected, in 1378, the Archbishop of Bari, who assumed the name of Urban VI., thinking that they should thus satisfy both parties, as he was not only an Italian, but also a subject of the French Sovereign of Naples.

Finding, when it was too late, that they had placed over themselves a Pope who made himself obnoxious to them by his harsh and imperious manner, the French Cardinals, anxious to retain the Pontifical Court in their own land, withdrew from their allegiance, and elected an anti-Pope, Robert of Geneva, who assumed the name of Clement VII. They alleged, in justification of the election, that they were under a constraint when they elected Urban VI. They would have remained quiescent under the dominion of Urban if he had not provoked them to anger by haughtiness and rudeness.

The world could not fail to regard the Popes and their office with well-merited contempt when they saw them afterwards wandering about Europe, blackening one another's character, exerting every effort to enlist the Princes of Europe in their cause, and hurling at one another their spiritual thunderbolts. The rapacity and venality of the Popes during this period surpass all description. New taxes constantly imposed, new methods of extortion constantly devised, were the means by which every one of them endeavoured to reimburse himself for the loss of the spiritual allegiance of Christendom. Thus men became more determined to oppose the Papacy. Thus an earnest desire was awakened in the minds of a large proportion of the inhabitants of Europe for the cleansing of the Augean stable of corruption, the noxious excrements of which sullied the purity of the robes in which the messengers of the Prince of Peace ought to be arrayed when they deliver the message of their Sovereign to the guilty and rebellious inhabitants of this district of His empire.

The Council of Constance, summoned to meet in 1414, first proceeded to adopt measures for the termination of the schism in the Papacy. The members agreed unanimously to depose the three Popes who claimed the allegiance of Christendom. The great question afterwards for their consideration was whether or no the election of the Pope should take precedence of the reformation of the Church. Many thought that, unless the Church was first reformed, the Pope, however pure he might be, would be unable, beneath the pressure of temptation, to hold fast his integrity. The Cardinals, on the other hand, were firmly convinced that, if they elected a Pope fettered by rules previously established, they would sign the death-warrant of that system of corruption which they were anxious, if possible, to maintain.

A fierce battle between the two parties raged during the summer months. At length the Cardinals were completely successful. Martin V., elected by the Council, soon showed that he was determined to resist any com-

prehensive measure of reform. The real question in the
Council was not the reform of the Church, but the ability
of the Bishops to maintain their position against the Pope.
No united policy could be obtained even in matters of
detail. The division of the Council into nations was a
hindrance to united action. This arrangement had been
made because, if the members voted by the head, the
Italians, being very numerous, could easily prevent any
measure of reform from being carried into effect. The
members of the Council could not discover the interests
of Christendom, because they were hidden by the conflict
of Churches and nations. The nations, deliberating
apart, were brought near enough to intensify national
jealousy, but not near enough to be induced to give up
that jealousy and to aim at the promotion of the best
interests of Christendom.

We must give a different report of the Council of Basel.
If a remedy for the evils of Christendom could have been
found, it would have been found within the walls of its
Council chamber. We find, indeed, that this world's
potentates did not honour with their presence the deliberations of the assembled fathers. The gay cavalcades, and
the banners emblazoned with the armorial bearings of
monarchs, princes, and warriors, were not seen amid the
streets of the city. But still the most learned and able
theologians in Europe were to be found in the Council.
Unlike the fathers of Constance, who merely pretended
to reform the Church, they displayed an honesty of purpose, a firm determination to heal the sores of the Church,
a high sense of responsibility to the nations of Christendom, and a determination, if possible, to overcome the
numerous difficulties in their way, which attracted the
admiration of many of their contemporaries. In some
matters the Council succeeded, but still the nations of
Europe were doomed to disappointment. The Council
failed because, in its anxiety not to represent the divisions

of Christendom, it represented the pretensions of a self-elected and self-seeking body of ecclesiastics. The failure of such a body of men, so earnest in their purpose, so devoted to their work, seemed to show far more plainly than the abortive attempt at Constance the difficulty in effecting by means of Councils the moral and spiritual regeneration of Christendom.

We have evidence in the works of Roman Catholic authors that the corrupt state of the Church continued after the Councils. 'For some years,' says Bellarmine, ' before the Lutheran and Calvinistic heresies were published, there was not any severity in ecclesiastical judicatories and discipline with regard to the Church, any reverence for Divine things ; there was not almost any religion remaining.' 'Concubinage,' says a good Bishop of Worms in the fifteenth century, ' is publicly and formally practised by the clergy, and their mistresses are as expensively dressed and as respectfully treated as if their connection were not sinful and indecent, but honourable and praiseworthy.' The Popes were now invested with a power almost despotic. They might have used it to check the progress of vice and immorality ; but they were themselves the slaves of the worst vices. The Popes of the period after the Council from Paul II. (1464-1471) to Alexander VI. (1493-1503) surpassed one another in wickedness. Paul was a great drunkard; he put up all offices to sale, and spent his days in weighing money and precious stones. Sixtus IV. (1471-1484) was dissolute and avaricious. As Bishop Creighton observes (' History of Papacy,' vol. iii., p. 116), ' He lowered the moral tone of Europe, and prepared the way for still unworthier successors in the chair of St. Peter.' Innocent VII. (1484-1493) was guilty of disgraceful profligacy and of the grossest bribery to secure his election. Alexander VI. (1493-1503) and Cæsar Borgia his son have been strongly condemned. He succeeded by the grossest bribery in obtaining the

2

Papal crown. His illegitimate children were now brought forward and acknowledged. The Vatican was often the scene of indecent orgies. Objectionable songs, swelled by a chorus of revellers, sounded through the banqueting-hall. Indecent plays were acted in the presence of the Pontiff. The grossest venality prevailed in the Papal Court. At length he perished by a poisoned draught which he had prepared for one of his Cardinals. Multitudes, while gazing on his corpse as it lay in St. Peter's, breathed a fervent thanksgiving for deliverance from the rule of one whose sins had polluted the land, disgraced human nature, and placed him on a level with the beasts that perish.

We have thus seen that the Popes from the time of Paul II. surpassed one another in wickedness. As an ardent patriot anxious to expel the foreigner from the soil of Italy, Julius II. might extort from us some admiration on account of the military genius which he displayed. But when we consider that he was the Ambassador of the Prince of Peace, and find him commanding armies and storming strongholds, we must visit him with unsparing censure, and need not be surprised to hear that he was a great scandal to his contemporaries.

A comparison of the Popes of this period with Gregory VII. and Innocent III. will serve to show us that the Papacy no longer exhibited the might and majesty which it formerly displayed. Gregory had rescued it from the deep abasement of the tenth century, and had laboured to make it the arbiter of the spiritual and temporal destinies of Christendom. Innocent III. had achieved great success as a statesman and conqueror. We must indeed strongly censure their ambition and arrogance, and must consider the kingdom thus established as the corruption of Christianity. But still there was a grandeur in the design of compelling men to cease from their dissensions which would command our admiration, if we could divest ourselves of the idea that they wished to gratify their love of power by planting their feet on the neck of the prostrate monarchs of Christendom. The Popes, however, of this period gave a very plain proof that they had not the same power as the giants of former days, and that they had sunk to the depths of degradation by limiting their ambition to the aggrandizement of their families, and to the consolidation and enlargement of their Italian principality. To dissolve a hostile confederacy, to surpass in craft a disciple of Machiavel, to make their sons the owners of splendid palaces, the possessors of vast estates, the Sovereigns of principalities—these became, from the death of Nicolas V. in 1453 to that of Paul III. in 1550, the objects of men who, if their lot had been cast in a former age, would have sought to 'bind kings with chains and nobles with links of iron.' The crimes of which they were guilty in the prosecution of their designs, the vices already enumerated, could hardly fail to be very injurious to the Roman Catholic Church. In the tenth and eleventh centuries, the crimes and impurities of the Popes, which were as great as those of a Sixtus, an Innocent, and a Borgia, had failed to shake the Papacy, because they were perpetrated in an age when 'darkness covered the earth and gross darkness the people.' But now, in the full blaze of day, the pollutions of the sepulchre were laid bare to the gaze of the nations. The armies of the invader, on their departure from Italy, published their crimes in their native land; the public press propagated them through Europe. Erasmus, whose works were read everywhere, lashed with his thrice-knotted scourge the perpetrators of these deeds of darkness. Preachers of righteousness, like Savonarola, lifted up their voices in indignant denunciation of their wickedness. The world stood aghast with horror at the contemplation of deeds as bad as those in the darkest period of Pagan antiquity. Men could not believe that those could be infallible guides who trampled on all laws, Divine and human, and set at naught all considerations of decency, in their anxiety to sweep away from their path whatever stood between them and the attainment of the object of their desire. These enormities were unquestionably a heavy blow to the Papacy, and served to prepare the way for the emancipation of the nations of Europe from their bondage to the Church of Rome.

The revival of a taste for ancient literature was also at this time very injurious to Romanism, because it led many of its leading members and ministers to breathe the spirit of the ancient world. The result might have been expected. The quick-sighted Italians, having the opportunity of going behind the scenes, had early discovered the hollowness of the pretensions of the Papacy. They had the opportunity of narrowly examining the lives of the Popes and discovering the motives by which they were influenced. They had thus lost the feeling of veneration for them entertained by those living in remote countries. The result had been an indifference to all religion, which on the revival of learning had settled down into scepticism. Men could not fail to be more and more alienated from the Church when they found that, to use Lord Macaulay's words (Essay on Ranke's 'History of the Popes'), the class just referred to consisted of those 'who, like Leo X., with the Latinity of the Augustan Age had acquired its atheistical and scoffing spirit ; who regarded those Christian mysteries of which they were stewards as the augur Cicero and the High Pontiff Cæsar regarded the Sybilline books and the pecking of the sacred chickens ; and who, amongst themselves, spoke of the Incarnation and the Eucharist and the Trinity in the same tone in which Cotta and Velleius talked of the oracle of Delphi or the voice of Faunus among the mountains.'

We cannot be surprised to hear that these abuses, vices, and the absolute irreligion of the clergy and laity, produced a deep impression on Adrian VI., who in 1522 was elected Pope on account of his holiness. He was impressed with a deep sense of his responsibility, and was most anxious to promote the spiritual welfare of Christendom. He did not, however, understand the age in which he lived. He thought that in a short time he could cease to be an Italian Prince, and that he could at once occupy the position of the spiritual head of Christendom. He did not understand that he could not at once sever the connection of the Papacy with the politics of Europe, which, he was convinced, had been a source of evil through many generations. He tried with vague promises of a reform, without a revision of the system by which the abuses had been fostered, to recover his hold on the allegiance of those who, as we shall see directly, had revolted from the Papacy. We cannot wonder, therefore, to hear that this old and feeble man, without resources, without a party, was utterly unable to make any progress towards the recovery of the spiritual allegiance of Christendom.

Many of the Roman Catholics themselves admitted that the abuses, vices, and irreligion, to which reference has been made, were causes of the rapid advance of the Reformers in their career of victory.

The Archbishop Antoine of Prague writes thus in 1565 to his provincial synod: ' Those are not far wrong who attribute the origin of the calamities of our Church to the vices of the clergy.' The Cardinal d'Altemps, the nephew of Pius IV., writes: ' The accursed and detestable conduct of the clergy has produced for the most part our misfortunes.' The walls of the strongholds of Romanism seem to have fallen prostrate, like those of Jericho before the first trumpet-blast of the armies of their foes. Some idea of the rapidity of the advance may be formed when we hear that in 1523 and 1524, soon after Luther began to preach, large and distant towns—Frankfort-on-the-Main, Magdeburg, Ulm, Strasburg, Halle in Suabia, Nuremberg, Hamburg, Bremen, and Stettin, had welcomed the principles of the Reformation. Before ten years had passed away from the time of the burning of the Papal Bull at Wittenberg, the States of Saxony, Hesse, Brandenburg, Luneberg, Mecklenburg, Holstein, and Pomerania, had cast off the usurped dominion of the Roman Pontiff.

The progress of the new opinions had been equally rapid in countries not included within the limits of the German Empire. In 1523 the Lutheran preachers sounded the trumpet-call through Eastern Prussia, and in 1525 the whole population crowded around the banner of the Reformers. The same Gustavus Vasa who had delivered Sweden from the yoke of her oppressor, Christian II., after some resistance from the people, which he at length quelled, succeeded in emancipating her from the spiritual bondage. Denmark, and Norway, too, through the instrumentality of the Sovereigns Frederick I. and Christian III., were, as we are informed by Ranke, numbered among the nations which had embraced the Reformed faith. The Reformation, too, advanced with great rapidity in Switzerland. Ulric Zuingle, its great apostle, first persuaded Zurich to accept it. Berne soon followed her example. In the course of three years from 1526, through his agency and that of others, half the Catholics of Switzerland had cast off the yoke of the oppressor. In 1559 a war broke out between the Protestant Lords of the Congregation and Queen Mary of Guise, which ended in the subversion of Romanism, and in the triumphant establishment of Protestantism in Scotland.

The public preaching of God's Word was the great agency by which the work of the reformers was carried on to a successful issue. Luther's doctrine was that they must 'know nothing among their hearers save Jesus Christ, and Him crucified.' They preached the doctrine of justification by faith, which Luther called 'the article of a standing or falling Church.' They lifted up their voices against the doctrine that God has pardoned sin as to its eternal punishment, but that its temporal punishment must be expiated by ourselves in purgatory. They denounced the system of human mediators, and reminded their hearers emphatically of the one Mediator between God and man, the man Christ Jesus. They condemned the pardons, the pilgrimages, and the indulgences, as a system invented for the purpose of inducing men to pour their wealth into the coffers of the Church. They opposed Transubstantiation because it is condemned alike by Scripture and by reason. Judging from their recent success, they indulged the confident anticipation that every part of Europe would be delivered from the yoke of its spiritual oppressor.

CHAPTER II.

Causes of the ultimate failure of the Reformation in Spain and Italy—
Reference to the final progress of the Counter-Reformation—The
Lutheran Reformation at first partially successful in Italy—Efforts
of Contarini, Valdés, Ochino, Flaminio and others for a Reformation on the Lutheran basis—Discussion at Ratisbon for a Reformation on this basis, and the failure of it—Character and views of
Paul III.—The work of the monastic Orders in regenerating the
Church—Reform in the Orders of Camaldoli, the Mendicants, and
the Capuchins—Foundation of the Order of the Brothers of Charity
by Jean de Dieu—Establishment of the Oratory of Love and of
the Theatins—Description of Gaëtan di Thiène, Caraffa, of their
work, and of the institution which they established—The Barnabites
—Philip de Neri—The establishment of these Orders, and of the
Jesuits, important causes of the Counter-Reformation.

WE have now seen that the Reformation had
advanced rapidly in the northern parts of
Europe. In the South, however, the Reformers
had not been equally successful. Spain and Italy refused
to cast off their allegiance to the Roman Pontiff. The
soil of the former country had been for centuries the
battle-field on which the inhabitants struggled with the
armies of the unbeliever. The Church had consecrated
their banners for this holy warfare. In obedience to the
summons of Spain, the swords of her warriors were
continually leaping from their scabbards. Scarcely had
the tumult of the conflict ceased, when the shock of
armies contending for the faith was heard in the newly-
discovered regions of the West. Multitudes hastened
over the ocean, influenced by the insatiable thirst of

gold, and by the desire of extending the boundaries of the Church. A rooted pursuasion existed in the minds of the Spaniards that they were delegated by heaven to propagate Romanism, and that it was their bounden duty to preserve the soil of Spain from being profaned by the tread of the heretic and the unbeliever. The Italians also had their reasons for remaining steadfast in their allegiance to the Pope. They felt that one consequence of the reforms would be that the golden tide which through ages rolled from foreign countries over the plains of Italy, would be arrested in its progress. They could no longer expect the rich benefices, the presentation to which was claimed by the Pope. The large sums of money arising from the first year's produce of livings after a vacancy, from the sale of absolutions, dispensations, and indulgences, from the lawsuits brought to Rome, from benevolences and the tenth of benefices, would no longer flow into the Papal treasury, and thence be distributed through Italy. They saw too that the sun of Rome had suffered an eclipse during the residence of the Popes at Avignon. They now began to see that the high dignity to which the Pope had been elevated, as the spiritual arbiter of Christendom, was a compensation for the loss of the glories of those days when Italy occupied a high place among the nations.

We cannot be surprised, therefore, to hear that the sudden outburst of zeal for the Reformation in the North of Europe had kindled a similar enthusiasm for Romanism in these two countries. We shall see in Chapter VI. the result of a careful calculation in 1563 that in the territory between them, including France, the Netherlands, Poland, Bavaria, Austria, Hungary, Transylvania, there seemed to be every probability of the triumph of the Reformation. But if we pass over a period of fifty years from 1563, we shall find that the tide of conquest had been checked in its course. Romanism was victorious in all those countries. We shall, after we have spoken of the progress of the Reformation in Italy, describe the reform of the old Orders, and establishment of new Orders beginning about 1520, because we believe that it is a most important cause of that memorable revolution in human affairs which we must now endeavour to investigate.

The first efforts of the Church of Rome to reform her institutions are not associated with opposition to the work of Luther and his associates. Protestantism, as we have just said, never took a firm hold of the large body of the Italians and of the Spaniards. But still we find that the steps of the Reformers are distinctly impressed on the soil of both countries. We shall describe the work of the Reformers in Spain, and the causes of the easy victory gained over them in both countries, in Chapter IV. We here observe that within two years of the appearance of Luther against indulgences, his works and those of Melanchthon were read with great delight in all parts of the country. Some of them were translated into Italian. They found their way to Rome, and were read, as we are informed, even in the Palace of the Vatican. The publication of the Scriptures in the original language was another means of promoting the Reformation in Italy.

In 1516 Erasmus published at Basle his improved version of the Greek text of the New Testament, accompanied by a better translation into Latin. Besides his own paraphrases, Erasmus published the notes of Laurentius Valla on the New Testament. They were recommended to the Italians as the work of one who had distinguished himself as a reviver of letters. By these means the minds of the learned were turned to the study of the Scriptures. We find that individuals in the Conclave, Egidio, Fregoso, and Aleander were skilled in the learned languages, and that some of them made translations distinguished for their Scriptural simplicity, which were published with the strong recommendation of the Head of the Church. We read that many, guided by them, dug deep into the vast mine of Christian truth, and brought up many gems of sound doctrine, which they exhibited in all their beauty and brilliancy to the astonished and delighted view of many thousands of their fellow-countrymen.

We must not, therefore, be surprised to hear that a little band of men had risen up in Italy who, enlightened by the study of the Scriptures and of the works of the great leaders of the Reformation in Germany, endeavoured to reform the Church on the basis of the doctrine of justification by faith, to which the Lutheran Reformation owed its origin. The leader of that band was Gaspar Contarini. He was a member of one of the noblest families in Venice, which traded very much with the Levant, and from his early youth had devoted himself very much to philosophical studies, to which he gave three hours a day. When he was admitted to the Council of the Pregadi, he did not venture at first to address the members; but afterwards, conquering his timidity, he spoke with so much energy, force of reasoning, and oratorical power, that he at once produced a deep impression on the minds of his hearers, and could always afterwards command the votes of the assembled senators.

One Sunday in 1535, as Contarini, who had been advanced to the most important offices, was seated at the ballot urn, proceeding to the election of State officers, a messenger arrived from Rome, to whom the proud Seigniory, as they were engaged on important business of their own, did not hesitate to refuse admission. The Secretary, however, left the assembly to receive the despatch, which had been brought from the Pope, Paul III. The object of it was to announce that Contarini had been made a Cardinal.

'A Cardinal!' exclaimed Contarini, with great surprise; ' no, I am a Senator of Venice.'

The republic was constantly coming into collision with the Holy See in spiritual matters. We shall now see that its determination not to submit to the interference of the Pope was expressed very strongly also in matters of State policy. While the ecclesiastics elsewhere swayed the destinies of States and empires, no mitred head was ever seen in that oligarchic assembly, that Council of Ten, which in Venice directed the movements of the body politic. No Cardinal, unless he came on a special embassy from Rome, could ascend the Giant's Staircase. The Patriarch of Venice, even when he was invested with that high dignity transferred to him from Aquileia, though he could officiate under the dome of St. Mark's with splendour, for the maintenance of which the Venetians were lavish in their expenditure, could never take a seat among the senators of the adjoining ducal palace. The priesthood were jealously excluded from all influence in political affairs. No ecclesiastic could hold a civil office. Church and State were as far as possible distinct in the constitution of Venice.

We need not, therefore, be surprised to be informed of the exclamation of Contarini when he heard that he had been created a Cardinal. He felt that he could not accept any dignity without the perfect approval of his fellow-citizens. That approval was immediately expressed. The Doge, the senators, and the people united in congratulating Contarini on his high dignity, only lamenting the loss which public affairs would sustain through his necessary exclusion from all interference with them. Contarini, after consulting with his friends in his own palace, decided on accepting the dignity. He was not yet a priest, but at once received the tonsure, and very soon, arrayed in the red robes of the Cardinal, paid a visit to the Doge and the Senate in one of the magnificent chambers of the palace.

We have full information from his treatise as to the basis of the Reformation which Contarini was anxious to promote both in Italy and Germany. We know that he brought forward more prominently than any other Italian the doctrine of justification by faith, which Luther, as we have said, declared to be the article of a standing or falling Church.

'If asked on what he should rely,' Contarini remarks, 'a pious man will answer he can trust to the latter alone.' 'Our righteousness,' he goes on to say, 'is only inchoate, and full of defects; the righteousness of Christ, on the other hand, true, perfect, thoroughly and alone pleasing in the eyes of God. For its sake alone can we trust to be justified before God.'

Cardinal Pole, whom Contarini knew well, when, as Papal delegate, he governed the portion of the Papal territory which lies round the city of Viterbo, cannot be sufficiently warm in his praise of this treatise. 'Thou hast,' he said, 'brought to light that jewel which the Church kept half buried' (Hook's 'Lives of the Archbishops'). But while he and other distinguished men wished to make this doctrine of justification the keystone of the arch of their salvation, we must remember that they did not surrender their belief in the other dogmas of Romanism, and that they still held that the Pope had a paramount claim on their dutiful allegiance.

Even in Naples, the enthusiastic daughter of the Church, whose zeal was often called forth in defence of its ritual and its festivals, its dominion and its dogmas, this dogma was widely propagated by Juan Valdés, one of the Viceroy's secretaries. On the Chiaja, not far from the road to Naples, where the tomb of the immortal Virgil arrests the attention of the traveller, Juan Valdés had a country-house standing by itself which commanded a view of the azure waters of the glorious bay, and of an unrivalled landscape, from which red, orange, and blue tints occasionally flashed out when the noonday sun bathes the country in a flood of brightness. Amid this scenery, so well suited to lead to high and heavenly meditations, Valdés delighted, especially on Sundays, in imbuing the minds of his friends whom he had gathered together around him with a knowledge of those great truths which, after laborious and prayerful meditation, he discovered for himself in the sacred Scriptures. His pale and delicately-cut countenance, in which the unseen world seemed to be reflected, his patient spirit, his courtly bearing, his eloquent conversation, the spotless purity of his life, the vast stores of learning which he constantly unfolded, gave him a great influence with the principal nobility and the enlightened men who, at certain seasons, flocked to Naples. His work 'A Hundred and Ten Considerations,' in which he does not attack the errors of Romanism, but confines himself to the inculcation of Divine truth, found its way to the distant parsonage of Bemerton, near Salisbury, and gave rise to the following observations of the holy and heavenly George Herbert in a letter to Nicholas Ferrer, of Little Gidding :

' I wish you by all means to publish this book for those eminent things observable therein ; that God in the midst of Popery should open the eyes of one to understand and express so clearly the extent of the Gospel in the acceptation of Christ's righteousness, a thing strangely buried and darkened by his adversaries and their great stumbling block. Secondly, for the great honour and reverence which he everywhere shows to our dear Lord and Master, setting forth His merit so piously for which I do so love him that, were there nothing else, I would print it, that with it the honour of my Lord might be published.' Another proof of the views of Valdés on the doctrine of justification is to be found in a little book, 'Il Beneficio di Cristo,' or 'The Benefit bestowed by Christ,' which had an enormous circulation in Italy, and was greatly instrumental in making the doctrine of justification popular in that country. Forty thousand copies of it were sold in six years. It was afterwards anathematized. Lord Macaulay writes: 'The Inquisitors detected in it the Lutheran doctrine of justification by faith alone. They proscribed it, and it is now as hopelessly lost as the second Decade of Livy.' Since he wrote those words, one copy has been found at Vienna, and another in the Library of St. Jòhn's College, Cambridge. Paleario does indeed claim the authorship of it ; but there is every reason to believe that Paleario derived from Valdés, who, in the manner just described, impressed his views on others, the great truths expressed in this book, the careful perusal of which made the doctrine of justification for a time very popular in Italy.

A very important person now demands our attention. Bernardino Ochino occupies a prominent place in the annals of the Reformation in Italy. He was born at Siena, a city of Tuscany, in the year 1487. Impressed from his early years with a deep sense of religion, he joined the Order of Franciscan Observants, and very soon surpassed others in his ritualistic zeal. He introduced the practice of meditating before the crucifix for forty hours at a time. Ochino became the most popular preacher of the day. 'In such reputation was he held' (writes the annalist of the Capuchins) 'that he was regarded as incomparably the best preacher in Italy. His powers of elocution, accompanied with the most admirable action, gave him the complete command of his audience, and the more so because his life corresponded with his doctrine.' His snow-white head and his beard, flowing down to his shoulders, his pallid countenance, on which mortification had set its seal, deepened the impression which his eloquence made on his hearers.

As a preacher, he was followed by the illiterate and the
unlearned, by the common people, and by the high and
mighty ones of the land. Charles V., who attended his
preaching when he was in Italy, is reported to have said:
'Ochino preaches with great power. He might make
even the stones to weep.' Even Cardinal Bembo, a
bigoted Romanist, who brought him to Venice, was so
dazzled by the glitter of his eloquence that he did not
discover the print of the cloven foot on the soil. We
see, indeed, in the nine sermons preached in Venice
in 1539, that he preached the doctrines of Transubstantiation and purgatory, and that he recognised the duty
of fasting, and submission to Papal authority. We
find, however, that he protested against the abuses
with which these doctrines were connected, and that he
appealed to the Scriptures in support of his opinions,
exhorting the people to build their hopes of salvation on
Christ, to the exclusion of every other ground of confidence. We may add to the class before us Flaminio,
who published an exposition of the Psalms decidedly
Protestant in its dogmatic spirit, which he addressed to
the Pope as the Vicegerent of God upon earth, and
Vittoria Colonna, Marchioness of Pescara, an intimate
friend of Valdés, who had imbibed his spirit, and expressed in her beautiful Tuscan verse, inferior only to
Petrarch's, the idea of Valdés as to the inability of man
to work out his salvation, and exhibited Christ as the
only ground of the sinner's confidence. We may include
in the list the beautiful Giulia Gonzaga Colonna, Duchess
of Tragitto and Marchioness of Fondi, who was the most
imbued with the spirit of Valdés, and who, while she did
not leave the Church of Rome, gave proof that she was
friendly to the Reformers by entertaining the preachers
of the new doctrine, who were constantly pursued by the
indefatigable Papal Inquisitors.

Contarini, with these and other members of his party,

was most anxious to impress on the Pope and the Germans the importance of a union of all parties on the basis of the doctrine of justification. The two parties never came nearer to each other than in the Conference at Ratisbon in 1541.

The Pope, Paul III., was certainly friendly to the project of the union, or he would never have sent to it his Legate Contarini, whom he knew to be the leader of a party favourable to it in Italy. By his appointment of him and four other members of the reforming party to the cardinalate he showed his willingness to recognise new elements of very various qualities in the Roman Catholic hierarchy. The discussion of the proposals began on April 5. Contarini had not, however, the unlimited authority to settle the matter which he urgently demanded. The Pope insisted at first on the recognition of his absolute supremacy. Contarini saw at once that on this rock the scheme would suffer shipwreck. He therefore arranged that this question should be the last for discussion, and that meanwhile they should consider fundamental doctrines. Morone, Bishop of Modena, who held the same views with himself on the subject of justification, aided him with his advice. Contarini was the ruling spirit in the debates at the Conference. Dr. Ecke, Luther's old antagonist, at first gave them some trouble, but by compelling him to discuss closely every difficulty, they at last brought him to an agreement with them. The two parties at last astonished the world by declaring that they were united in the belief that original sin and justification by faith were essential doctrines. Contarini added that faith working by love must be the constraining motive to all holy obedience. Many looked on this as a holy conference, and did not doubt that it would end in the regeneration of Christendom. Cardinal Pole thus expressed himself in a letter to Contarini: 'When I observed this unanimity of sentiment, I experienced a feeling of pleasure such as no harmony of tones could have afforded me; not only because I see the coming of peace and union, but because those articles are the foundations of the Christian faith. . . . We hope that he who has begun so successfully will also complete what he has begun.'

This was a crisis the importance of which cannot be exaggerated. If the moderate party in Italy which planned and conducted this effort for union had been successful, the course of events would have been very different in the nations of Europe.

But difficulties soon made their appearance. Luther never could be persuaded that this doctrine of justification had taken root among those who had constantly offered the strongest opposition to it. He thought that Satan must have suggested a compromise which would have the effect of nullifying a truth on which he had insisted with all the fiery energy of his nature. He therefore dissuaded the Elector of Saxony from attending the Conference. His presence would have given the greatest weight to its deliberations. The Pope and the Cardinals also thought that there was an ambiguity in the terms in which the doctrine was expressed, which operated as a difficulty in the way of acceptance of the recommendations of the Conference.

Political difficulties also came to the front. Francis I. of France was struggling with Charles for the supremacy in Italy. He saw that, as the head of the moderate party in a united nation, Charles would not only possess an influence which might prevent a successful struggle with him for the mastery, but which also might enable him to guide the deliberations of any General Council which might be summoned to deliberate on the doctrinal or general position of the Church. The Pope, too, opposed the acceptance of the terms of union, not only on account of their ambiguity, but also because the Emperor, in opening the Diet and declaring that there would be a General Council, had not announced that the Pope alone could summon it.

'The Emperor's enemies,' writes Contarini's secretary, 'in Germany and other countries, who feared that his power would be greatly increased if he should combine all Germany in unity, began to sow dissensions among the theologians. Carnal envy broke up the Conference.'

The Pope and the whole College of Cardinals at length announced to Contarini their unanimous determination that no toleration should be admitted for the dogmas which had been the subjects of their deliberation. His failure was more conspicuous than his short appearance of success. Public opinion would not accept a concordat founded on philosophical and political considerations. He could not contend with the fierce passions which raged around him. The Protestants disregarded his proposed compromise because he was a Roman Catholic. The Roman Catholics regarded him as a Lutheran in disguise, and would not tolerate his writings until they had passed the ordeal of the Papal Inquisitors. He returned to Italy to endure the slanders propagated at Rome regarding his conduct at the Conference, and to mourn over the failure of his design to unite both parties as moderate Catholics, that they might be better able to promote the onward march of moral and spiritual regeneration.

The new religious spirit, which was impregnated with Protestant opinions, but was unwilling to separate from the Church of Rome, showed itself in the formation of new Orders and the reformation of those Orders which were no longer animated in the spirit of their founder. This spirit led through those Orders to the formation of an impassable gulf between the Lutherans and their opponents.

Paul III. was not the man to guide this movement.

As we have seen, he showed his willingness to recognise the importance of introducing new men into the Catholic hierarchy. But still he could not shake off the influence of the old régime. He could not, as we shall see when we speak of the Council of Trent, abandon the medieval policy of opposition to the Holy Roman Empire, especially when he had for his opponent the Emperor Charles V., a man distinguished for his ability, and, in consequence of the wealth and wide extent of his dominions, wielding a greater power than any of his predecessors. He saw the necessity of fundamental reforms in the Roman Catholic Church, but he could not promote them, because he was fond of pomp and empty parade; because he wished to surround himself with all the embellishments of art and luxury, with statues and paintings by the hands of eminent masters; because he was the slave of unscriptural superstitions, and looked to astrology to guide him in all his important movements; because he had a son and grandsons for whom he wished to obtain principalities in Italy, deeming their advancement of far greater importance than those conquests which would be the means of extending the boundaries of his Church, and of adding new provinces to his spiritual empire.

The monastic Orders stood in the van of that movement which led ultimately to the regeneration of the Church of Rome. Like a river small at its rise, but gradually swelled in its progress by tributary streams, the number of these reformed Orders, at first limited, becomes more and more conspicuous on the page of history. At length they become like the rushing torrent which flows majestically forward, foaming over the rocks which interrupt its progress, until at length it expands into a bay where, ' laughing at the storm, rich navies ride,' and pours a large tribute of waters into the ocean.

The signal for religious reform was given by the Order of Camaldoli. It had been founded in 1012 by St.

Romuald at Camaldoli in Tuscany as a particular division of the strict Order of the Benedictines. The members lived as hermits in their cells, and never associated with one another except when they were summoned to public worship. They were obliged to be without food for a long interval. But gradually this rule was relaxed. They surrounded themselves with piles of wealth, and, in direct contravention of the direction of their founder, they came forth from their cells and associated freely with one another in their monasteries. Paul Giustiani, a learned theologian, the son of a noble family at Venice, becoming a member of the Order at the age of thirty-four, undertook to re-establish the institutions of St. Romuald. He lived for some time with his followers in the caverns of Misaccio in the Papal States, which the members of the Order had ceded to him. Very soon other hermitages were founded on the model of Masaccio. Rich persons, entering the new congregations, conferred all their wealth upon them. After the death of Giustiani, which happened in 1528, the centre of the new congregation was transferred from Masaccio to the hermitage of Mont de la Couronne. The rules of the new congregation were very strict in their requirements. When the members were allowed to meet, they were required to observe the law of silence, except during one or two days in the winter and three days in the summer, when they were allowed to converse. They were obliged to chant the matins at midnight. Their food was extremely simple. Giustiani so far conformed to the primitive rule of St. Benedict as to require from his disciples manual labour for one hour every day. This austere congregation spread very rapidly in Italy, Germany, and Poland. We merely mention this reform as a specimen of the spirit of reformation which was beginning to show itself in the Church of Rome. The Order exercised no influence on the laity. A few individuals under the influence of the spirit of melancholy and mysticism could not save from absolute ruin a Church which had been shaken to its very foundation.

The most important reform was in the mendicant Orders which was effected by Matthew de Bassi. They had very much departed from the rules of their founder, St. Francis of Assisi. These holy beggars, who had not at first where to lay their heads, had long rivalled, nay eclipsed, the secular clergy in their sumptuous style of living, in their gorgeous vestments, and in the pomp and luxury with which they were surrounded. They had long, too, ceased to stand on the world's highway, and to address to those around them the words of exhortation and remonstrance. But now we witness a remarkable change. Their zeal, the striking conversions effected by their preaching, the services which they rendered on the occasion of a contagious malady, made them very popular with the multitude. Very soon they founded monasteries for the accommodation of the large numbers who flocked to them. Their first Vicar-General was Matthew de Bassi. He required that their houses and churches should be devoid of ornament, and that their vestment and food should show that they attended to the requirement of absolute poverty, which was the fundamental rule of their founder. They were expected to look every day for subsistence to the voluntary contributions of the faithful. The multitudes, as they listened to the fervid eloquence of the preacher, showing that he was impressed with a deep sense of the importance of the truths which he was commissioned to declare, fancied that they were listening to an inspired messenger of Jehovah, proclaiming His mind and will to the guilty inhabitants of this district of His empire. Their poverty, too, their abnegation of self, their holiness, counteracted the effect produced by the preaching of the Reformers, who were constantly declaiming against the avarice and corruption of the clergy, and confirmed the wavering multitude in their allegiance to the Church of Rome.

The Order of the Capuchins often made themselves ridiculous by the importance which they attached to insignificant details, and by the means which they adopted for gaining an influence over the common herd of the people. We should, however, be unjust if we did not state distinctly that, especially in Italy, the Capuchins had really become the friends, the comforters, and the spiritual guides of the people, to whom they had given relief in famines, epidemics, and amid the miseries of war. The gross vulgarity which is a peculiarity of this Order has given the members a great influence with the lower orders, because the latter are rough in their manners and cannot appreciate that refinement which is a distinguishing characteristic of the upper class of the clergy. The Capuchins have undoubtedly done much to retain the lower orders in Italy in their allegiance to the Church of Rome, and they therefore ought to have a place among those who at this time contributed to the regeneration of the Church, and so enabled it to carry on successfully its conflict with the Protestants for the ascendancy in certain districts of Europe.

While the Capuchins were thus devoting their energies to the promotion of the spiritual well-being of the people, another class was labouring with indefatigable energy for the relief of the sufferings and the supply of the wants of the lower orders of the community. They could not listen unmoved to the recital of the woes of the poor, the stranger, the fatherless, and the widow. When they heard the cry of the distress ascending from the sufferers, they exerted every effort for the mitigation and removal of their calamities. That cry haunted them wherever they went ; it scared sleep from their eyes and slumber from their eyelids. They could not be satisfied until they had ministered to the relief of the victims of disease, until they had poured the oil and wine of heavenly consolation into the wounded spirit.

Jean de Dieu was the leader of this class. He was a native of Portugal, and had obtained employment as a shepherd, a soldier, and a maker of images. At length he was supposed to be mad, because he gave an exaggerated description of his sufferings, saying that he was enduring in his soul the torments of hell, that he saw before him a lake of fire, where ' the smoke of torment ascended up for ever and ever.'_ He was therefore shut up in a madhouse, where the inmates were lashed till the blood was drawn from them—a mode of treatment which caused them excruciating agony. After his release from this asylum, he determined to devote all his energies to the service of the poor. The Archbishop of Granada, who took an interest in him, provided him with the funds required to enable him to found a hospital, which he conducted with great skill, ability, and practical wisdom. While his hospital was supplied with all that was required for the victims of disease, he was in the habit of walking about clothed in rags. The Bishop of Tuy gave him the surname of de Dieu, in order to express his great piety and his inexhaustible benevolence, and he directed proper vestments to be given to himself and his assistants. When he died in 1550, he had not completed the organization of his congregation ; but he had created by his self-denial and by his sacrifices, by his activity and energy, the Order of the Brothers of Charity, which Roman Catholics affirm to be one of the greatest ornaments of their Church.

The Brothers of Charity have undoubtedly by their humility, by the services rendered to the sick and the unfortunate, done more for the advancement of Romanism than a hundred Bishops or doctors in theology. The diseased whom they have saved from death, the parents and the children whom they have restored to the bosom of their happy families, bear eloquent testimony to the value of their services, by which they had confirmed the wavering multitude in their allegiance to the Church of Rome.

But none of these foundations, if we look to their influence on the regeneration of the Roman Catholic Church, can be compared to the Orders of regular clergy which were instituted at the time before us. The first of these is the Order of the Theatines. Its founder, Gaëtan de Thiène, was born at Vicenza in the year 1480. He quitted a lucrative employment at Rome, to which he was appointed by Julius II., and took Orders soon afterwards. In 1519 he associated himself with some prelates and priests of the Church of Rome, in number about sixty, who, deeply grieved by the disorders in the Church, and by the commencement of the Lutheran revolt, formed a little community, determined to devote themselves to prayer, to the conversion of the unbelieving, and the removal of the doubts of those who were wavering in their allegiance to the Church of Rome. They called the body so created, the object of which was to combat heresy with the weapons of peace, the Oratory of Divine Love. The fame of this Order spread rapidly through Italy, and in many towns an endeavour was made to imitate it.

At Vicenza, his native town, he found a convent of Hieronymites, who were anxious to conform to the usages and practices of the Oratory of Divine Love. They asked Gaëtan de Thiène to take up his abode among them, and to aid them in carrying this design into effect. As he had long been desirous of a life of contemplation, he gave up the important post which he occupied at Rome, and took up his abode in the home of the Hieronymites at Vicenza, where he founded a hospital. Shortly afterwards he emigrated to Venice, where he introduced reforms into the hospital, and astonished the whole city by his pious zeal, and by the eloquence of his sermons, which had the effect of confirming many in their allegiance to the Church of Rome. He founded at the same time a hospital at Verona.

' I will never cease,' he said, 'to distribute to the poor all which I possess, until I shall have become so poor in the service of Christ that I shall not have more than enough to pay for my funeral.'

Very soon, however, this mystical piety, exclusively directed to the improvement of private life, was succeeded by a grand view of the public and practical purposes to which it might become subservient. The rapid progress of the Reformation led Gaëtan to reflect on the causes of the decline of the power of the Church of Rome, which became evident through the loss of several provinces of her spiritual empire. He came to the conclusion that the real cause was the evil life of the secular clergy, whose duty it was to preach to their people by the silent eloquence of a holy life, and to labour with indefatigable zeal for the promotion of their spiritual and everlasting interests. He resolved, therefore, to apply a remedy to this evil, and to found an institution designed to reform the character and education of the parochial clergy, and to lead them to exhibit the Apostolical virtues of the primitive Church. Anxious at once to carry this idea into effect, he returned to Rome to work it out in the capital of the world. His first friend and companion was Boniface da Colle, a lawyer of Alexandria in Lombardy, who lived in the Court of Rome, and had assisted Gaëtan in laying the foundation of the Oratory of Divine Love. The opinion, however, seems to have been that Thiène had not the energy, the intellectual power, nor the influence which would enable him to carry his resolution into effect. He was well adapted to the work of ministering to the wants of the destitute and the afflicted, of giving heavenly consolation to the wounded spirit, and of bringing back to the fold sheep which had wandered into forbidden pastures of Protestantism. He had not, however, the ability to found an important Order which might go forth into the world and contend successfully with the legions of Protestantism.

He was fortunate in an early stage of his career in an introduction to a prelate who was well qualified to enable him to carry into effect, on a large scale, the reforms in the system of his Church which he deemed to be essential to the recovery of her lost ascendency. John Peter Caraffa was the individual who greatly aided him in his work. We shall see that the one supplied the deficiencies of the other. Caraffa was born in 1476 in the kingdom of Naples, where his family possessed numerous fiefs, duchies, principalities, marquisates, and baronies. As a child he showed great intelligence, and made some progress in a knowledge of science. He was remarkable for an impetuous disposition, which even in early life led him to throw all his energies into his work. When he was fourteen years of age he determined to go into a monastery of the Dominicans. His father, who was very ambitious, and was anxious that he should distinguish himself in a secular position, or at least that he should rise to distinction in the Church of Rome, forcibly carried him off from the monastery. The young man was obliged to submit to the will of his father. After he had made some progress in a knowledge of Greek and Hebrew he went to Rome, holding one of the rich benefices in the gift of his family, and was appointed to an important office in the Papal Court in 1503. In the following year one of his parents gave to him a bishopric, which, being situated in the territory subject to them, was always considered to be at their disposal, the bishopric of Chieti or Theano. One of his uncles was at this time a Cardinal. We are not surprised, therefore, to hear that the young Bishop soon gained great influence in the Eternal City, that he was admitted to the most important meetings of the Curia, and that he was sent as Apostolic Nuncio to Spain and England. He was rewarded for his services by his appointment to the archbishopric of Brindisi, but he continued to be called the Theatine Bishop, by which title he has become generally known to the world.

After the commencement of the Lutheran revolt, Caraffa became one of the most earnest defenders of the Roman Catholic Church. He not only, along with Gaëtan de Thiène, with Sadolet, and many others, entered the Oratory of Divine Love, but he also published several theological treatises against Luther. His zeal for a reform in the Church of Rome, which might enable it to contend successfully with the Lutheran movement, recommended him very strongly to the Pope, Adrian VI., whose views on that reform were similar to his own. He drew him into his own circle, and this brought him into connection with Paul Guistiani, the founder of the Camaldolites at Mont de la Couronne. Adrian VII. was Pope only for a short time, and his successor, Clement VII. occupied himself with political matters which had not the remotest connection with a reformation of the Church. Caraffa had no hope of any progress in the work of reformation under this Pontiff. He therefore determined, with a view to his own soul, to bury himself in the seclusion of the cloister. But he had too much energy, too strong a desire for an active life, not to accept with pleasure a proposal of his old friend Gaëtan de Thiène that he should assist him in his work by combining with retirement in the monastery incessant work for the promotion of reform in the Church.

The Pope, who valued him very much because he possessed the qualities and qualifications which he wanted, endeavoured to retain him in the Pontifical Court. By a brief dated May 12, 1524, he gave him an absolute power of enforcing discipline among all priests living at Rome. But because he thought that his active work from his own monastery would be more likely to promote the general and permanent reform of the regular clergy, or because he thought that he could not show sufficient strictness in the position of which he had the offer under a very feeble Pope like Clement VII., he never wavered in his determination to decline the offered dignity. In vain the Pope spoke to him of the duty of every Bishop to be faithful to his own diocese, with which he was supposed to have contracted a mystical union, compared to the holy estate of matrimony. Jean Pierre, through his persistent importunity, obtained at length from Clement VII. the permission which he had often demanded in vain. Then, to the great astonishment of the Romans, little accustomed to events of this description, he resigned his two bishoprics, and exchanged the pomp of a Bishop and his luxurious style of living for voluntary poverty and work, which had for its object the reformation of the secular clergy. The Pope left to him the dignity and title of Bishop of Théano.

These two men, who were thus united in a common work, were a perfect contrast to each other. Caraffa was energetic, bold, violent, active — a practical man of business, as much inclined to destroy as to build up; and Gaëtan de Thiène was one 'who to the world appeared to be an angel, to himself a worm,' humble, gentle, pious, little inclined for conversation, and passing his time in prayers, in penitential sorrow, and in seeking to promote the Divine glory in the salvation of his ignorant and perishing fellow-creatures. The one, in fact, as we have said, supplied the deficiencies of the other. It will at once be evident that, in this alliance, Caraffa, who was already as Bishop superior in rank to Gaëtan, was more likely than the latter through that superiority, when he had become by his intercourse with Gaëtan more humble, and holy, and heavenly-minded, by his energy, practical ability, and knowledge of the world, to conduct the work of the new institute to a successful issue.

The original idea, due doubtless to Gaëtan, was to form a religious community, not of monks, but of priests, who should live together, who should take the three monastic vows of poverty, chastity, and obedience, but who should engage in the public celebration of Divine worship, and should administer the Sacraments like secular priests. This was the reason for giving to this institution the name of the Congregation of Regular Clergy. They were not called brothers, but priests. Their Superior had the title, not of Prior or Guardian, but of Provost. They wore a black robe and a baretta instead of a monastic cowl. They were free from all the ceremonies and all the acts of worship which occupy the greater part of the time of the monks. Assembled in a congregation, they wished to work together for the advancement of the moral and religious well-being of the world around them. This was at the time a new idea, which gave a great influence to this community, and especially to the Jesuits, who, as we shall see, subsequently adopted it. The real object of this institution was, however, not so much to advance the spiritual welfare of the laity as to show priests in what manner they should reform themselves. The idea was that their method should be, not to give them rules which were never kept, nor to inflict punishments upon them which were soon forgotten, but to teach them to set Christ constantly before them, to aim at the imitation of the graces and virtues for which He was conspicuous, and never to be satisfied until they stand before Him in heaven arrayed in garments of unspotted whiteness, like the angels and archangels who stand around His throne. In short, Caraffa, who was very ambitious, was anxious to make his institution a nursery for Bishops and high ecclesiastical dignitaries. His idea was that priests who were trained in this school would be more likely to take care that their clergy were remarkable for their personal holiness. He wished also to admit to this Order only those who were members of noble families. At length it became a rule of this institution that its members should decline to take charge of parishes, and that the institution should become a seminary of Bishops.

Boniface da Colle and Paul Consiglieri, both of them noblemen, were associated with Gaëtan and Caraffa in their work. They obtained from Clement VII. in 1524 a pontifical brief expressing approval of their institution, granting them the privileges of Canons Regular of the Lateran, placing them directly under the patronage of the Holy See, and allowing them to elect a Provost whose power should last for three years. They all of them at once gave up all their property, a very meritorious surrender on the part especially of Caraffa, because he not not only held many rich benefices, but had besides a large private fortune. He was the inspiring genius of the new association, and was therefore unanimously appointed its first Provost. They occupied a small house on Monte Riccio. There they passed their time in poverty, in the study of the Gospels, in those spiritual exercises and those Divine meditations which connected them with eternity. The quietude which reigned around them enabled them to rise above the world and the things of the world, and to hold high converse with the adorable Trinity. The distinguishing feature of this institution was that the members united with the vows of the monks the duties and sacred characters of the clergy. Gradually, as we have seen, it became a seminary for the training of Bishops. A distinguishing feature of the Order was, however, that they should go forth into the streets and lanes of the city and minister to the spiritual and temporal wants of the bond-slaves of sin and Satan. Caraffa and his associates, by their vigorous eloquence in public, and their work among the slaves of vice and the patrons of crime, produced a great impression on the masses of the population. They thus succeeded in time in arresting the progress of that revolt which was robbing the Church of Rome of one province after another of her spiritual empire. Several associations were subsequently formed on the model of the Theatines. The best-known among them were the Barnabites, or Regular Clerks of St. Paul, founded in 1530, and sanctioned by Clement VII. in 1533. The members of this Order aimed at the attainment of the same ends as the Theatines, but in a more democratical manner. They made it their great object to arrest the progress of infidelity. They went forth from their colleges and preached to the masses. They have thus succeeded in arresting the progress of the spiritual revolt, and in restoring to the Church of Rome many who had ceased to be her obedient subjects.

We must not omit to mention Philip de Neri, one of the most remarkable figures among the Roman ecclesiastics of the sixteenth century. He has been justly called the Apostle of Rome. No one has contributed more than de Neri to the reform of the Roman clergy, and the improvement of the moral and spiritual condition of the people of Rome. He was a man of shrewd common-sense. He instituted at Rome a society called the Trinity of Pilgrims; the object of which was to look after the pilgrims on their arrival at Rome, to superintend the moral training of all around him, to promote serious, frequent, and popular preaching, active ministration among the masses, and unsystematized, fervent, and private devotion.

We see, then, that a fever for the establishment of Orders at this time prevailed in the Church of Rome.

They were the expression of an earnest desire to retrieve the fallen fortunes of Romanism. Efforts for the reformation of the Roman Catholic Church had ended in failure. The thunder-clouds were hanging gloomily over the Church. Flash after flash had been seen, portending a storm which might shatter into fragments the gorgeous structure of Romanism. We now see that the Roman Catholics were awakened to a sense of their danger, and that they took the right course for their preservation from the destruction with which they were threatened. We believe that the reform of the old Orders and the establishment of new Orders were the first great means of the regeneration of Romanism.

A very full account of the Order of the Theatines has been given, because they suggested the idea of the establishment of the Order of the Jesuits, which acted an important part in the struggle between Protestantism and Romanism. We shall, therefore, in the next chapter explain the rules by which they were guided, and the training by which they were enabled to come off victorious in the deadly struggle with their foes.

CHAPTER III.

THE JESUITS.

THE Order of the Jesuits some time after it was established exercised a very wide but subordinate influence. Ignatius Loyola burned to achieve distinction in the ranks of chivalry. In the early part of his life, a vision had been constantly floating before him of captives rescued by him from the power of the infidel, of mighty warriors smitten down by the strength of his right arm amid the tumult of the battlefield. But a severe wound, which disabled him for life, compelled him to abandon the idea of the coveted distinction as a warrior.

Now, new visions presented themselves to him. During his seclusion in the sick-room, he read the history of the achievements of those spiritual warriors whose names fill a large space in the annals of Rome. He determined to rival their glory. If he could not win the chaplet with which the Queen of Love surrounds the brow of the warrior in some well-fought tournament, he would seek the undying wreath often conferred on those who have conducted to a successful issue some important spiritual enterprise. He made the alleged Queen of Heaven—the Virgin Mary—the mistress of his affections.

Just as the candidate for the honour of knighthood watched over his arms from the time when the light slowly faded into duskiness and the stars twinkled on the blue vault of heaven, and continued his vigil until the ruddy glow of the morning, which was to witness his investiture, made its appearance in the sky, so this spiritual paladin hung up his arms before the shrine of the Virgin Mary, and vowed that he would maintain the superiority of her attractions in mortal combat against all gainsayers.

The thought of this spiritual betrothal, the hope of laying at her feet his well-earned trophies, would, he was sure, animate him to perform prodigies of valour in the approaching conflict with the legions of Protestantism. At times, indeed, he wavered in his determination. In all probability, if he had regained his health, he would once more have cherished the fond hope of earthly glory. In this case he might have won a transitory honour as a knight distinguished for his prowess. But his name would not have been known to the world. The spiritual destinies of many countries would have been changed.

But Ignatius soon found that he must abandon the idea of the coveted distinction. Then he sought by mortifications and penances to obtain the same distinction as the spiritual heroes of past years. His flesh was torn by continual scourgings. The midnight beheld him lying on the cold pavement, the morning dawn saw him in the same place and posture, engaged in the performance of this painful penance. But, like Luther, he found that he could never do enough to obtain the approbation of his Maker. He did not, however, like him, go to the Source of peace and consolation.   He did not discover the doctrine of justification by faith in Christ.

At length he began to imagine that all his torments proceeded from the Prince of Darkness. Finding that the retrospect was a source of uneasiness, he determined no longer to think of his past life.   He would not take the Bible for his guide.   He would listen only to visions and revelations.   Once he deluded himself with the idea that he saw, in mystic symbols, the Almighty causing chaos to disappear, and calling the vast fabric of the earth into existence.   Afterwards, as he was standing on the steps of a church in an ecstatic trance, he saw the Trinity in Unity.   At another time, when he was sitting on the bank of a river, and gazing on its waters as they were sparkling before him in the noonday sun, he fancied that he was favoured with a sudden revelation of the sublime mysteries of Christianity.   Henceforth he fancied that he could dispense with the assistance of Holy Scripture.   A form unseen by those around him was, as he thought, continually beckoning him forward.   The battlements of heaven seemed to him to be lined with the heroes of his Church.   He heard their voices in every wind, animating him to press forward in the path of self-denial, to encounter trial, persecution, death itself, in the service of his Spiritual Leader.

The Pope, finding that he was, from the want of sufficient knowledge, teaching heresy in Spain, forbade him to take upon himself the office of a spiritual instructor till he had passed through a course of theology in one of the Universities.   He repaired to Paris, where he soon gathered round him a little band of followers, all of whom were animated by the same zeal for which he was distinguished.   He at first conceived the idea of repairing to Jerusalem, where he proposed to devote all his energies to the work of the conversion of the unbelieving and the edification of the faithful; but finding that war between the Turks and the Venetians would prevent him from carrying his schemes into effect, he determined to offer his services to the Pope for the establishment of a new Order.

He decided that the Order which he proposed to establish should be called the Company of Jesus, a body united to combat spiritual enemies, and that its members should be pledged to devote themselves body and soul to the Lord Jesus Christ, and to His true and lawful successor upon earth. Loyola at first experienced some opposition, but at length he gained a victory over his opponents. Paul III. by the Bull of September 27, 1540, ' Regimini militantis Ecclesiæ,' gave the Papal sanction to that celebrated Order, which has occupied an important place in the history of the world and the Church of Rome through many generations.

The ascetic reveries of Loyola had led, in the manner described by us, to the foundation of the most powerful, the most practical, the best-conducted Order which has ever existed. A strong weapon was thus placed in his hands, which he hastened to sharpen and to polish. Soon after its foundation the Society of Jesus became a power in the world. The first general was well qualified to conduct its work to a successful issue. That expressive countenance, that figure emaciated by fastings and mortifications, that high forehead, those small but bright and piercing eyes, that aquiline nose, that mouth showing, by the prominence and size of the lower lip, the difficulty with which he had overcome sensuality, gave evidence that Ignatius Loyola possessed all the qualities required to enable him to conduct a most important enterprise to a successful end. He had a firm conviction of the holiness and the importance of the cause to which he resolved to devote all his energies. He thought that he had been chosen by God to lay low his enemies, and to establish the Church in all its ancient grandeur.

'We ought,' he said, 'to have so much confidence in God that, if we have not a ship at our disposal, we should be ready to cross the sea on a plank, when our object is the promotion of His glory.' The advancement of the highest interests of the Roman Catholic Church became the paramount object of his life. 'If she teaches us,' he said, 'that anything which is white is black, we ought to declare it to be black immediately.' We must at once see that this sacrifice of reason has been the fruitful parent of all those absurd superstitions which have given to this Order an unenviable place in the annals of the world.

In defence of the cause of the Roman Catholic Church, Loyola displayed invincible energy and perseverance. Trial did not daunt, difficulties did not discourage him in her service. He regarded with disdain privations, injuries, fatigue, the injustice and opposition of the world. The struggle which he carried on against heresy appeared to him and his followers a benefit for the human race. In comparison with this object, every object seemed to them to sink into absolute insignificance. They thought that they were thus conferring a benefit on the world. They were ready to sacrifice every consideration to the advancement of this work.

A favourite maxim with him and his followers was that the power of denying our own will is worth more than the power of raising the dead. 'A tempest is not so great an evil as a calm, and it is a greater danger to be without enemies than to have a host of them arrayed against you.' Though a thousand hostile forms thronged the path which they were pursuing, he and his followers were still prepared to march forward. They planted their footsteps firmly in the breaches made in the outworks of Protestantism, and did not retire until they had beaten back their enemies, or, if they should fail in that object, they were determined to sacrifice their lives while endeavouring to stay the march of their adversaries. They refused to be satisfied while one hostile banner floated in the air, or while one province of Christendom continued in the occupation of the armies of their foes.

This cause appeared so important to Ignatius that he did not hesitate to employ any means for the advancement of it. He thought that great prudence in the choice of means was of far greater importance than a high degree of holiness without this quality. We believe that this maxim is the germ of all the moral errors of which the Jesuits have been guilty since the foundation of their Order. It led Ignatius to pay less attention to natural goodness than to a firmness of character and a great skill in the management of worldly business which he considered to be indispensable qualifications for admission to the ranks of his members. The members must be, as he states in a letter to the Rector of the Jesuit College of Coimbra in 1551, men of a certain height, of an agreeable personality, of exquisite tact, of unscrupulous energy, who will show great worldly prudence in the management of the important work committed to their charge. We must admit, indeed, that these are the qualities and qualifications well suited to a militant Order anxious to add recruits to the ranks of the Papal army. But they are not the principles of the sturdy Saxon peasant who at this time taught his fellow-countrymen to rise to their high destinies, to cast off the formalism and superstition of ages, and to become candidates for the imperishable crown.

Lord Macaulay, with that tone of brilliant paradox for which he was conspicuous, has attached an exaggerated importance to the work of the Jesuits in connection with the Counter-Reformation. He seems to consider that to them chiefly is due the restoration of Romanism to its lost ascendancy in many countries of Europe. We must admit that they acted an important part in this great drama. We must, however, maintain that they would have been utterly unable to govern masterfully the great Roman Catholic revival if the armies of Spain, conducted by the most skilful generals in Europe, who so improved the living machine under their guidance as to bring it to bear with irresistible force on the enemy, had not been placed at the disposal of the Roman Catholic Church ; if Philip II. of Spain, the most powerful monarch in Europe, who had the wealth of the most fertile territory in Europe at his disposal, and was lord of the rich empires of Mexico and Peru, had not poured his wealth into the Papal treasury, and had not laboured for the destruction of Protestantism ; if the decrees of the Council of Trent (to be described hereafter), to the paramount importance of which, in connection with their work, Lord Macaulay does not make the least reference, had not been so framed as to bring into prominence all the doctrines of the Church of Rome, and to render absolutely impossible a reconciliation between that Church and the Protestants ; if the dungeons of the Inquisition had not been full of victims, and the satellites of the Church of Rome had not inflicted on the Protestants unheard-of barbarities.

The truth is that the Jesuits were only good secondary agents in the work for which the Order was established— the advantage of the Church as represented by the Papacy. The record of the achievements of this remarkable Order is stamped in legible characters on the history of Europe through many generations. Their persevering labours, carried on in the spirit of obedience to the Pope, the pliability with which they adapted themselves to the tastes and prejudices of the world, their skill in theological controversy, the fascinating influence which they exercised, the success which attended their efforts to win over eminent Protestants to the faith, whose conversion carried with it the conversion of many others, because they looked on them as beings of a superior order, were no doubt the means by which they extended the boundaries of Romanism, and confirmed the wavering multitude in their allegiance to the Pope. In the prosecution of their object they gave their sanction to a system compatible with the indulgence of the worst passions of human nature. They were certainly to stamp with their strong disapproval any indulgence in fraud, violence, covetousness, or oppression. The following directions were given to them : Make no show of compromise with evil, but explain away the evil by distinctions and reservations until it disappears altogether. Explain to others the difficulty of knowing whether a sin be venial or mortal, and that there are many chances that it will not be found to be a sin; a way may thus be found for the gratification of every human desire.

In a country ruled by a despot who was friendly to them, they maintained ' the right Divine of Kings to govern wrong.' In another, the Sovereign of which was opposed to them, they would encourage the people in lifting up against him the standard of revolt, and even asserted that if the assassin should sheathe his knife in his bosom, he would not expose himself to any punishment when standing before the judgment-seat of Christ. In the company of men whose piety was of a morose character, they would stand forth the censors of their fellow-men. When they passed into the company of the gay and licentious who were smitten with remorse for their sins and crimes, they would administer an opiate to their consciences. They would call their sins venial trespasses, because they could not withstand the seductions of lust nor control the violence of their passions. In fact, they are chargeable with the great guilt of publishing a system of morality perfectly compatible with the indulgence of the worst passions of our nature. The analysis of their opinions cannot fail to justify the condemnation passed upon them by the Parliament in Paris in 1762 : 'These doctrines tend to destroy the natural law, that rule of manners which God Himself has imprinted on the hearts of men, and in consequence to sever all the bonds of civil society by the authorization of false-hood, perjury, the most culpable impurity, and in a word each passion and each crime of human weakness ; to obliterate all sentiments of humanity by favouring homi-cide and parricide ; and to annihilate the authority of Sovereigns in the State.'

If we wish to know the secret of their success, we ought to consider the system by which they have been trained for their work.   Every means is employed to conquer the soul, and to make the Jesuit a passive instrument in the hands of his superior.   The exact enumeration of his sins, often repeated in confession ; appeals to the imagination which have the effect of enabling him to realize spiritual visions ; frequent conver-sations with his own soul as well as with Christ, the Virgin, and the Saints ; a vivid representation of the Saviour agonizing and bleeding on the accursed tree ; a representation of the lost souls wandering over the waves of the lake of unquenchable fire, seeking rest but finding none—these were the means employed to conquer the soul of the disciple, and to prepare him for any work which might be committed to his charge.   The second stage is to hear in imagination the groans, the blas-phemies against Christ and the Saints, in order that he may have a deep sense of the horrors of that world of despair.   The impression produced on the conscience is supposed to be deepened when he is told to fancy himself on the other side of the gulf, to hear in an agony of re-morse the songs of the redeemed, to think that he has deliberately ruined his own soul, and that he has excluded himself from the society of that rejoicing multitude.

The senses are not less taken captive than the heart

and the imagination. When the object is to terrify the disciple now under training, human bones are placed before him. When, on the contrary, the work is to give a vivid idea of the resurrection, his instructors place in his hand fresh and fragrant flowers. Fastings and flagellations, peculiar postures of the body, the exclusion of the light of day in order that the soul may not be hindered in looking into the chambers of imagery, groanings and weepings, are prescribed as mechanical aids when the soul seems sluggish, and is unable to. have a realizing sense of spiritual and eternal realities. In fact, the individual subject to these influences becomes a mere automaton, under the absolute control of an imperious master; and the conclusion to which he is brought is that he is a mere machine which must obey the guiding influence of one who has a paramount claim on his dutiful obedience.

We are thus reminded that absolute submission to the Church of Rome is the end of these spiritual exercises. The third rule in them is that, in order to be identified with the Church, if she states that, 'if anything which appears to our eyes to be white is black, we ought at once to sacrifice our intelligence and 'to declare that it is black.' This obedience is the very basis of the Order of the Jesuits. We do not indeed mean to say that it is peculiar to this Society. On the contrary, since the days of Benedict of Nursia, absolute obedience is stated to be the principal object of the fraternities. The strongest expressions, which seem almost hyperbolical, have been employed to represent it. St. Basil, the father of the monastic Orders, told his members that they must be in the hands of their Superiors as the axe in the hand of the woodman. The monks of the Chartreuse are told that they must sacrifice their will as sheep led to the slaughter. The Carmelites are told that resistance to the order of a Superior is a mortal sin. St. Bonaventure tells us that a man perfectly obedient resembles a dead body which is moved without any resistance. We cannot find, however, that any one of these has brought forward so prominently as Ignatius Loyola this absolute, this blind obedience, as the very basis of his Order.

His ideas on this subject are fully expressed in his Constitution, in his letters to the Portuguese Jesuits, and in his ' Exercitia.' ' I ought to be subject to a Superior who endeavours to subjugate my judgment and to subdue my understanding. When it seems to me that I am commanded by my Superior to do anything against which my conscience revolts as sinful, and my Superior judges otherwise, it is my duty to yield my doubts to him, unless I am constrained by evident reasons.' ' I ought to be like a corpse, which has neither will nor understanding ; like a crucifix, which is turned about by him who holds it ; like a staff in the hands of an old man, who uses it at will for his assistance or pleasure.' ' I desire that you strive and exercise yourselves to recognise Christ our Lord in every Superior.' ' He who wishes to offer up himself wholly to God must make the sacrifice, not only of his will, but also of his intelligence.' ' A sin, whether venial or mortal, must be committed, if it is commanded by the Superior in the name of the Lord Jesus Christ.' ' Every part of the Roman Catholic creed, of Roman Catholic habits, of Roman Catholic institutions, must be defended with great valour.' ' It is our duty to uphold reliques, the worship of the Saints, stations, pilgrimages, indulgences, jubilees, the candles which are lighted before the altars.' Just as a subordinate was enjoined to sin, if sin were ordered by his Superior, so the whole company were bound to lie, to do the things which they disapproved, and preach the mummeries which they disbelieved, if they were ordered to do so by the Church.

Ignatius attained his object. Absolute, servile, blind

obedience became the distinguishing feature of the Jesuits. The Roman Catholic Church was passing through one of those crises which often decide the fate of nations. It was necessary to create a force, commanded by bold, skilful, and energetic leaders, which should combat heresy with secular as well as spiritual weapons. They must show in their exterior as little as possible which would identify them with monks. They should be exempt from those spiritual exercises, those communings with eternity, which occupy much of the time of those who bury themselves amid the gloom of cloistered seclusion. They must go forth on the world's highway, and should labour to arrest the progress of that revolt which was robbing their Church of one province after another of her spiritual empire.

In the prosecution of their work, Ignatius expected the same subordination, the same prompt obedience to orders from his followers, which are to be found in a regular army. Like the private in ordinary warfare, the Jesuit was expected, immediately after the command had been given, to fling himself into the deadly breach, or to plunge into the heat and sorest part of the battle, even though he thought he was rushing on certain destruction. But there was this difference between the two cases. The soldier may, while obeying the order, lawfully in his mind call in question the military skill and prudence of the general who had issued it. But the Jesuits were taught to regard the general of their Order as the incarnation of wisdom; they were bound to obey him, as if they recognised in him the presence of Christ. Their Constitutions (Part VI., chap. i., sec. 1) distinctly state that 'obedience is to be rendered in all matters, when only a sign shows us the will of our Superiors.'

The most characteristic passage is the following : ' They must show to the world that they are led by their Superiors, as if they were a carcase which can be carried wherever we wish, or as if they were the stick of an old man which guides his tottering footsteps.' The nature of this obedience is further stated in the fifth chapter of the seventh part of their Constitutions : ' It is necessary to obey the Pope without any restriction—even when obedience to his commands seems to lead us into ruin ; and we are equally obliged to commit a sin, whether mortal or venial, if our Superior commands it in the name of the Lord Jesus Christ.' We have here, then, the worst accusations of the enemies of the Jesuits fully justified by the Constitutions of Loyola.   Under the pretence of some advantage, the Superior may command the Jesuit to perpetrate the most atrocious crime, and the inferior is bound to obey the Order on account of his promise of obedience.   The motive for this detestable act is stated to be ' the glory of Christ our Creator and our Lord, who warmly approves of this act of the homicide.'

When the will, the passions, and the judgment of the Jesuits had thus been enslaved, they were sent forth to win the nations to the rule of the Pope.   They professed, indeed, to take a vow of poverty upon themselves. Loyola declared it to be the bulwark of religion, and that on that account he wished to preserve it in its primitive purity.   All the members are stated to be obliged to discharge gratuitously their ecclesiastical duties.   The priests are not allowed to receive money for the journeys which they have undertaken.   This rule at first seems exceedingly severe.   A close examination, however, will serve to show us that the apparent severity is so much mitigated that scarcely any of it remains.   The houses and churches of the members cannot have any revenues ; but if anyone should make a present to them, they may accept it, on condition that the Society should have the administration of the property.   All the colleges, the houses of novices, the institutes of education, were exempt from this obligation. On the contrary, the colleges may accept freely any donation or any legacy. Thus, then, it is perfectly evident that the Jesuits, notwithstanding their profession of poverty, may easily accumulate wealth. We constantly see proof that they may, by their exceptions, neutralize the strictest rules when it is contrary to their interest to observe them. The Constitutions of the Order direct the members to discharge gratuitously their ecclesiastical duties. The Constitution is easily evaded. ' If anyone should offer to recompense us for any service which we have rendered to him, we cannot refuse to accept this token of his gratitude.' The Constitutions, again, forbid anyone to travel on horseback. Permission is, however, in this case given when health has given way, or the business of the Society requires expedition. Thus, then, exceptions reduce to a nullity rules so strict in appearance that it would seem impossible to evade them.

Many of the Jesuits having been thus trained in the institutions established by Ignatius were to settle in various localities, and were to devote all their energies to the instruction of the rising generation. To the superior quality of the instruction given by them they owed a large part of their prodigious influence. Young persons learned more in a year with them than others in two years. New catechisms, grammars, and manuals of history enabled them to learn with facility in a few months what it had cost years to acquire under the former system of instruction. Even Protestants called back their children from distant lands and placed them under the direction of the Jesuits. By their skill in civil transactions they insinuated themselves into the favour of statesmen, and obtained admission to the cabinets of Princes. They were the secret spring of many political combinations, which affected the happiness and interest not only of their own generation, but also of generations then unborn. A great part of their influence was obtained through the confessional. All classes came to them for confession, because they fancied that from their superior knowledge of the human heart, and their superior skill in unravelling difficult questions in theology, which they had acquired through careful training, they would infuse balm into the wounded conscience, and guide them right in cases of difficulty and perplexity.

They were at length an omnipresent influence. Amid the snows of Lapland, amid the regions of eternal ice, beneath the burning sun of India, amid the busy marts of commerce, among those who pursued their occupations in the bowels of the earth, among the silken band of courtiers, in the 'perfumed chambers of the great,' in the rude hovels of the peasantry, the Jesuits were to be found in every character and every garb, violating indeed the plainest precepts of morality, but faithful in their allegiance to the Head of their Church, instructing the ignorant, soothing mental and bodily anguish, rekindling decaying zeal, fixing wavering resolutions, recovering those who had apostatized from Romanism, and adding new soldiers to the ranks of the Papal army.

We have now seen the nature of the organization called into existence to arrest the progress of the Reformation. We observe that in the early stages of their existence as an Order the Jesuits gained brilliant victories over their foes. The weapon must, however, be wielded by strong hands, especially trained for this warfare, if it was to mow down the powerful battalions drawn up against them. We must remember that independence and intellectual power are required to enable us to strike out and to carry into effect original ideas. A society in which every effort is made to repress individuality, which seeks to enslave the intellect of its members, which makes them a mere wheel in a gigantic machine, is doomed to become degenerate, and to fail in fulfilling the great end for which it was established. In its best times the Society of Jesus contained many remarkable men of gigantic intellect, but not one like Ajax, who towered by the head and shoulders above his fellows. No one could burst his fetters and come forth disenthralled into the land of light and life and liberty. Anyone who was gifted with original intellect saw at once that he could not as a Jesuit achieve the distinction which was the object of his desire, and bring to the birth the ideas struggling in his mind, which, worked out, would make him the benefactor of his fellow-men, and cause his name to descend with honour to future generations.

The terrible machine of war, the construction of which we have witnessed, has been worked during a long period with deadly effect against the powerful battalions of its foes. Sometimes allied with Kings against people, sometimes with people against Kings, the Jesuits have never known but one object, to maintain that the Supreme Pontiff has the first claim on the allegiance of the people and their rulers. Every nation may lawfully remove by murder every Sovereign who refuses obedience to him. The despotic power with which they have armed the Pope must, however, be wielded by themselves. We shall see the practical working of this theory in subsequent chapters. We shall find that, propagated among the people by themselves as the Pope's representatives, it led Jaques Clement and Ravaillac to sheathe their daggers in the bosom of Henry III. and Henry IV. of France. We shall see that they promoted the League of the Guises, which had for its object a change in the French dynasty; that they were concerned in the bloody massacre of St. Bartholomew; that they procured the revocation of the Edict of Nantes; and that they organized the bloody and terrible Thirty Years' War. Supported by the legions of their fellow-soldiers, they have made themselves obnoxious by their intrigues in every country where they

5

have been established. They were expelled from Venice in 1606, from Bohemia in 1618, from Naples and the Netherlands in 1622, from Russia in 1676, from Portugal in 1759, from Spain in 1767, and from France in 1764. The Order was abolished by Clement XIV. in 1773 on account of the anti-social spirit which it at that time exhibited. It was restored by Pius VII. in 1814 for the purpose of aiding him to promote the Papal reaction. The Jesuits have come in the nineteenth century everywhere to be considered as the factious enemies of all Governments which seek to restrain them in working out theories aiming a deadly blow at institutions beneath whose protecting shade a land has long enjoyed the blessings of liberty and independence.

We can now see that every effort is exerted by the Jesuits to place the Pope, through the Vatican decrees as to Papal Infallibility, in a position of ascendancy, not only in Italy, but throughout Europe. Bishop Reinkens, the Bishop of the German Old Catholics, has described the practical effect of the training now given to large portions of the Church of Rome. 'It is,' he says, 'to fix in the mind the conviction that Romanism has a Divinely-guaranteed right, under certain circumstances, violently to overturn all existing authorities.' No Bishop is now appointed who to the old oath does not add the Vatican decrees. No seminary is now training priests to deny the infallibility of the Pope. No catechism is now giving instruction against it or giving it ambiguously. The politics of the Syllabus are now forming the clergy of the future. The one commonwealth, with its one King, its glorious ceremonial, and its Divine law, is now made to appear as the fairest of visions. The Jesuits are transmitting and increasing the worst traditions of the Curia—that power behind the Papal throne by which the Roman Catholic Church is governed. The outward loss to the Church had been previously carefully calculated.

Roman Catholics say that it is more than compensated by the compactness obtained within the Church. When the preparations are completed, the hope is that a generation will have been trained in the course of years in obedience to the call of him who holds among Romanists the place of God, to cry 'God wills it,' and to march forward until every enemy has been cast down, and the Church alone shall stand, the one perfect society, embracing the whole human race.

We may confidently predict that their design will fail of the wished-for success. A conservative reactionary spirit cannot hope to be successful in a world which is constantly advancing. The uniformity of servitude created and maintained in Romanism by the Jesuits cannot conquer the modern world. The Church of Rome and the Jesuits will have to maintain a struggle which becomes increasingly difficult against the spirit of our epoch, which tends more and more towards liberty and independence. Notwithstanding its great influence over a part at least of the masses, Romanism is evidently losing its hold on the world. In the midst of the great Roman Catholic nations in France, Italy, Belgium, even in Spain, an insurrectionary movement, which is beginning to assume gigantic proportions, threatens the safety and independence of the Roman Catholic Church. In every country except Ireland, parts of Germany and Poland, where it seems to be endowed with energy, as it is obliged to maintain a deadly struggle with its foes, we find the inhabitants rebelling against the Church, because they wish to escape from an intolerable bondage. The Jesuits seem unable to realize that over the changes of the moral world we have as little power as over the changes of the physical world. They do not see that we can no more prevent time from changing the distribution of intelligence than we can change the courses of the seasons and the tides. In peace or in tumult, by means of old institutions, where those institutions oppose an unbending resistance, the great march of society proceeds and must proceed. The feeble efforts of individuals to bear back are overpowered in the great rush with which the species goes forward. Those who appear to lead the movement are only whirled along with it. Those who attempt to resist it are beaten down and crushed beneath it. Societies have their law of growth. As their strength becomes greater, as their experience becomes more extensive, they can be no longer confined within the swaddling bands, or lulled in the cradles, or amused with the rattles, or terrified with the spectres of their infancy. The Jesuits do not realize this truth. They are aiming at an impossibility. They will find to their cost that it is impossible to govern the men of the nineteenth century as the men of the days of Hildebrand, or even as the men of the sixteenth century; and that their Order has become a venerable relic of antiquity, a great anachronism in the midst of an advancing world.

CHAPTER IV.

THE INQUISITION.

WE have seen the progress of the Reformation in Italy. Even eminent Romish ecclesiastics had avowed their belief in the doctrines preached. Paul III. at once saw the importance of preserving them for the Holy See, because he felt that they would be useful to it in the coming struggle. He was persuaded that these men, not seeing clearly their way on the road along which they were beginning to travel, would be completely under the influence of the powerful ecclesiastical organization into which he wished to draw them, would be charmed by the honours which he conferred upon them, and would devote all their energies to the prosecution of the work to which he invited them. Accordingly, he made Contarini; Peter Bembo, chief of the Ciceronians; Sadolet, a poet and an elegant writer; the distinguished Englishman Reginald Pole; and Ghiberti, Bishop of Verona, all of whom were men favourable to a fundamental reform in the Church, and two of whom held Luther's doctrine of justification, members of the Sacred College. He likewise appointed in 1537 a commission of four Cardinals and five prelates to formulate a scheme for the abolition of abuses. They came to the conclusion that the abuses which were the subject of complaint had their origin in the constant practice of the Popes to choose for the highest dignities men who would second them in their worldly schemes, and who would perpetuate those abuses. These representations, addressed to Paul III., decided him to change his course in regard to the heretics. He came to the conclusion that the best plan was not to make a compromise with them, but to exterminate them.

Cardinal Caraffa, afterwards Paul IV., was the first to call the attention of the Sacred College and of the Pope to the rapid progress of the reformed opinions in Italy. The old Dominican institution of the Inquisition, established at Toulouse for the purpose of exterminating the Albigenses, no longer possessed the same vigour as heretofore. Caraffa therefore urged Paul III. to issue a Bull for the establishment at Rome of a general tribunal, on which all the other tribunals should be dependent. The majority of the Cardinals did not, however, wish to adopt these violent measures; they hoped to establish the peace of the Church by means of a General Council. But

Cardinal Caraffa triumphed over all opposition. He persuaded Paul III. to found at Rome, by a Bull issued on April 1, 1542, the Congregation of the Holy Office, consisting of six Cardinals (including Caraffa and Toledo), and to give them authority on both sides of the Alps to try all causes of heresy, to apprehend and imprison suspected persons, to punish the guilty, to nominate officers under them, and to appoint inferior tribunals in all places with the same or limited powers. The only restriction imposed was that they must not pardon, as that superior prerogative was reserved for the Pope. These were the rules of action :

1. In affairs of State there must not be a moment's delay, but on the slightest suspicion proceedings must be taken.

2. No regard must be paid to any prelate or potentate, whatever might be his dignity.

3. On the contrary, the greatest severity must be shown to those who seek to shelter themselves under the protection of a ruler. Only when confession is made are leniency and fatherly compassion to be shown.

4. To heretics, and especially to Calvinists, no toleration must be granted.

The Popes would not allow any consideration to induce them to mitigate the harshness of their decrees against heresy. At length it came to be asserted that a sin in thought rendered a man obnoxious to the sentence of the Inquisition. Sons were encouraged to bear witness against their fathers. The evidence of two witnesses was considered sufficient to ensure condemnation, and such as would have been rejected in other cases, as the evidence of those who had a personal enmity against the accused, was accepted in the case of a person charged with heresy. The person so accused might recant, but his recantation would not save him from the extreme penalty of the law.

The peaceable establishment of the Inquisition in Italy settled the fate of the Reformation in that country. The tribunal could never obtain a footing in France or Germany. We know that the attempt to introduce it into the Netherlands kindled a civil war which, after unheard-of barbarities, issued in the separation of seven flourishing provinces from the Spanish Crown, and in the establishment in them of civil and religious liberty. The ease with which it was introduced into Italy shows that the Italians were unwilling to cast off their allegiance to the Popes because they saw that the high dignity to which they had been elevated as the spiritual arbiters of Christendom was some compensation for the loss of the glories of those days when Italy occupied a high place among the nations. Other reasons for the failure of the Reformation in Italy have been stated at the beginning of Chapter II. The Italians also were destitute of the public spirit which would have inclined them to shake off the yoke of the oppressor. When we take into account the absence of that spirit, we may admit that the establishment of the Inquisition was, as Roman Catholics say, the salvation of the Roman Catholic religion in Italy. In places where the Inquisitors could not establish a local tribunal, they obtained liberty to employ their agents in searching for suspected persons, and prevailed on the authorities to send the accused to be tried by the Inquisition at Rome. A horde of spies was dispersed throughout Italy, who gained admission to families, and conveyed the secret information which they obtained to the Holy Office.

Caraffa had come to a correct conclusion as to the position of the Roman Catholic Church in Italy. The Inquisition which he had created was the only means of maintaining in Italy religious unity, if a hand as strong as his own directed its movements. We have seen that Protestantism had made progress in the Peninsula. The greater part, however, of those who were in favour of it were still unwilling to separate from the Church of their fathers. It was time, therefore, to terrify them by a persecution in which they would find no mercy. It was necessary to remove without delay the decided heretics, all the leaders of the new movement, and to take away from the weak their spiritual guides, in order that the large majority, terrified and deprived of their leaders, might be more easily brought back into the fold of the Church.

Guided by the rules which have come before us, Caraffa very soon laid his hand on numerous heretics. The prisons were soon full of them. One of the first of those whom Caraffa wished to apprehend was Ochino, Vicar-General of the Order of the Capuchins. Paul III. asked the Senate of Venice to surrender him, but they refused to do so. Then the design was formed to take him by craft. A polite invitation was given to him to come to Rome on important business. Ochino, well knowing that witnesses against him had been sent for to Rome, hesitated at first about obeying the summons, but, on receiving a peremptory order to come, he proceeded slowly on his journey. On the road he was informed that a terrible fate awaited him unless he abjured his heretical convictions. Accordingly, at Florence he made up his mind to disobey the summons, and to depart from Italy. One friend gave him a horse and a servant, and another friend supplied him with clothes and with the means of prosecuting his journey. He escaped all dangers, and arrived at Geneva, where he found a safe asylum from the persecution of the Inquisitors.

Another of the leaders of the movement, Peter Martyr Vermiglio, had also been cited before the tribunal of the Inquisition. He escaped, however, from the snares laid for him, and arrived safely in Geneva.

The Inquisition was inconsolable for the escape of those

heresiarchs. Caraffa, who believed himself to be especially invited by Providence to destroy them, published a letter in which he attacked not only their opinions, but their character. The members of the Inquisition, though obliged to give up these two victims, had attained their principal object : they had taken away from the Protestants their teachers and guides. We can have no doubt that the flight of these standard-bearers was a cause of the failure of the Reformation in Italy.

Paleario remained faithful unto death to his Divine Redeemer; but Ochino and Peter Martyr, by abandoning their native country, showed very plainly that they trembled and drew back when they surveyed the whole length and breadth of the danger to which they were exposed. Peter Martyr might indeed allege that he was leaving his country because he wished for a wider field of usefulness; but it was perfectly evident to all that he departed from it because he was deficient in the moral courage which should have animated him to endeavour to carry the standard triumphantly through the thick of the battle, and to plant it on the ruined battlements of the stronghold of his foes.

As Vermiglio had been the preacher of the Protestant community of Lucca, it was against this town that, in the first instance, the Inquisition directed its hostility. In its first year the persecutions had begun in the little republic, and had forced a certain number who were suspected to take to flight. The Senate was at first unwilling to obey the order of the Inquisitor; but, as the republic was constantly threatened by the ambition of Como of Florence, who, with the aid of his friend the Emperor, desired to incorporate it with his duchy, it did not wish to give its enemy an excuse for commencing hostilities against it.

One day, the agent of the republic, Louis Balbeni, being at Brussels, had been, with the connivance of the Chancellor Granville, concealed behind the tapestry of the chamber of the Emperor, where he heard a conversation between Charles V. and the Nuncio of the Holy See, in which an announcement was made of the design formed to deprive Lucca of its freedom if it continued to set a bad example in religious matters. This announcement disturbed very much the ancients of the little State. They therefore issued seven edicts against those who held heretical opinions or who had in their possession heretical books. They established at the same time, in 1545, on their own authority, a commission for the examination and punishment of the heretics.

Caraffa and the Inquisition were not, however, satisfied with this display of sanguinary zeal. They endeavoured at various times to induce the Senate of Lucca to receive into the town an Apostolic Inquisition. Lucca, however, succeeded in banishing them, and maintained its liberty and independence.

The Inquisition continued to pursue its disastrous course. 'Our brethren,' as Balthazar Altieri wrote in 1549 to Bullinger of Zurich, 'are persecuted more cruelly every day. Some are taken to the galleys, others are condemned to perpetual imprisonment; some, alas! from fear of death have apostatized; many have been banished with their wives and children; others have found safety in flight.'

These were very important results; but Caraffa wished to arrest the progress of the Reformation by measures of extreme severity. In 1543 he had published, as Grand Inquisitor, an edict forbidding, under a penalty of 1,000 ducats, of confiscation of all their books, of perpetual banishment, and of other penalties, according to the discretion of the Inquisitors, all the libraries of Italy to sell any book suspected of heresy, or which was not approved by the Inquisition. He threatened with the same punishment any printers who dared to print any books without

the permission of the Cardinal Inquisitors or the Master
of the Sacred Palace, or those who had bought, or even
possessed, heretical books.

This decree produced a painful impression on account
of the severity which it displayed against the liberty
of the press. This was a terrible blow for learning in
Italy, and it was at the same time an encroachment on
the province of the temporal power, because it inflicted
penalties without the consent of the Governments
of the different States in the Peninsula. But Caraffa
was determined to make an effort to establish the
absolute supremacy of the Church over the State. He
thought that if this terrible edict could not be immediately enforced, the ecclesiastical authority might
succeed by repeated efforts in imposing it on all the
provinces of Italy. In this manner heresy, which had
threatened the Church with destruction, would in the
end gain for it a new victory, and would aid it in its
progress towards universal dominion. When compared
with this result, the ruin of literature in Italy and of
some thousands of private individuals was a matter of
subordinate importance.

Caraffa could not under Paul III. and Julius III.
expect to be altogether successful. Both of them were
men of an amiable disposition, and had not the same love
for persecution which was the predominant feature in the
character of Caraffa. He would willingly have condemned
some Cardinals, known to hold moderate views ; but the
Popes would not allow him to carry into effect his
designs against them. He consoled himself for his disappointment by choosing for the office of Commissary-
General of the Inquisition the Dominican, Michael
Ghislieri, recommended to him for this important position
by the constant struggle which he had maintained in
carrying into effect the designs of the Holy Office, with
Bishops, Chapters, rulers, and the population of large

towns. This fanatical zeal for the Church militant had endeared him to Caraffa. Ghislieri was, in fact, more severe, more tyrannical, more fanatical, than the Theatine Bishop. Very soon the panic-stricken multitude gave him the name of Father Michael of the Inquisition.

These two men succeeded in gaining a complete mastery over the feeble and amiable Julius III. The Pope endeavoured to save several from their merciless vigour, but in general he did not dare to oppose them. The other members of the Holy Office were changed every year, but Caraffa always remained the President. At length he obtained the absolute control of its movements. The other members gave their signatures to his decrees. Caraffa was an object of terror to all with whom he came in contact. Full of vigorous life, walking rapidly so that he scarcely seemed to touch the ground, this man, sixty-five years of age, remarkable for his piercing eye, his angry temper, but at the same time displaying in all his actions an incredible grandeur and gravity, gave to everyone the impression that he was born to rule. He was very decided in all his political and ecclesiastical movements, and would not endure the least opposition. He thought that the Church was far superior to temporal Princes; he would not nominate any Cardinals on their recommendation. He was haughty, intolerant, scornful, and utterly regardless of the weaknesses of his neighbours. He was a man of extensive reading; he spoke very well the Latin, Greek, and Spanish languages; he could make eloquent speeches in his own language; he knew the Sacred Scriptures by heart, and was well acquainted with the principal commentators upon them, and particularly St. Thomas Aquinas, his favourite author. He had also a very retentive memory, never forgetting any injury done to him or the Church. We are not, therefore, surprised to hear that, after the death of Julius III. and the short pontificate of Marcellus I., the Cardinals, convinced that, on account of the difficulties of the Church, it was neces- sary to have a courageous pilot who, regardless of his inclinations and of the interests of his family, would make it his great object to steer the barque of St. Peter, assailed on all sides by violent tempests, should have elected, on May 23, 1555, Caraffa, who took the name of Paul IV. This election set the seal to the triumph of the Roman Catholic reaction, and insured the final victory of the Inquisition.

The new Pontiff remained faithful to his terrible rule, in the enforcement of which he displayed great courage, which was to strike especially the heretical leaders. His election was therefore the signal for the immediate departure of the Bishops and Italian nobles who had been seen in the streets of Rome and the chambers of the Vatican. No one in the worldly and frivolous crowd could deem himself safe from the austere and terrible Inquisitor. All the Cardinals who were inclined to hold moderate opinions, and even inclined towards peace with the Protestants, trembled for their safety.

Cardinal Pole was one of those dignitaries. He had been banished from England by Henry VIII., because he was a devoted member of the Roman Catholic Church. Paul III. had afterwards sent him back to England as Apostolic Nuncio to re-establish the Roman Catholic religion, with the aid of the Queen, Mary Tudor. We know that he had devoted all his energies to the accom- plishment of this object. But all this zeal was of no account with Paul IV., because he agreed with the Pro- testants in their views as to the doctrine of justification, and because he loved literature quite as much as theology. Notwithstanding the services which he had rendered to Romanism, Pole was deprived of his office of Apostolic Nuncio, and was recalled to Rome, doubtless for the pur- pose of being arraigned before the Inquisition. His

prompt obedience served to appease the anger of the
Pontiff. Pole died peacefully in England on November 18,
1558.

Paul IV., as we might have expected, gave a great
impulse to the Roman Inquisition. He directed that,
after an interval of three months, the heretics should
abjure their heretical opinions before their Bishops, and
that if they refused to do so, the Inquisition should proceed against them with merciless rigour. He commanded
also the Congregation of the Inquisition to meet once a
week under his presidency. He identified himself completely with the Holy Office. He never gave up the practice
of assisting once a week at the meetings of the Congregation, and even when his enemies had taken Anagni, and
were at the gates of Rome, he proceeded calmly to preside
over its deliberations. His object was to invest it with
absolute power, and with this view he endeavoured to
deprive the Bishops in Italy of the right to interfere in
the administration of its affairs. Centralization seemed
to him to insure the uniformity of its proceedings, a careful watch over the progress of heresy, and a strictness
always unconnected with local influence. The principal
Inquisitor in particular was invested with a terrible power,
because he was present everywhere, because he was feared
by the whole of Italy, because he compelled everyone,
even the Pope, to tremble before him, because he was a
supreme judge who had the power to discover the secret
movements of the mind, and to punish intentions as well
as acts. He placed in different towns Inquisitors, not
dependent on the Roman Congregation, who were required
to judge in the last resort, and without appeal, all the facts
connected with the heresy. In addition he appointed
certain zealous laymen to control the Inquisitors, and to
watch their proceedings.

‘ The resolution to establish this system was taken,’ as
we are informed by a historian of the Inquisition, ‘ because

not only a great number of Bishops, vicars, monks, and priests, but also because a great many people connected with the Inquisition were heretics.'

This singular admission serves to prove beyond the possibility of doubt that Roman Catholic historians have made a false statement when they affirm that Protestant-ism has found few partisans in Italy, that it was a foreign importation, altogether opposed to the national character. We see, on the contrary, that it had spread among all classes of the population, and that chiefly the savage violence of Popes, Inquisitors, and secular Princes, and a terrorism previously unknown, has destroyed it in the Peninsula.

The anger of Paul extended beyond individuals. He found it necessary to establish in Christendom a vast system of intellectual oppression. He had himself, as Cardinal Caraffa and principal Inquisitor, issued a Draconian edict against all printers or sellers of heretical books. But as these last were not mentioned in the edict, no one was aware of the books which were for-bidden. At last Paul IV., in 1559, directed the publica-tion of the first Roman Index, available for the whole Church, and serving as the model for all its successors. It was divided into three parts : the first part contained a list of the works which were forbidden, including even those which had not a religious character, but were written by avowed heretics ; the second part gave the names of the books specially forbidden ; and the third part stated the names of the works published since 1519. Even books hitherto read without opposition, and books such as the Annotations of Erasmus on the New Testa-ment, of which previous Popes had expressed their approval, found their place in the Index. The world had never seen a similar attack on literature and science. The consequences of this first index of prohibited books were disastrous. Nearly all of them quickly disappeared from Italy. Works like ' The Benefit resulting from the Death of Christ,' 40,000 or 50,000 copies of which had been printed, very soon could not be found. At Rome, at Naples—in fact, all through Italy—the forbidden books were burnt in enormous quantities. The campaign which Paul IV. had undertaken against free thought had been completely successful. No one could venture to hold any opinions but those which the Church had marked with its approval.

Paul IV. after this time constantly increased the privileges of the Inquisition. He conferred on the Inquisitors the power of inflicting torture on the accused, in order to wring from them the confession, not only of their own heresy, but also of the heresy of their accomplices. By a Bull of December 21, 1558, he withdrew the permission which he had given to certain persons to read prohibited books in order that they might refute them. He said that the advantage thus obtained had been neutralized because it had led many people into heresy. He was determined, in fact, that the Inquisition should hold on its course with disastrous rigour. It had never in any former period incarcerated, tortured, beheaded or burnt so many persons, several of whom belonged to the upper classes, as during the last months of the pontificate of Paul IV. He had addressed a letter to the Princes and Governors in Italy, requiring them to bring before his tribunal the unfortunate men who had been imprisoned in the different towns on account of religion. He had the boldness to declare in his Bull of February 15, 1559, that all Princes, Kings, or Emperors who showed the least inclination for heresy were to be deposed and were to be subjected to capital punishment. If they recovered their senses after torture, they were to be shut up for the rest of their life in a monastery, where, as penitents, they might eat the bread of affliction and drink the water of affliction. This defiance of the temporal power, breath-

6

ing the spirit of the thirteenth century, was perfectly ridiculous when half the Princes of Europe had cast off their allegiance to the Church of Rome, and she had not the same power as heretofore of controlling the destinies of mighty empires.

Paul IV. died on August 8, 1559, recommending with his dying breath the Inquisition to the special care of the College of Cardinals. A cry of relief ascended from all hearts after the death of this merciless fanatic. The people of Rome, orthodox as they were, detested him. At the moment when he was in his last agonies, they assembled at the Capitol, determined on the destruction of every object connected with him. They cast down his statue which they had erected, and having broken it in pieces, they cast the head into the Tiber. They also attacked the house which he had assigned to the Holy Office, and having taken it by assault, they delivered the prisoners, carried off everything on which they could lay their hands, particularly what belonged to Cardinal Ghislieri, the principal Inquisitor, ill-treated the officers of the Inquisition, threw all the papers into the street, and finally set fire to the building.

Pius IV., of whom we shall speak particularly in the next chapter, though he did not show the same blood-thirsty spirit as Paul, yet, urged on by his nephew, St. Charles Borromeo, continued the system of his predecessor. On November 1, 1561, he published a Bull in which, in order to make effective the process against heretics, he exempted the Inquisitors from the obligation to name their witnesses, or to give any account of their proceedings to anyone except the Pope and the Roman Congregation. After his death, in December, 1565, the man most in the confidence of Paul IV., the terrible ‘ Brother Michael of the Inquisition,’ was elected Pope and took the name of Pius V. This reign of more than six years witnessed the complete triumph of an institution of which he was the very soul. When we consider the exploits of this formidable tribunal in Italy since the pontificate of Paul IV., we shall see that its success had been so great that no Pope could hesitate to support it, until it obtained its greatest triumph under Pius V.

The agents of the Inquisition appeared at this time among the Calabrian Waldenses. They had quitted their valleys among the Alps, which were too barren to supply them with food, and had emigrated to Calabria. We find them here about the middle of the sixteenth century. They seemed to follow the rites of the Roman Catholic Church, but really they remained faithful to their former religious convictions. The Waldenses in the district of Guardia at length openly separated from the Romanists, with whom they had formerly attended Divine worship. One of them was dragged to Rome, was cruelly tortured, and was strangled in the presence of the Pope and Cardinals. The Inquisitors were afterwards sent to Calabria with orders to exterminate the inhabitants. They were shut up in different houses as in a sheepfold. The executioners brought them out one after another, and, making them kneel down in a neighbouring field, deliberately cut their throats with a knife. More than 2,000 innocent persons perished at this time. Such were the horrors committed by the ministers of a religion which was charged with a message of love to the human family.

The Waldenses were not, however, at this time always led as unresisting victims to the slaughter. In the year 1560, when the Count de la Trinitè invaded their valleys, entrenched behind the barricades formed in the mountain citadel of Prè-du-Tour, they hurled destruction for four successive days on the large bodies of men who were brought up in turn to assail those rocky ramparts. The assailants on the fifth day wavered, knowing very well that they were rushing into the jaws of destruction. The Waldenses, observing this hesitation, immediately sallied from their entrenchments, and drove them in utter discomfiture down the mountain-slopes.

But these were the only Waldenses in or near Italy who successfully resisted the oppressor; the others were compelled to submit to their enemies. At Faenza, a nobleman, honoured for his high birth and for his virtues, fell under the suspicion of the Inquisitors in that city. After having been detained for some time in prison, he was sent to the torture. As they could not extract from him the proof of his guilt which they wanted, they directed the torture to be repeated, and their victim died in agonies. In 1563, among the Milanese, scarcely a week passed without an execution for heresy. The execution of a young priest was accompanied by circumstances of particular barbarity. He was condemned to be hanged, and to be dragged to the gibbet at a horse's tail. In consequence of an earnest entreaty, the last part of the sentence was remitted; but after having been half strangled, he was cut down, and refusing to recant, he was literally roasted to death, and his body was thrown to the dogs.

The greatest resistance was made to the establishment of the Inquisition at Venice. After long negotiations, the Inquisitors were allowed to try causes of heresy within that State on the condition that a certain number of magistrates and lawyers should always be present at the examination of witnesses, and that the sentence should not be pronounced until it was submitted to the Senate. With this restriction the Venetian Protestants were cruelly treated in 1549. In that year Altieri writes: ' The persecution here increases every day. Many are seized, some of whom are sent to the galleys, others are condemned to perpetual imprisonment, and some, alas! have been induced by fear of punishment

to recant. Many have been banished with their wives
and children, while a still greater number have fled
for their lives.' But the Court of Rome at length
triumphed over patrician jealousy. Even foreigners,
who visited Venice for trade, were seized and detained
by the Inquisition.

The first death for heresy in Venice was in the year
1562. We have reason to believe that many whose
names have not been transmitted to us suffered death
at the same time in Venice, in addition to those who
suffered death from the diseases contracted during a long
and tedious confinement. The mode of martyrdom was
horrible in the extreme. We know that many have
witnessed a good confession while the flames raged
around them. But they have been animated by the
hope that the triumphant joy which they exhibited would
be a proof of the power of their faith to support a man
amid the agonies of dissolving nature, and would lead
many to cast in their lot with the followers of the Lord.
But to be carried out at the dead of night in a gondola,
attended only by the sailors and a confessor; to be rowed
into the sea beyond the two castles to another boat,
between which and their own boat a plank was placed,
on which the victim of the Inquisition was laid, having
his body chained, and a heavy stone affixed to his feet;
to be, on a given signal, by the withdrawal of the gondolas
from each other, precipitated into the deep—this was a
mode of punishment which might well have appalled the
stoutest heart and daunted the most determined courage.
We cannot wonder, therefore, if some shrank from the
appointed ordeal and apostatized from the faith. But
many rejoiced while sinking like lead in the deep waters.
Thus Julio Guirlanda, the proto-martyr of Venice, when
placed on the plank, ' cheerfully bade the captain farewell,
and sank into the deep calling on the Lord Jesus.'
Antonio Ricetto was in the same manner conducted to

execution.   As the night was cold, Ricetto asked to have his cloak restored to him.   One of the company then said, 'What, dost thou fear a little cold?   What wilt thou do in the bosom of the sea?'   When they were come to the place of execution, and the captain had bound him with a chain and weight, he lifted up his eyes and said, 'Father, forgive them, for they know not what they do.'   Then the heavy plunge was heard, and the sufferer fell asleep in Jesus.   Those who stand near the arsenal, now occupying the site of the castles, think little of the intolerance here displayed three centuries ago, which greatly aided in preventing the emancipation of Italy from the yoke of her spiritual oppressor.

The elevation of the terrible Ghislieri, Pius V., to the Papal throne spread consternation through Italy.   During his pontificate the liberty not only of writing and speaking, but even of thinking, was suppressed throughout the Peninsula.   A bigoted devotion, an anxious fear, took possession of a land once full of life, splendour, and joy. The great poets, the illustrious writers, the sublime artists, all disappeared from the country.   During his pontificate the Inquisitors assembled in solemn fashion, invoking the name of Christ, and summoning before them the prisoners whose names were reported to them.   Three kinds of interrogation by torture are described: the torture with fire, the torture with the bolt and bar, and the torture with the soldering pipe.   Allowance is to be made for weakness of constitution or tenderness of age. When the accused is brought to the place of torture, he is benignantly admonished to confess the whole truth, otherwise he must endure the appointed ordeal.   We see, then, that the opponents of the Reformation are terribly in earnest.   Rules are given with the utmost coolness for the infliction of exquisite pain.   We cannot wonder, therefore, that occasionally even the giant oak, the monarch of the forest, bent before the storm.   The

Republic of Venice might, if she had been so disposed, have resisted, as in former years, the great spiritual tyrant ; but even she had succumbed to the threats of the Papal Court, supported as they were by the great tribunal of the Inquisition. The Papacy carried all before it from the river Po to Sicily. When we remember that the Romish priests formed a united body, drilled into absolute obedience to their spiritual head, and that they aided the satellites of the Inquisition in the infliction of their terrible tortures, we cannot wonder that the Reformers in Italy were beaten down in the conflict, and that they were compelled to retire from the battle-field.

The Church of Rome has placed Pius V. in the number of her saints, not only on account of his blameless life, but also on account of his valuable services to her cause. He has succeeded in stifling the Protestantism of Italy. He has compelled the population to yield an absolute obedience to doctrines condemned alike by reason and Scripture. He has crowned with success the reactionary movement which his predecessors had commenced. Italy has been reconquered for the Papacy; she has paid an enormous price for her conquest. Rome has moved in her triumphal car over the prostrate forms of thousands whose only crime was their love to the Saviour. Neither sex nor age has softened her heart, nor turned her aside from her course of violence and outrage; she was utterly unmoved by the agonizing cries which issued from the lips of expiring multitudes, because she had cemented the stones of her spiritual fabric with their blood. The result of the triumph of the Inquisition in Italy has been to secure for the Church of Rome a vantage-ground, from which, in perfect safety, her satellites can exert every effort to compel the Italians once more to render to her a devoted allegiance. If the Roman Pontiffs have been able to render any assistance

to Romanism in her struggles in France, the Netherlands, Germany, or Poland, their thanks for their success
are due to Paul IV. and Pius V., to Caraffa and Ghislieri.
The advantage for the Church was so much the greater
that in Spain likewise, as we shall see directly, heresy
had been destroyed by Philip II., and that the first of
the Great Powers of Europe had entered into a close
alliance with the Papacy, the object of which was to
compel, by craft or by violence, the other Powers of
Europe to become her spiritual vassals.

We have seen that Spain was never likely to cast off
its allegiance to the Church of Rome. But still the
doctrines of the Reformers had found their way into this
country. Multitudes eagerly but unconsciously imbibed
the heretical poison contained in the Enchiridion of
Erasmus. 'There is scarcely anyone,' writes Alphonzo
Fernandez to Erasmus, 'in the Court of the Emperor,
any citizen of our cities, or member of our Churches—no,
not even a hotel or country inn—which has not a copy of
the Enchiridion of Erasmus in Spanish. This short
work has made the name of Erasmus a household word
in circles where it had been previously unknown.' We
shall at once see that this work would promote the
progress of the Reformation when we hear that it is full
of sarcasms against priests, against scholastic theologians,
and the doctrines, the vices, the follies, the impostures, and
the scandals, of the Court and Church of Rome. The
evil lives of the clergy were the cause of the rapid sale in
Spain, first of all of the writings of Erasmus, and
afterwards of the writings of Luther. Still, after many
years, scarcely a person was to be found who expressed
his agreement with the doctrine of the Reformers. The
great distance of Spain from the intellectual centres of
Europe, and its hereditary attachment to the Church of
Rome, would seem to account for the absence of any
sympathy with their opinions.

But at length Protestantism forced its way into the Peninsula. Its first centre was the great and wealthy city of Seville, then the mart of commerce for the Spanish Americans and the mother country. Thousands of strangers, merchants, sailors, soldiers, adventurers, and learned men, flocked into it from every country. We need not, therefore, be surprised to hear that the seeds of heresy were scattered through its streets. If Seville was the centre of the new doctrine in the south of the Iberian Peninsula, for the north the city of Valladolid was the centre from which the Reformed opinions were propagated. This was one of the most flourishing cities in the Peninsula. The concourse of strangers to it from all parts of Europe favoured the propagation of the Reformed opinions. The founder of the Protestant community at Valladolid was Don Carlos de Seso, an Italian Captain, who was firmly convinced of the truth of the Reformed doctrines. He gained to his views amongst others the eloquent Augustin de Cazalla, a celebrated preacher and chaplain to the Emperor, who had accompanied him to Germany and to the Netherlands. The noble family of Rogas, consisting chiefly of females, all of whom were nuns of Belen, ranged themselves on the same side. From Valladolid, Lutheranism spread to the neighbouring country, and chiefly to the town of Zamora. Even at Valladolid the heretics held frequent meetings.

The discovery was made by chance at Zamora in 1558 that there were in that place numerous partisans of the new doctrines. Scarcely were the leaders imprisoned when many of the Lutherans endeavoured to save themselves by flight, but they thus betrayed themselves. Many of them were arrested and imprisoned by the Inquisition. This institution had been for many years firmly established in Spain; it had grown every year in pride and pretension; it attacked even Princes of the blood; it filled every city in the kingdom with spies; ignorant and bloodthirsty monks were members of its principal tribunals. They spread lamentation and mourning and woe through the country. The Grand Inquisitor maintained a bodyguard of fifty mounted familiars and 200 infantry. Wherever they appeared, cities opened their gates to them, and magistrates rendered to them a devoted and dutiful obedience. Shrouded in secrecy, subject to no jurisdiction but their own, they delighted in the license of absolute dominion. The total number of heretics—chiefly Jews and Moors—condemned between 1481 and 1525 was 234,526, who were burnt alive, or banished from the country, or doomed to perpetual imprisonment. The multitude took a savage delight in the autos-da-fé, or public burnings, of those unfortunate men or women who made themselves obnoxious to the anger of the Inquisitors. Their bones, skulls, and braids of hair, occasionally discovered beneath the surface, attest the sanguinary violence of these monsters in human shape. The discovery of these remains now excites in those who have witnessed it a feeling of the greatest indignation; but in those days a brave and fanatical nation fell beneath the charm of the fascination of men who had for many years inflicted on their victims barbarities which were calculated to terrify the stoutest heart and to daunt the most determined courage.

The information which the familiars of the Inquisition at this time obtained led to the discovery of a large number who had embraced the opinions of the Reformers. The prisons of the Holy Office were very soon full of them. The same fate befell the Protestants of Seville. The members of the Inquisition in this town, panic-stricken and full of anger, at once cast 800 persons into prison. The Inquisitor-General gave an account of his important arrest to the aged Emperor Charles V. We shall describe the course which he took in regard to the propagation of the Protestant faith in the next chapter. He had lately abdicated the imperial office, and was in his retreat at St. Just. Exasperated by his failures in Germany with the Protestants, which will be fully described, and apprehensive that religious discord would be introduced into Spain, and would impair the royal authority, he determined to show no mercy to the heretics. He at once wrote to the Princess Jean, the Governor of Spain during the absence of his son, Philip II., in whose favour he had abdicated, and to his son in the Netherlands, directing them to take measures for the extermination of heresy. Philip and the members of the Inquisition did not want any exhortation to inflict vengeance on the heretics. He was at that time about to conclude with France a treaty, the principal object of which was to enable them to unite their efforts to arrest the progress of Lutheranism and Calvinism in their respective countries. Philip had already decided to establish in the Netherlands nine bishoprics, the object of which was to organize the Inquisition on a very extended scale. It was utterly impossible for him to tolerate heresy in his own native country, Spain. The Spanish Inquisition was also encouraged to prosecute its work by a special Bull from Paul IV., which conferred on it the power to give over to the secular arm, or to punish with death, all heretics, including even those who abjured their errors, not from conviction, but simply from fear of punishment, and with a view to their deliverance from prison. The same Pope, by a Bull of January 7, 1559, granted to it, to cover the expense of these numerous processes, several hundred thousand ducats drawn from the revenues of the Church of Spain. Thus, supported at once by the monarch and the Papacy, the Inquisition could inflict summary vengeance upon the heretics.

Charles V. did not hesitate to stimulate the ardour of

the judges, or, rather, of the executioners. Though he was at this time on the edge of the grave, he did not hesitate to direct that fires should be kindled in which the heretics should be bound to the stake, and should suffer a death of lingering agony. The flames blazing up shed a lurid light on the last days of his life. He had no need to stimulate the zeal of the Inquisitors. The preparations were made with great rapidity. The refinement of cruelty was shown in the tortures inflicted on their victims. May 21, 1559, was chosen for a solemn auto-da-fé. The people from all parts of Castile flocked with a savage delight to this terrible spectacle. Real Spaniards found more pleasure in these mournful sights than in the bull-fights. Such was at that time, as we have seen, the feeling of the nation, that the sight of the unutterable agony of those who had the boldness to think for themselves in opposition to the Church was the source of exquisite delight. The whole Court, Donna Juana the Regent, the young Prince Don Carlos, were present at the auto. Spectators who belonged neither to the Court nor to the constituent bodies paid for a place in the galleries a sum equal to about 50 francs. The celebrated Dominican preacher, Melchior Cano, Bishop of the Canaries, preached on the occasion. The Grand Inquisitor, Ferdinand de Valdés, Archbishop of Seville, directed the Regent and the young Prince to take a solemn oath always to be present at these spectacles. The Inquisitors burnt at that time alive, or when they had strangled them, hundreds of Lutherans. The decaying remains of the mother of Cazalla, who had been dead for many years, were taken out of the grave and cast on the burning pile. Some of those who had been condemned to death were reserved for the day on which King Philip II., after his return from the Netherlands, might by his presence show his warm approval of this terrible punishment.

On October 8, 1559, the King, accompanied by his son, by his brother, Don John of Austria, by the chief officers of State, and by the principal ecclesiastical dignitaries, came to an auto. Nearly 200,000 persons are said to have been present at it. They looked forward with a delight to the terrible spectacle about to be exhibited. The King drew his sword, and swore to defend the Inquisition, its officers, and its judgments. ' If my son,' he said, ' should become a heretic, I would gladly carry the wood to burn him.'

This was a terrible prophecy, fulfilled, however, in a different sense from that which he intended. Carlos hated the Inquisition, detested his father's policy, and was ready to place himself at the head of a party of toleration in Spain. He was therefore seized and imprisoned by the order of his father, and, having been condemned to death, died by the administration of poison. Some of the offenders were led to execution with a gag on their mouth, because they did not cease to preach loudly their heterodox doctrines.

Many Protestants who, not having the courage to endure this terrible punishment, had apostatized from Protestantism were sentenced to imprisonment for life. The Jesuits were sure to profit by their condemnation. They took possession of the house where Cazalla was brought up, and converted it into a college. They never lost any opportunity of making a gain from this expression of a firm determination to be faithful unto death to conscientious convictions.

The day of punishment came also for the Protestants of Seville. The women especially showed a courage which excites our admiration. Donna Maria Bohorgnes, who was only twenty-one years of age, did not hesitate to express her religious convictions in the midst of her terrible sufferings, and carried on an argument with the monks who had accompanied her to the funeral-pile.

She was burnt along with eighteen Protestants on September 24, 1559. A second auto was held on December 22, 1560, when eleven females were burnt, three of whom were young girls. It is said that the monks found the greatest pleasure in witnessing the agony of these women as they perished in the flames. In the following years the Lutherans were burnt at Toledo, at Saragossa, at Logrono, and at other important towns.

Bigotry after this time made rapid progress in Spain. Carranza, Archbishop of Toledo, had been highly esteemed by the Emperor Charles V. and by Philip II. The former had died in his arms at St. Just; but he had expressed in his Catechism the same opinions as Contarini, Pole, Morone, and other Cardinals of the first half of the sixteenth century. Times had, however, changed since the death of Charles V. The opinions which before his death were allowed, were, after his death, placed under ban and anathema.

The Counter-Reformation was, as we shall see, making rapid progress in the Church. The efforts of the Emperor to promote an agreement between the parties had ended in failure. Carranza was therefore, through the influence of the Chief Inquisitor, shut up in the prison of the Inquisition at Rome for seventeen years, and was compelled to renounce, just before his death, the opinions which had rendered him obnoxious to the vengeance of this formidable tribunal. The opinions which, as we shall see, the Emperor Charles V. wished to be tolerated could no longer be allowed in the Church of Rome.

The Inquisition had indeed stamped out the expression of these opinions when it compelled even the Archbishop of Toledo, the Primate of the Church of Spain, the next dignitary in Europe to the Pope, to abjure them. We can have no doubt that envy and political opposition acted an important part in the condemnation of Carranza, but we can see very plainly a firm determination in the mind of the Pope, the King and the Inquisition to crush with the pressure of its iron hand those who ranged themselves beneath the banner of the heretics. The Inquisition thus appears armed with a terrible grandeur when it carries on a war of extermination with those who, if Christianity be not a fable, are our very brothers.

The sanguinary violence exhibited at this time by Philip II. and the Inquisition rooted Protestantism out of the Peninsula. No one in Spain ventured to have any opinions but those which were sanctioned by the Inquisition. Those who did not wish to renounce the right of private judgment took refuge in foreign lands. Some thousands of courageous men, who would not do violence to their conscientious convictions, settled in Geneva, Germany and England, where they were received with open arms. The number of these emigrants increased so much that Spanish politicians began to tremble for the safety and independence of their country.

Some Spanish emigrants settled in London and at Frankfort. They translated the Bible, and published theological treatises in the Spanish language. But they were disappointed in the expectation that they should by these means revive Protestantism in the land of their fathers. The dread of the Inquisition rendered the attainment of this end absolutely impossible. Many men and women, since placed by the Roman Catholic Church in the number of its saints, were shut up for a time in the prisons of the Inquisition. Amongst them were to be found such men as Ignatius Loyola, John de Ribrera, John de la Cruz, the ecstatic doctor, and Joseph de Calasanz, who were deprived of their liberty because the Inquisition wished to condemn any opinion seeming to have the remotest connection with those on which the dominant Church had pronounced a distinct and emphatic condemnation.

Philip was determined that an impassable barrier should separate Spain from the intellectual life of Europe. He forbade his subjects under the penalty of the loss of their nationality and the confiscation of their property, to study in any foreign school or University. But he has thus greatly hindered the development of the intellectual life of the inhabitants of Spain. In fact, when we witness the great superiority which the anti-Papal state of England possesses over Spain in arms, arts, letters, science, commerce and agriculture; when we remember that at the beginning of the sixteenth century the Spaniard was in no respect inferior to the Englishman; when we see that after that time Spain was fearfully misgoverned; that her natural resources remained undeveloped, and that a land which, with proper cultivation, might have become very productive, became for some time a barren and desolate waste; when we see that England is remarkable for the productions of nature and art; that the colonies planted by England in America have immeasurably outgrown in power those planted by Spain; that she has her fleets on every sea, and that she is enriched by the choicest productions of foreign countries, we cannot help coming to the conclusion that the Counter-Reformation has caused the decay of Spain, and that the Protestant religion has raised England to its present 'high and palmy state' among the nations of the earth.

This system of violent repression, both in Spain and Italy, would, in fact, have hindered to a much greater extent the development of the social power of Rome, if she had not exerted a sustained, a vigorous, and a persevering effort to raise the religious life of the nations which acknowledged her supremacy. Brutal violence rested on a real moral and religious revival. The barbarous and sanguinary violence which has been described was accompanied by a real reaction both in discipline and doctrine. The Council of Trent, whose work we shall now describe, aided by the Jesuits, has promoted the onward march of Romanism through the length and breadth of the Continent of Europe.

CHAPTER V.

THE COUNCIL OF TRENT.

Determination of the Emperor that a Council should be summoned—
Opposition of Clement VII.—His character—Arrangement at
length made that it should meet at Trent—Description of the place
—Final meeting after adjournment—Different views of the Pope
and Charles as to the matters before it—The objects of Charles in
connection with it impracticable—The Pope's means of defeating
his designs—Decrees of doctrine passed—Some show of compliance
with Charles's wish as to reform—Connection between political
events and the alteration of Paul's policy—Council removed to
Bologna—Death and character of Paul III.—Election of Julius III.
—Council brought back to Trent—Dogmatic decrees passed by it
—Protestants invited, but not allowed a voice at it—The hope of
peace with the Protestants a mere chimera—Disappointment of
Charles on account of his failure, and his withdrawal from the
world—Dissolution of Council—Reflections upon it—Marcellus II.
—Paul IV.—Character of Pius IV.—Council summoned at Trent—
Design of Pius to make the Pope supreme—Final success after
much discord—Catherine de' Medici and the Cardinal of Lorraine,
and their designs in connection with the Council—Death of the
Legates—The new Legates successful in persuading the Emperor to
make concessions— Dictation of decrees by the Pope—Opposition
of France and Spain overcome—End of the Council—Its decrees
not universally accepted—Its settlement of the doctrines of the
Church which were previously uncertain — Extreme doctrines
sanctioned by it, including especially the supreme power given to
the Pope—Re-organization of the College of Cardinals not effected
—The Jesuits the authors of the changes made at it—The character
of Pius IV.—His retirement from the world, and the success of his
policy.

GENERAL Councils were not at this time popular in
Europe. The two last Councils had, as we have
seen, altogether failed in effecting the regeneration of Christendom. But still the Emperor, Charles V.,

was convinced that a Council was the only means of reforming the Church. The Lutheran Princes were also favourable to a Council, based on Holy Scripture and called by the Emperor, where the laity could sit and vote. They were not sanguine as to the result, but still they thought that they would make another effort to promote by means of it a reform of the Church.

Clement VII. was at this time Pope. He had by a subtle intrigue obtained the Papal tiara. A very strong feeling existed against him throughout his pontificate. Italy was exhausted by the wars which his ambition had occasioned. We shall see at the end of this chapter that one of them had led to the sack of Rome by the Constable Bourbon, and to the perpetration of deeds of cruelty compared with which the indignities offered to her by the Huns and Vandals fade into insignificance. His son also, whom at the cost of great crimes he had raised to the throne of Florence, was proving himself a worthless tyrant.

Another cause of his unpopularity as Pope was the illegitimacy of his birth. He was unwilling to summon a Council, because he thought that it would depose him on account of it. At last he gave his consent to a Council where the Bishops only could sit and vote. Protestants might have a safe-conduct, and might be heard, but they were not to be allowed to have a vote. Clement annexed this condition to his consent, that the Council should not be held in Germany.

He had now been brought to see that, whether he liked it or not, the Council must be held. The prospect was dreadful to him. Thus matters remained during the lifetime of Clement. Paul III., who succeeded Clement, was as much opposed as he was to the summoning of a Council. Charles, however, and the Cardinals insisted that it should meet. He obtained the tiara only on the condition that it should be summoned. Charles would allow the Pope to preside, but he insisted that the Protestants should be invited to it.

Another condition was that it must be held outside Italy. If it were held in Italy, it would be too much under the control of the Pope. The latter objected to Germany, because Charles and the German Princes would have great influence over it. At length it was decided that it should be held at Trent. All parties were agreed as to this place. Charles and his brother wished that it should meet here because Trent was in the dominions of Ferdinand, who was Count of the Tyrol, and King of the Romans, Bohemia, and Hungary. Paul was satisfied with Trent, because, on account of the disturbed state of Europe, it would be difficult for the German and French Bishops to attend in large numbers. The Italians must predominate. The distance from Rome was not great, and therefore couriers could constantly pass to and fro. Paul could be in frequent communication with the Legates. He could easily direct them what to do and what to leave undone, and could, in fact, guide, as we shall see, the deliberations of the Council.

The Fathers had a delightful residence during summer. The town of Trent, which thus became for many years the centre of the religious life of Europe, the place on which the eyes of all Christian nations were fixed, is situated in a large and fertile valley through which the river Adige runs like a thread of silver, and is overshadowed by lofty mountains. The sultry heat of summer becomes endurable through the fresh air from the Alps. The fields bathed in the brightness of the sun, covered with may-blossom, with the purple clusters of the vine, with chestnut and olive trees, form an admirable contrast to the lofty mountains, which have snow upon them during a great part of the year. The population was at this time 10,000. The number of palaces was large. The most remarkable of them was the residence of the Bishop, which was built in the Roman style. The Bishop was the nominal Sovereign of the country; but he was connected with the House of Hapsburg, not only because he was a Prince of the Empire, but also because the Count of Tyrol was, as we have said, the brother of the Emperor.

Paul, in giving his consent to this arrangement, knew well that he had one circumstance in his favour. In winter the climate would be so trying, that he indulged the sanguine hope that the session would be short. Notwithstanding the constant expression of this wish that the Council should meet, it was the conviction of his intimate friends that he intended to exert every effort to prevent its deliberations from having a successful termination. On May 22, 1542, he issued his Bull directing the Council to meet in the following August. Patriarchs, Archbishops, Bishops, and Abbots were summoned to it. The object of it was stated to be to determine certain articles of the Christian faith. Secular Princes were invited to attend or to send ambassadors. A special invitation was given to the Princes of Germany. An intimation was, however, conveyed to them that Bishops only could deliberate and vote on the matters which came before them. The Pope seemed at the time to be in a conciliatory mood, because he named as his Legates the Cardinals Pole and Morone, both supposed to be in agreement with the Lutherans on the doctrine of justification. These prelates on their arrival found only a few Italian and German prelates at Trent. They neverthe- less opened the Council, and waited in vain for six months for the arrival of other Bishops. Paul therefore directed the adjournment of the Council on July 6, 1543. The reason of the absence of the French and Spanish prelates was that a war, occasioned by the struggle of the two nations for the supremacy in Europe, had broken out between them. On the conclusion of peace Paul

summoned it to meet at Trent on March 14, 1545. On
this day, under the presidency of the Papal Legates,
Cardinal de Monte and Cardinal Cervino, in the
Church of St. Mary, a structure of red marble, still
adorned with the portraits of many of the prelates who
attended the Council, the Fathers began deliberations,
the issue of which was the means of rescuing Romanism
from the dangers with which it was threatened, and
of promoting its triumphant progress throughout the
world.

Charles V. thus seemed to have been successful. He
always pursued his object with unfailing patience and
with unfaltering courage. Trial did not daunt, difficulty
did not discourage him; no defeat, no deception, caused
him to abandon his designs. He regarded the Council
as the great remedy for the evils of Christendom. He
wished to show himself, by bringing together this august
assembly, to be a powerful Emperor, the champion and
ruler of the Church, who might unite the nations which
had acknowledged him as their leader in a holy confederacy for the advancement of Christianity throughout the Continent of Europe. This was a glorious
design, but impracticable because it brought him into
collision with three adversaries, who were equally formidable: the Pope, Paul III., that subtle fox who
did not hesitate to have recourse to any intrigue
designed to prevent the Emperor from having the first
place in Christendom; the Protestants, who were determined not to make the least compromise with Rome,
even when she approached them with the winning
accents of conciliation, and told them that they need
not accept her more obnoxious doctrines; and foreign
nations, especially France, who were determined that
Germany should not direct the course of events in the
nations of Europe.

The wish of Charles was that the Pope should take up

morals in earnest. The Fathers would be better able to deal with spiritual mysteries when their hands were clean. The secular Princes, the Bishops, and the faithful members of the Church in France and Germany wished to have from the Council, above all, a reform of the Church in its Head and in its members. The Pope, however, never intended that the Council should interfere with him and his Court. He did not wish the Germans to attend, because he knew that they would insist on reform, and by hurrying forward the doctrines he hoped to make the refusal a certainty. In fact, he wished the blame of the refusal to be thrown upon the Diet. Charles, on the other hand, said that doctrines should wait till the theologians had been heard upon them. He commanded the Fathers to purify morals and discipline. The Pope offered a strong opposition to him. He knew that the Church might be regenerated, but that the pomp and wealth of the Papacy would be gone for ever. He did not wish to give to the Bishops any power over the Holy See. He did not wish to make an end of the pretexts under which the Popes had pillaged the Bishops, the Churches, the monasteries, and the nations in general throughout Europe. The means of escape was to appeal to the dread of heresy, and to stand forth as the uncompromising champion of the orthodox faith. De Monte was therefore directed to open the Council on heresy, to take up the articles of the Confession of Augsburg, to examine and condemn them, and to do the work so quickly that no question might be raised about hearing opponents. When he had obtained this result, he wished to dissolve the Council. The reform of abuses might be entrusted to him as the judge in ecclesiastical matters, or, in other words, might be postponed to the Greek Kalends. In this sense we are to understand the ·following instructions to the Legates : ' As to reform, it is not necessary to discuss it before dogmas, nor, indeed, at the same time with them, because it is quite a secondary end of the Council. But you ought to act in this matter with prudence.' The instructions were, too, in direct opposition to the precedent of former Councils, 'to make all the decrees run in the name of the Holy See and the Legates.'

The intention was that the articles of Augsburg should be condemned before a Synod could assemble in Germany. The Emperor could not bring before a lay Synod articles passed by the Church. The Council therefore proceeded rapidly with the declaration of doctrine. Throughout the sessions of the Council, Spanish, French and German representatives, whether Fathers or Ambassadors, maintained the subjection of the Pope to the authority of the Council. The French and Germans were united in the wish to favour Protestants by reasonable concessions. We see, therefore, that the Papal supremacy had to encounter a serious opposition. But the Pope had a sure means of triumphing over his opponents. He could inundate the Council with Italian prelates. These were far more numerous than the Bishops of other nations. In Italy the dioceses contained a population of 6,000; while in Germany, France and Spain the population in every diocese was on the average 200,000. The Italian Bishops knew very well that the eye of the Pope was fixed upon them, and that if they voted exactly in accordance with his views they would obtain high preferment from him, and that they might even rise to the dignity of Cardinal. Moreover, the Jesuits, when the Council was transferred to Bologna, began those doctrines which ended in the declaration of the doctrine of Papal supremacy.

We need not, therefore, be surprised to find that the decrees, having been elaborated in congregations and proposed to the assembled Fathers by the Papal delegates, who had the initiative, were with a little dexterity passed by the Council when the Court of Rome strongly insisted upon them. They now made an impassable gulf between the contending parties. After having declared that a belief in the Bible, including the Apocrypha, is an integral part of Roman Catholic doctrine, they proceeded to affirm doctrines on which the Protestants were strongly opposed to them; they settled the authority of tradition as a rule of faith; they condemned the Lutheran doctrine of justification by faith, affirming that a man can by faith, by repentance, by mortification of the flesh, by obedience to the commandments of the Church, by good works, obtain the grace of God. They affirmed also the efficacy and authority of seven Sacraments. They showed great dexterity in working out this system of doctrine, and in closing up every avenue by which the Protestant could come within measurable distance of them.

The Fathers showed an increasing determination to disregard the wishes of the Emperor. The arrangement was that an alternate session should be given to reform. The Emperor complained that they had altogether neglected it, and hurried on the definition of doctrine. They now made some show of a desire to propitiate him. They proposed a decree as to the residence of Bishops. They allowed the Cardinals who held several bishoprics to choose in six months which one of them they would keep. This Bull, however, designed to deceive the Emperor and the public, remained a dead letter. Under various pretexts the Cardinals continued to procure a large number of rich benefices. The decree was brought forward for a third time, but it made slow progress, while the dogmatic decree respecting the Sacraments advanced with startling rapidity. The Cardinals continued to challenge the Protestants to mortal combat. The Emperor blamed them because they had paid no regard to the opinions of the Protestants. But they turned a deaf ear to his warnings and his remon-

strances. They continued to set him at defiance.
But now Paul began to have a dread of the Emperor.
Charles had advanced rapidly in his career of victory.
Germany seemed likely to be subject to his dominion.
He thought that this overwhelming power would act
upon Italy, and would soon show itself both in
spiritual and temporal affairs. With a view of diminish-
ing that power, strange to say, while he was urging the
Fathers to oppose the Germans in the Council, he now
encouraged the Northern Germans to resist the Emperor.
His anxieties concerning the Council, too, had greatly
increased. Some members of the imperial party, made
more daring by victory, ventured on measures of very
great boldness. The Spanish Bishops, too, now brought
forward some remarkable articles, called censuræ,
designed to diminish the authority of the Pope. Under
these circumstances he removed the Council to Bologna,
the second town in the Papal States, where it was
immediately subject to his control. He did not long
survive this transference. Heart-broken by the rebellion
of his grandsons, on whom he had conferred independent
principalities, he breathed his last in November, 1549.
The impartial historian must be his stern censor. If it
be a merit to have defeated by his crafty policy the
honest designs of an Emperor anxious to purify the
Church, and to have made absolutely impossible a union
between Roman Catholics and Protestants, Paul III.
deserves a high place among those spiritual heroes whom
his Church embalms with her praises because they have
advanced her best interests, and have given her a high
place in the annals of the world.

The conclave which elected the next Pope, Julius III.,
showed a different spirit from its predecessors. The
Cardinals made an honest effort to secure the best man
for the Papacy. They had, however, failed altogether.
Julius III. was elected because he was considered the

least objectionable of those whom it was possible to elect. He was utterly unequal to the work of guiding the vessel of the Church over a stormy ocean.

The great desire of Julius was, as far as possible, to pass his time in voluptuous enjoyment in the villa which he built near the Porta del Popolo, to be at peace with all the world, and especially with the Emperor. He immediately complied with his demand, and summoned the Council to reassemble at Trent. Charles was most anxious that the Princes of the Empire, the Roman Catholics and the Lutherans, should be present at the Council. The Germans, however, would not go without a safe-conduct. The Council agreed, as far as possible, to give security to both parties, secular and spiritual. The safe-conduct, when it arrived, was found to be unsatisfactory. It must be amended, and words must be removed which would have enabled the Pope to disregard it. At length it was brought into a form to which no objection could be made. All Germans might attend the Council. Nothing, however, was said about the right of the Protestants to vote—nothing about the revocation of the dogmatic decrees, without which attendance would have been a mockery.

The Fathers had gained by the delay occasioned by the reference of the safe-conduct to the Diet. They went to work and heaped canon upon canon. They rejected the doctrine of Luther which asserted that the bread and wine did not change their qualities, and that Christ was present under them; and affirmed distinctly that the bread and wine were changed into the very body and blood of Christ. They would not allow the cup to be given to the laity. They established also the Sacraments of Penance and Extreme Unction. Charles endeavoured to stay their hand. He was anxious to have such a reformation as would satisfy the Lutherans and reconcile them to the Church. But his own Bishops would not.

obey him in doctrinal matters. They and the other Bishops were anxious to see the doctrines fixed in so decided a manner that the Protestants should be completely vanquished, and should find themselves in opposition, not only to the Holy See, but to the whole Roman Catholic Church. They and the other members of the Council declared without any circumlocution that they insisted on all the decrees of the first Council of Trent, notwithstanding the contrary wish of the Emperor and the Protestants. They came to this decision when the Emperor and the Pope were firm allies, and they expected every day the arrival of the Lutherans. They were encouraged in this resolution by the Jesuits Lainez and Salmeron, whom the Pope had sent to the Council as his representatives. The Legate so far gave way to the Lutherans that they were allowed to plead their cause before the Fathers. They made a deep impression upon some of the Bishops. The Legate was horrified by the bold language of the Protestants who had dared to say that all the decrees of the Council ought to be tried by their agreement with Scripture. He and his adherents would not make the least concession to the Protestants, and said that they would rather dissolve the Council than allow the admission of men who thus disturbed the belief of the Fathers.

Julius III., when he heard of the bold language of the Protestants, directed the Legate not to allow the Council to renounce its office of supreme judge. He complained to the Emperor of the impudence and impiety of the Protestants, and declared that he would never allow a seat in the Council, or a right to speak, to heretics and schismatics. He was not satisfied with words. Notwithstanding the loud complaints of the Protestants, he directed the Council not to pay the least attention to their devices, and to hurry on their resolutions. In fact, the Pope, the Curia, and all their partisans were determined not to allow them to change one iota of any decree of the Council. The hope of Charles V. that he should solve the religious question in a Council under the influence of Rome was a mere chimera.

The Emperor was deeply grieved when he found the impossibility of an agreement between the Council and the Lutherans. A reformation of the Church and the moderation of its system of doctrine had been the passion of his life. All the forces which his opponents had at their command—calumny, treachery, and hypocrisy—had been tried against him. He had fought on, and he did not believe that he should fail. The final manœuvres at Trent showed him that he had failed. Romanism and Protestantism had hardened into irreconcilable antagonism. When the safe-conduct had been granted, the Emperor's object seemed to have been gained. But the advantage had been neutralized by the precipitation with which the doctrinal canons had been passed. A general reform conducted by the Church would have reunited Europe. The Pope and his Legates were determined not to have it. Decrees on complicated points of doctrine had made difficulties cries of battle. The longer the Council now sat, the more mischief it would do. The Emperor must have led the Revolution, falling back on the German Diet, or he must have raised a Roman Catholic army in the Pope's interest, and begun a religious war. His orthodoxy prevented him from doing the first, and the second course he could not take. He could, therefore, only withdraw from the struggle and watch the course of events. Very soon he retired from the turmoil of the battlefield, and brought a shattered mind and body to the monastery of Yuste, in one of Nature's green solitudes, where he hoped by meditation and by devotional exercises to prepare himself for that eternal and unchangeable state on which he felt that he must shortly enter.

The Council had thus, so far as the Protestants were concerned, proved a failure. The Emperor saw that their presence at Trent could not again be expected. The general feeling was that the Council must now be dissolved. The Roman Catholics wished for the dissolution. The Germans said that they would not submit to the dictation of a single nation, the Italians. They would not accept any of its decrees. The Emperor had been reluctantly obliged to direct the suspension of the Council on March 5, 1552. Its useless existence was, however, prolonged because the representatives of the Pope and the Emperor did not like to take upon themselves the responsibility of dissolving it. The course of events now settled the matter for them. The soldiers of Saxe, of Hesse, and of the Marquis Albert of Brandenburg, were now on full march towards the south to chase the Emperor from Germany. On April 4 they took possession of Augsburg. The King of France received the keys of Metz. The Elector of Saxe was at the entrance of the Tyrol. These events decided the Pope to direct the suspension of the Council on April 28, 1552. The Bishops now fled for their lives. Only a few Spaniards were left with the Legate, Cardinal Crescentio. They passed a hurried vote that all those decrees already sanctioned, and those which awaited the Pope's approval, should be held valid for ever. The Council which met ten years afterwards was a new assembly, with no pretence of desiring peace, but determined to renovate the Roman communion for the recovery of its lost dominions. It met to divide nations into factions, to set subjects against Sovereigns and Sovereigns against subjects, to break the peace of families, and to deprive men of that liberty which is their inalienable birthright.

We have now seen that for the present the regeneration of the Church through a Council was hopeless. If the life of Marcellus II., who succeeded Julius III., had been prolonged, it is not unlikely that he might have guided the deliberations of the Fathers to a successful issue. It is even possible that the inhabitants of England might have been numbered among his obedient subjects. He was determined to purify the Church from its abuses, and to avoid those political complications which had tarnished the glory of the Papacy, and had become in the course of God's Providence subservient to the advancement of Protestantism. But the bright vision of a Church regenerated through his disinterested zeal soon vanished away. Like another Marcellus, cut off in the spring-tide of life, who, if he had lived, would have shed an imperishable glory on the land of his birth, he decorated only for a short time the sphere to which he had been elevated. He died on the twenty-second day of his pontificate. In the one case as in the other, the Tiber, as it glided by the walls of Rome, heard the loud lamentations of his friends, and witnessed the funeral pomp which accompanied him to his last resting place.

'Ostendent terris hunc tantum fata.'

The reign of Marcellus might, then, have healed the schism in the Church. The reign of his successor, Paul IV., effectually prevented that consummation. We have seen when we described the Inquisition that he regarded Protestantism with intense abhorrence, and that he was determined to wage with it a ceaseless warfare. It was his favourite boast that there was no need of a Council to restore the Church to its purity, since he was restoring it.

The successor of Paul IV., Giovanni Angelo Medici (Pius IV.), was a man of a totally different character. A jurist, remarkable for that subtlety which inclined and enabled him to follow the law through all its turnings and windings, ignorant of theology, exhibiting that political

cunning and unscrupulousness for which his great countryman, Machiavelli, was distinguished, he was as different
as possible from the fiery Neapolitan nobleman, the
haughty fanatic, who trampled upon Kings, and wrote
his arguments in defence of Christianity in the blood
of his fellow-Christians.   He was a man of inferior
ability, but possessed an adroitness gained by his legal
training.   When he ascended the Papal throne the
Reformation had run like wildfire through Europe.
Nation after nation had cast off their allegiance to
the See of Rome.   Paul's impolitic pretensions had
alienated England and Scotland.   Pius saw that a
Council was the only remedy for the evils of Christendom.   He therefore at once summoned it to meet at
Trent, and sent four Legates, who opened the Council
on January 15, 1562.   He was convinced, however,
that, to be successful, he must not follow the example
of his predecessors.   Their desire from the time of
Hildebrand had been to plant their feet on the neck
of the monarchs of Christendom.   He, on the contrary,
had made up his mind to prove that their interests
were identical with those of the Popes, and to enter into
the closest alliance with them.   The reconstruction of
Christendom which opened a new era in the history of
Europe was settled in the Courts and by the Cabinets
of Rome, Spain, France, and Austria.

Pius saw at once that he must endeavour by subtle
intrigue, by political unscrupulousness, always to secure a
majority in the Synod.   He inundated the Council with
Italian prelates who were carefully instructed as to the
votes which they were to give.   Couriers were constantly
on the road who conveyed information to the Pope of the
minutest details of the Council.   It soon became evident
that the Pope directed the deliberations of the assembled
Fathers.   The murmur was heard that the Holy Ghost
was sent to Trent in carpet bags.   He showed, too, all

the wisdom of the serpent in his dealings with the
monarchs of Europe. He did not arrange his proposed
decrees through information obtained from his Legates,
but endeavoured by means of agents, through whom he
held communication with the monarchs of Europe, to
frame by mutual concessions measures which might be
safely submitted to the assembled Fathers.

We must not, however, suppose that this method of
procedure, contrary to the precedent of former times, was
established without opposition. The Legates had induced
the Fathers to assent to their proposal that they alone
should bring resolutions before the Council. The object
was to make the Pope the supreme authority in it. The
Spanish prelates afterwards saw the importance of this
resolution, and remonstrated against it. The Legates,
however, disarmed their opposition by vague assurances
that they would not take an undue advantage of the
privilege thus conceded to them.

Other causes of discord soon made their appearance.
The Spanish prelates contended that the residence of
Bishops in the diocese had been divinely commanded,
and that their authority was derived directly from Christ.
The Pope, however, persuaded Philip to command them
to abstain from their opposition on the grounds that
the independence of the Bishops would lessen his own
authority, and that it would render them independent
of the Papal See.

Other demands were made. The French and imperial
prelates demanded that the cup should be given to the laity.
The Germans also stipulated for the marriage of the clergy.
The Spaniards, however, would not hear of the Communion
in both kinds. The Spaniards and French were alike
opposed to the marriage of the clergy. Thus discord
reigned in the Council. The Spaniards further insisted
that every prelate and Prince should have the right of
making propositions, and that the Pope should approve

8

and publish them, but that he should not examine them. The Pope and the Curia were thus in a very difficult position. If they avoided Scylla, they would steer the vessel into the whirlpool of Charybdis. The dissensions of the Fathers saved the Pope. The French and Spaniards were opposed to one another, not only on religious, but also on political questions. If the French and Germans had followed the example of the Spaniards, and had sent learned men to the Council, the destinies of Europe might have been changed. The result would have been that the Fathers would have come to an agreement on the disputed questions. Pius was, however, able through the absence of effective opposition to keep the vessel stationary, and to avoid the dangers with which he was threatened.

Once, indeed, the better genius of Pius deserted him. He forgot the doctrine which he had previously professed, and asserted that he, as Bishop of the Universal Church, had the right of forcing Bishops to reside. This announcement raised a storm in the Council. If he had endeavoured to exercise that power, the dissolution of the Council would have been a consequence; for the Spanish, the Germans and the French would not have consented to place the Council in absolute subjection to the Roman See. The Germans also insisted, in opposition to the Pope, that the Council should be considered a new assembly, and not a continuation of former Councils. They threatened otherwise to withdraw from it. The Pope afterwards saw his mistake. The Legates, acting in conformity with his instructions, postponed the questions, the discussion of which would have led to a disastrous result. The vessel, though shattered, was able to pursue her course, and was saved from sinking beneath the boiling surges.

But still it was likely to encounter violent storms. Discord still reigned in the Council. The King of Spain took one view of important questions; the Emperor and the King of France took another view of them. The Pope and the Cardinals were anxious to maintain their authority and revenues without the least sacrifice. The Synod seemed as the Councils of Constance and Basel, not unlikely to break up in confusion, and to fail altogether in effecting the regeneration of Christendom.

At length this pupil of Machiavelli, this master of political intrigue, who seemed profoundly versed in all the mysteries of statecraft, saw that he must change his course if he hoped to gain a triumph for his Church. He determined to make a retrograde movement. He could the more easily take this course because his campaign against the Council of Trent had produced important results. Those of the Fathers who had the courage to oppose his dictatorship were altogether discouraged and vanquished. As they were exposed to violent attacks from those to whom they looked for advancement in the Church, the Italian Bishops determined to withdraw from the struggle with the Council. Pius had been equally successful in his struggle with the Kings. Philip II. commanded the Spanish Bishops for the present not to bring forward the question of the Divine origin of episcopal residence. The King also, in order to propitiate his uncle the Emperor, agreed that the question whether the Council of Trent was a new Synod, or a continuation of former Synods, should remain undecided.

Pius now, having asserted his authority, determined to change his angry tone for the winning accents of reconciliation. He determined to adopt two courses which soon enabled him to bring the Council of Trent to a successful termination. The first was to give a cheerful consent to a searching reformation of the Church, but to insist on a reform in the ecclesiastical relations of the States. The second was no longer to assert the political pretensions of his predecessors which were a manifest anachronism, and to cultivate friendly relations with the monarchs of Europe.

The events of the spring hastened the adoption of this course. Charles, Cardinal of Lorraine, whose presence was dreaded by the one party and eagerly desired by the other party, arrived at Trent on November 13, 1562, with a train of eighteen Bishops and three Abbots. He was at once a prelate and a statesman, remarkable for his refinement and for his acute intellect, but at the same time for his disregard of the fundamental rules of morality. Every course seemed to him lawful if it only led him to the enjoyment of power and wealth. Avaricious, vindictive, tortuous in his policy, he only used his profound knowledge of public affairs, and his great eloquence, for the advancement of his own interests. But he tried to conceal his abominable egotism and his utter want of religion beneath the cloak of a dignified manner and a pious hypocrisy.

At this time the Queen-mother, Catherine de' Medici, was very favourable to the Reformers. This unprincipled woman was, as we shall see when we speak of the Counter-Reformation in France, engaged in balancing the advantages of rival alliances, and was strongly inclined to favour the Huguenots. No one was, therefore, surprised to find this time-serving prelate placing himself on the same side. He was now commanded to urge a series of radical reforms : the establishment of a pure worship free from all superstitious ceremonies; the use of the national language in preaching and in the administration of the Sacraments ; the Communion in both kinds, and other important concessions which were recommended with the view of establishing the unity of the Church.

The acceptance of these proposals by the Italian Papists and by the fanatics of Spain was almost hopeless. Thus discord reigned in the Council. The Germans joined the French in insisting on radical reforms. Charles of Lorraine threatened to bring sixty French prelates to enforce his views on the Council. This dissension showed itself in a singular manner. Even the servants of the rival parties fought in the streets. The prelates did not dare to leave their houses, lest they should be exposed to personal injury. At this time an important event occurred, of which Pius was not slow to take advantage. The Legates, the Cardinal Seripando and the Cardinal of Mantua, died after a short illness. He appointed in their place Cardinals Morone and Navagero, who by their political cunning and dexterity enabled him to gain the victory over his opponents. Morone was sent on a special Embassy to the Emperor. He was greatly aided by a discreet and able agent of the Pope, the Jesuit Canisius. The latter quite gained his confidence, and was able to convince him that he would obtain much more from the Holy Father by concessions than by menaces, and that by constant opposition he would promote the progress of heresy, and prevent the deliberations of the Council from having a successful issue. At first the Emperor was proof against all these arguments. At length his mind began to open to the conviction that it would be for his advantage to listen to Morone and the Jesuit. They were commissioned to give him a private assurance that the Pope would allow Communion in both kinds immediately after the termination of the Council. They also showed the Emperor a number of articles of reform to be immediately placed before the Council, which astonished and delighted him. He was thus induced to consent to the requirements that the Legates alone should make proposals of reform to the Council, and that the secular Princes should not exercise any influence on the deliberations of the Fathers. The instructions which he sent to his representatives at Trent were, in fact, dictated by the Pope and his Nuncios. Thus the unity of the independent party in the Council came to an end. A breach was made in the wall of the citadel through which the soldiers of the Papal army could easily pass and plant their banner triumphantly on the ruins of ecclesiastical liberty.

The formidable opposition of the French Government, and of its representative, the Cardinal of Lorraine, remained to be overcome. Pius and Cardinal Morone showed in their dealings with him all the wisdom of the serpent. Morone, on the arrival of the Cardinal at Trent, flattered him, and would undertake no measures of importance without consulting him. Pius followed the same course, directing his Legates to ask his advice on all occasions. He also invited him to Rome, received him with great state, honoured him by visiting him in his house, held out to him the vision of succession to the Papacy, and laboured to convince the Cardinal that only by a close alliance with the Holy See could he establish the power of the House of Guise on a firm foundation, or maintain the ascendancy of Romanism in France. He also mingled threats with flatteries, and thought to embroil the Kings with their Protestant subjects, by raising the question of their right to interfere with the administration of National Churches. The end was that the French prelates, led by the Cardinal, cast in their lot with the Papacy. Catherine de' Medici, conscious of having made too many concessions to Protestantism in France, was glad of this opportunity of conciliating the Papacy. The Spanish prelates, led by the Count of Luna, remained firm until they had a distinct assurance that their King was favourable to the decrees, and until they had fully discussed the articles bearing on the independence of the Princes and their legal rights over their ecclesiastical subjects. An alarming rumour of the dangerous illness of the Pope, however, soon brought the sittings to an end.

On December 4, 1563, the decrees of the Council were signed by 234 prelates present at Trent. Pius ratified the decrees by a Bull dated January 26, 1564. We shall now see, in the concluding observations which will be made upon them, that a useful victory had been gained for the Roman See, that a conciliar sanction had been given to Roman absolutism, and that the great dogmas of the Roman Catholic Church had been clearly declared, and guarded with fresh definitions which no one could deny without endangering his soul's salvation.

We find that the decrees of the Council were not universally accepted. The Emperor alone had accepted them without limitation for his hereditary dominions. France had, however, firmly rejected them ; Spain had accepted them with some qualifications. Venice followed the example of Spain. Poland and Portugal gave their unqualified assent to them.

We shall find, however, that those decrees have exercised a great influence on those countries which acknowledge the supremacy of the Pope. We may say that they have saved the Church ; that they have given a constitution to it, and a direction to the energies of its members which lasted through the following centuries.

Let us recall the history of the period which preceded the Council. We shall find that very many were uncertain as to the doctrines which they ought to believe. Very few were inclined to admit the necessity of a religious reform. Others, while admitting it, did not see how far it should proceed. This uncertainty led many to waver in their allegiance to the Church of Rome, and to adopt many of the opinions of the Protestants. Contarini, Pole, and Morone agreed with the German and Swiss Reformers on the doctrine of justification by faith and the freedom of the human will. Even the Pope and his Legates were inclined at times to adopt some of the opinions of the Protestants.   The books of the latter were numerous, and were written in a popular style.   The divine, the man of learning, the refined scholar, the artisan, the soldier, and the peasant, could find books which explained the Bible in the sense given to it by the German Reformers.   The Roman Catholics had no books fully explaining the articles of their faith.   Even after the first meetings of the Council of Trent, the great preacher of the Court of Maximilian, Jean-Sebastian Phauser, could pretend that he had never left the Roman Catholic Church, while he was teaching doctrines exactly the same as those of the Reformers.

But when the decrees of the Council of Trent were published, this state of things ceased to exist.   The Roman Catholics then knew exactly the doctrines of their Church and those of the Reformers.   No doubt on the subject could any longer exist.   The long arguments which accompanied the theses of the Ecumenical Synod explained to them fully the reasons for their belief. They found an arsenal full of weapons which they could use for their defence when they were attacked by their enemies.   The Church of Rome showed that she hoped to withstand the assault.   She had well compacted and consolidated the stones in the grand and imposing structure which astonished the inhabitants of Europe. She hoped that she had not left a single breach through which the enemy could force his way into the heart of the fortress.   The Council of Trent stayed the triumphant march of the Reformers.   The garrison of the Roman fortress, strong, courageous, well disciplined, and enterprising, resumed the offensive, and drove back the enemies from many positions which hitherto had been supposed to be impregnable.

We who differ from them must admit that they had showed wisdom, zeal, and energy.   In 1546, 1547, and 1551, they had developed their system of doctrine.   They

had declared that the Scriptures had no authority except
in the version of the Vulgate. They condemned the
doctrine of justification by faith ; and affirmed the
efficacy and binding authority of the seven Sacraments.
No concession was made to Protestantism. The Church
of Rome did not wish her position to be misunderstood.
She was determined rather to alienate for ever the
countries in the North of Europe than to incur the
reproach of having shown the least vacillation in the
declaration of her fundamental doctrines. The party
which triumphed at Trent declared in effect its conviction that the half of the Christian Church ought rather to
perish than that any doubt should exist as to any one of
the doctrines which she had placed in her Creeds, and
brought prominently before her members.

We are now explaining the views of the Fathers of
the Council. They said that the Protestants had a book,
the Bible, to which they could turn for the explanation
of their doubts and the removal of their difficulties. If
the Church had not demanded their unqualified assent
to the dogmas which she brought before her members,
she who did not allow private judgment would be utterly
unable to carry on the conflict with her opponents. The
Protestant opinions of a large number of the members
of the Church of Rome ought to convince them that
a firm opposition could alone save them from their
enemies. If they had left one or two doors open,
the enemy would at once have forced his way into the
citadel.

The Order of the Jesuits was in its infancy during the
first two sittings of the Council. But even now they
were beginning to exercise that influence which enabled
them to guide the deliberations of the Fathers. They
had begun by affirming that the tradition of the Church
has the same authority as the Bible. They had then
established the doctrine of justification in a manner to

preclude the possibility of a reconciliation with the Protestants. They had heaped up on this foundation with great energy and perseverance dogma after dogma, until they had reared an imposing structure. They had thus begun, even in the infancy of their Order, to form a united body, as strongly as possible antagonistic to the Reformers. In the fourteenth and fifteenth centuries a certain latitude had been given to the members of the Church of Rome. If they attended to certain ceremonial observances, no one would be disposed to challenge their religious belief. Now they must close their ranks, and must present a united front to the enemy. Every soldier who did not render implicit obedience to the word of command must be punished as a traitor to his cause, and must at once be expelled from the Papal army.

If the Jesuits could exercise this influence when their organism was incomplete, we shall not be surprised to hear that they were armed with an authority almost despotic, when at the time of the last Council of Trent they had fully developed their system, and, ' breathing united strength,' had come forward as the leaders of the Papal army. Lainez, the ablest of the lieutenants of Loyola, had on his arrival at Trent asserted an authority almost despotic over the Council. He strongly opposed the independence of the Bishops ; he would not allow the least concession to the Reformers ; and he affirmed the absolute authority of the Pope. He attacked in the most violent manner all those who wished for reform. ' What,' he cried, ' have we to do here with reforms ? The Pontiff alone has a right to propose them.' He had even the effrontery to assume the authority of the Pope, and to threaten the Council with an early dissolution if the Fathers continued their innovations, and forgot that they were merely the creatures of the Pope. He constantly and proudly affirmed the superiority of the Bishop of Rome to the Council. He and the other Jesuits were determined not to stand on the defensive, nor to make the least concession to Protestants, but to carry the war into the enemy's country. They did not merely reproduce the teaching of the Church in the sixteenth century; they excluded all elements from their teaching which had the least appearance of giving a sanction to the doctrines of the Protestants, and brought forward dogmas hitherto debatable, to which, because they were opposed to the teaching of their opponents, they attached paramount importance. They thus carried without much difficulty decrees to which there had been strong opposition in the early stages of the Council. Absolute power had been given to the Pope. He had been called the Vicar of God upon earth (Session VI., on Reform, chapter i.). The following addition had been made to this decree: ' The supreme power in the Universal Church has been conferred on the Roman Pontiff ' (Session XXIV., chapter vii.). The Fathers declined to affirm the Divine origin of episcopacy. The Pope had an absolute right to regard himself as the Universal Bishop, who would not confer any of the power entrusted to him on other Bishops. Thus, then, this Council, which he so much feared, had made him the absolute master of the Bishops, who were more dependent on him than they had ever been in former ages of the Church. They had become simply delegates of the Apostolic See (Session VI., on Reform, chapter iii.). Certain crimes could be judged, not by the Bishops, but by the Popes (Session XIV., de Pœnit., chapter vii.).

The Pope could also confer several benefices on ecclesiastics, and could dispense with the obligation of residence. He could give a certain abbey to secular priests, especially to Cardinals and Bishops who were his favourites. He retained the annates, or the payments made by every Bishop to the Holy See on his promotion, notwithstanding the attacks made upon them in the Council, affirming that they were absolutely necessary for the maintenance of the dignity and grandeur of the Holy See. All the abuses which the Council and the Kings had wished to abolish remained in the Church, and some of them were greatly intensified.

The re-organization of the College of Cardinals, which had come prominently before the Council, had not been effected. The Popes were enjoined to make their selection from all nations, and to be guided by the consideration of the fitness of the individual for the office thus conferred upon him. It seemed, at first sight, an arrangement which cannot be justified, that a small number of Roman priests should be allowed to choose one who asserts a claim to the spiritual allegiance of Christendom. The selection of the candidates from a much wider field, while the Pope adheres to the ancient plan by the titles given to the Cardinals, served to lessen this objection. But the Popes have disregarded this consideration. They have appointed a large majority of Italians. They have often utterly neglected the idea of suitableness for the appointment. Shortly before the last Council of Trent, Julius III. had made a Cardinal the boy who kept his ape ; Paul III. had made his nephew a Cardinal at fourteen, his grandson at sixteen, and his cousin at twelve ; and Pius IV. made Ferdinand de' Medici a Cardinal at fourteen. Thus the Popes have utterly set at naught this and every direction of the Council which was disagreeable to them. We believe that this mode of appointment will be like the canker at the root of the widely-branching tree, which will ultimately be the cause that it no longer puts forth its branches, like the glory of Lebanon, seen far and wide on the summit of the mountain, and that it becomes a lifeless trunk, which the genial influence of the spring shall revisit no more.

The Council of Trent affirms more strongly than ever

the erroneous doctrines and mistaken requirements of the Roman Catholic Church. The marriage of priests was rejected in the most energetic manner. ' If anyone shall say that a priest having received sacred orders can marry, let him be accursed ' (Session XXIV., can. ix.). It forbade the celebration of Mass in any other language than the Latin. The worship of the saints and the adoration of images and relics were plainly recommended in the twenty-fifth session of the Council. The traffic in indulgences had been the cause of the Lutheran Reformation. The Council on the second day of the twenty-fifth session directly enjoined it.

We must see, then, that the Council had altogether failed in effecting the reunion of Western Christendom through the reconciliation of the Protestant and Roman Catholic Churches. This was the favourite project of the Emperor Charles V. We have seen that the Popes, the Jesuits, and the Councils exerted every effort to prevent it from being brought to a successful issue. Their object had been to draw a broad line of demarcation between the rival communions. Councils in the preceding centuries had restricted Papal prerogatives. The work of the Council of Trent was to invest the Pope with a power almost despotic. The Council had given to him the right to explain its decrees. We cannot, therefore, be surprised to find him in the Bull ' Benedictus Dei,' of January 26, 1564, distinctly affirming, ' We forbid all prelates, who do not wish to be deprived of their bishoprics, or to be excommunicated, to publish without our permission commentaries, glosses, annotations on the decrees of the Council. We reserve to ourselves the explanation of the difficulties and controversies arising out of the decrees, in accordance with the decree of the Council.' The Council has thus prepared the way for the Vatican Decrees of 1870 and the affirmation of the dogma of Infallibility. To the Fathers of Trent we owe the assertion of the late and present Pope and the Jesuits, that our duty is to accept whatever the present Church teaches. The words of Pius IX. and Leo XIII. are as truly inspired by God's Holy Spirit, and are to be accepted with as much reverence, as the words of St. Peter and St. Paul. The defenders of Romanism have taken up this position because they have been dislodged from every other. But they have taken it up at an immense loss. They have given a triumph to infidelity. It is a very short distance from the doctrine as to the inspiration of Pius and Leo to the doctrine that Peter and Paul were no more inspired than Pius and Leo. The Fathers of Trent are thus answerable for the changes which are now made with great rapidity in the Roman Catholic Church. We may count them on the minute-hand, not on the hour-hand, of the watch. Many now keep pace with the times, and watch with intense interest the shifting phases of Roman defence. We think of the Council of Trent when we remember that the changes in the system of her who formerly called herself the unchangeable Church, rendered necessary by the doctrine now before us, have been, and will be, the means of inflicting on her an irreparable injury.

We must see also that the Council applied no remedy to the numerous abuses which had through ages prevailed in the Church of Rome. We must, however, admit that many remedies of practical evils, many improvements in matters of discipline, followed immediately from the enactments of the Council. The ecclesiastical authorities acquired by means of them powers not previously possessed for bringing offenders to justice. The abolition of pluralities, the enforcement of residence, the more careful education for the ministry in the new seminaries, the stricter supervision of monastic institutions, tended to give the clergy a stronger hold on the spiritual allegiance of her members. We must, however, remember that we can give the Council only a very small share in effecting these salutary improvements. The facts that it was unwilling to reform, that it resisted the strongest pressure put upon it by the Roman Catholic Sovereigns, that its motives and proceedings had been strongly censured, not only by Protestants, but also by Roman Catholics who were loyal members of their Church, afford us very strong evidence that these improvements did not owe their origin to the Council. We believe that the Jesuits are the real authors of these changes. We have described their system in a former chapter. They have shown in the prosecution of their work a great disregard of the fundamental rules of morality; they have done evil that good might come; they have also brought forward, and are still bringing forward, doctrines condemned alike by reason and Scripture—for instance, the worship of the Virgin Mary, by which they raise a barrier between us and Him who wept over the grave of Lazarus and the foredoomed Jerusalem. They have, however, as we have seen, shown a spirit of devoted obedience to the Pope, being ready when he commanded them to go through difficulties and dangers to the limits of the world. The Inquisition aided them in their work; the Jesuits rallied the scattered forces of the Church, disheartened by the rapid victories of the Reformers; they disciplined them by precept and example; they inspired them with a superhuman courage; they animated them to go forward in their victorious career until they wrested from the Reformers many of the territories which they had conquered, compelling the inhabitants, often by persecution and fire and sword, to cast in their lot with the obedient vassals of the Papacy.

We see, then, that to Pius IV. and the Jesuits belongs the merit of completing this victory for the Church of Rome. The success which attended the designs of Pius is a wonder to those who reflect that men with ' strength surpassing Nature's law'—a Gregory I., a Gregory VII., an Innocent III.—were required in former times to enable the Church of Rome to go forth 'conquering and to conquer,' and to reign with despotic power over the nations of Europe. We have said enough to show that Pius was a mediocrity. He found his chief pleasure in conversation and diversion. He was remarkable for his gaiety and cheerfulness. The Fathers elected him because he was a perfect contrast to the gloomy and fanatical Caraffa. We have already partly explained the secret of his success. He possessed that legal ability, that political prudence, that knowledge of the world, which enabled him, with the assistance of the Jesuits, to control the deliberations of the Fathers, and to make even Kings his obedient subjects. Thus this moral mediocrity, this son of pleasure, this man gifted with political prudence, guided safely the vessel of the Church among the rocks on which she might have foundered.

In the year 1527 the storm of war had smitten down the battlements of Rome. The soldiers of Constable Bourbon had practised every refinement of cruelty on the Cardinals to induce them to show where they had buried their treasures. Clement VII. had been obliged to take refuge in the Castle of St. Angelo, and to submit to the terms imposed by his conquerors. The long dominion of the Papacy seemed to have come to an end. But now Pius IV. and the Jesuits had enabled it to rise like a young phœnix from the ashes of its parent. Not an article in the decrees of the Council had passed without the sanction of the Pope. No stipulations had been made with the Roman Catholic Sovereigns of which he had not expressed his full approval. The Fathers had, as we have seen, made him and his successors a court of ultimate appeal. The Pope was thus invested with a greater power than any of his predecessors. He now thought that he might commission others to carry on the warfare.

He determined to release his mind from the tension as soon as the conclave was closed. He retired from public life, and directed his nephew, Carlo Borromeo, to discharge the ordinary duties of the Papacy. The world thought that he was neglecting preparation for the eternal and unchangeable state on which he must shortly enter. He passed his time in the society of buffoons, in convivial banquets, in pomp and luxury and empty parade. In two years after his retirement he sank into the grave. We, who disapprove so strongly of his policy, must admit that it has produced permanent results. God 'makes even the wrath of man to praise Him.' Pius has given the Papacy a new lease of power, and begun a policy which has left a deep impression on Europe and the Church during the three following centuries.

CHAPTER VI.

THE RAPID PROGRESS OF THE COUNTER-REFORMATION.

Rapid progress of the Reformation—The influences which checked it—The first cause mentioned is the greater zeal of the Popes Paul IV., Pius IV. and Pius V.—Description of Cardinal Borromeo and of his work—Philip II. of Spain and his influence on the Counter-Reformation—Gregory XIII.—Sixtus V. and his schemes —The progress of the Counter-Reformation in Germany—The Jesuits, who were aided by the decrees of the Council of Trent, the agents in it—The progress of it in Austria and Illyria—Promoted by the dissensions of the Protestants—Progress in the Netherlands —The cruelties of Philip and Alva—Resistance of the inhabitants under William of Orange, which was for some time unsuccessful— Its end and results—Progress of the Reformation in France—The reaction and its causes—Character of Charles IX. and Catherine de' Medici—The Massacre of St. Bartholomew—Advance of Romanism chiefly through the Jesuits—League to exclude Henry of Navarre from the throne—Events connected with the league— The assassination of the Duke of Guise, and subsequent assassination of Henry III.—His assassination recommended by the Jesuits, and extolled by Sixtus V.—A description of the designs of the Jesuits— The success of Henry IV. in battle, which the Duke of Parma made of no avail—The altered position of the Pope in consequence of the Counter-Reformation manifest during the pontificate of Sixtus V.—His fantastic designs, including Rome as the capital of the world, and at last the prevention of Henry's accession—Dispute on this matter with the Venetian Ambassador—Withdrawal of Sixtus from opposition to Henry, and his support of his pretensions —His death and character—Short reigns of the next three Popes— The designs of Gregory XIV., which might have been successful if they had not been prevented by his early death.

WE learn from contemporary documents that before 1563 the Reformers had advanced rapidly in their career of victory. We have already, in Chapter I., glanced at this advance. We need not speak of England, Scotland, or the Scandinavian kingdoms, which had for ever cast off the yoke of the Roman Pontiff. On the shores of the Baltic, Prussia had secularized the property of the Church. The Lutheran rites were established by charters in the great cities of Prussia; the smaller cities were secured against the encroachments of the powerful Bishops. In Poland the greater part of the nobility had embraced Protestant opinions.

During the reign of Sigismund Augustus, the Protestants had gained possession of some of the episcopal sees, and had thus obtained a majority in the Senate. In Hungary, Ferdinand I. had endeavoured in vain to induce the Diet to oppose Protestantism. Transylvania severed itself entirely from the Papacy; the property of the Church was confiscated by a formal decree of the States in 1556; the Crown seized the greater part of the tithes. But in Germany Protestantism had advanced more than in any other country beyond the limits which now separate the rival religions.

The present Protestant States are but a small part of the territory which the Reformation had obtained from its adversary. The great prelates in Franconia had in vain opposed the progress of the Reformation. In Würzburg and Bamberg the greater part of the nobles and of the officers of State, and the great body of the magistrates and of the burghers in the cities, had embraced the Protestant faith. In Bavaria, the greater part of the nobility professed Protestantism. In Austria the Revolution had advanced still further. The nobility had gone to study at Wittenberg. The colleges of the country were filled with Protestants. 'It was calculated,' as Von Ranke states, 'that not more than a thirtieth part of the inhabitants were Romanists.' The Archbishop of Salzburg could not succeed in prohibiting Lutheranism in his territory. In Salzburg the Mass was neglected; neither fasts nor holidays were observed.

'In short,' as Ranke states, 'from the East to the West, from the North to the South, throughout Germany Protestantism had a decided superiority. The nobility had been attached to it from the beginning; the civil officers, already a numerous and distinguished body, were educated in the new opinions. The common people would no longer hear of certain doctrines, such as purgatory, or certain ceremonies, such as pilgrimages. A Venetian Ambassador calculates, in the year 1558, that in all Germany not more *than a tenth part of the inhabitants* were true to the ancient faith.'

We must now endeavour to ascertain the powers at the command of the Papacy for the purpose of checking the progress of the Reformation. Rome had at first maintained a passive attitude, excepting in Spain and Italy. The Reformation had never, as we have seen, the least chance of success in either of those countries, especially in Spain. A description has been given of the stern system of repression exercised by the Inquisition in both those countries. In Spain it was much aided in its work by Philip II. We shall see presently that his was a most important influence in connection with the Counter-Reformation, and that he lived and laboured for the advancement of Romanism.

We shall find that the strength of the Papacy was in its own reviving energy and activity. The Popes had armies under their command more powerful than the men-at-arms who marched beneath the banners of Alva and the Guises. The reformed and the new Orders aided them in their work. When the revolt had only reached a certain point, the Dominicans were the efficient soldiers employed for its suppression. They bathed their swords in blood. But in provinces which were almost totally alienated from the Church of Rome, where Protestantism had gained a hold upon the body of the people, especially on the educated classes, a different policy must be adopted. The Jesuits, aided by the Council of Trent, were the subtle influence employed in this and in other countries to arrest the progress of the Reformation.

The advance of the Protestants had compelled the conclaves to discontinue the gross simony of former days, and the intrigues, difficult to unravel, which ended in the appointment of unsuitable men to the Papacy. The Popes during the age which preceded the Reformation had been the slaves of every vice. Public opinion now required the appointment of a different class of men from their predecessors. To this change it is very important to invite the attention of our readers.

The whole life and conduct of many Popes were condemned by the stricter spirit which had arisen in the Church. Greater zeal was now required in the Popes. Paul IV. was under the influence of this spirit. He has already come before us in connection with the Inquisition. He had a high idea of the power of the Papacy. He regarded Protestantism with intense abhorrence, and longed to wage with it a ceaseless warfare. He was for some time under the influence of political considerations. At length the failure of his ambitious schemes led him to devote his energies to the reformation of the Church. He determined to remove every abuse in its temporal and ecclesiastical polity. He prohibited strictly the sale of offices, from which the Roman Catholic Church drew a large revenue. He insisted that a holy and devoted life should be a qualification for those who were raised to the highest dignities. He had a medal struck, representing him, under the likeness of Christ, as driving the money-changers from the temple.

Ranke (Book III., sec. 4) says of him:

' If there was a party which purposed the renovation of Catholicism in all its strictness, that party possessed in him who now ascended the Papal chair not a member merely, but a founder and leader.   Paul IV. was already seventy-nine years, but his deep-sunk eyes retained all the fire of youth.   In his personal habits he bound him-self by no rule.   He often slept in the day, and studied by night.   Woe to the servant who should enter his room before he had rung the bell !   He was very tall and thin.   His step was rapid, and he seemed to be all nerves. In all matters he followed the impulse of the moment ; but that impulse was always governed by a habit of mind so as to become a second nature.   He seemed to know no other occupation than the restoration of the old faith to its former dominion.'*

We need not dwell upon the career of Pius IV.   We have seen that he has a claim on the gratitude of his Church because he converted the Council of Trent into an instrument for promoting the Roman Catholic reaction.

The next conclave could not resist the spirit of the times.   It appointed as a zealous Pope one whom the Church has since canonized.   He carried on the work begun by Paul IV.   The austere party were delighted at the elevation of Pius V. to the Papacy.   He has already come before us.   He was Michel Ghislieri, the chief of the Inquisitors.   We need not repeat the more or less doubtful information contained in the book on conclaves, respecting his election.   We know that he owed it to the celebrated Cardinal Borromeo.   The latter had gained great influence in Italy by his zeal and irreproachable life. In the time of the plague at Milan he spoke words of peace and consolation to those who were shunned by all the world.   He would stop at the doors and under the windows to address to those stricken with the plague words calculated to support them amid the agonies of dissolving nature.

* Ranke's description is taken from the relation of the Venetian Ambassador.

We have a letter from Borromeo which gives a sufficient explanation of his election. We know that he had
great influence in determining the choice of Pius V. 'I
resolved,' he says, 'to look to nothing so much as religion
and faith. As I knew well the piety and holy life of the
Cardinal of Alessandria, I exerted all my efforts in his
favour.' No other motives could have been expected
to influence Borromeo. Philip II. of Spain thanked
Borromeo for the part which he took in his election.
The austere party were delighted at his elevation. If
he had followed the course of life to which his inclinations led him, he would have buried himself amid the
gloom of cloistered seclusion, because he fancied that
he could thus hold that communion with heaven which
he regarded as the perfection of earthly happiness. This
elevation to the Papacy appeared likely to hinder him in
the attainment of this end. He carried into his exalted
station the same zeal for which he was conspicuous in
the early part of his career. Those who saw him at the
head of some procession, ' his rapt soul sitting in his eye,'
while on his wan and wasted countenance was seen a
brightness which seemed to be derived from the source
of uncreated light, deemed him a being from a higher
sphere, who had descended to declare God's mind and
will to the guilty and rebellious inhabitants of this district
of His empire. By his piety and zeal, and by his reform
of various institutions, he gained great influence throughout the Roman Catholic world, and promoted the success
of those measures which had for their object the regeneration of the Church. His religion was, however,
tainted with extreme bigotry. He sent a jewelled hat to
the Duke of Alva in the Netherlands because he had
written his arguments in defence of Christianity in the
blood of thousands. He also told Charles IX. and his
mother in France that they could not do a deed more
acceptable to God than to sacrifice hecatombs of victims

on the altars of the Church. To Catherine de' Medici he said : ' Under no circumstances, and from no considerations, ought the enemies of God to be spared.' These and similar exhortations repeated through many years issued in that bloody massacre of St. Bartholomew which has consigned Charles IX. and his mother to eternal infamy.

The influence which ruled this and following conclaves up to the election of Clement VII. was Spanish influence. Philip II. made the members of the conclave the creatures of his will, so that he appointed all these Popes in succession. The benefices and abbeys to which he had the presentation in his extensive dominions had a great influence in determining their choice. Philip lived and laboured for the advancement of Romanism. In comparison of that object every other object seemed to him to be insignificant. He was the King of Spain, including Aragon, Castile, and Granada. He was the King of Naples and Sicily, and Duke of Milan. He was the King of the Low Countries, at that time the richest territory in Europe. He also possessed the riches of the empires of Mexico and Peru. The Protestants trembled when they saw that all this wealth, all this power, were employed to arrest through severe persecution the progress of the Reformation on the Continent of Europe.

Gregory XIII., elected under Spanish influence, was at first addicted to pleasure. He would have followed the example of Innocent VIII. if he had lived a hundred years before this age. But he could not resist the spirit of the times. He sought in every land for suitable men to elevate to bishoprics. He spent immense sums of money on the enlargement of the Jesuit College at Rome, and called it the Seminary of all Nations. By this title he seemed to intimate that his purpose was to extend the influence of the Roman Catholic Church throughout the world. We have distinct evidence in the letters of Cardinal Allen, published a few years ago by the Fathers of the Oratory at Brompton, that ' he did not express the slightest disapprobation of the plot formed to assassinate Queen Elizabeth, but spoke only of the advantage it would be if in some way or other the wicked woman were removed by death.' He thus showed that he was under the influence of the same bloodthirsty spirit as Philip II., to whom he owed his elevation to the Papacy. Though he did not recommend, he expressed his strong approval of that bloody massacre of St. Bartholomew at Paris, enjoined, as we have seen, by Pius V. He commanded it to be celebrated with special services and 'brilliant illuminations; also he directed a medal to be struck, and a jubilee to be held that Roman Catholics from all parts of the world might render thanks to Heaven for what he considered to be one of the most brilliant deeds in the history of Christianity.

Sixtus V., Pope from 1585 to 1590, was also elected under Spanish influence. He it was who fixed at seventy the number of electors of the Sacred College, which had constantly varied through the ages. Under him the territorial possessions of the Papacy became very important to the Pope and Roman Catholic Powers. His predecessor, Gregory XIII., had endeavoured to make them available for the propagation of the faith by seizing the estates of the Roman nobility under the pretext of lapsed titles and tributes unpaid. The result, however, had been that many of the dispossessed nobility had broken out into open insurrection, had taken the law into their own hands, had established a system of brigandage, and had laid waste the territory of their neighbours with fire and sword. Sixtus, by the adoption of strict measures, struck terror into the insurgents, succeeded in restoring the order essential to the collection of the taxes, and consequently, as we shall see, to the prosecution of his schemes. The income arising from the constant creation of offices, and the loans effected by the Pope, the interest on which was paid by very heavy taxes on the Roman States, both of which plans had been adopted by his predecessors, was employed by him in beautifying the city, in promoting works of public utility, and above all in carrying on the war with heretics and unbelievers. He sold offices, taxed necessaries, debased the coinage, and raised loans (*monti*) on a scale far surpassing any of his predecessors. Thus he contrived to amass a sum of 4,500,000 scudi, which he kept stored in the Castle of St. Angelo. Palaces, which astonished spectators by their grandeur, once more towered on the seven hills of Rome. His desire was to have buildings rivalling those in the days of the Emperors, when Rome sat as a queen among the nations. But this restoration was carried on in the spirit of the Roman Catholic reaction. He waged war with the monuments of antiquity. Works which defied the storm and waste of ages were levelled with the ground. The breathing figures of Jupiter and Apollo were taken from the Capitol and that of Minerva was suffered to remain on condition that for the spear should be substituted a gigantic cross. By this iconoclastic spirit he showed very plainly that the restoration of Romanism was the absorbing subject of his attention.

We are thus led to contemplate the tremendous war which the regenerated Papacy waged with new weapons for the recovery of her lost ascendancy over the nations. The religious action is closely connected with political impulses. Every passion which stirs the human frame was pressed into that warfare. Profound politicians, great captains, fierce demagogues, and desperate assassins were enlisted in it. We believe that the pontificate of Sixtus V. is the period of the great crisis in the history of the Papacy, the turning-point in the endangered fortunes of the Roman Catholic system. Sixtus V. had, indeed, other objects for the promotion of which he had collected his treasure. He hoped to combine all North-eastern and South-western Europe for the annihilation of the Turkish Empire. He hoped also to effect the conquest of Egypt. He had heard from his earliest days a voice in every wind urging him to climb the steep ascent which leads to the Temple of Fame. And now, when the largest wishes of his ambitious heart had been gratified, he believed that he had been chosen by a special Providence to carry his scheme into effect. But still with him, as with other Popes during this era, every object compared with the regeneration of Romanism seemed to sink into insignificance. The conflict in which they were engaged raged as far as earth's remote boundaries. Several nations threw themselves ener-getically into it. Germany, the Netherlands, and France were, however, the principal battle-fields. To them, therefore, with an occasional reference to other countries, we shall now invite attention.

We shall begin with Germany. We shall find that the Jesuits were the agents employed to stay the progress of the revolt against the Church of Rome in this district of her spiritual empire. We have fully described their qualities and qualifications for this important work. This remarkable Order, founded by enthusiasm which seemed very much like insanity, but regulated by wisdom which seemed very much like craft, pledged to absolute submission to the Holy See and to their General, now came prominently forward in every part of Europe to which the members could obtain admission. In Germany their success was very rapid. Urban, Bishop of Laibach, was confessor to Ferdinand of Austria when he attended the Diet of Augsburg in 1550. In Augsburg he met the Jesuit Le Jay, who was attracting great notice by his con-versions. With the full consent of Ferdinand he invited Le Jay to Vienna. The arrangements were soon made. In 1551 Le Jay with thirteen Jesuits arrived at Vienna.

Ferdinand granted them a mansion, a chapel, and a pension, and shortly afterwards assigned to them the superintendence of the University. They were two years in establishing themselves at Cologne. Here, however, also in the year 1556, they obtained a settlement. In the same year they were recalled to Ingoldstadt, from which they had been expelled. Here also they obtained a firm hold.

From these three places they spread throughout Germany; from Vienna over the Austrian dominions; from Cologne over the Rhenish provinces; from Ingoldstadt over the whole of Bavaria. They gradually gained a footing at Spires. At Würzburg they received a hearty welcome. They obtained a settlement in Innspruck, in Munich, and in Dillingen.

'In 1551,' to use Ranke's words, 'they had no firm station in Germany. In 1566 their influence extended over Bavaria and the Tyrol, Franconia and Suabia, a great part of the Rhineland, and Austria; they had penetrated into Hungary, Bohemia, and Moravia.'

In the year 1561 the Papal Nuncio affirmed 'they gain over many souls, and render great service to the Holy See.' They laboured especially at the improvement of the Universities. They were ambitious of rivalling the fame of the Protestants. Their teaching might claim to be ranked with the teaching of the restorers of classical learning. The scholars of the Jesuits learned more in one year than those of other masters in two, and even Protestants recalled their children from distant gymnasia, and committed them to their care. Schools for the poor, modes of instruction suited to children, and catechizing, followed. Their catechism satisfied the mental wants of the learners by its well-connected questions and answers. The children who frequented their schools were remarkable for the firmness with which they rejected the forbidden viands on fast-days, while their parents partook of them without scruple. In Cologne it was once more regarded as an honour to wear the rosary, while relics which no man had dared for years to exhibit publicly began once more to be held in reverence. The sentiments of which these acts were demonstrations were disseminated through all the population by preaching and confession. The decrees of the Council of Trent aided them in their work. They told their pupils that they were engaged in a war in which there could be no neutrality, that they must not, like Pole and others, make the least compromise with the Protestants; and that they must render to the Pope a devoted and absolute obedience. Professor Ranke has the following strong and just observations on this remarkable movement (Book V., section iii.): ' This is a call perhaps without a parallel in the history of the world. All the other intellectual movements which have exercised an extensive influence on mankind have been caused either by great qualities in individuals or by the irresistible force of new ideas. But in this case the effect was produced without any striking manifestation of genius or originality. The Jesuits might be learned and pious in their way; but no one can say that their learning depended on the free impulse of their mind, or that their piety sprang from the ingenuousness of a simple spirit. They were learned enough to obtain reputation, to command confidence, to form and to retain a strong hold upon their scholars; they attempted nothing more. Neither their devotion nor their learning struck into free, unlimited or untrodden paths. Yet they had one peculiar distinction—rigid method. Everything had its object. Such a union of wisdom sufficient for their purpose with indefatigable zeal, of study and persuasiveness, of pomp and the spirit of caste, of universal propagandism and unity of the main principle, has never been seen in the history of the world.'

We are thus reminded that the Jesuits obtained their success because they brought forward prominently the decrees of the Council of Trent. From the moment when the decrees were accepted in a meeting of the ecclesiastical Princes we may date the commencement of a new religious life in the Roman Catholic Church in Germany. These rigid decrees, which absolutely exclude neutrality, were subscribed alike by the high and the low. The ecclesiastical Princes felt that it was important that their subjects should embrace the Roman Catholic faith, because they opposed them strongly on account of their ecclesiastical character. The Popes also at this time showed all the wisdom of the serpent in their dealings with royal and noble houses. We have no doubt that the possession of Church property was the great argument which induced many to embrace the Protestant faith. The Popes followed their example. The Sovereigns of the smaller sees installed their sons, with the sanction of the Pope, into the Chapters of which they had obtained possession. The stern and bigoted Pius V. allowed the son of the Duke of Bavaria to hold the bishopric of Frisingen. The Duke fully succeeded in restoring the territory of Bavaria to Romanism. He sent his High Steward with a Jesuit into lower Bavaria, who proceeded in a summary manner ' to set free the ears and the spirit of the simple multitude for the reception of the heavenly doctrine.' They compelled the monks who had not remained strictly orthodox to abjure all deviations from the true faith, filled the schools, both primary and superior, with Roman Catholic masters, and sent into exile the laity who refused to conform. Thus in two years, 1571 and 1572, the whole country was slowly restored to Romanism.

The dominions of Austria gradually submitted to the same impulse. As late as 1578, in all the provinces, German, Slavonian, and Hungarian, except the Tyrol, Protestantism had maintained the predominance. The Emperor Rodolph II., by his own personal example, in 1578 succeeded in rekindling the devotion to Romanism. He performed all the acts of devotion with the greatest

strictness. Men saw him with astonishment attending the
procession, even in the most severe winter, bareheaded,
and carrying a torch in his hand. A Protestant preacher,
inflamed with anger on account of this open profession
of Romanism, declaimed against him in the Landhauss
at Vienna with such vehemence that, in the language of
a contemporary, as the congregation left the church they
would have 'torn the Papists to pieces.' A riot subsequently compelled the Government to take stronger
measures. Opitz, the preacher, was ordered immediately
to leave Vienna and the Austrian dominions in eleven days.
The submission of the Protestants, who did not offer any
opposition to this edict, and were satisfied with escorting
him out of the city, shows the altered condition of the
country. The Government had the strength and courage
to expel the Protestant preachers. It could force the
laity into conformity, or compel them to abandon their
homes, because the popular mind was already estranged
from them. The Archduke Charles effected the same
Counter-Reformation in Illyria. Wolf Dietrich, Archbishop of Salzburg, compelled his subjects to emigrate
from his territory or to embrace the Romish worship.
The Romanists also gained the ascendancy in Cologne,
Aix-la-Chapelle, Augsburg, and Ratisbon, and even individual Counts and nobles and Knights of the Empire,
who had been converted by some Jesuit, undertook the
resuscitation of Romanism within their small territories.
Thus the persevering labours of the Jesuits had been
rewarded. The tide was now on the ebb, and soon,
rushing on with great violence, would sweep away the
dams and mounds, and carry all before it.

We must not, however, attribute to the Jesuits only
the success which attended the Counter-Reformation.
The Protestants had been their own worst enemies. The
Jesuits succeeded because they were bound to hold and
to declare their belief in all the decrees and dogmas of

the Council of Trent, and because they thus presented an
unbroken front to the enemy. But endless divisions and
contentions interrupted the harmony and endangered the
existence of the Protestant Churches. The great master-
spirit, Luther, had disappeared, who alone could still the
raging of the tempest and hush the troubled elements to
peace. Two classes of a totally opposite character had
appeared who wished to guide the course of the Reformation. The one party strove to emancipate itself from
Rome, but did not care to define too closely the articles
of Christianity. The other party laid down the dogmas
in the same peremptory style as the decrees of the
Council of Trent, to which it required Protestants to
yield their unqualified assent. The members would not
accept Melanchthon as a leader, because it was supposed
that he wished to make a compromise with the enemy.
The questions of justification, of good works, and of the
Sacraments, were contested with as much bitterness of
spirit as if the fate of empires depended upon the settlement of them. The places where their meetings were
held were the very Babel of discord. Every discussion
seemed to disclose new points of difference, and to make
them more antagonistic to one another. The wild revolutionary dogmas of the Anabaptists, which led to an
armed insurrection, were supposed by many to show that
the doctrines of the Protestants were the fruitful causes
of social disorganization. Thus it came to pass that the
Reformers by their disunion inflicted a grievous injury
on the Reformation. That disunion, as contrasted with
their own union, was constantly brought forward by the
Jesuits as a plain proof of their own superiority to them.
They thus inflicted an injury on their own cause, when
they ought in the presence of the enemy to have sought
points on which they agreed, rather than points on
which they differed, and when they ought to have been
united as one man to beat back foes who were robbing

them of one province after another of their spiritual empire.

Immediately after the days of Luther the Reformation had made progress in the Netherlands. Charles V. endeavoured to arrest it by persecution. During his reign 30,000 of the inhabitants were barbarously murdered.

Philip had no sooner ascended the throne than he determined to labour for the extermination of it in his hereditary dominions. The clouds gathered with portentous blackness over the Netherlands. In the year 1555 the Inquisition, armed with additional powers, began to lay its terrible hand alike on the young and the old. Deeds of cruelty were perpetrated surpassing in horror any in the darkest period of pagan antiquity. All lay persons who held in their house conventicles, or who conversed or disputed concerning the Holy Scriptures, openly or secretly, or who entertained any of the opinions of Luther or of others, were, if they were men, executed with the sword, and if they were women buried alive, if they did not persist in their errors ; but if they did persist in them, they were committed to the flames. They had previously been subjected to a terrible apparatus, by which the sinews could be strained without cracking, the bones bruised without breaking, and the body racked without being deprived of life. The King, with a refinement of cruelty which deserves the strongest condemnation, fearing that the heretics might glory if they passed through the ordeal of a public execution, directed that their heads should be bound between their knees, and that they should be slowly suffocated at midnight in tubs of water.

The iron now entered into the soul of the inhabitants. In streets which once resounded to the busy hum of industry now reigned a stillness as deep as the stillness of the tomb. The inhabitants, in order to escape the fury of the persecutor, emigrated in great numbers to England, which they enriched with the manufactures of their native

10

country. An urgent appeal addressed to the King, to mitigate the severity of the sufferings, was answered by a direction to substitute the halter for the faggot. But this persecution only served to inspire the Reformers with a firmer determination to continue in the profession of their faith. Thousands, prohibited from carrying on their worship in the churches, assembled in the fields, and listened with eager attention to the preachers as in animated discourses they brought before them those truths which are the delight of the angels and of the spirits of the just. Anthems from multitudinous voices ascended from the grassy meadows to the throne of God.

Exasperated by this disregard of his edict and by the iconoclastic fury of the multitude in Antwerp, who shivered every stained-glass window in the gorgeous churches to atoms, and hurled the statues of the saints from their niches to the ground, Philip determined on an invasion of the provinces. In 1567 the Duke of Alva, at the head of a body of veterans, whose courage and military skill had been proved on numerous well-fought fields, was sent to the Netherlands as the executioner of his vengeance. His person is well known to us by the grand portrait of Titian. Tall and upright, with a stern and dark visage, with black and gleaming eyes, with close black hair, and a waving beard descending over his magnificent armour, and wearing the collar of the Golden Fleece, he looks the personification of the resolute and haughty grandee who delighted in war, and was convinced that he ought to devote all his energies to the extermination of the heretics. He exhibited a bloodthirsty spirit and a patient vindictiveness in union with stealth and ferocity seldom found in a human being, which have obtained for him a high place in the annals of persecution.

The Blood Council, established by him soon after his arrival, now cast its awful shadow over the land. Not

only avowed heretics, but even those who had tolerated
field preaching, and who asserted that the King had not
the right to deprive the provinces of their liberties, made
themselves obnoxious to its vengeance.   Men, women, and
children were burned before slow fires, pinched to death
with red-hot tongs, starved, flayed alive, or broken on the
wheel, and were thus subjected to a death of lingering
agony.   Even Counts Egmont and Horn, good Roman
Catholics, who suggested that, as a matter of policy,
Philip should moderate his fury, became the victims of
his wrath.   The country was one vàst sepulchre.

But the deliverer was at hand.   The Prince of Orange
now came forward, determined to break the fetters which
the tyrant had forged to enslave his fellow-countrymen.
He was the Count of Nassau on the Lahn, and titular
Prince of Orange on the Rhone, and in Brabant the Baron
of Breda.   He was commissioned as the Governor of
Holland, Zealand, and Utrecht.   He was a Roman
Catholic, but as a politician, not as a theologian, he
offered a strong opposition to the persecuting designs of
Philip and of Alva.   He now, however, enrolled himself
for life as the soldier of the Reformation.   The patient
zeal with which he laboured in the service of his country,
the magnanimity with which he sacrificed himself in order
to secure for his fellow-countrymen the blessings of civil
and religious liberty and independence, are written in
indelible characters on the pages of the history of Europe.
He went into exile on the appearance of Alva, and was
very soon outlawed as a traitor and rebel by the Government.   He formed three independent expeditions to
invade the Low Countries, all of which were ignominiously defeated.   Thirty thousand men whom he had
himself armed and equipped were afterwards mustered
beneath his banner; but he was doomed to the sickness
of hope deferred.   Alva, by declining a battle which, if
the Prince had been successful, would have roused the

martial spirit of the inhabitants, caused in a short time
the dissolution of the army. He afterwards continued
his career of butchery. The Pope, Pius V., who like
this bloodthirsty tyrant contended with weapons not
drawn from the armoury of heaven, sent him a jewelled
hat and sword in acknowledgment of his services.

Meanwhile the Prince seemed the sport of adverse
fortune. Germany, torn by religious factions, refused to
strike a blow on his behalf. He was unprovided with
funds to organize new levies; the blackness of darkness
had gathered round him.

But now a ray of light struggled through the gloom,
and fell on the dark path along which he was passing.
A band of rovers, ranging the sea in quest of booty,
suddenly descended, in 1572, upon the seaport town
of Brill in Zealand, took it by surprise, and planted on its
walls the standard of the Prince of Orange. This
capture was the foundation-stone of that building which,
augmented by fresh materials, gradually rose majestically
towards heaven. Animated by this success, all the cities
of Holland, by one spontaneous movement, formed themselves into a confederacy to fight the battles of their
country, and to eject from it the armies of the
invader. Flushing, in the Isle of Walcheren, was lost.
Mons, the capital of Hainault, was captured. City after
city in other provinces threw off the yoke of the
oppressor. One thunder-bolt after another descended on
Alva. The Prince's fortunes had been ruined in the service of his country ; but he persevered in the high and holy
enterprise which he had undertaken. The States, roused
by the impassioned eloquence of St. Aldegonde, willingly
poured their silver and gold into his treasury. The King
of France announced his determination to employ his
forces in rescuing the Netherlands from the yoke of
bondage. The Prince of Orange had a right to cherish
the hope that he should soon achieve the independence

of his native country. But 'the gorgeous palaces, the cloud-capped towers,' soon dissolved 'like the baseless fabric of a vision.' The bloody massacre of St. Bartholomew, of which we shall speak hereafter, at once converted Charles into the most powerful ally of the King of Spain. The Prince of Orange could no longer trust one who had been guilty of perfidy and murder unexampled in the history of the world.

Heart-broken the Prince struggled on. If he had been a great master of the art of war, at the head of a well-disciplined body of patriots, he might have crushed Alva, and roused all the Netherlands to arms. But he was not skilled in war, and he led only a loose body of mercenaries. Alva's army, though not so large as William's, consisted of unconquered veterans led by consummate generals. The issue did not remain long in suspense. A night surprise, which disorganized his army, compelled William to return to Holland. He was now compelled to disband his army. Mons, to the relief of which he was hastening, was obliged to surrender to the enemy. The keys of the city unlocked the gates of every town in Brabant and in Flanders. Crimes were perpetrated by the Spanish soldiers in the sacred name of the King of Heaven, unparalleled in the history of Christianity. In obedience to the orders of Alva, the inhabitants of these towns were slaughtered with barbarities which fill us with astonishment and horror. At Naarden laughing soldiers, intoxicated, not with wine, but with blood which they drew from the veins of their victims, found a savage pleasure in the agonies of those whom they tossed to and fro with their lances. Harlem in Holland, after a heroic resistance of seven months, in which her defenders —men, women, and children—displayed prodigies of valour in their struggle with Spanish veterans, after seven months of terrific suffering, was compelled by famine to surrender to her savage foe. The inhabitants of this city were literally baptized with a baptism of blood.   But its resistance nerved the arms and animated the hearts of the inhabitants of Batavia.

The flame glowed more brightly on her hearths and her altars.   The waves of the fiery deluge rolled against Alkmaar, but they recoiled like the surges from the rock-bound coast.   Its walls still remained immovable, rising from them like Mount Ararat from the flood.   The Spaniards, fearing to be submerged by the ocean which the patriots brought in upon them by opening the dykes, retired from the city.   This memorable repulse, the first retreat of a great Spanish army, the exhausting siege of Harlem, and the still more exhausting and disastrous repulse from Leyden, soon to follow, mark the turning-point in the heroic struggle which ended in the expulsion of the Spaniards from the Northern provinces.   Alva now, finding that the slaughter of 18,000 persons during his administration had been in vain, and that, though the Prince of Orange was defeated, he was unconquerable, resigned from disappointment the government of the Netherlands.   He has made himself infamous by his unheard-of barbarities and by his monstrous tyranny.

We do not propose to describe minutely the war in the Netherlands.   When William of Orange was assassinated by Balthazar Gerard in 1584, his devotedness to the cause of his country had been rewarded by the establishment of the Government of the United Provinces, which is nearly identical with the modern kingdom of the Netherlands. Our surprise at his success will be the greater when we hear that, at this stage of the conflict, the soil of Holland and Zealand was unproductive, and that they were occupied by only half a million of inhabitants, while Spain had a powerful navy, a formidable and well-disci-plined army, under the command of the most skilful generals, and had the riches of her own and other countries at her disposal.

Partly through diplomacy, partly through liberal bribery, partly through conquest, Alexander Farnese, Prince of Parma, at the time Governor of the country, had succeeded in re-annexing, in 1579, the south-west portion of the Netherlands, including Hainault, Artois and Douay, with the flourishing cities of Valenciennes, Arras, Lisle and Tournay, to the dominions of Philip of Spain. Afterwards, by the persevering exertions of the Jesuits, they were confirmed in their allegiance to the Papal See.

We wish that we could say that the Protestants had been equally successful in winning converts from Romanism. But we grieve to say that the violent disputes between Lutherans and Calvinists served to alienate many Romanists who would otherwise have become Protestants, and caused many who had joined the Protestant Church to return to their allegiance. Thus then, as we before stated, these miserable disputes aided the cause of the Counter-Reformation.

Parma afterwards gave proof of his military skill by capturing the important city of Antwerp, which was so strongly fortified by Nature and Art as to be almost impregnable. The capture of this city was soon followed by the submission of the provinces of South Brabant and East Flanders to their former Sovereign. A tract of country was thus added to the dominions of Philip, corresponding to the modern kingdom of Belgium.

Our wonder that Parma should have been successful is the greater when we remember that his soldiers were half starved, and ready to mutiny from want of pay, and that he had only 10,000 of them with whom to carry on a difficult siege. If only England had come sooner to the assistance of the Netherlands, he must have been compelled to abandon the rich prize when it was almost within his grasp. But that parsimony which was a defect in the character of Elizabeth caused her to dispute with the United Provinces the pecuniary conditions on which she should assist them till it was too late to save Antwerp from the foe, and afterwards hindered the success of important operations by leading her to withhold the money and the well-trained soldiers required to enable the projectors of them to conduct them to a successful issue. A vigorous campaign carried on at this time by the Earl of Leicester, another general of the Netherlands, with an efficient body of men against Parma would, as he was paralyzed by famine, pestilence, poverty, mutiny, and want of men, in all probability have changed the destinies of the Southern provinces by smiting down the heroic champion of Romanism.

Holland must have been in danger if Philip had listened to the pathetic appeal for men and money which Parma addressed to him, and had concentrated his energies on the conquest of this country. But she was safe, because Philip poured his treasures and sent his armies into France, partly that he might promote the designs of the league, which had for their object to aid the Roman Catholic reaction. Thus the republic, aided by the ambitious designs of Philip, was able to proceed onward in her career of victory. The little vessel was occasionally shattered by the violence of the tempest, but again she bade defiance to the fury of the elemental war, and rode triumphantly over the billows.

At the time when she most needed a heaven-sent general, one was raised up to her in the person of Prince Maurice of Nassau, the son of William of Orange. By a careful study of the art of war before he ventured to assume the command of an army, he was able so far to improve the living machine, whose movements he guided, as to bring it afterwards to bear with overwhelming force on the enemy. Siege operations conducted on a new system to a successful end; veteran soldiers, through a new method of attack, scattered in ignominious flight by greatly inferior numbers, astonished hoary generals, and showed that a new master of the art of war had risen in Europe.

At length Philip III., who succeeded his father in 1598, or, rather, the Duke of Lerma, who was the real Sovereign of the country, found that Spain had no money to pay her soldiers, and that her once-splendid army was disorganized and in a state of mutiny. This state of affairs will excite no surprise when we hear that, in consequence of defective financial arrangements, the territories subject to Spain could only just pay their expenses; that labour was discouraged in that country; and that from this and other causes a land which might have been the granary of the world had not food enough for her own population. On the other hand, the rebellious provinces had wrung from an ungrateful soil the wealth which it seemed to deny to them, possessed the richest manufactures in the world, and had fleets on every sea which brought to them the treasures of Europe and of Eastern and Western regions. At length Spain, influenced by all these considerations, but especially by the knowledge that their naval supremacy enabled them to strike a deadly blow at their former masters, was induced in the year 1609, after a negotiation of two years and a quarter, to consent to a truce of twelve years with the United Provinces. The conclusion of this truce was galling in the extreme to the pride of the Spaniards, for it was a confession that the rebels, with arms in their hands, had gained the victory, and that the unexampled tyranny and bloodshed had not coerced them into submission to the See of Rome and to Spain. The Southern provinces won back to Philip by Parma, and confirmed in their allegiance to the Papacy by the exertions of the Jesuits, were, in consequence of the banishment of the Protestants, the emigration of the manufacturers, the loss of commerce through the blockade of the coasts by the fleets of the provinces, and the tyranny and misgovernment of the Spaniards, reduced to the greatest poverty; while the Northern provinces were rewarded for all their heroism, and all their exertions, and all their sacrifices, by the possession of all the advantages just referred to, and of the invaluable blessings of civil and religious liberty and independence.

We must now speak of the reaction in France. The fruit of the persevering labours of the Reformers was not altogether satisfactory. They rather tended to the development of the intellect than to the promotion of the onward march of doctrinal and moral improvement. Francis I., who was anxious to inaugurate an Augustan Age, was the professed patron of men of letters, and was disposed to favour the Reformers because they were men of learning, eloquence, and intelligence. But when they published placards in the streets of Paris, in which, with biting sarcasm, they attacked the Sacrament of the Mass, and when they had the effrontery to nail up a placard on the door of the royal bed-chamber, he vowed irrecon- cilable enmity to the Reformation. He thought that the doctrine of Transubstantiation thus assailed was one of the fundamental doctrines of Christianity, and that the tone of the placards revealed a contemptuous disregard of kingly authority. Thus he kindled the flames of persecu- tion, and directed the use of a new instrument of torture. The victim was suspended by chains over a blazing fire, and was alternately lowered into and pulled out of it, that he might die a death of lingering agony.

On the accession of his son, Henry II., as he was guilty of flagrant immorality, and as the courtiers were intent on the pursuit of riches and honours, the Reformers thought that the spirit of persecution would not be so strongly displayed as it was under his predecessor. But, on the contrary, while Francis chastised the heretics with whips, Henry chastised them with scorpions. The King was anxious to make atonement by persecution for the immorality of his past life, and the courtiers wished to enrich themselves with the spoils obtained by the death of the Reformers and the confiscation of their property.

But, notwithstanding this persecution, Protestantism increased to an alarming extent. The Reformation was openly avowed by the first men in the kingdom, including the King of Navarre, the Prince of Condé, and the brother of Admiral Coligny. Even the judges appointed to investigate cases of heresy showed sympathy with those who were accused of it. One of them, Anne du Bourg, because he lifted up his voice in Parliament in eloquent denunciation of the persecuting rigour of the Court, perished amid the flames. The serene courage with which he and others encountered the King of Terrors as he approached in his most forbidding form, preceded by the dark executioners of his mandates, their holy and blameless lives when contrasted with the vice and immorality of the King and courtiers at whose bidding they suffered, showed the reality of the faith to which they had given an enlightened and conscientious adherence. The multitude listened with breathless interest to the sermon which Du Bourg addressed to them. 'As we returned from the execution,' writes a very bitter enemy of the Protestant cause, 'we were melted to tears ; and we pleaded his cause after his death, anathematizing the judges who had justly condemned him. His sermon at his death did more than a hundred ministers could have done.'

There were other causes of the wonderful propagation of the Reformation during the last two years of the reign of Henry II. The mind, enlightened by the new learning, began to push its inquiries into the vast system of error which the Church of Rome had imposed on Christendom. Next to the Bible, the 'Institutes' of Calvin, expressed in nervous language, charmed the ear and made a deep impression on the hearts of the multitude. A metrical version of the Psalms, sung in the cottage, the barn, and on the open heath, cheered the soul of the peasant and artisan with the prospect of the bliss of the unfading inheritance, and animated them to endure persecution in the service of their Divine Master. But the youths trained at Calvin's school at Geneva were the most effective instruments in promoting the progress of the Reformation. As the King no longer supported the movement, it came into the hands of these Reformers sprung from the people. Unlike those in its early stages, who were more studious of popularity than zealous for the truth, they persevered in their work of faith and labour of love. Under the influence of their preaching France seemed waking up from the sleep of ages. In 1561, letters recently brought to light from Paris and Geneva show us that a cry for ministers of the Gospel was heard from all parts of the country. In two months we read that an infant Church of thirty had grown to 600. The history of hundreds of towns and villages was the counterpart of its history. In the year 1561 there were 2,150 Protestant churches in France, and in 1564 the number of Reformers was about one million and a half.

In the year 1560 the Reformers assumed the name of Huguenots. Some have supposed that it is a corruption of the German ' Eidgenossen,' or confederates. Others have assigned a different meaning to the word. On this point we do not give an opinion. We can only say for certain that a powerful party seemed to have sprung up in a night immediately after the unsuccessful conspiracy of Amboise, which had for its object to overthrow the power of the Guises, and that within a week the name of Huguenots was given to it. They soon became too powerful to submit to arbitrary violence. It was soon evident that an edict obtained in 1562, allowing them to assemble for worship by day outside the walls of the cities, would not be observed ; and that the Duke of Guise, who

with Montmorency and St. André, had obtained the paramount authority in the State, was determined on their
extermination. They had therefore no alternative but to
take the field under the command of the Prince de Condé
and of Admiral Coligny. It is the deliberate conclusion
of a Venetian Ambassador, who had remarkable oppor-
tunities for observing the history of the time, that this
war prevented France from becoming a Huguenot country.
The Huguenots had gained converts by the serene courage
which they showed in the burning fiery furnace. But
now the indifference of the multitude to the Reformation
was changed into actual aversion when they saw them
in the tumult of the battlefield, and heard of the crimes,
which they tried in vain to prevent, perpetrated by those
who had allied themselves with them, because they thirsted
for revenge, or from the lust of gain, or with the view of
promoting some selfish or worldly purpose. The Jesuits,
finding that this war had prepared the way for the triumph
of their principles, established themselves in France, and
by their high-toned morality, which they could exhibit
when it suited their purpose to do so, as well as by their
indefatigable zeal, both of which were their credentials
to the common herd of their fellow-countrymen, prevented
many from joining the Huguenots, who were wavering in
their allegiance to the Pope, and won back many who
had apostatized from Romanism. They had at the same
time among them some men of fervid eloquence and of
brilliant talents, who, by their apparently lucid explanation of Scripture, and by their burning words, produced a
deep impression on the minds of their fellow-countrymen.

We see, then, that the civil wars which desolated the
country before the massacre of St. Bartholomew, though
unavoidable, were a misfortune for the Reformation in
France. The first war would probably have ended disas-
trously for the Huguenots if Francis of Guise had not been
struck down by the hand of an assassin. There was no

other general qualified to lead on the army of the Court to victory. Repeated infractions of the Treaty of Amboise, concluded after that war, impressed the Huguenots with the conviction that Catherine de' Medici, the Queen-mother, who was now their decided enemy, had determined on their destruction. They were thus led once more to fling wide their standard to the winds. Money, gold chains, silver, articles of every kind, were lavishly contributed to replenish the empty coffers of the army. A peace was concluded after a war of half a year, because the Court was not nearer the attainment of its ends than at the outbreak of hostilities, and because the Roman Catholic forces, swollen to 40,000 men, were confronted by an army of 30,000 Huguenots in the neighbourhood of the capital. Referring to their common faith, their well-ordered form of Church government, and their common danger, the Venetian Ambassador Correo writes : 'They were so bound together by this Order and by their objects, that there resulted a concordant will, and so perfect a union that it made them prompt in rendering instant obedience, and most ready to execute the commands of their superiors.' This peace was soon followed by the third war, in which Condé and Coligny, the Huguenot leaders, having narrowly escaped falling into the hands of a per-fidious Court, now in the interest of the Guises, who had ordered their arrest, stood forth manfully in defence of the lives and liberties of their fellow-believers. After the defeat of Condé and Coligny at Sarnac and the death of the former and the defeat of Coligny at Moncontour, the Court thought that the Huguenots were subdued. But Coligny soon convinced them that they had gained unprofitable victories. He proved his right to be considered a great general, by leading his army in nine months, in the face of an enemy flushed with victory, a distance of 400 leagues, through a hostile territory, to the immediate neighbourhood of the capital. Charles and his mother, now convinced that it was in vain to attempt to exterminate the Huguenots by force of arms, concluded the Peace of St. Germain with them, which seemed to secure to them, within certain limits, the blessings of religious liberty and independence.

Catherine de' Medici acted a conspicuous part in the scenes and events which have passed rapidly before us. The character and motives of this unprincipled woman have been misunderstood and misrepresented by historians. When her son, Charles IX., ascended the throne of France, her great object was to govern the country in his name. She found, however, that she could not accomplish this object without the assistance of one of the great parties struggling for supremacy in France. We learn, from a recently-discovered contemporary account, that on one occasion, when she feared that the growing power of the Guises would cast her influence into the shade, the Huguenot leader and the Chancellor L'Hospital spent two or three hours alone with her, day after day, in earnest argument. Sometimes they imagined that they had gained everything, and that she was ready to set off to Condé's camp; then, all of a sudden, so violent a fright seized her that she lost all heart. At that time, 1562, she wrote a letter to Condé, in which she called herself his good cousin, and said that she was no less attached to him than a mother to her son. For a long time she balanced the advantages of rival alliances; at length she decided against the Huguenots. She wished to reign unfettered by their love of liberty. Their superior industry and intelligence, and the circumstance that their strength lay in the middle classes and in the nobility, had awakened her jealousy. We cannot suppose that at the time just referred to she was so well inclined as, we learn from a letter written by the Ambassador Throkmorton to Queen Elizabeth, Admiral Coligny thought, to advance the true religion, or that afterwards, from religious zeal, she ordered the bloody massacre of St. Bartholomew; for there is evidence that she was a freethinker, and probably an atheist. Historians, till recent times, have supposed that the massacre was arranged at a conference at Bayonne, seven years previously, between herself, her daughter, the Queen of Spain, and the Duke of Alva. But the Duke's own correspondence with his Sovereign, recently discovered, shows not only that Alva did not distinctly declare himself in favour of a massacre, but that he was disappointed because Catherine said that she would not have recourse to violent measures.

The truth is that papers recently examined, not only at Simancas, but also at Paris and Venice, show us very clearly that she never long premeditated any course of action ; that she was fluctuating in her purposes and false in her promises ; and that, having been brought up in the school of her countryman Machiavelli, she was a dissembler, thought that the end justifies the means, and was ready to sweep away any who stood between her and the power which was the object of her desire. We would not, indeed, affirm that she did not wish to remove the leading men of the Huguenot party, but it seems plain that the design of the massacre was really formed only the day before it was carried into execution. Catherine had discovered that Admiral Coligny, who after the Peace of St. Germain had been summoned to Paris for the purpose of giving his Sovereign advice in regard to an expedition projected in aid of the revolt in the Low Countries, had gained an influence with Charles, prejudicial to her ascendency over him. She therefore determined on his assassination. If Coligny had died from the wound given him by the pistol fired at him, without the knowledge of the King, from a window in Paris, a massacre would not have been perpetrated which has excited the horror of the whole civilized world. But as the wound had not proved fatal, Catherine, the Duke of Anjou, the Duchess of Nemours, and the Duke of Guise, determined that he should perish in a massacre of the Huguenots. Charles was at first unwilling to consent to the death of the Admiral. He told Coligny's son-in-law that a crowded Court had become a vast solitude, and that the only person to whom he could have recourse for advice was that Christian hero whose figure stands out prominently through the mist of ages, from the mass of meaner men, the stern old Huguenot warrior. A voice from his young days might at this time have fallen upon his ear, reminding him of a conversation in 1561 with his aunt, the Queen of Navarre, in which he told her that he would not, if he could help it, go to Mass, and that as soon as he became a man he should cast off the superstitions of his fathers. But now the early buds of promise had been blighted, and a monarch whose fair natural endowments and love of goodness might have enabled him to act a conspicuous part in the history of Europe had become, through the education given to him, and the example and counsels of his mother, the slave of every vice and the patron of every crime. We cannot wonder, therefore, that his good feelings towards the Admiral should have passed away, and that when Catherine and Anjou told him that the Huguenots would soon rise against him on account of the wounding of the Admiral, but that if he were put to death their designs would perish with him, he at once, in a fit of frenzy, declared that he should be murdered, and that all the Huguenots should be murdered also, that no one might hereafter reproach him with their death.

We must, however, remember that without the teaching of the Church of Rome the massacre would have been an impossibility. Various motives may have influenced those who dyed their hands in the blood of the Huguenots. But we may certainly say that Charles IX.

and his mother, who aimed at a political object—those
who were anxious to sweep away from their path a
fellow-creature because they were eager for revenge,
or because they were anxious to seize his property, or
because he had taken a different side from themselves
in the civil warfare which desolated the country—the
religious assassins, too, whose number was small in comparison with those who made religion their pretext, would
not have been guilty of this crime if their savage
passions had not been excited by Pius V. and his
emissaries.   The former, in his letters to Charles IX. and
his mother, the latter, who traversed the country in
all directions, in their addresses to the populace, told
them that they could not do a deed more acceptable
to God, than to sacrifice hecatombs of victims on His
altars.   Pius had exhorted Charles and Catherine 'to
punish the heretics with all severity, and thus justly
to avenge not only their own wrongs, but those of
Almighty God ; to pursue and destroy the remnants
of the enemy, and wholly to tear up not only the roots
of an evil so great, and which had gathered to itself
much strength, but also the very fibres of the roots.'
To Catherine he said : ' Under no circumstances, and
from no considerations, ought the enemies of God to
be spared.'   These and similar exhortations, repeated
through many years, at length issued in that bloody
massacre which has consigned Charles IX. and his
mother to infamy.

Gregory XIII., who became Pope in 1572, though he
did not suggest, certainly applauded this terrible crime.
It was the greater because Charles had, by treaty, taken
the Huguenots under his protection, and because he
had invited them to Paris to celebrate the marriage of
his sister Margaret with Henry of Navarre, so that,
as the historian Thuanus says, ' her marriage robe was
sprinkled with their blood.'   When the bell in one of

the churches of Paris sounded early in the morning of August 24, 1572, the assassins, armed to the teeth, and distinguished by the white crosses on their hats, issued from their hiding-places on their errand of violence and blood. Coligny first fell a victim to their vengeance. A massacre was perpetrated, the atrocities in which make us shudder as we read of them. The air was rent with the oaths and blasphemies of the murderers, with the sound of fire-arms which they were continually discharging, with the groans of the dying, with the shrieks of the women whom they dragged along the streets by the hair, and with the rumbling of the carts, some laden with booty, others with the dead bodies which they cast into the neighbouring river. Murder raged uncontrolled through the city ; some were shot on the roofs of houses, others were cast out of the windows into the water, and were knocked on the head with violent blows of clubs ; some were killed in beds, some in the garrets, and others in cellars ; wives were slain in the arms of their husbands, husbands on the bosoms of their wives, and sons at the feet of their fathers. Neither sex nor age availed to soften the hearts of the murderers nor to turn them aside from their career of violence and outrage. The streets were literally paved, and the gateways were blocked up, with ghastly heaps of the dead and the dying. The small streams were filled with blood, and rolled in red torrents to the river. Thus 15,000 Huguenots in Paris, and 30,000 throughout the kingdom, fell victims to the savage fury of the Romish Church. This, then, is that massacre of St. Bartholomew which Gregory XIII. commanded to be celebrated with special services and brilliant illuminations, in honour of which he commanded a medal to be struck, and directed a jubilee that Roman Catholics from all parts of the world might render thanks to Heaven for what he considered to be one of the most glorious deeds in the history of Christianity.

But this crime was ineffectual for the purpose designed by it. The Huguenots had lost their most able leaders, but they were not crushed. As soon as they recovered from their consternation they once more took up arms. They held out at Rochelle and Sancerre against the whole power of the French crown, and compelled the Government, in 1573, to renew its concessions to them. But still Romanism continued to advance. Jesuit missionaries traversed the kingdom in all directions. Protestantism fell 70 per cent. The result of their efforts is seen in the circumstances connected with the history of the following times. In consequence of the failure of the direct line, Henry of Navarre, a Protestant, became, after the death of the Duke of Anjou, in 1584, the heir to the throne. A League formed between the leading Roman Catholic nobles for the suppression of heresy now added to its objects the exclusion from the French throne of Princes who were heretics, or who treated heretics with impunity. They concluded an alliance with the King of Spain in 1585, who agreed to assist them in their purpose. Pope Gregory directly encouraged the League. He was rejoiced to see the members of it forgetful of their country in their anxiety to propagate Romanism. An association called the League of the Sixteen, from the circumstance that Paris was divided into sixteen parts, and that an agent was appointed in every one to collect men and money in aid of the design formed to oppose the party of Henry of Navarre, was established in the city. The League very soon extended to other parts of France. Henry III., the successor of Charles, no doubt, as a good Romanist, would have been glad to see one of that religion guiding the helm of government in that country; but he well knew that the consequence of the triumph of the Roman

Catholic party would be that Philip would have acquired a predominance distasteful to him on account of their ancient rivalry, and prejudicial to the balance of power in Europe. The League regarded this vacillation on the part of Henry as a proof that he really favoured the designs of the Huguenots. The question was now discussed in the Sorbonne, whether the allegiance of the people was due to a King who did not do his duty to the Pope. The Pope, Sixtus V., lent his aid to swell the popular clamour against Henry, encouraged Cardinal Bourbon in his pretensions to the crown of France, exhorted the Roman Catholic cantons of Switzerland to come to the assistance of the League, declared Henry incapable of reigning in France, and extolled the Duke of Guise as the champion of Romanism. Henry, exasperated, interdicted the Duke of Guise from coming to Paris. But, notwithstanding his prohibition, he entered the city, and, in a tone of insolent dictation, required him to prosecute the war against the Huguenots, and to take effectual measures to prevent the accession of a heretic Prince. The King, in order to free himself from this dictation, filled Paris with his soldiers. Immediately the fierce democracy of Paris, who were eager for the glory of Rome, flew to arms, erected barricades formed of paving-stones, rafters, carts, and barrels, at all the principal thoroughfares, made a desperate attack on the King's troops, and compelled them to surrender at discretion. Guise, having shown his power by appeasing, as if by magic, the raging multitude, soon compelled Henry to submit to his arms and to prohibit Protestantism in France.

The King soon afterwards, anxious to be delivered from the thraldom in which he was held by the Duke of Guise, caused him to be assassinated. The intelligence of this murder produced a terrible explosion of popular fury at Paris and throughout the country. Sixtus V.

was indignant at this murder, and anathematized Henry. Then the Jesuits afforded undoubted evidence of their determination to adapt their views to times and circumstances. They at first found great difficulty in obtaining admission to France. The Parliament of Paris refused to register the royal edict for their admission. The Sorbonne also condemned them as likely to disturb the peace of the Church. At length, in 1561, they obtained admission on condition that they should submit to the authority of the diocesan Bishops. But, with their usual subtlety, they freed themselves from every restraint. They now saw plainly how they could guide the course of events. Those who in one country maintained the absolute power of the monarch, now asserted that the people are the only fountain of legitimate authority, and propounded the dogma that a King who neglects to maintain in its integrity the Roman Catholic faith may be assassinated. The Sorbonne, which had hitherto opposed these views of the Jesuits, now unanimously asserted that the people are absolved from their allegiance to King Henry. This assertion led him to make peace with the King of Navarre, to join his forces with those of the King, and to march upon Paris, before the walls of which city he was assassinated on July 31, 1589. Sixtus V. extolled the deed as the most glorious in history. His authority, however, passed to his legitimate successor, Henry IV. The League, in conjunction with the Pope and the King of Spain, now exerted every effort to prevent him from reigning in France.

But Henry bore up against his adversaries with undaunted courage. He beat back the vastly superior forces which the Duke of Mayence brought against his little band of warriors, who were entrenched in a strong position at the little village of Arques. This success, and other advantages gained during this campaign, were followed in the next year by the victory of Ivry, which has shed an imperishable glory on his arms. The Leaguers, in number about 10,000, advanced to the charge. The fray was bloody and terrible. The white plume on the helmet of the King shone like a guiding star amid the combat, wherever it glowed most fiercely. Pressing after it, according to his own directions, his warriors plunged amid the foe, and in two hours

' Their ranks were breaking like thick clouds before a Biscay gale,
The field was heaped with bleeding steeds and flags and cloven mail.'

This victory seemed likely to contribute to the success of his cause. The Duke of Parma, however, sent by Philip from the Netherlands, arrested Henry in his career of victory. He obliged him to raise the siege of Paris, which would have been soon compelled by famine to capitulate. The King, foiled by the superior skill of his adversary, who resolutely declined a battle, was soon obliged to abandon the field. Thus the Battle of Ivry has indeed a place among those battles which, on account of the deeds of heroism performed in them, will live in records more durable than brass or marble, but which have not affected in the remotest degree the destinies of States and empires.

This Counter-Reformation, as we have said, took place chiefly during the Papacies of Gregory XIII. and Sixtus V. The altered position of the Pope might well have gratified the ambition of the latter Pontiff. Instead of seeing province after province revolting from him, he saw them gradually returning to their allegiance. He now stood at the head of a powerful Roman Catholic confederacy. Spain was his ally. The ruling party in France depended on him for support. His power was steadily advancing in Germany. A large part of the Netherlands had been reduced to submission to his will. He was called, as we shall see hereafter, to give a blessing to that great Armada which was designed to subjugate England and to lay low the fabric of Protestantism. We cannot be surprised to hear that, inflated with arrogance, he indulged the wildest dreams of ambition. 'The stern virtue which he enforced, the severe financial system which he introduced, his rigid and minute domestic economy, were mingled with the most fantastic political schemes' (Ranke, vol. ii., p. 142). If he, the son of a swineherd, was Pope, to what height might he not aspire? He thought that he might even be a Papal Cæsar, reigning supreme over the monarchs of the earth.

'He flattered himself for a long time that he was destined to put an end to the Turkish Empire. He entered into relations with the East, with Persia, with the heads of some Arab tribes, and with the Druses. He armed many galleys; Spain and Tuscany were to furnish others; and the sea-armament was thus to come to the assistance of the King of Poland, Stephen Bathory, who was to conduct the invasion by land. The Pontiff hoped to unite the whole forces of the north-east and south-west in this enterprise; he persuaded himself that Russia would not only join, but subject itself to the King of Poland' (Ranke, vol. ii., pp. 139, 140).

Another of his schemes was the conquest of Egypt, the union of the Mediterranean and the Red Sea by means of a canal, and a new Crusade for the recovery of the Holy Land. He thought even of hewing the Holy Sepulchre out of the rock, and transporting it to Italy. But the grand vision which presented itself to him was Rome as the religious capital of the world. After a certain number of years, all the nations were to come, even from America, to Rome. All the monuments of the ancient world were to become indications of the triumph of Christianity. We thus see that there were mingled together in the mind of this singular man religious enthusiasm, a determined perseverance in action, and the most consummate worldly prudence.

But his Oriental visions vanished in useless negotiations; scheme after scheme was rejected as visionary. At length he concentrated his energies on a scheme which he had no doubt that he should be able to conduct to a successful issue. That scheme was to exert every effort to prevent the accession of Henry IV. to the throne of France. He had not the least doubt that on that point the whole Roman Catholic world would agree with him. Words cannot describe his astonishment when he found that Venice differed very strongly from him. She had actually recognised Henry's title to the throne, and had congratulated him on his accession. He at once directed the preparation of the old form of monition, in which anger with Venice and admiration of her are strangely blended.

'There is no misfortune so great as to fall out even with those we do not love; but with those we love, that indeed goes to the heart. It would indeed be a grief to us to break with Venice. . . . Has the republic any fears of Navarre? We will protect her, if necessary, with all our powers; we have strength sufficient. . . . The republic should esteem our friendship higher than that of Navarre. I intreat you, retrieve this one step' (Ranke, vol. ii., pp. 143, 144).

The following significant sentence occurs in the note: 'There have been three persons excommunicated: the late King, the Prince of Condé, the King of Navarre. Two have perished miserably, the third is doing our work, and God preserves him for our service; but he too will come to an end, and that a wretched one; let us not doubt about him.' These words were addressed to Donato, the Ambassador of Venice, a man strongly opposed to the doctrine of the Jesuits, that the Pope ought to reign supreme over the monarchs as well as over the Churches of Christendom. We shall see presently that many of the Jesuits maintained that it was perfectly lawful to assassinate those who opposed them in their design.

Now, this was a theory to which Venice offered the strongest opposition. She was often, as we have seen, coming into collision with the Pope in spiritual matters. The crowds bowing down before the shrines of the saints were a very plain proof that Venice would not cease to be a devoted daughter of the Church. But she would not allow any interference of the Pope with the affairs of the republic. Donato did not urge this argument; but he spoke strongly of the danger of establishing Spain in an autocracy, which was inevitable if she succeeded in destroying the independence of France. The Pope for some time struggled against his convictions. At length the politician gained the victory over the Churchman. The Pope declared that he could not approve of the conduct of the republic, but that he would suspend the threatened measures of hostility.

The change in the Pope's views became still more apparent when M. de Luxembourg, the envoy from the Roman Catholic nobles, who had joined Henry IV., obtained an audience of the Pope.

' Truly,' he exclaimed, ' I repent that I have excommunicated him!'

The Roman Catholic zealots were struck dumb with amazement when they heard that the famous Sixtus, who had thrown himself energetically into the movement for the advancement of Romanism, was now disposed to sanction the claim of the heretic to the throne of France. The Ambassador from Spain forced his way into the apartments of the Pope, with the view of expressing the conviction entertained by the world, that there were many in Christendom who surpassed the Pope in orthodoxy. He knelt before him and expressed the opinions of his master :

'His Holiness must declare the partisans of Navarre without distinction as excommunicated, and Navarre himself, under all circumstances and at all times, as incapable of succeeding to the throne of France. If not, the Catholic King will renounce his obedience to His Holiness; the King will not endure that the cause of Christ shall be thus betrayed and ruined.'

The Pope scarcely allowed him to proceed. ' This,' he cried, ' is not the duty of the King.' The Ambassador arose, threw himself again on his knees, and wished to go on. The Pope called him a stone of stumbling and turned away. But Olivarez was not satisfied. He said that he must and he would finish his protestation, even if the Pope should strike off his head. Sixtus, on the other hand, broke out into fire and flame.

' It belongs to no Prince on the earth to instruct the Pope, who is appointed as the master of all others.'

' The Ambassador was behaving with gross impiety; his instructions only empowered him to deliver his protestation if the Pope should appear lukewarm in the affairs of the League. What ! will the Ambassador direct the steps of His Holiness ?' (Ranke, vol. ii., p. 148).

The unparalleled difficulties of his situation caused a change in his character. This Pope, who had been remarkable for his promptitude in action, no longer displayed his accustomed energy. He halted and hesitated between opposite courses. One cause of his hesitation was that he had a great admiration for Henry, which he did not dare openly to avow. He also felt that, as a politician, he must strongly oppose the designs of Philip on the French crown. But he could not openly oppose him. He therefore dismissed Luxembourg, but under the pretext of recommending him to go on a pilgrimage to Loretto. He concluded a new league with Spain, but secretly entertained Envoys from the Protestant Courts.

The mental struggle through which he passed probably hastened his death. He died in August, 1590.

' A storm burst over the Quirinal while he was dying. The simple populace was persuaded that Fra Felice had made a compact with the Evil One, by whose assistance he had risen, step by step. Now that his course was run, his soul was carried off in the storm. Thus did they embody their discontents on account of so many newly-imposed taxes, and those doubts of his perfect orthodoxy which, during his latter days, had become prevalent. In wild uproar they tore down the statues which they had before erected to him. There was even a decree affixed in the Capitol that no one should henceforth raise a statue to a Pope during his lifetime ' (Ranke, vol. ii., p. 224).

Three Popes—Urban VII., Gregory XIV., and Innocent IX.—passed like shadows in one year (1590-91) over the Papal throne. Urban was Pope less than a fortnight. During their pontificate, the war between the two parties was carried on with unabated vigour. This was a momentous crisis in the world's history. The Jesuits had been only too successful in persuading the people that, if Henry should return to the Mass, he would become a double apostate, and could not be absolved, and that the Papal absolution was indispensable to the assumption of the regal dignity.

Gregory XIV., Pope from December 5, 1590, the devoted adherent of the League, never faltered in his determination. The treasures amassed by Sixtus V., in the manner already described, which he himself, on account of his vacillation at the decisive moment, had allowed to lie unemployed in his coffers, were now applied by Gregory to the purpose of arming and equipping his own and the Spanish troops for a struggle, the issue of which did not at first seem likely to remain in suspense for a moment. But he sat on the Papal throne only ten months and ten days. His successor, Innocent IX., died two months later, still in 1591. If the life of Gregory had been prolonged, it is possible, if we may judge from his stern determination and the vast resources at his disposal, that he would have excluded from the throne a monarch who claimed to reign by hereditary right, even though he was willing to return to the bosom of the Roman Catholic Church, that he might ultimately have fused together all Roman Catholic countries in a unity, embracing their religious ideas, their social life, and their political existence, and that he might have gained a paramount influence in all matters affecting the general interests of the body politic. He might thus have saved Philip and his Church from the consequences of a calamity which, as we shall see in the next chapter, seemed to have paralyzed his energies and to have dissipated his visions of their universal empire.

CHAPTER VII.

THE COUNTER-REFORMATION IN ENGLAND.

The Bull of Deposition of Elizabeth issued by Pius V.—The truce between Protestants and Romanists not broken for some time after its publication—The celebrated Cardinal Allen the breaker of the truce—A description of his career, including an account of his seminary at Douai—The object of that seminary the training of priests for the conversion of England—Description of the training—Severe Act caused by the Bull of Deposition—A description of the spy system for the discovery of the agents of Rome—The means employed to elude the vigilance of the spies—The Jesuits afterwards engaged to assist the seminary priests—The Jesuits not at first numerous—Description of Parsons and Campian, and of their work in England—Severe measures of government—Description of the torture system—Severe Act against Romanists—The capture and death of Campian—Inquiry into the justice of the punishments inflicted—The raid on England a failure, and injurious to Romanism —Allen's political designs—Gregory XIII., Sixtus V. and Cardinal Allen at length successful in inducing Philip to undertake the invasion of England—Their original letters to him—Preparations for the Armada, and the sailing of it—Enthusiasm excited among the Spaniards and English—The country long warned of it—False economy of Elizabeth—Defeat of the Armada, and subsequ? dispersion by the storm—Reflections upon it.

PIUS V. had, as we have seen, carried on with great energy his war against the Reformers. In 1569 the triumph of the Counter-Reformation seemed to be near at hand. Pius saw at this time only one Power in Europe—England—which stood in the way of the complete success of the Papacy. He determined to strike a blow at her which, he hoped, would be fatal. He issued against Elizabeth the Bull of Deposition, as Hallam calls it, 'almost the latest blast of that trumpet which once thrilled the souls of monarchs,' and absolved the inhabitants of England from their allegiance.

The Bull was a challenge to Protestant England, summoning it to a mortal combat. The war was to be carried on with all the forces of the Papacy. The single-hearted Christian missionary was to go forth with the wily conspirator and intriguer, whose object was to stir up disaffection, and to prepare the way for the triumph of a spiritual and temporal despotism.

A truce between Protestants and Roman Catholics had existed which does not seem to have been broken for some time after the publication of the Bull of Pius. The laws against the services of the Church of Rome were certainly very severe. Elizabeth was, however, unwilling to enforce them. They had for the most part slumbered in the Statute Book. The Romanists generally attended the services of the Church. Mary's clergymen, commonly called the old priests, were found in every part of the land. Their work was to keep alive the flame on the hearths and altars of Romanism.

Dr. Bellesheim, in his recent life of Cardinal Allen, states that he has ascertained that as late as the year 1596 there were still forty or fifty Marian priests at work in this country. They served as chaplains in private families. By stealth, at the dead of night, in private chambers, in the secret lurking-places of an ill-peopled country, with all the mystery that subdues the imagination, with all the mutual trust that invigorates constancy, these proscribed ecclesiastics celebrated their solemn rites, more impressive in such concealment than if surrounded with all their former splendour.

The truce between the two parties above referred to was broken mainly through the efforts of the celebrated Cardinal Allen. A careful examination of the Diaries of the English College at Douai (1878), of the Letters of Allen (1882), and of the additional information in the life of him by Dr. Bellesheim, enables us to see that he was the leader of the Counter-Reformation in England, and that he was the centre of all those efforts which had for their object the restoration of that country to its allegiance to the See of Rome. These works should be studied by all who wish to form a correct idea of the history of this eventful period.

Allen was born in 1527, in Lancashire. He belonged to a family the members of which, amid all changes, adhered to the religion of their fathers. He went to Oriel College, Oxford, in 1547, became Bachelor of Arts in 1550, and in the same year was unanimously elected a Fellow of his College. In 1556 he became Principal of St. Mary's Hall, which was then, as now, connected with Oriel. About the year 1558 he became a Canon of York. His strong religious views obliged him to resign his office of Principal when Elizabeth ascended the throne. But he could still reside at Oxford, because conformity to the new religion was not strongly enforced in the University. Roman Catholic Fellows retained their Fellowships. Roman Catholic students were not required to take the oath of supremacy when they were admitted to their degrees. Allen's zeal at this time attracted the notice of the authorities. He was constantly engaged in rekindling decaying zeal, and in making new converts to the Roman Catholic faith. He thus gave so much offence to the civil authorities that he was soon obliged to leave Oxford for the Continent. He crossed over to Flanders in 1561, and took up his abode at the University of Louvain. He afterwards spent three years in England, from 1562 to 1565, in his native county, Lancashire, where he exerted every effort to arouse Romanists to a sense of their duties and responsibilities. The success which attended these efforts soon obliged him to leave Lancashire, and to cross over to Flanders, where he was ordained to priest's orders at Malines. After spending two years in Flanders, he

went on a pilgrimage to Rome, in company with Dr.
Vendville, Regius Professor of Civil Law in the University of Douai. On his return to Belgium in the spring
of 1568, he persuaded Dr. Vendville to assist him in
establishing at Douai a college where English students
might have the benefit of college training, and where
men might be trained to take the place of those who were
gradually gathered to their fathers.

But a grander design than the one just described presented itself to Allen. Other men might be satisfied with
the conversion of a few individuals. He would be satisfied with nothing short of the conversion of the whole
nation to the faith of their forefathers. He was impressed with a deep conviction, which remained on his
mind after years of disappointment, that this expectation
would be realized. He laboured with indefatigable
energy for the accomplishment of his object. He was
ready to conquer or to die in the service of his Church.
His whole life is comprised in the words which Dr.
Bellesheim has chosen to occupy a prominent place
in the title-page of his book: ' Oportet meliora tempora
non expectare, sed facere.'

The grand design which he had formed shall be stated
in his own words in a letter from Dr. Vendville to
Dr. Biglius, the President of the Council of the new
University established by Philip II. of Spain for the
preservation of the Roman Catholic religion in Lower
Germany.

' It is now six or seven months,' he writes, ' since two
or three pious or zealous men have entertained the thought
that it would be for the benefit of many souls in Belgium,
or in some countries near it, to collect together in a
house certain English theological students of great ability
and promise who are living here on account of their
religion in much poverty, and are proficients in theology.
After providing them with a modest board and lodging,

we must exercise them in controversial questions, and we must give them a more than ordinary knowledge of ecclesiastical history and antiquities. Thus, after having been trained for about two years, they may be employed in promoting the Catholic cause in England, even at the peril of their lives. If God at length takes pity on that country, they may speedily and openly restore in it the orthodox faith, and win many souls, every one of which is precious in the Lord's sight.'

On Michaelmas Day, 1568, he took possession of a large house at Douai, and began to live there in collegiate form with a few students, English and Belgian, whom he had invited to join him. It was a kind of hall, from which the students attended University lectures. It ranks first in order of time among the different seminaries which the Council of Trent ordered to be established in Christendom. Gradually students flocked to this seminary. A large proportion of the early students came from the University of Oxford, where they had been trained by Allen and others in the Roman Catholic faith. Wandering amidst its colleges, associated in their minds with the Roman Catholic prelates and others who had endowed them, they brooded over their master's teaching, the effect of which was heightened by that association, and resolved, one after another, to devote themselves to the propagation of the Roman Catholic faith. Many, year after year, severed the ties which bound them to their native land, and, fired with enthusiasm, which Allen and others knew how to turn to account, took up their abode at Douai in order to prepare themselves to labour in the high and holy work of restoring England to its allegiance to the Papacy.

The great object of the instruction at Douai was to prepare them for their missionary work in England. The more advanced students were required to preach in English on every Sunday and festival, in order that they might acquire a greater facility in the use of that language, and that the cause might not suffer by a comparison with the fluency of their opponents. The object of those sermons and of the instruction given to them in the seminary, was to inflame them with a holy indignation against the heretics. With this view they were often reminded of their own privileges, surrounded as they were with the pomp and ceremonial of Romanism, allowed and encouraged to bow in solemn adoration before the sculptured effigies of the saints, and to adore the mystic presence in the sacred elements. They were then told to compare their prosperous condition with the disadvantages of those who were destitute of these blessings, who were compelled to attend the churches of the heretics, who were perishing in schism and ungodliness, who were buried in the gloom of the dungeon, and were often cruelly tortured because they would not forsake the worship of their forefathers. They were not all required to be great students in theological science, but they were expected to have a burning love for immortal souls. But those who were gifted with great intellectual powers were expected to apply the whole force of their minds to the investigation of truth, because they would thus be better able to promote the Divine glory in the salvation of their fellow-countrymen. They were all most carefully instructed in Holy Scripture, on which a lecture was given every day. Also, after dinner and supper, there was a running commentary on one chapter of the Old and another on the New Testament. They were required to take down from dictation the explanation of those passages of Scripture which were brought forward to establish the dogmas of Romanism. They were also instructed in Greek and Hebrew, in order that they might not be taken at a disadvantage by those of the Protestants with whom they might engage in controversy. The scholastic theology trained their intellectual powers, and pastoral theology supplied them with rules for their guidance in the high and holy enterprise committed to their charge.

The time had now come when, having polished their armour and exercised themselves in the use of their weapons, they were to go forth to smite down the oppressors of God's Church. In 1574 the first priests were sent to the English Mission. By 1579 about 100 priests had landed in England. They must expect to encounter trials and tribulations, and 'a great fight of afflictions' in their spiritual enterprise. In 1570, very soon after the publication of the Bull of Deposition, an Act of Parliament had been passed by which it was forbidden to put in force within the realm any Bull, writing, or instrument obtained from the Bishop of Rome, or any person claiming authority from him. An Act was also passed to the effect that 'if anyone shall by colour of any such instrument take upon himself to absolve or reconcile anyone within the realm, or if anyone shall willingly receive such absolution or reconciliation, or if anyone shall obtain from the Bishop of Rome any manner of Bull, writing, or instrument containing any thing, matter, or cause whatsoever, or shall publish or put in use any such instrument, every such act shall be deemed to be high treason, and these offenders, with their procurers, abettors, and counsellors, shall suffer death as traitors, and forfeit all their lands, goods, and chattels to the Queen.'

The great difficulty of the mission priests was to avoid detection. The spies of Elizabeth were everywhere. The spy system had been brought to great perfection. The Government was peering with the eyes of Argus into every part of the country, even into the most secluded haunts of Romanism. Some spies were wandering about the country in disguises, hearing confessions, giving absolution, and thus obtaining important information as to the treasons, stratagems, and schemes of the Roman Catholic party, which was at once conveyed to Government. They were often wretches who had everything to gain by straining the penalties of the law to the utmost, because they obtained their share of the spoil. They were robbers, protected by the law, sent forth with an order from the Privy Council, easily obtained, against that portion of the community which they might rob with impunity. Chief among these miscreants was one Richard Topcliffe. His cruelties would fill a volume. We have his own information as to the detestable nature of the expedients which he adopted to hunt down his victims, recusants, seminary priests, and Jesuits, during a quarter of a century. ' I have helped,' he said, ' more traitors to Tyburn than all the gentlemen of the Court.' In one case he seduced the daughter of one of his victims, and used her for playing on her father, in whose house one Southwell was apprehended.

We find that some spies crossed the seas, and with great skill and address insinuated themselves into the confidence of the leaders of the Roman Catholic army. They even obtained admission to the seminary at Douai, and afterwards at Rheims, where they became remarkable for the reverence with which they bowed down before the consecrated shrine, and for the devoted adoration offered by them to the transubstantiated elements. But, as we learn from the Douai letters, by the polished sarcasm, by the well-turned objection, by the doubt insinuated rather than expressed, they endeavoured to shake the confidence of those with whom they associated in the Sacrifice of the Mass, in purgatory, and in the other dogmas of Romanism. We are informed in a letter of Cardinal Allen that a spy of this description had obtained admission to the seminary at Rheims, and had for years been engaged in plotting for the spiritual and temporal ruin of those with whom he was associated. At length, without his knowledge, Allen having obtained information of his schemes, and having carefully watched him for a time in order that he might have full evidence of them, threw him into prison, just as he was about to carry them into execution. He proposed to reveal the designs formed at Rheims against the Queen and Parliament, and said that he could give such evidence of the complicity of Mary Queen of Scots in them as would cause her immediate execution. He was alleged by his accusers to have proposed to murder Allen, to poison all the wells at the college so as to cause the immediate death of its residents, or, as he knew that the Queen showed more fear of the college than of France or Spain, to be the means of an explosion which would cause its walls to lie a mass of ruins on the ground. He hoped that he should be rewarded for his treachery by a large sum of money from the Treasury, or by notoriety through preaching at Paul's Cross and revealing the designs of the Roman Catholic party, or by an appointment in the service of some distinguished man who would raise him to the pinnacle of worldly greatness. We have other proofs of the care with which this spy system was organized. Drawings and paintings were made of men obnoxious to the Queen and Government, as to whose movements they were particularly anxious to obtain information. When Father Parsons and Campian, of whom we shall speak directly, were expected in England, the Custom House officers at every port at which they were likely to land were provided with drawings of them that they might discover and apprehend them immediately after their arrival.

Allen and his associates used every effort to track these spies through their turnings and windings, and to prevent them from obtaining full information as to their designs. We find in the Calendar of State Papers, the Domestic Series, a paper dated August 25,

1582, stating that Allen was reported to be at Rome, watching for English spies. He thought that they would obtain admission to the college established in that city, of which we shall speak directly. Again, in the same Calendar, on April 4, 1582, we read that 'fifty Englishmen, as well Papists as Protestants, were taken in Rome for English spies.' The latter were supposed to have assumed the garb of the former. But still the seminary priests could not, on landing, always elude their vigilance· They were often obliged to land in Scotland, or to go by some other circuitous route to the place of their destination, in order that the spies might not track them. They lived, after their landing, as much as possible in concealment, and they were in constant fear of their lives. 'I could reckon unto you,' writes Cardinal Allen on August 10, 1557, 'the miseries which they suffer in their night journeys in the worst weather; from perils of thieves, of waters, of watches, and of false brethren ; from their close abode in chamber, in prison, or dungeon, without fire and candle lest they should give token to the enemy where they are ; from their frequent and sudden rising from their beds at midnight to avoid the diligent searches of heretics ; all which and divers other discontentments, dangers, and reproaches, they willingly suffer for their " feathers " (their secular disguises) ; and all to win the souls of their dearest countrymen, which pains few men pity as they should do, and not many reward, as they ought to do.'

We have other proofs of the dangers to which these priests were exposed. In the Roman Catholic houses which were the resort of the seminary priests there was generally a secret chamber to which they could retire in case of a hostile search. Very great precautions were taken as to the admission of persons to attend the service in those houses. Some confidential person was always on the watch for the examination of all who approached them. The following extract from a diary may give us some idea of the danger :

'Sometimes, when we are sitting merrily at table, conversing familiarly on matters of faith and devotion (for our talk was generally of such things), there comes a nervous knock at the door, like that of a pursuivant. All start up and listen, like deer when they hear the huntsman. We leave our food, and commend ourselves to God in a brief ejaculation ; nor is a word or sound heard till the servants come to say what is the matter. If it is nothing, we laugh at our fright.'

When there was a night alarm, they betook themselves to thickets or ditches or holes. They often for some time hid themselves in obscure caves or excavations in fields or woods. A tangled dell in the neighbourhood of Stonor Park, near Henley-on-Thames, is still shown as the place where Campian wrote his 'Decem Rationes.' While he was in that retirement books and food were privately conveyed to him.

'The feathers,' or disguises, to which reference has just been made were of various kinds. Parsons, just referred to, disguised himself as a volunteer officer returning from the Low Countries. His buff uniform, his gold lace, his hat and feather, and his well-appointed servant, were a passport quite sufficient for the Dover searchers. Campian disguised himself as a jewel-merchant. Others, as Allen states in his letter, disguised themselves with colours, ruffs, and rapiers. Allen, while he gave his sanction to these disguises, because otherwise they would not have been able to prosecute his design for the conversion of his fellow-countrymen, still thought them objectionable, because he feared that they would thus form a habit of dissimulation, catch the spirit and imitate the example of those whom they represented, and in consequence of their low standard of personal piety lose their influence for good with those among whom they were appointed to minister.

As the work was both difficult and dangerous, he thought that they ought to be men who stood out prominently from the common mass. They were not to be under thirty years of age, because it was supposed that at that time of life they would be prudent and discreet. They must be men of whom their enemies must say, ' I find no fault in this man.' They must preach by the silent eloquence of a holy life; they must show that they are living for eternity, that they are different in their tastes and habits from the ignoble herd of sensualists and world-lings around them; they must walk as seeing Him who is invisible, and as now mingling with the inhabitants of the world of glory. Thus it was hoped that their labours for the conversion of their fellow-countrymen to the Roman Catholic religion would be crowned with the wished-for success.

Allen had laboured with indefatigable zeal in training them for their work. Their preparation was interrupted in 1578 by the removal of the college to Rheims for political and religious reasons. The insufficient supply of money for carrying on the work had hitherto been a constant source of trouble to him. Their principal support had been a pension of 100 crowns a month which Gregory XIII. in 1575 gave to the college, afterwards increased in 1580 to 150 crowns. The work had been before Allen's time carried on, as we have stated, by the Marian clergy.

They had been instrumental in gaining fresh converts to Romanism, and in confirming many in their wavering allegiance to the Pope. The diary shows us that the seminary priests had given a great impulse to the work thus carried on in England. But now other labourers were to give help in gathering in the harvest. Allen visited Rome for the purpose of obtaining them. He found that the Jesuits were in charge of the college at Rome, founded by Gregory XIII., in which many of his own pupils had been trained. He thought it right that they should teach them both by precept and example to lay down their lives in England at the bidding of their Church. A great inducement for the Jesuits to come to this country was that Ignatius Loyola, the founder of the Order, in a letter dated January 4, 1555, a year before his death, had expressed 'the ardent desire which the Divine and supreme charity had imparted to him, of saving the souls in that realm.'

Allen now urged the General of the Order to send the Jesuits to the English Mission. The General at first hesitated, because he thought that the Protestants would be offended, and that divisions would be caused among the Roman Catholics. At length the Society consented to send them, and Father Parsons and Campian were chosen for the work. We must not, however, suppose that the English Mission was exclusively or mainly carried on by the Jesuits. There were often not more than five or six of them at a time on the mission. Even so late as 1598, eighteen years after the arrival of Fathers Parsons and Campian, they numbered only sixteen Fathers.

The list of martyrdoms enables us to come to the same conclusion. During the forty-four years of the reign of Elizabeth, 116 secular priests and seven Jesuits suffered death. For twelve years and a half, between December 1, 1581, and July 4, 1594, no Jesuits were executed, but eighty-nine priests, thirty-five laymen, and two women suffered during that period. These numbers are significant when we remember that the battle always raged very fiercely against the Jesuits. We cannot explain this fact except on the supposition that there were at that time very few of the Jesuit Fathers in England. The brunt of the battle fell on the seminary priests, of whom in 1596 300 were engaged in carrying on the work in England. Only from the early part of the seventeenth century the Jesuits became very numerous in England. Dr. Bellesheim in his work gives the names of no less than 135 old students of Douai who, between the years 1577 and 1618, suffered martyrdom in their native land. A careful examination of these old documents has therefore enabled us to correct a popular fallacy, and to show that not the Jesuits, but the seminary priests and their leader, Allen, as we shall see presently, summed up in themselves the Counter-Reformation in England, being the principal parties in the work, the object of which was to shake to its foundation the throne of Elizabeth, and to batter down the walls of the citadel of Protestantism.

Campian and Parsons were, as we have seen, the first of the Jesuits sent on a mission to England. Campian was born in 1540, and was the son of a book-seller in London. Parsons was born at Stowy in Somersetshire. The first became a Fellow of St. John's College, Oxford, the other a Fellow of Balliol College. Campian displayed at Oxford those oratorical powers for which he was afterwards distinguished. He made a remarkable English oration at the funeral of Amy Robsart, the wife of the Earl of Leicester, at St. Mary's ; and he afterwards showed his eloquence in an address on an academical subject, before the Queen and the Earl, which elicited the warm approval of Her Majesty. In 1561 he was the most popular man in Oxford. He saw that he might aspire to the highest ecclesiastical dignities. But he soon found that he could hope to achieve that distinction only by a public surrender of his belief in the dogmas of Romanism. He could not make that surrender. He determined, therefore, to sacrifice the worldly honours, the prospect of which at one time animated him to exertion, and proclaimed his determination to be a faithful subject of the Pope by joining Allen at Douai.

After spending a few years at Douai, he was gradually

led to the conviction that he ought to join the Order
of the Jesuits, because he knew that he could in connection with it gratify that ardent zeal for the propagation of Romanism which now became a distinguishing
feature in his character. He was admitted to the Order
in April, 1573. He and Parsons were appointed to the
English Mission. Parsons, though he was younger than
Campian, became the head of the mission because he was
supposed to have talents better suited than Campian for
administration. Bold in his schemes, fertile in his
expedients, remarkable for his force and vehemence, he
was discouraged by no difficulty and alarmed by no
danger. This vigour marks him as one of the giants
of the age. He was a great enthusiast ; but he was not
at all skilful in the conduct of his enterprises. Though
he knew that every Jesuit who landed in England
exposed himself to certain death, yet he persisted with a
horrible recklessness in hurling man after man against
the entrenched camp of the enemy. He deluded himself,
like Cardinal Allen, with an idea which gained possession
of his nature and clouded his judgment, that England
would be recovered for the Church of Rome. His great
blunders, his desperate ventures, and his consummate
arrogance, are enough to disprove the assertion of
Romanists, that he was a cool, far-sighted, and sagacious
diplomatist. On the contrary, he was a violent partisan,
utterly deficient in those qualities which were required
to ensure the success of any enterprise which might
be committed to him. Men like Parsons, audacious and
terrible, are not those who will convert nations. In this
matter the enthusiasm of love and self-sacrifice can alone
be successful. Campian resembled him in some par-
ticulars, but he surpassed him in eloquence and in the
determination to do and to dare in the service of
his Church. He knew that he was marching to certain
death ; but still, while he shuddered at the prospect

before him, he loved the danger, and determined to cast himself into the midst of the fiery furnace.

Furnished with full instructions, they took their departure from Rome. Parsons was entrusted with the deeper secrets of the Papal policy, but Campian was directed to confine himself to the work of conversion. The Jesuits had resolved not to risk their whole venture in one boat, but to go in different detachments to England. Parsons went through Calais to Dover, furnished, as we have seen, with a captain's uniform of buff, with hat and feather, and passing through Calais and Dover, where he eluded the vigilance of the searchers, arrived safely in London. Campian followed, disguised in the manner just described. He was not so successful in baffling the searchers, and was taken before the Mayor. The latter had given an order for him to be conveyed to London, but he seems suddenly to have changed his mind. While Campian was trembling with anxiety, and praying, as he tells us, to God and St. John, a messenger came forth from the chamber and dismissed him. The next day he arrived in London.

Parsons, who was still in the country, had directed him to remain in London till his return. On their arrival there was an outburst of Roman Catholic fervour which had not been witnessed for many years. Recent researches have served to show us that some time previously a large and carefully organized society had been formed for the purpose of co-operating with the Jesuits and seminary priests. A number of young men in the upper classes had banded themselves together to devote their time and substance to the Roman Catholic cause. The fame of Campian's eloquence had preceded him, and his co-religionists were very anxious to hear him. An arrangement was therefore made that he should preach at a house in Southwark. His sermon produced so strong an impression that his hearers went everywhere

proclaiming that if those who were halting and hesitating
between Romanism and Protestantism could be brought
to hear him, they would soon cease to waver in their allegiance to the Church of Rome, and would become champions
of her cause. The consequence was that the Council heard
that Parsons and Campian were in London, and issued
warrants for their apprehension. As it was considered
no longer safe for them to remain in London, they determined to visit every English county for the purpose of
strengthening the weak, encouraging the desponding,
ministering the Sacraments, recovering those who had
lapsed to Protestantism, and adding recruits to the ranks
of the Papal army.

Before, however, they took their departure from London,
they held a conference with the Romanists, the object of
which was to satisfy them that they had not come for
treasonable purposes, but simply with a view to spiritual
work. Parsons and Campian had given an explanation
of the Bull of Deposition, designed to relax its severity,
to the effect that Romanists were to accept Elizabeth as
Queen until circumstances should allow the Bull to be
executed. This was undoubtedly a message of treachery.
Under its apparently softened rigour was concealed the
assertion of a right to take up arms when a Sovereign
should come forward who had a claim on their allegiance.
We can prove, in the case of Parsons, that this oath was
subsequently broken. Campian devoted himself to
spiritual work during the fourteen months which followed
their arrival in England. Parsons, however, not only
engaged in this work, but also availed himself of every
opportunity of gaining a knowledge of the political state
and circumstances of the Roman Catholic gentlemen
who spoke to him about matters of conscience. Besides,
enthusiastic Catholics might be expected to rise and join
the invading army if ever the banner of the Spaniards
were unfurled on the shores of England. Thus, even if

they confined themselves to spiritual matters, they would be aiding the movement which had for its object the deposition of Elizabeth, and the elevation of a Roman Catholic Sovereign to the throne.

The Queen's Government was now alarmed, and determined to proceed to extremities against the spiritual invaders of England. We do not wonder that this alarm should have existed. Briefs declaring the Queen to be a Queen no longer were found lying about the streets of London. The system of espionage which Walsingham had organized enabled him to discover a scheme formed by the Roman Catholic powers, which included first the conquest of Scotland, and of Ireland from that country, and next a descent on the coast of England. In consequence of these fears, and of the Jesuits and seminary priests, the statutes against the Romanists were put in force, and gentlemen discovered in hearing Mass were thrown into prison. Walsingham also directed six of the younger priests to be seized and stretched on the rack in the Tower in December, 1582, with the view of extorting from them information as to the hiding-places of Campian and Parsons, and the designs of the leading members of the Roman Catholic party. The excruciating agony thus inflicted, borne with a fortitude worthy of a better cause, was not the means of eliciting any important information from the priests and the Jesuits. This barbarous treatment was, of course, deserving of the strongest condemnation. We can only say, in extenuation of it, that the danger was real ; that Walsingham had not risen above his age ; and that the cells of the Tower were less horrible than the torture chambers of the Inquisition. We have a proof that this cruelty was to be found even among Protestants, when we read, in a letter from Hugh Latimer to Cromwell, in the reign of Henry VIII., that he asked for a platform on which he might play the merry-andrew on the occasion of the barbarous execution of an aged priest named Forest, whose only crime was that he had opposed the divorce of Henry VIII. The poor old man was hung over a fire and roasted alive. No wonder that it is said that he had not taken to his death kindly. We can only say that the sentiment of humanity is of recent growth, and that though torture was never recommended by the English law, it was constantly employed as a means of extorting confession, and that it gave an additional horror to many kinds of death.

The tortures inflicted were horrible enough to excite our detestation, as the following enumeration of them will show. The pit was a subterranean cave twenty feet deep, and entirely without light. Little-ease was a cell where the prisoner could not stand, but must lie at length. The rack was a wooden frame, with rollers at each end, to which the prisoner's ankles and wrists were attached by cords, gradually tightened by turning the rollers till the bones were ready to start from the sockets. The scavenger's daughter was a broad hoop of iron, opening by a hinge. The hoop being applied to the prisoner's spine, the two ends were put, one between his legs, and the other over his head, and were forced together till they could be fastened. The iron gauntlets, after having been put on the hands, were contracted by screws, by which the wrists were compressed. The sixth and seventh tortures were manacles for the hands and fetters for the feet. We cannot read this description without shuddering at the barbarity of our forefathers, and without a feeling of gratitude that we have left far behind us these execrable instruments of cruelty of another and a darker age.

These severe judicial proceedings were followed in March, 1581, by a very strong Act against the Romanists. This Act made it treason to absolve any person or convert him to Popery. The saying of Mass was forbidden under a penalty of 200 marks, and the hearing of Mass under a penalty of 100, with a year's imprisonment. Any person above sixteen years of age who did not come to church for one month was fined £20. The same penalty was inflicted every month for twelve months, at the end of which time he was to be arrested, and bound in a penalty of £200 to good behaviour.

Campian had been at the time of the passing of this Act labouring for nearly a year in England. He and Parsons had been successful in 'reconciling' many in the different counties, including lords, knights, and the old nobility, to the Roman Catholic faith. During the session of Parliament he was in London, engaged in superintending the printing of his 'Decem Rationes; or, Ten Reasons for being a Catholic,' which he had composed, as we have stated, in hiding near Henley-on-Thames. The publication of this book increased the determination of the Government to punish the author. He was therefore obliged to take great precautions for his safety.

Parsons intended that Campian should go into Norfolk. The latter, however, applied for and obtained his permission to visit the moated grange of Lyford, near Abingdon, the house of a Mr. Yates, who was at this time a prisoner for religion in London. Mrs. Yates was in the house, and had with her eight Brigittine nuns who had migrated to Belgium, but had been compelled by the troubles in that country to return, and were now residing at Lyford, with the approval of the Queen. It was natural that, when they heard that Campian was in the neighbourhood, they should be anxious to see and hear him. Their imagination was fired by the prospect of confessing to him, receiving absolution from him, and taking the Holy Communion from his hands. As the house was notorious, and there would be a large concourse from the neighbourhood, the visit might be dangerous to him. Parsons, however, at length allowed him to go, but on condition that he should not stay more than one day and one night. The

13

nuns, of course, were in an ecstasy, and wished him to prolong his visit, but he was obliged to fulfil the condition on which he had been allowed to go to them.

The next day a large party from the neighbourhood came to Lyford to see the nuns. They were grieved that they had missed him, and sent a messenger after him, imploring him to return. The messenger found him at Oxford, surrounded by delighted students. Emerson, a lay brother, in whose charge he had been placed so far as the journey was concerned, yielded to the importunity of the messenger from Lyford and the friends at Oxford. Campian had refused the request of the latter that he would preach to them, on account of the danger of doing so in a public place. They thought that, if he would return to Lyford, they could return with him, and so both parties would be gratified. Emerson, though very unwilling at first to allow him to go, at length, for a reason which seemed satisfactory, yielded to their importunity.

Of course, he was received with joy. For two days the nuns and the visitors at Lyford were in paradise, but soon their raptures came to an end. Eliot, a spy of Leicester's, was in the neighbourhood, attended by a pursuivant, and armed with full powers to summon Sheriffs and constables to his assistance. Just as Campian was about to say Mass Eliot presented himself at the door, and obtained admission through a cook who had known him in former years as a devout Roman Catholic, and was not aware that he was now a spy on the movements of those with whom he had been associated. He stated that he was anxious to be a guest at the spiritual banquet. Mrs. Yates, to whom the cook applied, gave a reluctant consent to his admission. He found the opportunity, before he entered the house, of whispering to the pursuivant to go to a neighbouring magistrate, and to summon him and a body of men to his assistance.

Eliot heard him preach one of his most brilliant and

moving sermons. Perhaps Campian was the more subdued because he saw that the glorious termination of his career could not be far distant. Eliot immediately afterwards left the house, having refused an invitation to dinner. This abrupt departure excited some suspicions, and led Mrs. Yates to place a man on one of the towers of the house to give warning of the approach of danger. Very soon he rushed into the room where the party assembled was dining, and informed them that the house was beleaguered with armed men.

Campian wanted to leave the house immediately, and perhaps might have succeeded in effecting his escape; but the inmates compelled him to remain. They told him that the house was pierced in every direction with secret galleries, and that there were chambers excavated in the walls into which anyone might retreat in case of danger. Into one of those chambers in the wall above the gateway they hurried him and two priests who were with him.

Just as they had taken refuge in their hiding-place the men-at-arms had completely surrounded the house, and had placed a guard at every outlet of it. A chosen number, led by Eliot, demanded and obtained admission to the house. They searched for Campian and the priests in all the chambers, and sounded the walls all the afternoon, but they were unsuccessful. The magistrate and the men then retired, the former apologizing to Mrs. Yates for the trouble and vexation which he had given to her, and the latter ridiculing Eliot for his credulity.

But Eliot was determined not to be baffled. He felt sure that the men were in the house. He therefore required that the party should return and institute a closer search. The men were obliged to attend to Eliot's order. The priests had crept out of their hiding-place, and were congratulating themselves on their safety, when, to their dismay, they found that the magistrate and the party had returned. They at once retreated to their hiding-place. The house was again examined, and the walls were broken through where they seemed hollow. The search was continued till late at night, but without success. Mrs. Yates then ordered that the men should be well entertained. In consequence of their long excitement, their fatigue, and of the beer which they had drunk, they were soon buried in a profound slumber. Mrs. Yates, in her anxiety to hear them once more, forgot prudence, summoned them from their cell, which was just behind her bedroom, and insisted that Campian should preach to her and her household. The congregation, excited by his eloquence, forgot prudence, and made a noise which disturbed the sentinels at Mrs. Yates's door. They gave the alarm. The searchers entered the chamber, and almost caught sight of the men as they retired to the secret chamber; but they once more searched for them in vain. Meanwhile the congregation had glided away through the secret passages, and left no trace of the course which they had taken.

After part of a day and a night spent in fruitless search and destruction of the walls, Eliot and his men despaired of success, and prepared for their departure. The latter were unmeasured in their abuse of Eliot for having brought them into this labyrinth. Eliot was now descending the stairs, accompanied by the man whom Mrs. Yates had appointed ostensibly to wait upon him, but really to give the house information of his proceedings, when suddenly he placed his hand on the wall over the stairs, and exclaimed: 'We have not broken through here.' The man, who knew that the priests were hidden behind that wall, at once turned pale, and stammered out that he thought that a sufficient number of walls had been broken up already. Eliot observed his confusion, and immediately asked for a smith's hammer. He smashed in the wall, and there, in a small cell, on a narrow bed, Campian and the two priests were found lying side by side, with their hands uplifted in prayer. They had confessed their sins, and had invoked John the Baptist three times. For John had once before saved Campian from a similar danger. On the fourth day after his capture, the Sheriff of Berkshire, under whose custody he had been placed at Lyford, received instructions from the Council to send him and the priests under a strong guard to London. They had been treated by the Sheriff up to the time of their arrival at Colebrook, ten miles from London, with marked courtesy, but they were now to be made ridiculous. They rode in mock triumph, having their elbows tied behind them, their hands in front, and their legs under the horses' bellies. Campian, who rode first, was decorated with a paper stuck in his hat, on which were written the words: ' Campian, the seditious Jesuit.' They were thus paraded through London on Saturday, July 22, especially through those places where, as it was market-day, the greatest crowds were assembled, amid the jeers and hisses of the multitude, until they arrived at the Tower, where they were delivered over to the custody of Sir Owen Hopton, the Governor. The gloomy gates of the Tower then closed behind them.

We do not propose to give a minute description of the trial of Campian. We know that he was convicted of treasonable designs; that on a cold and dismal morning in December, 1581, he and Sherwin and Bryant, who were condemned with him, were brought out of the Tower lashed on hurdles; that they were dragged through an immense crowd in the streets of London to Tyburn, and that they were hanged in the presence of a large concourse without that quartering before death which was a disgrace to the barbarous penal legislation of our forefathers.

We must now inquire into the justice of the sentence passed upon them. We have a document before us which enables us to come to a correct conclusion. Mr. Butler discovered in the Library of the British Museum an account published by Government in 1582 of the answers made by twelve priests to certain questions which were put to them before their execution. They were asked if the Bull of Pius V. was lawful and ought to be obeyed by the subjects of England, if the Pope had power to discharge any of Her Majesty's subjects from their allegiance, and what side they would take if the Pope, or any other by his authority, should invade the kingdom. We find that nine of the priests, including Campian, Sherwin, and Bryant, refused to answer the questions, or gave evasive answers to them, or such answers as expressed their belief of the deposing doctrine or else a hesitation of opinion regarding it. The pardon of the three priests who answered the questions satisfactorily seems to show that if the others had disclaimed explicitly the Pope's dispensing power they would not have been executed, and that a declaration to the same effect from the general body of the Roman Catholics would have shortened the term of their sufferings.

We have now seen enough to show us that the hand of Elizabeth's Government had been laid heavily upon the Roman Catholics. She had, indeed, often pleaded for mercy; but she yielded to the pressure which her Ministers put upon her when they assured her that mercy to them meant danger to her throne. We know that it has been stated that she ought to have made it evident that she was attacking the political conduct of the Roman Catholics, and not their religion ; and that she often punished the innocent as well as the guilty. But the preceding statements ought to satisfy us that, to use the words of Mr. Hallam, 'there seems to be good reason for doubting whether anyone who was executed might not have saved his life by explicitly denying the Pope's power to depose the Queen.' He does indeed say afterwards : 'That which renders this condemnation of Popish priests so iniquitous is, that the belief in, or, rather, the refusal to disclaim, a speculative tenet, dangerous indeed and incompatible with loyalty, but not coupled with an overt act, was construed into treason.' But surely when the air is charged with electricity, we ought to be very careful about our stores of gunpowder. A speculative opinion might in those days, when treason was abroad, have been easily carried out into action. A regard for the safety of society would therefore dictate the measures taken against the priests. We learn also from a letter to Walsingham, quoted by Mr. Froude, that ' none was put to the rack that was not first by manifest evidence known to the Council to be guilty of treason ; so that it was well assured beforehand that there was no innocent man tormented. . . . Nor was any man tormented for matter of religion, nor asked what he believed of any point of religion, but only to understand of particular practices against the Queen for setting up their religion by treason or force.'

Perhaps sufficient discrimination may not always have been exercised. We must remember that the passions of the two parties were roused ; that Englishmen looked upon the war as a death-struggle for the maintenance of Protestantism and of civil and religious liberty ; and that Romanists looked upon it as their last cast for ascendency in England. This deadly struggle would serve to cloud the judgment. Words may have been tortured into a confession of treason, which did not properly bear that construction. This would be more likely to be the case when it was ascertained, through the agency of the numerous spies, that men like Parsons, as we have seen, who had just taken a solemn oath that they were aiming at a religious object, were really, under the seal of confession, mixing themselves up with political matters, and carrying on treasonable designs. The idea must have been generated in the minds of Elizabeth's Ministers that they were living in an atmosphere of deceit, and that they could not depend on the plainest statements.

When we hear afterwards that Allen's priests, who, as we shall see, were not allowed to mingle in the strife of politics, suffered in batches, we are apt to think that here at least we have a proof of the injustice which is made matter of accusation against Elizabeth and her Ministers. But we must remember that they were fired with ambition for the martyr's crown, and that Allen had gained so strong a hold upon them that they would be ready to be guilty of some treasonable act which would enable them to obtain the tribute of his applause. Thus Harte, one of his priests, in a letter to Walsingham, writes: 'There is nothing that can please Dr. Allen better than to hear of his scholars' stoutness in suffering for the Catholic faith.' We must remember, also, that evidence was given at the trial of Campian that copies of an oath had been found in Roman Catholic houses disclaiming obedience to the Queen, and that evidence was given of language used by the Jesuits to their penitents preparing them for the time when tyranny would end, and the Church of Rome should again reign supreme in this country.

We think then that it is quite evident that the air was impregnated with treason. A mine was about to be sprung which would have shattered into fragments the throne of Elizabeth. We shall explain hereafter Cardinal Allen's connection with the subject before us. The din of warlike preparations was very soon to resound in a foreign land. We are thus reminded of the destruction of the Armada, and of the severe treatment of the Roman Catholics after that event. A recent writer has the following observations upon it: 'It appeared as if the Government were determined to prove that it was not the political but the religious belief of its subjects that it was attacking. The throne of Elizabeth was now safe from the armed attempts of Pope or Jesuit. Though her person was still in danger from plots of assassination, those plots were now the work of a small section of obscure fanatics, and were no longer countenanced by ecclesiastics or hatched by Cardinals. Nevertheless the penal laws were put into force relentlessly.'

This statement is not correct. The Government had the same reason for alarm as in the time of Campian. We know that the Roman Catholics who had emigrated to Spain and Flanders issued publications bearing on the succession, which excited no small alarm in the Queen's Government. She was also disturbed by a report that preparations were being again made by Philip for the invasion of England and Ireland. She therefore issued a proclamation to the effect that her forces should be increased, and that she would provide a very severe remedy against seminary priests and Jesuits who were suspected of being guilty of traitorous practices. We must see, then, that they were prosecuted, not for their religious opinions, but for their political conduct. The persecution carried on at this time was different from the persecution carried on by Queen Mary. The former had in view the maintenance of our ancient institutions; the latter sprang from religious bigotry, and, not attempting to shield itself beneath the pretext of policy, endeavoured, in violation of the direction of our Saviour, to write its arguments for the faith in the blood of the Reformers.

This raid upon England, which will again come before us in a religious and political form, was, in the judgment of the Roman Catholics themselves, a failure: Mr. Simpson, the biographer of Campian, has expressed that opinion. After speaking of the work of Parsons in its political and religious aspect, he thus expresses himself:

'I suppose that it is mainly due to the political element among the missionary priests that the martyrdoms of so many, and the sufferings of such endless numbers both of priests and laymen, bore so little permanent fruit. It was not only that the treason of a Ballard or a Robert Catesby was, in its insulated effect, almost as pernicious as the martyrdom of a Campian was beneficent, but also that through them, in the old Protestant language, religion was turned into rebellion, and faith into faction, by which means not only was the adversary confirmed, and even on political grounds justified in his determination to persecute even to extermination, but also the faith itself began to lose its attractions for the faithful. . . . When the Catholic found not only that the Protestant Government, but also that the Pope and the King of Spain, and the wiser and more politic sort of the priests, considered that he, as a Catholic, was a probable rebel, he must have grown by degrees convinced that his religion was in a manner rebellion, and so have become in time either a confirmed conspirator or a wavering Catholic, and in either way have both weakened if not lost his own faith, and become a scandal to those who might have occasion to judge of Catholicism by his conduct.'

The mission just described had also been injurious to Romanism because it led to the passing of an Act which compelled Romanists, under a heavy pecuniary penalty, to discontinue attendance at the Mass in private houses, and to attend the public services of the church. They had hitherto been allowed to attend those services. But now they were told that they could not go to them 'without the danger of damnable schism.' The consequence was that many disregarded this prohibition, and by attending the services of the Church showed that they had cast in their lot with the Protestants. Many also ceased to be Romanists on account of the heavy and ruinous fines inflicted upon them. Many rebelled against the Pope, because he had compelled them to abandon a position of neutrality. Many also, who submitted to the fines, did not, for this cause, exhibit the same burning zeal for which they were formerly distinguished. As the hold of Romanism upon them had been thus weakened, they did not pour their money with the same liberality as before into the coffers of the Church of Rome. The seminaries at Rome and at Rheims languished from want of funds. Those who were willing to subscribe found that on account of the fines they could not contribute the same amount as heretofore. Thus a very small number of reapers could be sent to gather in the spiritual harvest. The consequence was an interruption in the work. Allen might boast that Campian had converted many of the most distinguished of the nobility and gentry to Romanism. But if we penetrate beneath the surface, if we examine the papers in public and private archives in recent years laid open to us, we shall see another side of the question. Disaffection was spreading through the camp of Romanism. The opposition to the claims of Romanism was beginning to be extended to the creed. We observe here the commencement of that revolt which, completed by the destruction of the Armada, dissipated the hope of the reconciliation of England with the Holy See, and led many members of the Church of Rome to come forward as the opponents of the Papacy.

Allen had now for some time been engaged in promoting through his priests the conversion of England; but he was now to plunge into the stormy sea of politics. Henceforth he becomes a prominent figure in the designs of Gregory XIII., the successor of Pius V., for the deposition of Elizabeth. Gregory had renewed the Bull

of the latter. Pius was annoyed at the continued disregard of it shown by the monarchs of Europe. His
admonitions and entreaties addressed to Philip II. of
Spain had hitherto been in vain. Allen was now specially
urged by Gregory to engage in this work. He engaged
in it the more readily because he was not obliged to
abandon the spiritual work of his seminary. He appears
to have kept this work unconnected with his political life.
He does not seem to have allowed the seminary priests
to take any part in his political designs. All questions
relating to the Pope's power of excommunicating and
deposing Princes were carefully excluded from the college
course. He might have thought that the ardour of their
zeal for the conversion of England to Romanism might
have been damped, if not quenched, if they engaged in
secular enterprises. He would not employ in political
work the friends and disciples who helped him to carry
on the college. He carefully avoided all conversation
with them on political subjects. Even when his mind
was full of the impending expedition against England, of
which we shall speak directly, we do not find one syllable
with reference to it in his letters to his friends in the
college. He seems to have employed a different set of
agents for this work. These were probably the men
whose deaths were proclaimed afterwards through Europe
with the view of inflaming the minds of men against the
great Antichrist of England.

Allen came forward as a gladiator in the political arena
in the spring of 1582, when he entered warmly into the
intrigues of the Guises, the object of which was to effect
a rising in Scotland. After its failure in the spring
of 1583, they and the Duke of Mayence agreed to pay a
large sum of money to anyone who would assassinate
Elizabeth. The agent of Spain thus writes respecting it
to Philip II.: 'The project which Hercules [*i.e.*, the Duke
of Guise] was pursuing was *a deed of violence* against this

lady, and it has for the present disappeared, and no further mention is made of it.' The italicised words in this extract are underlined in the original by the King, who has written with his own hand in the margin : ' I fancy thus, I believe, that we understand it here ; and if they had done it, it would have done no harm.' We have this information in the ' Records of the English Catholics,' consisting of a series of letters and memorials of William, Cardinal Allen, from 1532 to 1594, and despatches, reports, and other official documents which passed between the Courts of Rome, Spain, and France, now for the first time published by the Fathers of the Brompton Oratory. The Pope, Gregory XIII., who caused a medal to be struck to commemorate the bloody massacre of St. Bartholomew, 'did not express the slightest disapprobation of it, but spoke only of the manifest advantage which it would be to religion if in some way or other the wicked woman was removed by death.' Allen most probably had cognizance of it. He seems to have been from this time possessed with the spirit of religious and political fanaticism, and to have laboured for the dethronement and death of Elizabeth with all the passionate energy of his nature.

The design for the success of which he determined to labour with indefatigable energy was the restoration of England to the supremacy of the Pope. Sixtus V., of whom we have spoken fully, was not long in discovering that Philip II. would afford invaluable assistance in the prosecution of his designs against England. We learn that Allen and Parsons came to Rome in November, 1585, in compliance with the wish of the Pope and of Philip, in order that they might give the Pope full information as to the affairs of England. The despatches published by the Fathers of the Oratory afford abundant evidence that the Pope exerted a vigorous and a sustained effort to induce Philip to undertake the invasion of

England. We may refer especially to the despatch of
Count Olivarez, the Spanish Ambassador, to the Holy
See, as confirming the truth of the preceding assertion.
From this despatch we learn that Allen was employed to
stir up the zeal of the Pope, who was even then anxious
for the success of the enterprise. In this despatch we
find a summary of the several points submitted by Count
Olivarez to the Pope, and a report of the reply given by
the Pope to every one of them. The first point submitted
to the Pope was:

‘Although His Majesty Philip II. has been at different
times admonished by the predecessors of His Holiness to
undertake this enterprise, he never felt so convinced of
the reality of the assistance he should obtain from them
as he now confidently expects it from the courage and
vigour of His Holiness, which consideration, together
with the great favour with which His Holiness regards
the enterprise, and the desire which His Majesty has to
give him satisfaction, moves him to engage in it.’

Upon this point the Pope replies as follows:

‘His Holiness returns infinite thanks to God that he
has been the instrument of setting in motion His Majesty,
to whom he gives many blessings for the zeal with which
he is disposed to engage in an undertaking so worthy of
the calling of the Catholic King.’

The second point submitted was:

‘That the end and declared ground of the enterprise
shall be to bring back that kingdom to the obedience of
the Roman Church, and to put in possession of it the
Queen of Scotland, who so well deserves it for having
remained firm in the faith in the midst of such great
calamities.’

The Pope’s reply was:

‘His Holiness praises and agrees to what His Majesty
here proposes.’

The third point submitted was as to the succession to

the throne of England after the death of the Queen of Scotland. We gather that Philip's object was to prepare the way for securing the succession to himself or some member of his family on the death of Mary Queen of Scots, and to exclude James from the throne as a confirmed heretic. To this point the Pope gives a doubtful answer, saying 'that this is a matter for grave consideration.'

The fourth point submitted to the Pope was:

'His Majesty finds himself so much drained by the long wars of Flanders, and his subjects of every state so distressed, that, much as he regrets it—for he would have rejoiced to be able to carry out this enterprise without asking anything of His Holiness—its magnitude, and the preparations which are necessary to resist those who in great numbers will endeavour to hinder it, make it requisite that His Holiness should contribute for his share two millions of gold.'

The answer was the following:

'His Holiness, while he thinks that every assistance given to this enterprise is very well employed, is grieved that he cannot fully satisfy His Majesty's request, as he has found the Pontifical treasury much exhausted, and the revenues of the Apostolic See in great part spent and pledged. Hence, being unable to offer the sum which he would readily contribute, and being ready to go beyond every subsidy which has been granted by his predecessors for any enterprise hitherto undertaken on behalf of the Catholic religion, he offers to His Majesty, as soon as the expedition has set sail for the enterprise against England, to give 200,000 crowns, and he will give 100,000 more the moment the army has landed on the island, and yet further, 200,000 more at the end of six months, and in like manner after another six months 100,000 more ; and if the war lasts longer, His Holiness will continue to give each year 200,000 crowns. . . . Besides this, he will not fail to excite and animate all the Italian Princes to so glorious and holy an enterprise, which, if it turns out prosperously, as with God's favour is hoped, His Holiness' intention is that the Apostolic See should recover, and be effectually replaced in possession of, the revenues, rights, jurisdictions, and actions which it formerly had in that kingdom before Henry VIII. apostatized from the faith.'

We see, then, that the Pope and the King were both desirous that the crusade should be undertaken, and that England should return to its allegiance to the Holy See. To the persevering energy of Cardinal Allen and the Popes this change in the feelings with which Philip regarded the enterprise is to be attributed. We have thus an answer to the assertion of some Roman Catholic writers that Philip undertook it of his own accord, in order that he might reduce England to the position of a Spanish dependency. The anxiety of the Pope that the enterprise should not be delayed was manifested in a very striking manner. Olivarez writes to Philip that 'what grieved the Pope was his inability to induce your Majesty to undertake this enterprise. Would that he could persuade you!' We also learn from these despatches that the Pope had laboured to excite an insurrection; but there were difficulties in the way of no ordinary magnitude. The first was the succession difficulty. The Pope was opposed to the aggrandisement of Philip; and the English nobility, though so anxious for a Roman Catholic Sovereign that, as we read in the despatch of February 24, 1586, 'they had several times made an offer to pay whatever is spent in the enterprise,' were determined not to purchase his accession by the sacrifice of the inestimable blessing of national independence.

The insufficient sum of money offered by the Pope was, as we have seen, another cause of the delay in the commencement of the enterprise. This difficulty was, however, subsequently overcome. Sixtus promised to increase his subsidy. He was probably induced to do so by the assurance which Philip gave in a letter to Olivarez, dated July 22, 1586, that the effectual reintegration of the Apostolic See in the jurisdiction, contributions, rights and actions which it possessed before King Henry's apostasy seems to His Majesty to be most just.*

The regeneration of Romanism, and the great religious war which Roman Catholic Powers were carrying on for the recovery of her ascendency, were, as we have seen, the objects for which Sixtus had chiefly collected his treasure. Allen wrote a stirring letter to Philip in which he urged him to engage in this enterprise. 'Gird yourself,' he wrote, 'great King, to the work which Christ has reserved for you. Delay no longer. Listen to the groans of the priests who are crying out to you from their dungeons; listen to the voice of the Church, which calls you through the tears of the faithful. While you linger, souls are perishing, friends are murdered, and the enemy grows strong. Be not frightened by any delay or difficulty. With the sword of the Lord and of Gideon, with which you have crushed the Turk and triumphed over your rebels, you will chastise the English heretics and this woman who is hateful to God and man, and you will restore our noble nation to its ancient glory and liberty.'

At length arrived the intelligence of the execution of the Queen of Scots. In her had centred various plots for the assassination of Elizabeth. At length Babington's plot, in which she had a part, brought matters to a crisis. The blow descended, and her head fell on the scaffold. Allen, soon after this time raised for his services to the rank of Cardinal, again in spirit-stirring language urged Philip to plant the Castilian banner on the Tower, saying that the tyrant had quite filled up the measure of her iniquities. Now, he said, was the time to strike, when France was engaged in

* 'Letters and Memorials,' pp. lxxxv, 265.

14

civil war.   Philip acted on his advice, and determined to strike suddenly.   He had been busy for four years in making naval preparations for the invasion.   The crusade had been preached from the pulpits and platforms of Spain.   The hearts of the Spaniards had been fired with the same enthusiasm which they had exhibited during their warfare with the infidel.   Thousands of swords were leaping from their scabbards ; thousands of warriors arose in every part of the land, determined to conquer or to die in the service of the Church.   An army had been assembled at Dunkirk under the command of the Prince of Parma, which, after the navy of England had been annihilated, was to scatter in ignominious flight the armies of England. But the sailing of the fleet in September was delayed till the bad weather came, which rendered absolutely necessary the postponement of the invasion.   The consequence of the delay was that Philip lost by death the services of the Marquis of Santa Cruz, under whom the flag of Spain had been carried triumphantly through the thick of many battles.   The Duke of Medina Sidonia, appointed after some delay, was very far inferior to him.   If the Spanish fleet had sailed, as it was proposed, in January, 1588, the probability is that, as Elizabeth in a fit of economy had broken up her own fleet, and left the Channel undefended, the fatal blow might have been struck, and England might have again become the bond-slave of the Church of Rome.

At length Allen and the Jesuits triumphed.   The time —the important time—arrived, big with the fate of England and the Reformation.   On May 28 and 29 the Armada had sailed down the Tagus, but it encountered a storm, which compelled it to return.   On July 22 it took its final departure from the shores of Spain.   In reading the description of the morning when it sailed, we seem, to use the words of the poet, to have before us

'The torrent's smoothness ere it dash below.'

The sun was tinging with a ruddy hue the long chain of the Gallician mountains, and shedding a soft radiance on the white walls and vineyards of Corunna. The sea was reposing in the soft quiet of an infant's slumber. We may gather from contemporary records and State Papers of the period much valuable information respecting the Armada. The fleet was the most powerful which the world had ever seen. The treasures of the Indian mines had been for three years freely lavished upon it. The Armada consisted of 130 vessels. In the six squadrons there were sixty-five large ships ; the smallest of them was 700 tons, seven of them were over 1,000 tons, and the largest of them was 1,300 tons. Besides, there were four gigantic galleys, carrying each of them fifty guns and 450 soldiers and sailors. In addition to these were four galleys and fifty-six armed merchant vessels. The number of cannon was 2,430, brass and iron of various sizes, the finest from the Spanish foundries. The English fleet was altogether unequal to the Spanish, containing only eighty vessels. Fifty of them were little bigger than yachts, and of the thirty Queen's ships which formed the main body only four equalled in regard to tonnage the smallest of the Spanish galleons.

The Spanish fleet glided majestically over the ocean, manned by 30,000 men, 20,000 of whom were never again to see the shores of their native land. We may form some idea of the importance attached to the crusade, and of its religious character, when, as State Papers recently examined state, the most rigid discipline was enforced among the soldiers and sailors, and the ships were christened after the saints, evidently with the view of securing the guardianship of the Almighty. We learn, also, that, according to the 'orders set down by the Duke of Medina, Lord-General of the King's fleet, to be observed on the voyage towards England,' gambling and profane language were forbidden, and no women were allowed to

accompany the expedition.   Private quarrels and mis-
understandings were to be made up, and everything
calculated to defile the Armada was to be avoided.   It
was further ordered that, every morning, the boys,
' according as is accustomed, shall give the good-morrow
at the foot of the mainmast, and at the evening shall say
Ave Maria, and some days the Salve Regina, or at the
least every Saturday, together with the Litany.'   In order
that nothing might be wanting to add to the complete-
ness of the Armada, we find there were sufficient provisions to feed an army of 40,000 men for six months, while
powder and lead for small arms were in great abundance.

We learn also from the State Papers that, through the
spy system, which has been described, the preparations
of Philip and the approach of the Armada had come
under the notice of the English authorities.   Sir George
Casey, Governor of the Isle of Wight, wrote to Sir Francis
Walsingham, the Secretary of State, on January 30, 1583-
1584, informing him that he had received tidings from
one Jacob Whiddon, the master of a ship just returned
from Lisbon, that ' great preparation be in hand for arming a navy this summer.'   Among further numerous
entries in the State Papers relative to the Spanish movements, we may quote the important correspondence of
Thomas Rogers, alias Nicholas Berden, one of Walsingham's agents, undoubtedly the basis of the secret intelligence which enabled Walsingham to counteract the
designs of Spain.   At the close of 1586, Walsingham
hears from Sir John Gilberti that the King of Spain is
preparing a fleet with 60,000 soldiers ' to have his revenge
on England '; and in the following April Sir Francis
Drake, writing to Secretary Wolley, says that he intends
to intercept the Spanish fleet coming out from the Straits
before it joins the King's forces.

The country, therefore, had long warning of the intended invasion.   Patriotism proved stronger than the

internal differences on which Philip confidently reckoned. From every quarter Elizabeth received the warmest promises of support. Thus the aged Shrewsbury wrote: 'Though I am old, yet your Majesty's quarrel shall make me young again; though lame in body, yet lusty in heart, to lend your greatest enemy one blow; to live and die in your service.' Numerous similar entries in the State Papers show that the whole nation was animated with enthusiasm. Instinct told England that its work was to be done on the sea. To quote Mr. Green's words: 'The royal fleet was soon lost amid the vessels of the volunteers. Coasters put out from every little harbour. Squires and merchants pushed off in their own little barques for a brush with the Spaniards.'

The night of July 30, after the day when the Spanish fleet was seen on high ground above Plymouth Harbour, will never be forgotten in the history of England.

> ' Night sank upon the dusky beach, and on the purple sea;
> Such night in England ne'er had been, nor ere again shall be.
> From Eddystone to Berwick bounds, from Lynn to Milford Bay,
> That time of slumber was as bright and busy as the day,
> For swift to east, and swift to west, the ghastly war-flame spread.
> High on St. Michael's Mount it shone : it shone on Beachy Head.
>
>   *   *   *   *   *
>
> Till the proud Peak unfurled the flag o'er Darwin's rocky dales,
> Till like volcanoes flared to heaven the stormy hills of Wales,
> Till twelve fair counties saw the blaze on Malvern's lonely height,
> Till streamed in crimson on the wind the Wrekin's crest of light.
>
>   *   *   *   *   *
>
> Till Belvoir's lordly terraces the sign to Lincoln sent,
> And Lincoln sped the message on o'er the wide Vale of Trent,
> Till Skiddaw saw the fire that burned on Gaunt's embattled pile,
> And the red glare on Skiddaw roused the burghers of Carlisle !'*

We learn from contemporary documents that the news of the arrival of the Armada which the beacon-lights flashed through the country kindled a spirit of resistance which has never been surpassed in the history of England.

* Lord Macaulay on the Armada.

Meanwhile, the ocean was the scene of events which will never be forgotten. The English fleet, under the command of Lord Howard of Effingham, issued from Plymouth Harbour, and hung upon the rear of the Spaniards, as, in a broad crescent, they held on their course with the intention of effecting a junction with Parma at Dunkirk. Vessel after vessel was sunk, boarded, or driven on shore. We may form some idea of the difficulties with which the English were called on to contend, when we hear that they had not a sufficient supply of powder and shot, and that they were often obliged to obtain a supply from the vessels which they had captured. The fact is that a struggle was going on at this time in the mind of Elizabeth between parsimony and patriotism. The entries in the State Papers afford an admirable illustration of Elizabeth's false economy, which, to use Drake's words, ran the risk of hazarding ' a kingdom with saving a little charge.' In another letter he writes : ' The proportion of powder for the largest ships was sufficient but for a day and a half's service if it was begun and continued as the service might require.' This was not the limit of her false economy, for in the ' Provision of Victuals for the Fleet ' we are told that whereas ' every man's victual of beef standeth Her Majesty fourpence the day, it was proposed to alter "that kind of victual to fish, oil, and peas." '

This false economy threatened to counteract the unrivalled seamanship and bravery of the sailors. As Mr. Ewald has pointed out in the *Gentleman's Magazine,* ' the one cry throughout the correspondence at this time is, " Nothing can exceed the patient and willing spirit of both sailors and soldiers ; but send us provisions, send us powder, send us money, clothes, and drink, else we be too enfeebled to fight." ' But still they were animated with patriotic ardour. They were struggling for the safety

and independence of their native country. The feeling
was that the time had now arrived when it was to be
decided whether England was to return to the darkness
of medieval superstition, and to lose through subjection
to Philip that valuable constitution of King, Lords, and
Commons, which has made her the greatest nation in the
annals of the world. The Armada had dropped anchor
in Calais Roads. The hours of Sunday, August 7, were
rapidly passing away. Before dawn the fleet of Medina
Sidonia would have effected a junction with the fleet
of Parma, and England would be lost. To attack the
ships where they were was impossible. They must be
compelled to move out into the open sea. With a view
to that end, a plan was adopted which, as we learn
from the State Papers, was completely successful.

When the Spanish bells were striking twelve, and all
except the watch on deck were stretched in sleep, certain
dark objects, which had been seen dimly drifting on the
tide near where the galleons were thickest, on a sudden
shot into pyramids of light. Flames leapt from sail
to sail, and the vessel was soon a lurid blaze of conflagration. A cool commander might have directed his boats
to move out and tow them away; but Medina Sidonia was
terrified, and was altogether unequal to the emergency.
The whole Armada was in consternation. The enemy
whom they dreaded most was advancing towards them.
A shot was fired from one of the vessels as a signal for
them to move out into the open sea. Amid the greatest
confusion, they set sail and cleared away, congratulating
themselves on the ease with which they had evaded the
designs of the enemy. They thought that they should
return in the morning and resume their position. But
really they were visited with a judicial blindness. That
departure from Calais Roads was the cause of the destruction of the Armada.

Now comes the turning-point in the history of the invasion. The master mind of Drake comprehended the situation at once. The vessels must not be allowed to return to the Calais Roads, but must be driven into the North Sea. When the morning came, they were scattered over a large surface off Gravelines. The English poured in upon them during the day a well-directed fire ; while the Spaniards, who worked their guns on rolling platforms, sent their shot harmlessly into the sea or into the air. The result was that they were driven in upon their own centre in one confused mass, a mere target for the English guns, and that they became mere slaughter-houses. Six galleys were sunk or had drifted helplessly on the coast of Flanders. A council of war was held, at which it was resolved that they should return to Spain by the only course open to them, a voyage round the Orkneys. The members of that council knew that, if they returned to Calais, and risked a second battle with the English, the consequence would have been the immediate annihilation of the Armada. But in the North Seas they encountered a worse foe than the English. The storms which rage in those Northern regions burst violently upon them for eleven days. During that time many of the ships were sunk, many were hurled against the dark cliffs of Ireland and many came on shore, scattering their drowned crews by hundreds on the beach. More than 1,100 dead bodies were counted, and many more perished. The sea was not their only enemy. Those who came safe to land were slaughtered by the Irish for their velvets, gold brocade, and for their rich chains. Eight thousand Spaniards perished between the Giant's Causeway and Blasket Sound. Of these, 3,000 were murdered by the Irish ; the rest, more fortunate, were drowned. Of that large Armada, containing 30,000 men, only fifty vessels returned to

Corunna, bearing 10,000 men, stricken with pestilence and death.

We must see in these events the interposition of the Almighty King of Heaven. We know that there is a common belief that to the tempest, irrespectively of any other cause, is due the destruction of the Armada, falsely styled Invincible; but we must remember that it would never have sunk beneath the boiling surges if the master spirit of the English navy, Sir Francis Drake, had not first defeated it by his superior skill before Gravelines, and then driven it, crippled as it was, into the region of storms. On the result of that action before Gravelines were suspended the spiritual and temporal destinies of England. But even if we could suppose that the annihilation of the Spanish Armada was due only to the tempest, we should still be able to trace in its destruction the agency of God. We ask: 'Shall there be evil as well as good in a city, and the Lord hath not done it?' We say that 'fire and hail, snow and vapour, wind and storm, fulfil His word.' We must protest against that refined idolatry which consists in overlooking the Great First Cause of all things, and attributing to the operation of second causes events which have flowed from the direct providential interference of God. We should tremble for the safety of that nation whose leading men banished Christ from their councils, and denied that interference. We should shortly expect to see Him visiting that land with His four sore judgments, laying bare His arm in anger, and casting it down from the high place which it may now occupy among the nations of the earth. We must admit that this great destruction was due to Him whom we are thus reminded that the Psalmist styles 'the Lord mighty in battle.' We know that many of the Spaniards were conscious of an emotion of pride when they gazed on those ships of war, those monarchs of the deep, which were floating triumphantly before them. They thought in the vanity of their hearts, that, having ruffled up their plumage and issued from their harbours, they would ride triumphantly over the billows, and scatter destruction among the navies of their opponents. They trusted in an arm of flesh, and not in the arm of the Lord God omnipotent.

Let us learn, then, that God is 'the only Giver of all victory.' We must also come to this conclusion when we hear that the English fleet had in it far fewer vessels than the Spanish fleet ; that it was far inferior to it in other respects which have come before us ; and when we remember also that the greatest service ever performed by an English fleet had been performed by men whose wages had never been paid from the time of their engagement ; by men half starved, with their clothes in rags, and falling off from their backs; by men so ill-found in the necessaries of war that they supplied, as we have seen, the want of ammunition by ammunition taken from the enemy; men in whom the tendency to disease was so aggravated that boatloads of them were carried on shore at Margate, and set down to die in the streets, as there was no place in the town to receive them. Let us, then, look away from ourselves, our own wisdom, our own resources, and our own armies, and let us look to Him who is 'a buckler to them who trust in Him.' Let us learn to depend on Him without whose blessing on our warriors the strongest arm must fall palsied and powerless, and the stoutest heart must quail. Let us ascribe the victory to Him who by the breath of His mouth can blast the strength of the most powerful army which ever marched beneath the banner of this world's potentates, and lay low the pride of the proudest navy which ever ploughed the waters of the ocean.

The attempted invasion of England was a most momentous crisis in the world's history. If it had been successful, in all human probability the power and policy of England would have been employed to promote the progress of Romanism throughout the world. The result of the struggle in the Netherlands would not have remained in suspense for a moment. The Prince of Orange had indeed broken the fetters which the tyrant had forged to enslave his fellow-countrymen. The patient zeal with which he laboured in the service of his country was rewarded, as we have seen, by the establishment of the government of the United Provinces. But if Philip had been successful, the Armada and the unexhausted resources of Spain, augmented by those gained through the conquest of England, would at once have been successfully employed by Philip to win back the United Provinces to their allegiance to himself and the Papacy. Another result would have been that he would have interfered with success in that conflict which Henry of Navarre, the Protestant King of France, was waging with the whole force of the League, formed for the purpose of excluding from the throne a monarch who claimed to reign by hereditary right, even when he was willing to return to the Roman Catholic Church. We should never have heard of the Edict of Nantes, establishing universal religious liberty in France. The Jesuits would have been successful, and France would have been placed in absolute subjection to the Pope. The Thirty Years' War, of which we shall speak in a future chapter, would never have been fought, or would have been brought through the vast resources placed at the disposal of the Roman Catholic Church to a speedy termination. The Pope would have reigned supreme throughout the continent of Europe.

The tide in 1588 was swelling continually higher and higher. Onward it was rushing with a violence which seemed likely to carry all before it. If only the army of

Philip had set foot in England the conquest would have been certain. The fortresses were dismantled or un-garrisoned. In consequence of the change in the art of war the peasantry were hardly prepared to form an efficient body of soldiers. The heroism of Elizabeth and the chivalrous loyalty of her troops were as nothing when compared with that well-disciplined valour which carried the banner of Spain successfully through the thick of a hundred battles.

But the chief danger of England lay in religious disputes. The Roman Catholics far outnumbered the Protestants. Philip's designs had alienated many who were Roman Catholics more from descent than from fanaticism, men whose hearts were beating high with love to their country and Queen ; but, still, there was a large party under the influence of the Jesuits who would have aided the soldiers of Philip in imposing on their country the yoke of an intolerable bondage. But we see the agency of the God of battles. The utter inability of the English army to contend on equal terms with the army and navy of Spain afforded the plainest evidence that, if they were to be successful, the Omnipotent Leader of the armies of heaven must interpose on their behalf. This expectation was well founded. The arm of Philip was palsied as it was being raised to strike the fatal blow. The strength of God was magnified in human weakness. The defeat of the Spaniards, with its terrible features, the storms and tempests, the artillery of His vengeance, to complete the work which Drake had begun, was accepted as the received judgment of Heaven. Many of the Roman Catholics, seeing the agency of God in this deliverance, at once placed themselves under the banner of Protestantism. Thus the Armada was as a sermon which completed the conversion of England. Thus Protestantism was saved from annihilation in Europe. But we need not dwell on those glorious results. They form part of the heroic traditions which have nerved the arms of our soldiers and mariners, and have animated them with the pleasing assurance that God would still, as in past ages, interpose to preserve us from those mighty foes who are combined in a dark confederacy to lay low the stronghold of the Reformation.

CHAPTER VIII.

THE CONTINUATION OF THE STRUGGLE.

Failure of the designs of the Jesuits to exclude Henry IV. from the throne of France—Their partial success in that country—Ferrara added to the Papal States—The Archbishop of Cologne and his ejection from his States on account of his marriage—The Counter-Reformation successful in Poland, but a failure in Sweden—Extension of conflict connected with it to distant lands and seas—Death and character of Philip II.—Divisions among Protestants a hindrance to the advance of the Reformation—Disputes among the Jesuits injurious to Romanism—Description of the election of Paul V.—His character and designs—His contest with Venice, and its results—The importance of that contest—Fra Paolo Sarpi, and the aid which he rendered to Venice—His own work on the Council of Trent, and his opposition to the designs of the Jesuits, as shown in it—His attempted assassination—Strong observations on the Jesuit system of morality—Assassination of Henry IV. of France—Opposition to the claims of the Pope to temporal supremacy in France—Apparent progress of Romanism in France, but not of real religion—Cardinal Allen's work in England—Description of his seminaries after his death—General expectation of ultimate success in England, which is shown to be unfounded—The perseverance of the priests notwithstanding failure—Description of the work of a Jesuit Father—Severe treatment of Romanists by James, which caused the Gunpowder Plot—Relaxation of the laws against Romanism under Charles I., and consequent revival of the work of the seminary priests—Proof of the revival of Romanism in England from the works of Panzani—His intercourse with the King and Queen—Progress of Romanism in England—Strong tendencies towards Romanism in the works of Bishop Montague and others—Proofs of a desire to unite the two Churches in England and Europe—The scheme proved to be impracticable on account of the opposition of the Puritans and of the Church of Rome.

WE have seen that with the defeat of the Armada Philip's hopes of universal dominion had passed away. A gleam of light darted athwart the clouds when Gregory ascended the Papal throne. We have stated that he proposed to employ the treasures accumulated by Sixtus V. in the promotion of the Papal reaction. But after the death of Gregory the clouds once more gathered thickly around Philip. Amid the raging of the tempest, a voice of irresistible authority might have been heard saying to the waves dashing wildly against the spiritual fabric, 'Hitherto shall ye come, and no farther.'

The scales now fell from the eyes of many who had heretofore been the bigoted adherents of the wild and wicked dogmas of the Jesuits. They began to be fired with patriotic ardour. They saw that they must contend for liberty and independence. They felt that, if they submitted to the dictation of the Pope, they would with their own hands rivet on their own limbs the manacles of a foreign despot. They were now impressed with the conviction that whoever resists a lawfully appointed monarch shall, to use the words of St. Paul in the thirteenth chapter of the Epistle to the Romans, 'receive to himself damnation.' They began to remember that Henry possessed that magnanimity and those personal qualities which were so well suited to win the affections of his people, and that he had carried his banner triumphantly through the thick of many battles. Still, they thought that he must submit to the Roman Catholic Church before they could submit to him as their lawful monarch. Even those gallant adherents who had stood by him with unwavering loyalty from the first, and who held that even heresy could not interrupt that order of lineal descent which they believed to have been appointed by God, thought that he must abjure Protestantism before he could be finally established on the throne of his ancestors. The difference between them and the other party was that they were content to wait for a change which the latter regarded as indispensable to their allegiance.

Henry at length declared his intention of joining the Church of Rome, and applied for absolution to the Pope, Clement VIII. A valiant soldier, a skilful general, and a great statesman, he had been rather the political leader of the Huguenots than the champion of Protestantism. Pope Clement was at first unwilling to grant that absolution. He had hitherto, from the time of his elevation to the Papacy in 1592, laboured to support the League, and to promote the designs of Philip II. on the French crown, and he would not withdraw from his party. The conflict, therefore, between the Huguenots and their opponents continued; but now defections were constantly taking place from the ranks of the latter. At length the strength of the kingdom was mustered beneath Henry's banner. The favourable opportunity for the Papacy— the

'Tide in the affairs of men
Which, taken at the flood, leads on to fortune'

—had now for ever passed away. The opinions at first held by a small section had become those of the whole community. Henry's superiority now became evident. The King of Spain was obliged to abandon his designs. At length Henry entered Paris in the presence of thousands, who rent the air with acclamations as he rode in his triumphal car through the streets of the city of his fathers.

We see, then, that the Jesuits had decided the conflict in favour of Romanism when we find that a Protestant monarch could not ascend the throne of France; but the success fell far short of their sanguine expectations. The bright vision of a Pope reigning over the nations had vanished away. Clement had failed in excluding Henry as a relapsed heretic from the throne; nay, more, the Papal absolution had not been considered as indispensable to the assumption of the regal dignity. His coronation in the cathedral of Chartres preceded,

in fact, was the cause of, the solemn ceremonial in front
of St. Peter's at Rome on December 17, 1595, connected
with his absolution. This was the great event of Clement's
pontificate. It is true, indeed, that the Pope on this
occasion appeared surrounded with the ensigns of that
temporal and spiritual authority which, fifty years before,
it was supposed had passed away for ever. But, still, the
circumstances connected with the elevation of Henry to
the throne showed very plainly that he had lost much of
his power, and that he could no longer wield at will the
fate and fortunes of mighty empires.

Romanism had gained a victory in France, not by the
efforts of the extreme party, but rather of those who,
having come forward at first in opposition to Henry, had
afterwards become animated with ardent patriotism, and
had coalesced with those who had supported him from
the very first for the purpose of saving the nation from a
foreign yoke. We have an additional proof of the decline
of the Papal power in the Edict of Nantes, issued by
Henry on April 13, 1598, which established universal
liberty and equality as to religious profession and worship.
We see, then, that a well-laid scheme formed by the
Jesuits had failed of the wished-for success, and that
Europe was saved from that bondage to the Pope which
would have palsied its energies, and would have retarded
the onward march of spiritual, moral, and political improvement.

Rome was successful at this time also, not only in the
enlargement of her spiritual dominions, but also of her
temporal possessions. Alfonso II., Duke of Ferrara, the
gaoler and patron of the immortal Tasso, had died without children, and his relation, Don Cæsar, at once took
possession of the sovereignty. But Clement VIII., under
the pretext that he was of illegitimate descent, determined
to resume this fief of the Holy See. Accordingly, he
smote the duchy with an interdict, marched an army into

15

the territory, and compelled Don Cæsar to abandon his dominions, which he added to the Papal States. His predecessor, Gregory, had been successful in another quarter. Gebhard Truchess, Archbishop of Cologne, had married and embraced Protestantism, hoping that the Lutheran Princes would stand by him and enable him to maintain his principality. But, as Gebhard was a Calvinist, they would not espouse his cause. This was one of those little wars in which the Romanists prevailed through the divisions of the Protestants. The issue was that the Pope persuaded the Duke of Bavaria to march his army into his territory, which ejected him from it, and compelled him to take refuge with his wife in the Netherlands. Sigismund III. also, assisted by the untiring efforts of the Jesuits, and by divisions in the ranks of the Protestants, succeeded in banishing Protestantism from Poland, in which it made great progress.

But in other quarters the Papacy did not come off victorious. We have seen that the grand expedition of Philip against England, designed to recover England for the Holy See, had altogether failed. The Papacy was also unsuccessful in other countries. Sigismund, chosen King of Poland in 1587, a zealous Roman Catholic, had succeeded, on the death of his father, to the crown of Sweden. His uncle Charles, who was appointed Viceroy, availed himself of the opportunity afforded by his delay to return to Sweden to enact very stringent laws against Romanism, because he was afraid that Sigismund would re-establish it in the land of his ancestors. Sigismund, angry on account of these enactments, invaded Sweden, and attempted to reduce it to subjection to the See of Rome; but he was vanquished in battle, and expelled from the kingdom. The Diet then conferred the crown on Charles, the father of that immortal hero, Gustavus Adolphus, who, as we shall soon see, saved Protestantism

in Europe from the destruction with which it was
threatened.

The war had hitherto raged with undiminished violence.
Europe had long re-echoed to the tread of contending
armies; but the battlefield of the two faiths was not
confined to it. The warfare was not carried on only
by land : it raged on the ocean. It reached to the ends
of the earth. It was fought on the shores of Brazil and
amid the Eastern Archipelago, in the Persian Gulf and
on the Pacific Ocean. As Sovereign of Spain and
Portugal, Philip was the King of both the Indies. He
had an American, an Asiatic, and an African empire. In
whatever part of the world he reigned, to it came his
Protestant enemies of Holland and England. The Dutch
repaid his invasion and devastation of their own land by
the invasion and devastation of his vast dominions in the
farthest East and West—India, Mexico and Peru—and
by the conquest of a portion of them. They smote their
Spanish oppressors with almost unbroken success, wrested
from Philip realms of gold and islands of spice, and in the
contest for faith and freedom erected a magnificent
empire in the East Indies. The seamen of England
ventured as far and smote as severely ; but they did not
make the same splendid conquests.

Distant continents, heathen and Mohammedan nations,
were disturbed by the convulsion of Christendom. Shah
Abbas, the great ruler of Persia, and Sultan Akbar, the
Great Mogul who so vigorously, gloriously and beneficently
reigned over Hindoostan, heard how the Christian unbelievers were smiting one another along the shores of
their extensive dominions.

At length, in 1598, the great master-spirit, the bloodthirsty tyrant, Philip II., passed to his account. He was
the prey of a loathsome disease, and died a death of
lingering agony. After all his expenditure of blood and
treasure, he had been only partially successful. He had,

15—2

indeed, made Spain more than ever the devoted slave of
the Papacy, thus causing her, as we see in the present
day, to descend in the scale of nations, and had brought
back the inhabitants of Belgium to their allegiance to
their spiritual mother; but he had strengthened the
determination of England to spurn his yoke, and had
enabled the Northern Netherlands to burst the bonds of
her temporal and spiritual oppressors.   Shortly before
his death, wearied by this warfare, and feeling that he
was standing on the brink of eternity, he had concluded
a peace with Henry IV. of France.   In the year 1609,
Philip III. of Spain, who, though he was as great a bigot
as his father, was very far inferior in ability to him, concluded, as we have seen, a twelve years' truce with the
United Provinces.

The war between Rome and the Reformation now languished because no conspicuous champion appeared for
either cause.   In Germany, Protestants and Roman
Catholics occasionally engaged in petty contests, fought
for the possession of a bishopric, or for supremacy in an
imperial city.   In those little wars the Roman Catholics
generally had the advantage, through the divisions of the
Protestants, who, divided into Lutherans and Calvinists,
sought the defeat of one another rather than of the common
enemy.   The Lutherans were the chief offenders.   The
Saxon Electors distinguished themselves as persecutors of
their fellow-Protestants, and by their submission to the
House of Hapsburg.   The Calvinists showed a nobler
spirit.   Their chief, Frederick, Elector Palatine, urged
cordial union and vigorous action, and at length, in 1597,
formed an alliance among the lesser Princes and imperial
towns, which was renewed and strengthened in 1608, and
is known as the Union.

'The Papacy' at this time, as Professor Ranke observes,
'appears under its proper and praiseworthy character as
the mediator and pacificator of Europe.'   Clement VIII.

conducted the two events of his reign, the reunion of France to the Roman See by the absolution of Henry IV., and the incorporation of Ferrara with the temporal dominions of the Pope, to which reference has been made, with consummate dexterity. The feud within the Jesuit Order, and the collision of that body with other bodies, were matters of the greatest importance to the interests of Romanism. We have seen that the Jesuits were Spanish in their origin. Of the twenty-five who composed the General Council, eighteen were Spanish. The first three Generals were of Spanish birth.

Gregory XIII. seems to have felt some apprehension that the Order would be more at the command of the King of Spain than of the Pope. He therefore used his influence to make Mercurio, an Italian, the fourth General. Mercurio was a weak man, and was governed by those around him. Factions were now formed between older members in the Spanish and the younger in the foreign interest. Mercurio was succeeded by Acquaviva, a Neapolitan. Uniting the perseverance of the Spaniard with the subtlety of the Italian, he endeavoured to establish the ascendency of the Pope in the Order. Acquaviva's enemies, however, at length succeeded in calling in question his administration of the Order, and obtained from Clement VIII. his consent to the convocation of a general assembly to inquire into the matter. Acquaviva made some concessions, and came forth triumphant. The subsequent collision of the Jesuits with the Dominicans in Spain weakened their authority. The Dominicans watched with jealousy the rapid growth of a rival Order. The Inquisition seized a provincial and some of the brethren who were accused of concealing the heretical opinions of some of their Order. The affair created an extraordinary sensation in Spain. A rumour spread that the Jesuit Order had been found guilty of heresy. At a somewhat later period real differences of religious belief arose between the Jesuits and the Dominicans. The Jesuits revolted from the tenets of Thomas Aquinas, and adopted those of Molina on the subjects of grace and free-will. This was exactly in character. The austere and bigoted Dominicans adhered to the definite dogmas ; the learned and pliant Jesuits inclined to the more moderate opinions. Thus the Jesuits became a Papal, but even more a French, power. This is no doubt the secret cause of their readmission into France, from which they had been expelled by Henry IV., who appalled his old Protestant friends, and alarmed his warmest Romanist partisans by his appointment of the Jesuit Cotton as his confessor. We shall see presently that their political doctrines excited more misgivings than their speculations in theology. His own light speech that he would rather have them for his friends than his enemies was as true as it was characteristic. We shall find directly that there were stronger reasons for this change in the policy of France.

This agitation in the Jesuit body lasted till the accession of Paul V. Leo XI. reigned only twenty-seven days. The conclave which elected Paul V. is a specimen of the way in which business was conducted in the early days of modern times, and in the period of Church earnestness which intervened between the scandals and heathenism of the Italian renaissance and the general orthodoxy and propriety of the succeeding period.

This conclave ' was disgracefully conducted. Four parties in it were struggling for the ascendency. They were the party led by Cardinal Aldobrandino, the nephew of the late Pope ; the independent party, led by Cardinal Montalto ; the Cardinals in the interest of Spain, and those in the interest of France. The total number of votes was fifty-nine. The party led by Aldobrandino had · possession of the Paoline Chapel, and the party led by

Montalto occupied the Sistine Chapel. Sometimes the two rivals, surrounded by their adherents, conducted the man chosen by them into one or other of the chapels. They planted themselves opposite to one another, and tried to force one another into the chapel occupied by their own faction. The extent of the confusion and the violence of the emotion among those holy and reverend men may be estimated by the fact that Cardinal Visconti was thrown down in the confusion, and Cardinal Serapino's arm was sprained before the two parties could be separated. Even Baronius, though he struggled violently, was once forced away into the Paoline Chapel. Those who are familiar with the Sistine Chapel when it is the theatre of the magnificent pomp of the Roman Catholic Church, with the dignitaries arranged in decorous order along its sides, may amuse themselves with the picture of the exhausted Cardinals sitting on its pavement, some eating their suppers, some fast asleep on an extemporized pallet, some engaged in conversation carried on in a whisper, some taking off their purple and scarlet vestments, that they may have a few hours' rest at the foot of the altar.

The day was occupied in negotiations between the two parties; the night, however, found them as far as ever from the election of a Pope. At last Aldobrandino and Montalto agreed that, as all combinations had failed, they must look for a candidate among the younger men. Borghese was then mentioned. He was a member of Aldobrandino's party, the 'creature' of Clement VIII., a personal friend of Montalto, and acceptable to the Spanish party. It only remained to be ascertained if he would be acceptable to the French party. Aldobrandino was earnest enough in the matter, as it was his only chance of making one of his own party Pope. He found Cardinal Joyeuse, who represented the French party, in his cell. He was not indisposed to Borghese, but said

that he must consult Montalto before he gave his consent.   Aldobrandino, in order to overcome his reluctance,
flung himself on his knees before him.   Just at that
moment, as the conclavist informs us, Montalto entered
the cell.   The latter joined his representations in favour
of Borghese, as his election seemed to offer the least
objectionable solution of the difficulties which surrounded
the conclave.   Joyeuse, therefore, at once consented in ·
the French interest.   Thus three old men, not one of
whom was qualified to direct a parish, settled one of the
most important elections in the history of the Papacy.

Paul V. sprang from a family of Siennese gentlemen
expatriated by the Medici.   He was so courteous that he
was known by the name of His Benignity.   But after
his election he laid aside his benignity, and showed himself rigorous in the administration of justice.   He believed
himself able to revive the high claims of Hildebrand and
Innocent.   He hoped to compel the monarchs of Europe
to crouch before him.   He never seems to have entertained the least doubt that he should be successful.   He
had compelled the secular powers in Parma, Malta, Lucca,
and Genoa to submit to his imperious will.   He thought,
therefore, that other States would acknowledge his claim
on their allegiance.   He did not doubt that even Spain
would submit to him.

Venice had always asserted its independence of ecclesiastical control.   The pomp and glare of her worship,
the clouds of incense rolling up from innumerable altars,
the crowds bowing down before the shrines of the saints,
gave a very plain proof that she would not cease to be a
devoted daughter of the Church.   At the same time she
would not submit to Papal dictation, nor allow any interference on the part of Rome in the affairs of the republic.
She aimed at the mean between subservience to the
Church of Rome and the maintenance of her spiritual
independence.   Paul was determined to see if he could

not compel Venice to be a vassal in his train. Two ecclesiastics had been thrown into prison in Venice for notorious
crimes. He directed his Nuncio to demand that these
persons should be handed over to the ecclesiastical
authorities. The Senate showed a dignified resolution in
maintaining its own rights, and would not give up the
prisoners. At the same time the answer evinced that the
Papacy had a hold on the allegiance of the senators.

The thunderstorm of anathema and interdict then
burst over Venice. But it was utterly disregarded by the
Venetians. They would not yield to the imperious
demands of the Pope. The laws remained unrepealed.
Henry IV. of France sent Cardinal Joyeuse to reconcile
the contending parties. But he found the Senate as
unyielding as the Pope. The Venetians were aided in
their conflict with the Pope by the celebrated Father Paolo
Sarpi. To the State Papers which he issued it is owing
that Venice came off victorious in the conflict. A reconciliation was, indeed, effected between the Pope and the
Senate, but it involved a surrender on the part of the
Pope, and was, in fact, a complete defeat under the form
of a reconciliation—the greatest defeat in the history of
the Papacy, which, as Mr. Hallam says, 'shook the fabric
not only of Papal despotism, but of ecclesiastical independence and power.' These preposterous Papal pretensions led also to the consolidation of the Gallican
Church. The passions, jealousies, and fears of these
three old men in their narrow cell in the Vatican were
the means of conferring this advantage on Pius V., that
they enabled him to found a great family at Rome, celebrated for its palaces, gardens, and galleries. They
inflicted, however, an injury on their Church, because they
showed the weakness of the Roman power even on the
Italian side of the Alps, and that it was an act of folly
to assert at this time of day the preposterous claims of
Gregory, Hildebrand, and Innocent.

The conflict which has just been described was one of the greatest importance. When we reflect that a Roman Catholic alliance was exerting every effort to arrest the progress of the Reformation, that the Jesuits had been enforcing everywhere absolute obedience to the decrees of the Council of Trent, and the paramount authority of the Pope, both in ecclesiastical and civil matters, this opposition of Venice, who had always held all the dogmas of the Papacy, while she had occasionally differed from her in other matters, was an important element in the struggle for liberty which was now carried on throughout Europe.

Rome, re-constituted by the Council of Trent, and led on to battle by the Jesuits, had not yet come into collision with any State which still remained in her communion. The importance of the struggle between Venice and the Papacy consisted in the fact that if she had yielded Rome might have come off a victor in the conflict. But her effective resistance, in which she was aided by Sarpi, showed that the days had for ever passed away when Rome could set her foot on the neck of the monarchs of Christendom. He thought that the Church ought not to interfere with secular matters, and that the State ought not to interfere with Church matters. We can hardly do justice to his boldness when we remember that in every parish sermons were heard in which the assertion was made that Rome was supreme over Princes and people, that she could even direct the assassination of Sovereigns if they did not obey her will, and that they could not be saved if they did not render to her an absolute and unconditional obedience.

But Rome was determined that Venice should not brave her with impunity. She would display her might and majesty before the nations. Sarpi was assailed by assassins as he was walking through the streets of Venice. Fifteen blows were aimed at him, which struck him in the neck and face.   He fell to the ground dangerously wounded.   He was carried to a neighbouring monastery, where for some days he hovered between life and death. At length he recovered.   We have presumptive evidence of the connection of the Papal camera with this attempted assassination.   The assassins drew 100 crowns from it, and had a triumphal progress through the Papal States. They were afterwards received in the palace of Cardinal Conolla at Rome.   Attempts were made on the life of Sarpi in succeeding years which were certainly instigated by the Cardinals.   His enemies could not fix on him the crime of heresy; he was a devout Roman Catholic.   The head and front of his offending was that he had employed the large stores of learning which he had acquired and his amazing intellectual powers in demolishing those arguments for the new system of Papal supremacy which the Jesuits were labouring to impose on Christendom. The object of Sarpi was to show that the State and the Church were independent organisms; that the Church had no right to supremacy over the State, and the State had no right to supremacy over the Church.   As his opponents had not sound reasoning on their side, they were driven to employ the arguments of personal abuse and the stiletto.

We may well, then, ask what was the value of this Reformation.   Treachery and violence were to be the means by which the Church was to be restored to primitive simplicity.   Men whose hands were stained with the blood of their nearest relations were to be the agents employed to bring into subjection Kings and learned historians who would not admit that the Pope ought to sit as God in the temple of God and arrogate to himself the attributes and prerogatives of Deity. Great sins might be expiated, and eternal grace might be obtained, by the murder of those who entered an indignant protest against the morality of the Jesuits.   Thus

Mariana approved of the assassination of Henry III. of France by Jacques Clement, whom he praises as resembling the heroes of antiquity. Those who rendered this service to the Church were sure of happiness both here and hereafter. Sarpi had also made himself obnoxious to the Jesuits because, though not a Protestant in the sense that he held the distinctive doctrines of the latter, in that history of the Council of Trent which Lord Macaulay places on an equality with the works of Livy and Tacitus, he had made it perfectly clear that human diplomacy rather than Divine inspiration had guided the deliberations of the assembled Fathers, and had injured their cause by asserting that a purer discipline and a sincere spirituality must be a distinguishing feature in the system of those who made it their great object to promote the spiritual and moral regeneration of Christendom.

The Jesuits after this time gave another proof of their dark and dangerous designs. Ravaillac, instigated by them, assassinated Henry IV. of France. The inhabitants of Europe, when they heard of this event, thought that it had been really disadvantageous to the Pope because it prevented that monarch from endowing him with the kingdom of Naples at the expense of the House of Austria, and making him the head of a grand Italian confederation. If, however, the secrets of futurity had been unfolded to them, they would have seen that it had given her another chance of universal empire ; for it saved the House of Austria from those territorial losses which would have paralyzed her energies, and would have prevented, as we shall see presently, the Emperor Ferdinand, the most devoted of the sons of Rome, from raising his arm for the purpose of striking a blow at the liberty, religion, and independence of Germany.

Paul V. thus failed in increasing his temporal predominance. We find also that the King of France and the clergy were as determined as the State of Venice not to admit his claim of temporal supremacy over the Gallican Church. Paul after the severe lessons taught to him remained quiet and moderate. We find, however, that during his Papacy, partly through the work of the Jesuits, Romanism was everywhere in the ascendant. In France, in Germany, in the Netherlands, in Hungary, in Poland, and in Switzerland, zeal and power, the preaching of the Jesuit, and the royal edict, the encouragements addressed to the ardent, the bribes offered to the wavering, the re-established splendour of the services attracting to the Church ; the decree of banishment which severed the ties of home and of kindred ; the unwearied charity, the careful education given ; the persecution to which the Protestants were often exposed ; the careful training ; the discharge of the pastoral office with its gentle spirit of conciliation ; the favour of the Sovereign, the promotion to the highest offices of the State, were influences which worked together against divided Protestantism, and in favour of regenerated Romanism.

Protestantism, too, had ceased to be the active force which once exercised a predominant influence. It had become a hereditary faith. The bitter persecution which puts to the test the reality of a man's religion had ceased. Endless divisions and contentions interrupted the harmony of the Protestant Churches. The revived Romanism, too, had all the charm of novelty. In France the virtues and the vices of men all contributed to the advancement of Romanism. The Christian virtue of men like St. Francis de Sales ; the learning of the Benedictines ; the active beneficence of the several female monastic communities, which began to act as Sisters of Charity, to attend the hospitals, to visit the sick, to pour the oil and wine of heavenly consolation into the wounded spirit, contributed to the regeneration of Romanism. On the other hand, we cannot help coming to the conclusion that the religion of many was hollow, heartless, and unmeaning. They embraced Romanism because it was an easy religion, because the Jesuits condescended to allow them to make any compromise with sin for the purpose of gaining converts. The undisguised atheism of many of the courtiers was greatly encouraged by the light-hearted gaiety with which Henry transferred his allegiance from the Protestant to the Roman Catholic faith. We have thus the explanation of his friendship for the Jesuits. They had encouraged him in a religion which was perfectly consistent with the indulgence of every vice and the perpetration of every crime.

We must return to the missionary work in England. We have seen the utter failure of Cardinal Allen's political schemes. Some success had indeed at first attended the missionary work of his priests. Many had avowed themselves the adherents of the Roman See. But really the enterprise ended in failure, and prepared the way for the triumph of the Reformation. The knights and squires scattered through England formed the Protestant party after the destruction of the Armada and the High Church party of which we read in the following reigns. The number thus converted very far exceeded the number through Allen's priests converted to the Church of Rome. We must strongly condemn his objects. We cannot fail, however, to admire his marvellous zeal and self-sacrifice, and his persevering efforts, notwithstanding the want of material resources and great difficulties, to aid the Counter-Reformation, of which he was in his own person the embodiment in England, by winning back his fellow-countrymen to their allegiance to Romanism.

Allen died at Rome on October 16, 1594, at the age of sixty-two. His indefatigable labours had worn out the material tabernacle. We are much touched when we find him writing that ' he is overpowered with work and with care ; and that he cannot attend so quickly as he could wish to the duties which devolve upon him.'* The partial success which attended his work was no doubt due partly to his loving disposition, to his power of sympathy, his patient gentleness, by which he won the hearts of all who approached him, and to the excellent training given to his priests, by which they were well prepared for the work committed to them. Parsons thus wrote of him :

' Allen possesses the hearts of all. He enjoys such authority and respect with the whole nation, that his mere presence, though he only occupied a private position, will weigh more with the English than several thousand soldiers ; and not only the Earl of Westmoreland, who is more difficult to manage, but all the exiles bear him such reverence that at a word from him there is nothing they would not do.'

No one possessing Allen's qualifications for the work was found to take his place. But his seminary did not perish with him. In 1592, when all his schemes seemed to have failed, he expresses a confident expectation that England would be recovered for the Holy See, even when all hope of Philip II.'s successful intervention by force of arms had passed away. He thus wrote to the priests in England on December 12, 1592 :

' Doubt ye not, my most sweet and faithful coadjutors and true confessors, that our adversaries' iniquities are now in God's sight near accomplished, and at the height. On the contrary side the number of our brethren that are to suffer for the truth is near made up, and shortly to receive, not only in the next, but in this world, the worthy fruits of their happy labours. God, almighty and all-merciful, will not suffer long the rod of the wicked to lie so heavy

* ' Letters of Cardinal Allen,' p. 208.

upon the lot of the just, neither let us be tempted more than by His grace we shall be able to bear, but will shorten those days of affliction for the elect's sake.'*

We find that the older Orders of the Church of Rome, beginning work again with energies quickened by the general revival, shared Allen's expectation. They did not for a century from this time relinquish the hope of one day again establishing themselves in England. Many illustrations of the prevalence of this feeling on the Continent might be given. One may be cited as occurring in the provisions of a deed by which, in the year 1611, the Abbot of St. Vedast, at Arras in France, conveyed to the seminary priests at Douai a country house belonging to his abbey. A clause in the deed of gift specified that the property was to revert to its original owners 'when the Catholic religion should be restored in England.'† The foundation of many new colleges for the English Mission, and the energy infused into the management of them, had raised in their minds the confident expectation of the ultimate triumph of Romanism in England. Allen's College of Douai survived till it was swept away in 1793 because it was considered dangerous to the Revolutionary Government. In furtherance of Allen's views, Parsons founded three secular colleges to be carried on under Jesuit rule in Spain, at Madrid, Seville, and Valladolid, and another at Lisbon. To him also is due the formation, in 1593, of a Jesuit lay college at St. Omers, which, for upwards of two centuries shared with the second Jesuit lay school at Liége the glory of instructing the Roman Catholic laity of England and Ireland. It still exists at Stonyhurst. The Benedictines, with the same object in view, founded a priory at Douai, a priory in Paris, an abbey at Lammspring in Westphalia, and soon afterwards a third priory at a place called Dieudwert in France.

* 'Diaries of Douai,' p. xcvi.
† Alban Butler's Travels, p. 47.

The Franciscans, or the Grey Friars, from the Minories in London, reconstituted themselves at Douai, while the Dominicans, or Black Friars, also from London, established themselves at Louvain. Dr. Bellesheim has given in his work a curious list of all the English houses founded on the Continent—belonging to Jesuits (4), Benedictines (12), Carthusians (1), Dominicans (3), Franciscans (7), Carmelites (4), Austin Nuns (4), Brigittines (1), and the house of ' Marie Ward ' (1). The colleges just enumerated are the most important of the sixteen founded in different countries of Europe in addition to those founded by the Jesuits for their own Society within twenty years of the death of Elizabeth, having for their united object the restoration of Romanism to its ascendency in England.

The men who went forth from these seminaries well knew that they were about to engage in a war in which no quarter would be given. The Government spies were not only keeping a watch upon the colleges, but were waiting for them at the different ports, so that it was a wonder if any of them escaped detection. They were still obliged, as we have already seen, to take refuge in ' dens and caves of the earth.' They knew that they must expect hardships and indignities, and they had the prospect before them of being stretched on the rack or of perishing ignominiously on the scaffold. Occasionally, like Campian, they would shudder when they thought of the terrible doom which awaited them. But they generally went forth without any sinking of heart to this warfare, displaying a heroism and a patient perseverance to the end, which, while we condemn their object, ought to obtain the tribute of our applause. Occasionally, as we see in the following reigns, the harsher enactments of the penal law were relaxed when the King was in a merciful mood, or when, as was the case with Charles II., he was their friend, or when his political necessities or private

16

schemes rendered that relaxation desirable. The Governments and the English people in those days seem to have thought that our self-defence rendered that rigour absolutely necessary. The law gradually fell into abeyance. But we may say that for nearly a century from the latter part of the reign of Elizabeth they were liable to be arraigned and visited with a terrible punishment for celebrating Mass or administering any other religious rite to the members of their own faith, or for any effort which had for its object the extension of the boundaries of Romanism in England.

The description of the successful missionary work of a Jesuit Father may serve to illustrate this portion of our history. A few weeks after the destruction of the Spanish Armada a young Englishman, John Gerard, landed by night on the coast of Norfolk. He was the son of Sir Thomas Gerard, a Lancashire Baronet. He never, in consequence of imperfect education, became a scholar; but he understood the training of a falcon, and was well acquainted with all the pastimes and accomplishments of town and rural life. Gerard went first to Oxford, and afterwards to Rheims, where, through the influence of a young friend, he was induced to resolve to become a member of the Society of Jesus. Cardinal Allen, whom he met at Rome, at once saw that he would prove a valuable emissary to send to the English Mission. He at once obeyed his summons, and proceeded to England, animated with the desire to labour with all the fiery energy of his nature for the conversion of his fellow-countrymen.

Gerard landed about the end of October, 1588. The great difficulty was to avoid the spies and officers who were on the look-out for seminary priests and Jesuits. After two or three narrow escapes, he was guided, providentially for him, to a gentleman as enthusiastic as himself. The latter did not further the plan of Gerard, which was to present himself as soon as possible to his superior in London, but induced him to remain in Norfolk. The part of the county to which he had come was like a harbour of refuge to the mariner after a voyage over a stormy sea. The squires were Romanists almost to a man. He was in as safe a neighbourhood as there was in England, south of the Humber. The gentleman who detained him saw at once that he was no ordinary man, and that he might be very useful as a proselytizer in Norfolk. His knowledge of the ordinary sports of a country gentleman was a recommendation to many of the nobility and gentry of Norfolk. He had also personal advantages. He was tall, erect, and well-set; his complexion was dark; he had eyes with a strange piercing look in them; he had a prominent nose, full lips, and hair that hung in long curls. Gerard could accommodate himself to any society; but he was especially, through his courtly manners, a favourite with the nobility and gentry. He was always polite; but, still, he could assert himself with decision. The flashing eye, the indignant expression of countenance, and the stern rebuke whenever he heard any ribaldry or any observation which seemed to cast a reflection on the dogmas of Romanism, his occasional gravity and silence amid his gaiety and vivacity, like a thick mist coming over a landscape illumined with the bright beams of the noonday sun, showed his friends at once that he was something more than themselves, a mere Romanist—that he was a Jesuit in disguise, and that his mind was occupied with high and heavenly meditations.

The success of Gerard in Norfolk surpassed his most sanguine expectations. He gained converts through that subtle and indefinable charm of manner which is more likely to win them than the most laboured process of reasoning. Recent research has enabled us to see that his influence was felt during seventeen years to a wonderful extent in the upper ranks of English society. At least ten young men of high rank, from the counties of Norfolk and Suffolk, through his influence left England, and joined the Society of Jesus before the end of Elizabeth's reign. Closely dogged by spies, he passed safely through imminent perils and had hair-breadth escapes. At last he was apprehended in 1594, and imprisoned in the Tower. Here he was exposed to the dreadful agony of being hung up by his hands and arms to the roof of his dungeon for hours. When he fainted from the excessive torture he was restored to consciousness, only to be tortured over and over again in a similar manner. He tells us that even his gaolors were moved to compassion by the sight of his sufferings. He bore them with heroic fortitude, and resolutely refused to give any information which could implicate a single friend or associate. In consequence of his sufferings he lost the use of his hands for months. We must condemn this terrible persecution. It hindered the progress of the cause which it was designed to promote. The only extenuation of it which can be made is that, as stated in the last chapter, our countrymen had not risen above the spirit of the age, and that far severer sufferings were inflicted by the Inquisition.

At length he escaped from the Tower in 1597, and persevered in his work, in which he displayed great tact, courage, and ability, administering the Sacraments at the risk of his life, sustaining the drooping courage of the Romanists, confessing the penitent, and adding soldiers, as we have seen, to the ranks of the Papal army. He at last died quietly in his bed, leaving an example to us who profess to be the disciples of a purer faith to lead a life of holiness and self-denial, to labour zealously for the salvation of immortal souls, and to submit to the lesser sufferings of ridicule and obloquy in the service of our Divine Master.

When James I. ascended the throne, it seemed as if the danger to English independence from the Counter-Reformation had passed away. The Pope, Clement VIII., wrote a letter to James before the death of Elizabeth, assuring him of his support in the event of opposition to him, and the English Roman Catholics aided in securing his peaceful accession. No nation in Europe was likely to stir up those plots for the enforcement of the Bull of Pius V., which had for their object also to secure the predominance of Romanism in England. The sceptre was beginning to fall from the grasp of Spain ; the empire on which the sun never set would soon vanish away. The struggle of the Counter-Reformation was likely soon to be transferred to another land. The storm-clouds were beginning to gather over Germany ; flash after flash was breaking from them over the mountains of Bohemia and the waters of the Danube.

The sword of persecution might, therefore, it would seem, have slumbered in its scabbard in England. A confident expectation prevailed that as James was the son of Roman Catholic parents, and as he was fond of the solemnity of the religious services of the Roman Catholics, he would be much more favourable to Romanism than his predecessors. This expectation was so far justified by the event that, a few months after his arrival in England, he declared to the Roman Catholics that he would not enforce the fine collected from those who refused to attend the services of the Church, provided they remained quiet and did not organize any plots against himself and the State. The fines, which in late years had amounted to more than £10,000, decreased in the year 1603 to £300, and in 1604 to £200. He determined, however, to enforce the laws against the seminary priests and the Jesuits. He directed that they should be banished from the kingdom. He thought that he should thus avoid all the consequences of the hostility of those who were still very powerful in the world at large and among his own subjects.

The penal laws were no longer vigorously enforced in any respect. The result was that the chapels of the Roman Catholic Ambassadors were numerously attended, so that, in some provinces, especially in Wales, Roman Catholic sermons were delivered in the open air, and were attended by thousands of hearers. This result of his policy created very great dissatisfaction among his subjects. They said that he was very much to be blamed for relaxing laws which were enrolled among the statutes of the realm. The Roman Catholics, too, were dissatisfied. They saw that they were absolutely at his mercy if political necessities or his personal fears compelled him to enforce the laws vigorously.

These fears were well founded. The King and Council had determined to inflict great severities on the Puritans. They felt, however, that they must be even-handed in their administration of justice. They therefore determined to enforce the laws against the Romanists with great severity. James felt himself insulted if anyone doubted his intention to make the laws operate in both directions. The result was that, in June, 1604, an Act was passed for the due execution of the statutes against Jesuits, seminary priests, and recusants. In the autumn of 1605 the laws against the Romanists began to be executed. The priests were not, indeed, punished with death, but they were thrown into prison, where they very soon succumbed to the severe treatment which they had undergone. In September a Commission was appointed to carry out their banishment. The King also charged the Bishops to see that the fines for recusancy which were in arrears should be levied.

But even the laity suffered much more from the spies who forced their way into their houses. They complained loudly and bitterly of the insecurity of their position.

They could find no tenants to take their farms. The consequence would be that they would be deprived of their patrimony, and would become needy dependents on the precarious charity of strangers. They said that the King had mocked them with the semblance of liberty. He had only mitigated the laws that he might afterwards enforce them with greater severity. It is said that 5,560 persons were convicted of recusancy. The result was that terrible Gunpowder Plot which shattered into fragments that fabric of toleration which the King had been taking pains to compact and consolidate.

The Gunpowder Treason was the last design formed by the agents of Rome against the life of the Sovereign of England. The Counter-Reformation in this country in the reign of Charles I. took the form of Court intrigue, and of a scheme for bringing the Church of England into closer agreement with the Church of Rome. The minds of the Puritans, and of those who upheld Parliamentary authority, were harassed by the fear that this last design would be successful. The severe laws against the seminary priests and Jesuits were greatly relaxed in consequence of a promise made by Charles on his marriage with Henrietta Maria, a Roman Catholic daughter of France. The fines on a profession of Romanism were reduced to one half, or were redeemed altogether by compositions made under the Great Seal. The bloody and barbarous executions of former days were no longer allowed in England. The spies, who were almost an omnipresent influence, were no longer visible. The Queen exerted every effort to prevent them from executing the commission against the priests and Jesuits with which they were entrusted.

We shall at once see the importance of this relaxation from a Roman Catholic point of view when we hear that the spy system was the great hindrance to the success of the missionary work in England during the two preceding reigns. The most insidious means of obtaining information as to the movements of the priests and the Jesuits were adopted. Very often it happened, as we have already seen, that the spies obtained admission to the colleges as students. They were so exemplary, and showed so strong an opposition to Protestantism, that no one could suppose them to be Protestants in disguise.

Very often it happened that a student found, on his arrival in England, that every particular of his past life was known to the authorities. The Superiors of the colleges were often obliged to practise deception in order to elude the vigilance of the spies. The destination of a missionary was kept secret till the time of his departure from the seminary; or he would go to England by a different track from that which was noised abroad, in order to throw the bloodhounds off their scent; or he would often change his name, in order that he might escape detection on arrival in England.

The work was thus stripped of the charms which it possessed with men remarkable for their nobility of spirit and dignity of character, and became repulsive to them. A residence in the college became distasteful on account of their bad food, their coarse raiment, and the deprivations of another kind to which they were obliged to submit. Their ardour for the enterprise cooled when the romantic associations connected with the work began to pass away, partly through the operation of the causes just stated, partly also on account of the dangers and difficulties which they were sure to encounter, and the small measure of success which had attended the labours of their predecessors. The consequence was that the fountain-head in England was for a time nearly choked up, and that only a scanty stream issued from it for the supply of the missionary colleges.

This difficulty was overcome, to a certain extent, by an appointment which Clement VIII. made in 1598. Dr. William Blackwell was appointed Arch-priest of the

Roman Catholic congregations in England. In 1623 a Bishop *in partibus*, Dr. William Bishop, was appointed, after a long controversy on this point between the secular priests and the Jesuits, the former desiring a Bishop, and the latter opposing the appointment as limiting their authority. A part of the business of both of them was to examine candidates, and to send a constant supply of them to the seminaries. Thus the work was carried on with greater zeal and regularity than during some preceding years, until at length, through the relaxation of the laws and the removal of the spies at the time before us, students for the colleges and missionary priests for England, thick as autumn swallows, spread their wings over the ocean.

The real state of the feeling at Court and in parts of the country at this time with reference to Romanism is well stated in the memoirs of Gregory Panzani, who arrived in London as a Nuncio from the Pope in December, 1634. This work was published in England in 1793 by Mr. Berrington, a Romish priest, to explain the object of his mission, which was to settle a dispute between the Jesuits and the English secular priesthood. Panzani, ' who was a secular priest of experienced virtue, of singular address, of polite learning, and in all respects well qualified for the business, was sent by the Pope to obtain information not only of the true state of affairs among the Catholics, but also to feel the pulse of the nation in regard to other concerns.' He was desired to keep his mission from public observation. His object was, in fact, if possible, to negotiate terms of union between England and Rome. Panzani made no attempt to deal with the project of reconciliation till he had been for some time in England, beyond a private communication to the Queen, to whom he had constant access ; but in January, 1635, he had an interview on the subject with Secretary Windebank, who is described as ' a Protestant by profession, but no enemy to the Catholics, and prepared to go all lengths with the King and the Court party.' Windebank proved very friendly to the project. He was soon able to arrange that he should meet the King in a remote and unsuspected place, the Queen also being present. Charles was most courteous in his reception of the Envoy, and received very graciously the Pope's acknowledgments of his mild treatment of the Catholics. The particular form which the result of their interview was made to assume was the establishment of a reconciliation agency between the Court of Rome and the Queen, by which cautious experiments towards a reunion might be made. The young wife had been taught in France to consider herself as entrusted with the commission of comforting and protecting persecuted members of her Church. Charles certainly did not give any countenance to the idea that he intended to change his religion, but he endeavoured to show that he did not feel any abhorrence for Romanism. Panzani had frequent interviews with Windebank on the subject, and stated that the Holy See was very favourably disposed towards a reunion of the Churches. We shall see presently that this projected reunion between the Church of England and the Church of Rome ought to have been considered as a palpable chimera. Romanism was regarded with abhorrence by the majority of the clergy and the religious laity. In some parts of England, however, it was making a little progress. We are informed that a great change in London is daily visible. Sometimes in sermons before the King and the Court the schism with Rome is condemned, and the King is exhorted to make some advances towards a union with the Church of Rome.

The practice of auricular confession is praised, and images as well as altars are constantly commended. The Roman Bishop and the Roman Church have their full share of praise given to them. The preachers declare that it is the best of Churches, and that the Bishop of it is the Patriarch of the West. They talk much about a reunion. The Queen has, besides her private chapel, a public one at which the Mass is celebrated with great pomp. We learn not only from Panzani but from other sources, that the Roman Catholic services were celebrated in numberless places, but with most splendour in the residences of the Ambassadors, where they vied with one another in keeping Holy Week with fine music, with sensuous representations, and with a gorgeous ceremonial. Panzani states expressly: 'Every one of the Roman Catholics acknowledges how much their condition is improved, and that easier times had never been.'

Many passages are to be found in the writings of Montague (Bishop of Chichester), Pocklington, and other ecclesiastical writers, showing the strong tendency towards Romanism which existed among many of them in those days. They support the practice of setting up crucifixes, pictures of God the Father and the Holy Ghost, and images of saints in churches. Montague and Pocklington discuss as a curious question the doctrine of purgatory, to which they seem to consent. Many passages may also be found in their books, and those of others, showing the value and necessity of prayers for the dead. A large array of quotations from the writers of this period may be found in 'Catena Patrum,' No. 81 of the celebrated 'Tracts for the Times,' showing that Jesus Christ and His Passion are offered up to God in the Sacrament of the Altar, which, it is stated, is a sacrifice as well as a Sacrament.

We may further illustrate the tendency towards Rome which existed in those days by a reference to a work entitled 'Deus, Natura, et Gratia,' which bears the name of Franciscus a Santa Clara. The author was Damport or St. Giles, both Roman priests of the Franciscan Order. It was first printed at Leyden in 1634, and was dedicated to King Charles. The object was to show that a man might with a safe conscience sign the Thirty-nine Articles of the Church of England, and yet remain in communion with the Church of Rome. In fact, it was intended to prepare the way for that scheme of reconciliation with Rome to which reference has already been made. A translation of this work, slightly modified, forms the well-known ' Tract for the Times ' No. 90, published in 1842 by the Oxford party. The argument by which the writer prepared the way for his well-known interpretation of the Thirty-nine Articles was the absolute coincidence of the theology of Mountague, Pocklington, Mainwaring, and others with the theology of the Church of Rome. From this coincidence Santa Clara inferred the very minute and unimportant difference between Anglicanism and Romanism, with a view to the restoration of the unity of the Catholic Church. Meanwhile the writer proceeds to show that it was not a matter of the least importance to which Church anyone belonged, as the Thirty-nine Anglican Articles presented no barrier to communion with the Church of Rome.

We have no doubt that these attempts to re-unite the two Churches had their origin in a conviction that Protestantism was now firmly established in Europe. The failure of the various efforts of the Counter-Reformation, especially the last desperate efforts of the Emperor Ferdinand in Germany which will be fully described in the next chapter, had impressed the world with the conviction that Romanism would never recover its ascendency in Europe. The hope of this restoration of Romanism thus appeared to be a mere chimera. Thus the way was prepared for the revival of the plans for a reconciliation between the two Churches. The breach between them was by no means regarded in those days as irreparable. We think that the existence of this feeling furnishes us with a clue to the offer of a Cardinal's hat which was made to Archbishop Laud on the morning after his predecessor expired. He does not show any astonishment at the offer, nor any indignation because it had been made to him. He calmly replied that 'something dwelled within him which would not suffer *that*, till Rome was otherwise than it was at that present time.' The existence of the feeling just referred to supplies us with the reason for the calm indifference with which he regarded this offer. We meet with plans of union in France, Germany, Bavaria, Poland—in fact, all over the Continent. They were maintained by Kings, by powerful Ministers, by learned theologians, and by men who had achieved distinction in literature and science.

The complimentary style of intercourse between Rome and her revolted subjects may serve to show us the feeling which existed in regard to a union with her. Sully, the celebrated Minister of Henry IV. of France, received a very courteous letter from Pope Paul V. in which he paid him high compliments for his abilities, and expressed an ardent wish for his conversion. Sully does not take any notice of that wish, but replies to him in an equally complimentary strain, and 'hopes that he may have the honour of kissing the Pope's feet.' We know also that James I., who prided himself on being a strong Protestant, was invited to send his son to Rome for education, a proposal which, though declined, was declined with courtesy. Charles I., too, addressed the Pope in a style which was hardly consistent with a sincere profession of Protestantism. A plain proof was thus given that a closer union with Rome was by no means regarded in those days as visionary.

We have no doubt that, when Laud gave the answer above referred to, he contemplated such a union with Rome as could be maintained without a surrender of the principles of the Reformation. On his trial he repelled with great indignation the charge that he had formed a design against the Protestant faith. ' I do here make my solemn protestation in the presence of God and of this great Cóurt that I am innocent of any thing greater or less, that is charged in this article or in any part of it.' But he was deceiving himself. The union with Rome which he contemplated involved a departure from essential and fundamental doctrine. Such a scheme was impracticable on account of the strong Puritan spirit prevalent in the country and actively manifested in the House of Commons. The doctrinal Puritans felt with ourselves that the image of the Crucified One must be printed on our hearts. They attached the greatest importance to the Lutheran doctrine of justification by faith in the merits of the Saviour. They lifted up their voices against the mediation of the saints, against purgatory, against the worship of the Virgin Mary, against all those doctrines which nullify and abrogate the truth as it is in Jesus. The men who held these doctrines constantly reminded the members of the Laudian party that they were departing from the principles of the English Reformation. They did not refuse to wear the surplice, to kneel at the Eucharist, nor to use the sign of the cross in baptism. They did not look upon episcopacy as a relic of Antichrist. They delighted in holding real communion with God in our beautiful Liturgy. Under Archbishop Abbot and Bishop Hall the true spirit of the English Reformation revived. They were the true Evangelists of the age. Sound doctrines were taught and Christian virtues were inculcated by them. But they disappear from our view when the storm thickened, and the blackness of darkness gathered over the land. If Laud had attended to their warnings, they would have saved the Church. If the Parliament had followed their example of moderation, they would have saved the monarchy. They were raised up like the prophets of old to foretell impending ruin, and to leave

both parties without excuse.   The neglect of their warnings led to an appalling retribution, when the Church and
monarchy were overthrown, and the heads of Charles and
Laud fell upon the scaffold.

The reconciliation proposed by Laud and his followers
was impossible, even when the Bishops had surrendered
some of the fundamental dogmas of Protestantism,
because the Jesuits and the Court of Rome were strongly
opposed to it.   They could not entertain it on any terms
which implied independent rights.   They required an
unconditional surrender on the part of England to the
Papacy.   We have a proof of the truth of this assertion
in the attempt made to show that a man might be a
member of the Church of Rome while he held the Thirty-
nine Articles.   The authorities at Rome strongly censured
that scheme, but they did not make the decree public.
They required, however, the author to come and clear
himself at Rome of the suspected heresy.   He pleaded
bodily infirmities as his reason for not obeying the summons.   When they found that he did not come, they took
pains to circulate in England the censure of the book.
He published an apology for it, and submitted himself
and the book to the judgment of the Pope.   But still they
were not satisfied, and exerted every effort to effect his
expulsion from England.

We come to the same conclusion as to the impossibility
of a union, even with important concessions to the Papacy,
from the instructions sent to Panzani after he had reported
a conference held with Montague, Bishop of Chichester,
who was, as we have seen, one of the chief sympathizers
with the project for reunion.   That project had gone so
far that the King actually nominated two persons in succession to act for the Queen, who had been selected rather
than himself as the chief persons to conduct the negotiations, not only on account of his creed, but also because
the laws distinctly prohibited diplomatic relations with

Rome. Charles felt that it would have been dangerous to himself to attempt to violate them. We see, then, that Charles, while repudiating the leading dogmas of the Church of Rome, deluded himself with the idea that a reconciliation was possible. Panzani soon dispelled that illusion. He gave him to understand that it was useless to discuss particular subjects of controversy, not only because such deliberations had produced no result, but because the Catholic Church would not admit these disputations till the fundamental point of a supreme judge was established. In other words, Rome would not admit any reconciliation until the Church of England confessed that it had erred fundamentally, acknowledged the supremacy of the Pope, and then humbly asked him to prescribe the conditions on which he would restore her to his favour.

We see, then, that the Counter-Reformation, when it assumed the form of union on equal terms with the Church of Rome, ended in failure. The voice of God forbids us to look for this union. We cannot unite with her as she is now, because she does not hold fundamental doctrines, and we cannot expect that Rome will ever be different from what she is. The Scriptures plainly reveal to us that Rome will be Babylon to the end. They tell us that she will be burnt with fire (Rev. xvii. 16), and they show us the smoke of her burning (Rev. xviii. 9). We are filled with awe and wonder and sorrow as, looking through the ages, we see her for her manifold sins and perversions of the truth consigned to final and everlasting destruction. Then will this song of praise ascend from the spirits of just men made perfect: 'Great and marvellous are Thy works, Lord God Almighty; just and true are Thy ways, Thou King of saints' (Rev. xv. 3).

CHAPTER IX.

THE THIRTY YEARS' WAR AND THE END OF THE STRUGGLE. '

The Catholic League and the Protestant Union—The revolt in Bohemia the beginning of the Thirty Years' War—The Elector Palatine induced to become King of Bohemia—Defeated near Prague—Count Mansfield, Christian of Brunswick and Christian of Denmark, and their efforts on behalf of Frederick—Ambition and fanaticism of the Emperor Ferdinand—His proceedings in regard to the restoration of Romanism in Germany—The Edict of Restitution issued by Ferdinand—Gustavus Adolphus of Sweden summoned by the Germans to their assistance—His character, and his freedom from ambition—His difficulties and encouragements—The treaty of Gustavus with France and Cardinal Richelieu—Inadequate support of Gustavus in Germany—His defeat of Tilly at Leipsic—The victory of Gustavus at the Lech, and its consequences—Victory of Lützen, and death of Gustavus—The work successful notwithstanding his death—The Peace of Westphalia, and its important consequences.

WE here return to the progress of the struggle in Germany and Austria. The Catholic League and the Protestant Union had been formed— the latter to maintain the principles of the Protestants, the former to promote the designs of the Roman Catholic party in Germany. The head of the first was Maximilian of Bavaria; the leader of the latter was Christian of Anhalt. The Emperor Matthias, in an evil hour for the peace of Germany, abdicated the crown of Hungary and Bohemia in favour of his cousin Ferdinand. The latter was remarkable for the zeal with which he had laboured for the propagation of Romanism in his hereditary dominions of Styria and Carinthia. He had no sooner

17

taken possession of his new territories than, in direct violation of the oath taken on his election, he advanced Roman Catholics to the vacant offices at his disposal, and endeavoured to limit the freedom of Protestant worship in Bohemia. Affairs were in this situation when Count Thorn endeavoured to stay the approaching subjugation of his country. He entered the Senate and pronounced a distinct and emphatic condemnation on the arbitrary proceedings of Ferdinand. Inflamed by his spirited harangue, the assembled members proceeded to an unjustifiable act of violence. They hurled out of the window in March, 1618, two members of the Council who had made themselves obnoxious by their persecution of the Protestants. This act led to the Thirty Years' War.

At this juncture Ferdinand, by the death of Matthias, obtained, in 1619, the imperial dignity. He was chosen by the aid of the Elector of Saxony. He and the other Protestant Electors might have prevented a choice which would arm him with additional power in dealing with the affairs of Germany ; but they distrusted one another, and were therefore unable to oppose it. Fully expecting that he would inflict vengeance upon them, they raised the standard of revolt and prepared for their defence. Finding that they could not defend themselves, they offered to Frederick, the Elector Palatine, the crown of Bohemia.

Dazzled by the splendour of the prize, and urged by his wife, the daughter of James I. of England, he was induced to accept it. They hoped that his father-in-law and the other members of the Protestant Union would come to his assistance. But James, who was intriguing for the marriage of his son with the Infanta of Spain, was unwilling to offend her kinsman, the Emperor, by allying himself with his enemies. The other members of the Protestant Union were deterred by the Calvinism of

Frederick from joining him. The Protestants were, in consequence of their dissensions arising from this cause, unfitted to cope with their opponents, who were closely united, and were full of zeal and energy. To those divisions, and the lukewarmness of Protestant Europe, we may attribute the long duration of the Thirty Years' War. The inhabitants of Bohemia were not hearty in supporting him, because he had made himself unpopular by his personal demeanour and his Calvinistic proceedings. The result was that in a battle in front of Prague on November 18, 1620, he was defeated by the forces of the Emperor, and was driven into exile not only from his own dominions, but also from his paternal inheritance.

But Frederick still found friends who exerted every effort to wrest the Palatinate from his foes. These were Count Mansfield and Christian of Brunswick. The latter engaged in the cause of Frederick partly from the love of enterprise, and partly because he was smitten with a romantic passion for the Queen of Bohemia, whom, like a true knight, he vowed that he would reinstate in her dignity. Christian of Denmark aided them in this war. In all probability, if they had been opposed by an inferior general, their efforts would have been successful. But they were called upon to contend with Barclay Tilly, one of the most distinguished generals of the age. The result was that the Palatinate was soon cleared of the armies of Christian and Mansfield.

The Emperor Ferdinand, now finding that all opposition had vanished, called a Diet at Ratisbon, the object of which was to render legal the ban of the empire, which, in a most arbitrary manner, he had himself pronounced against Frederick. His power so overpowered the other members of the Diet that a sentence was passed in accordance with his wishes. The Palatinate was bestowed on the Duke of Bavaria.

These arbitrary proceedings opened the eyes of the

17—2

world to the rapid strides with which Frederick was
advancing towards the assumption of an authority incompatible with the independence of Germany, and prejudicial to the best interests of the nations of Europe.
Accordingly, we find that a confederacy, of which the
leading members were the Dukes of Brunswick and
Mecklenburg, was formed against him. Christian of Denmark was selected as the commander of their army. But
his defeat on the plain of Lutter by the army of Tilly
showed that he had undertaken a task to which he was
unequal. He might have been successful if Charles of
England, who, like James I., was anxious for the restoration of Frederick, had aided him with money. The
English Government was largely responsible for this
defeat. He had also to contend with the celebrated
Bohemian Baron, Albert de Wallenstein, who now
came prominently forward with an army levied and
equipped at his own expense. The latter, having defeated
Mansfield, pursued the retreating monarch, and, having
been victorious in several encounters, compelled him to
embark with such precipitation that he left behind him
half his army, which was compelled to surrender.

The ambition of the Emperor might well be gratified
by the dissolution of the formidable confederacy against
him. The Elector Palatine was an exile from the land of
his fathers. The Protestant Union was humbled in the
dust. Not a single member of the League formed against
him remained to arrest the progress of his arms. If we
turn to foreign countries, we shall find that they were incapable of interfering to avert the fate with which Germany seemed to be threatened. France, still suffering
from that civil warfare which had raged for some time
between Huguenots and Roman Catholics, had not
been able to develop her resources, and could not offer
to the Germans effectual assistance. England was unable to co-operate with them because she was now in-

volved in those dissensions which ended in the Civil War and the death of her Sovereign. Ferdinand, therefore, finding that none of his adversaries could make head against him, proceeded to carry into effect a plan which he had formed for the annihilation of Protestantism in Germany. He was assisted in this war by Philip IV. of Spain, who, urged on by his Minister Olivarez, made the elevation of the House of Austria his principal aim, and exerted extraordinary efforts, on the termination of the twelve years' truce in 1621, to recover the United Provinces, which were, however, unsuccessful.

Ferdinand had been a zealot from his earliest youth. On his knees before the shrine of the Virgin at Loretto, he had sworn to exterminate Protestantism. So great was his fanaticism that he looked upon a victory gained in one part of his dominions as a reward for persecutions carried on in another. The common opinion in Europe was that not only the German Empire, but also Sweden and Denmark, would be brought, as he expressed his own idea of the last political constitution, under 'one King, one law, one God.' In fact, his design was to aim a fatal blow not only at the religion, but also at the liberties of Germany.

At length Ferdinand, deeming that he might safely do so, proceeded to the execution of his designs. He was in those designs the tool of the Jesuits. He first commanded all Protestants to withdraw from the Austrian territories. By 1628 Protestantism existed as a proscribed religion not only in Bohemia and Austria, but also in the Palatinate. In Southern Germany the inhabitants were compelled to attend Mass, and the churches which had been in the occupation of the Protestants for half a century were delivered to the Roman Catholic clergy. Then Ferdinand issued the famous Edict of Restitution, by which the Protestants were required to surrender all the ecclesiastical property of which they had become possessed since the date of the Treaty of Augsburg into the hands of the Commissioners appointed by Ferdinand, to be by them restored to the Roman Catholic Church. This arbitrary proceeding convinced all—both Protestants and Roman Catholics—that Ferdinand was seeking to destroy the independence of Germany. Even the Duke of Bavaria, the head of the Roman Catholic League, remonstrated with him on the impolicy of these proceedings. Wallenstein was furious. Ferdinand had prevented the execution of his designs. The unity under the Hapsburg monarch was further off than ever. From that time Wallenstein hated worse than before the Jesuits, whom he rightly regarded as the authors of this unconstitutional Act. The people of Germany, groaning beneath the exactions of Wallenstein's troops, cried aloud to Gustavus Adolphus, the heroic King of Sweden, to hasten to their assistance. He was the only person in Europe who was able to strike off the chains with which Ferdinand had bound them. He was unable at first to assist them because he was engaged in a war with his Roman Catholic relation, Sigismund, King of Poland. The object of the latter was to recover his kingdom, of which he had been, as we have seen, deprived, and to restore Romanism in Sweden. At length a peace was concluded, one of the articles of which was that Sigismund should renounce his title to the crown. Gustavus was now to be transferred to a sphere where he was to gain distinction as a benefactor, as the mighty conqueror who by the strength of his right arm broke in pieces the yoke of the oppressor.

Now, some have represented him as not influenced by disinterested motives in undertaking this enterprise, and as having an intense longing for military glory. This opinion is not correct. He thought that, if the Emperor extended his authority to the Baltic, the national independence of Sweden might be in danger. The defence of

Protestantism, and not the desire of glory, was his paramount motive. His conduct and his recorded utter-ances show that he was under the influence of Christian feelings, and that he had conquered the love of fame, called by Milton ' the last infirmity of noble minds.' Just before his last battle he knelt down and offered up this prayer : 'O Lord Jesus Christ, bless our arms and this day's battle for the glory of Thy Holy Name !' That he strove to be in private what he was in public appears from the following story which is told of him, that on one occa-sion, when he did not expect that anyone would intrude on his privacy, he was found by one of his counsellors busily engaged in reading the Scriptures. He at once observed to him : ' Steinberg, the greatest consolation I receive is from the study of God's Word ; and, believe me, those placed in exalted stations are of all men the most exposed to the attacks of the enemy of the souls of mankind.'

We have here casually disclosed to us his inner life. To the Senate of Nuremberg he said : ' Your own preser-vation has been effected in a manner little less than miraculous, and in the choice which the Almighty has made of me to accomplish it I see a no less striking evidence of the power of His arm.' This freedom from the love of praise is the more remarkable when we hear that he has been placed among the most distinguished generals of all times. The eight best generals whom the world has ever seen were, according to Napoleon, Alexander, Hannibal, Julius Cæsar, Gustavus Adolphus, Turenne, Prince Eugene, Frederic II., and Napoleon. In this renunciation of self, he stands in remarkable con-trast with those generals who have 'sought the bubble reputation at the cannon's mouth.' Thus, Alexander the Great wept because there were no more worlds to conquer. Napoleon used every effort to erect to himself a pyramid of glory designed to reach to the clouds. But Gustavus Adolphus was influenced throughout his career by prin-

ciples and feelings of a totally opposite character. To
use the words of Alison, the eloquent historian of modern
Europe, applied to the Duke of Wellington: 'He was a
warrior, but he was so only to become a pacificator; he
has shed the blood of men, but it was only to stay the
shedding of human blood; he has borne aloft the sword
of conquest, but it was only to plant in its stead the
emblems of mercy; he has conquered the love of glory
by the love of peace, the first grace of the Christian
character.' He was, in fact, a warrior not from choice,
but from necessity. His achievements were designed for
the preservation of the Protestant institutions of Sweden
from the Imperialists, who had gradually advanced until
they established themselves in the Hanse towns on the
Baltic; for the deliverance of Germany from Papal and
imperial domination; for the safety and independence
of his own country, of Europe, of the whole civilized
world.

The wonder is, when we consider the formidable difficulties which Gustavus was called on to encounter, that
he should have had the least expectation of bringing the
war to a successful issue. In fact, he could not have
engaged in it if Philip had been successful in England.
He would have employed the additional resources which
he had gained in aiding the League in France to beat
down Henry of Navarre. Thus France, instead of being
against Spain, would have been with her and the Jesuits
during the Thirty Years' War. We see the full signifi-
cance of this statement when we remember that France
could at this time bring into the field the enormous
number of 132,000 men. This army, combined with the
100,000 veterans under Tilly and Wallenstein, the greatest
captains of the age, and the numerous and well-disciplined
forces of Spain, would have constituted a body of men
to which the Bohemians would have shrunk from bidding
defiance. Thus, as we have said, we might never have

seen the beginning of this war. At all events, Gustavus would never with 15,000 men have thrown himself into the heart of Germany. His own army was a handful when compared with the 100,000 veteran soldiers under Tilly and Wallenstein, the greatest generals of the age, whom Ferdinand could bring into the field. Sweden was a thinly-peopled and small country. The conscription would soon exhaust the flower of the population. The expenses of the war would be so great that the scanty revenues of Sweden would be scarcely equal to the payment of them. But he had also great encouragements to enter on the war. He was beloved by his soldiers. In obedience to his command they would willingly fling themselves into the deadly breach, or cheerfully plunge into the heat of the battle. The Protestants, alienated from Ferdinand by his arbitrary proceedings, were quite ready to cast off their allegiance to him, and to range themselves beneath the banner of Gustavus. Wallenstein had made himself very unpopular by his arrogance and by the excesses of his soldiers. For these reasons the Princes and Electors made his dismissal from the command of the army an indispensable condition of the assistance which they offered in driving the invader out of the country.

But Gustavus derived most assistance from a treaty concluded in 1631 with France. Richelieu, the celebrated Minister of that country, was jealous of the predominance which the House of Austria was likely to gain through Europe. He therefore undertook that France should give Gustavus an annual subsidy of 1,000,000 livres. Without this treaty he would have soon found that he had been rash in undertaking this enterprise, and that the right arm of his strength was paralyzed at the very time when he was raising it to strike a blow for the deliverance of Germany. Richelieu could not have thought of negotiating this treaty with a heretic if the

Pope, Urban VIII., who was elected in 1623, had expressed
his disapprobation of his object. Formerly he had been
obliged to dissolve the combination which he had formed
against the House of Austria because the Pope was
opposed to him. But now the latter continually urged
him to prosecute his designs against the Emperor.
Herein he differed greatly from his predecessor, Paul V.,
who, baffled, as we have seen, in his warfare with Venice,
sought to revenge himself for his defeat by assisting
Ferdinand in his designs for the extirpation of Protestantism in his dominions. Though Urban was most
zealous for the propagation of Romanism, yet he was still
more anxious to maintain the balance of power in Europe,
and to defeat the ambitious designs of the Emperor
Ferdinand. When Cardinal Borgia complained of the
desertion of the House of Austria by the Pope, he
answered : ' I know very well that the violence of the
modern Goths offends neither against consciences nor
altars, that the conquered are left free to exercise their
religion, the churches in possession of their ornaments,
the ecclesiastics of their benefices, the colleges and con-
vents of their property.' The truth was, that both the
Pope and Richelieu thought that they were saved from
the scandal of having given, the one an indirect, the other
a direct, sanction to the prosecution of the war by the
insertion of a clause in the treaty between France and
Gustavus that the Roman Catholics should not be
molested in the exercise of their religion throughout the
empire. Richelieu would rather have attacked Spain
and Austria through the instrumentality of the League
than through the instrumentality of Gustavus and the
Protestants; but he saw that the future was with Gustavus,
and not with the League. He sacrificed his wishes to his
policy. He coquetted with the League, but he supported
Gustavus. This alliance, however, is a very plain proof
that the former state of things was passing away; that

the religious wars between Protestantism and Romanism would soon exist only in the memory of days gone by ; that the time was coming when neither party would disturb the other in the occupation of the territories which they had gained during the warfare, and that hence-forth the nations of Europe would form new combinations, dictated not by religious considerations, but by the desire of preventing any one people from gaining an ascendancy injurious to the balance of power which ought to exist between the nations constituting the great European commonwealth.

But the support given to Gustavus in Germany was not as yet equal to his expectations. It was in vain to hope that he would be successful until the Elector of Saxony and the Elector of Brandenburg had joined him. He had hoped that his rapid conquest of Pomerania and his capture of Frankfort-on-the-Oder would have induced them to come to his support. But he found an obstacle in their intense selfishness. They alleged that, after they had declared themselves, Gustavus might return to his country, and might leave them to bear the full weight of the Emperor's indignation. He longed to hasten to the relief of Magdeburg, at that time besieged by Tilly, which had raised the standard of independence immediately after he had landed in Pomerania. But without the support of the two Electors he could not venture to go to the assistance of the inhabitants. He demanded from the Elector of Brandenburg the surrender of the fortresses of Küstrin and Spandau in his rear, that he might occupy them with his forces ; for he knew that, if they were seized by the forces of the Emperor, now on their march to Italy, he should be exposed to certain destruction. Overcome by his importunity, the Elector placed Spandau in his hands ; but to his astonishment and indignation a request to the Elector of Saxony that he would allow him to occupy the town and bridge of Wittenberg till he had

effected the relief of Magdeburg was met with an unqualified refusal.   The best commentary on the conduct
of the Elector is to be found in the cry of anguish and
despair which only a few days afterwards was heard from
the city of Magdeburg, where deeds of cruelty were perpetrated from the contemplation of which the mind recoils
with horror ; where the soldiers bathed their swords in
the blood of unoffending women and helpless children ;
where a conflagration, reddening the Elbe with its glare,
continued to rage till it had destroyed 6,000 houses;
where headless forms and mutilated trunks told a tale of
unheard-of barbarities.

Gustavus was now in great danger.   The friends of the
Protestant cause trembled when they saw Tilly, the hero of
a hundred battles, advancing against one who seemed its
only remaining champion.   Wallenstein, through jealousy,
had been dismissed from his command.   Having only
half the number of the forces of Tilly, Gustavus abided his
attack in an entrenched camp near the confluence of the
Elbe, which he fortified with great judgment.   Tilly
attempted in vain by a furious cannonade, which was
returned with murderous precision, to batter down the
ramparts.   He was obliged to retire from the siege like
the lion who, longing to slake his thirst in the blood of the
flock, is prevented by the vigilance of its faithful guardian
from accomplishing his object.   This success induced the
Landgrave of Hesse Cassel to join Gustavus with all his
forces.   The Elector of Saxony at last, irritated against the
Emperor, sent a message of defiance to Tilly, and effected
a junction with the army of Gustavus.   Tilly, having
invaded Saxony and compelled Leipsic to surrender,
hastened to meet him.   Now he should conquer the foe
who had so often baffled him.

The celebrated battle which we are now about to
describe was fought in the immediate neighbourhood of
Leipsic.   Gustavus, fearing that, as the Saxons were new

levies, they might not withstand the charge of the veteran troops in the imperial army, placed them on the left wing in such a position that, if they were routed, they might not spread disorder among the Swedish battalions. Tilly then made an impetuous charge upon the Saxons. The latter were immediately scattered, and never halted until they were many miles from the field of battle. Meanwhile the imperial cuirassiers advanced against the Swedish cavalry on the right wing, commanded by Gustavus, hoping by the impetuosity of their charge to complete their discomfiture. But the galling fire of the musketeers whom Gustavus had posted among the cavalry aided the well-disciplined valour of the latter, who fell upon the cuirassiers as soon as the musketeers had checked them in their charge, and, having several times beaten them back, drove them in tumult and disarray from the battle-field.

While this conflict was taking place, Gustavus observed the rout of the Saxons. His army was thus reduced to half its original number, but he did not give way to despondency. He hastened at once to Horn, who commanded in the centre, and directed him to throw back the regiments under his command so as to form a front to meet the Germans on their return from the pursuit of the fugitive Saxons. Tilly, on his return, hurled his columns against the Swedes. But they stood firm like the rock amid the boiling surges. But now the King, having finally driven his foes from the field of battle, advanced to the crest of the hill where Tilly had originally drawn up his army, and, seizing his artillery placed upon it, directed it with deadly aim against the Imperialists. Meanwhile he directed some parties of Swedish musketeers to move round the masses, and to pour in from three sides a deadly fire upon them. They were at the same time charged in the rear by the Saxon cavalry, which alone stood firm when their brethren in arms had fled from the field of battle. Still, amid these disadvantages the battalions maintained their high reputation, and fought with desperate valour. The stillness of a lovely autumnal evening was broken by the groans of the dying, the roar of the artillery, and the shouts of the combatants, as they fought, hand to hand, in the ranks of war. The landscape, sleeping in soft repose at a short distance from the field of battle, resembled the smoothness of the torrent before it dashes into the boiling caldron at the foot of the precipice. Sword, lance, and armour were flashing in the farewell beams of the sun as he was descending in his glory. As soon as the shades of night gathered around them, the greater number of the Imperialists, throwing down their arms, fled under cover of the darkness from the field of battle. A scanty band, shorn of its pomp and glory, was all that remained next morning of the magnificent array which, burning with high hope, had threatened destruction to the Swedish army.

This battle may be regarded as one of the most important in the world's history. Gustavus by this victory saved Protestantism from destruction, and secured the independence of Germany as well as of neighbouring countries. The Swedish hero was now at liberty to choose the direction in which he would turn his arms, and to march to almost certain victory. He might, if he chose, pursue his course without interruption to the walls of Vienna. The moral results of the victory, too, were most important. Henceforth men began to look upon Gustavus as a being of a superior order, as the first general of his age, and as quite equal to the task which he had undertaken of breaking in pieces the yoke of the oppressor.

Gustavus afterwards continued his career of victory. Half of Germany had, since he landed, acknowledged his authority. He now commenced his last campaign. He carried the war into Bavaria, and, having secured the command of two important passes over the Danube, laid waste the country between that river and the river Lech. Tilly had lined with his troops the right bank of the Lech for a distance of sixteen miles. Gustavus gained a victory at this river which may be justly regarded as shedding more glory on his arms than any previous victory. To have constructed a bridge across a rapid river in the face of a furious cannonade, to have beaten back after he had landed, and to have gained a victory over, a foe firmly entrenched in a commanding position, may be justly regarded as an achievement without parallel in the history of the world. This victory spread consternation among the Austrian and Roman Catholic factions in Germany. Nothing seemed impossible to a general who had gained a victory in spite of obstacles which others would have deemed insurmountable. No fortified place nor army now remained between Gustavus and Vienna. The French Ambassador, on asking him how far he intended to carry his arms, was told that he should do so as far as his interests required.

In this situation the eyes of all turned to Wallenstein as the only general capable of retrieving the fortunes of his country. Tilly had been mortally wounded at the Battle of Lech. Sixty thousand men influenced by the desire of serving under a general profuse in his liberality soon flocked to his standard. Now, as he would have to contend with an army four times as numerous as his own, the general opinion was that Gustavus was exposed to certain destruction. Troops, however, summoned from various quarters, whose movements Gustavus guided with great skill, so that they fell in with another army at Metz, like a river swelled in its progress by tributary streams, advanced towards the camp of Gustavus and effected a junction with him. Wallenstein saw in their union a disappointment of his long-cherished expectations. Gustavus, having attempted with a terrible carnage to storm the camp of Wallenstein, defiled his army before him, offering him battle. Finding, however, that Wallenstein still declined an engagement, he withdrew, having brought back his army in safety from an enterprise which, it was confidently predicted, would lead to its destruction. Wallenstein followed his example. The storm-clouds proceeded in different directions, discharging the bolts of death on other regions in their desolating progress.

But the day of battle, big with the fate of Protestantism in Germany, at length arrived. Wallenstein determined to take vengeance on the Elector of Saxony for his defection from the cause of the Emperor by laying waste his country. Gustavus at once advanced by forced marches to his assistance. Wallenstein, hearing that Gustavus was approaching, withdrew to the plain of Lützen, where he determined to abide the attack of his great enemy. This celebrated battle was fought on November 6, 1632, two years and four months after Gustavus entered Germany. The latter, when he arrived late in the day in front of Wallenstein's camp, found that a thick mist covered the country, and during its continuance it was utterly in vain to attack the enemy. He therefore postponed the attack till the morning. While he was waiting anxiously for the time when he could give the signal for battle, he ordered Luther's paraphrase of the forty-sixth Psalm to be read, and a hymn to be sung at the head of the regiments. The mist then suddenly rolled away. Immediately the sun poured a flood of light over the plain, and disclosed to the view the two armies arranged in battle-array, eager to begin the conflict. Gustavus then rode along in front of the regiments, and addressed a few spirit-stirring words to the soldiers. His voice passed along the ranks like the blast of the clarion, breathing heroic fire and strength.

They burn to plunge amid the battle-tide and to do deeds of high emprise in the service of their heroic leader.

Gustavus then, waving his sword, placed himself at their head, and led them against the enemy. The Swedes rushed on with impetuous valour, carried the trenches at the first charge, and gained possession of the enemy's guns. They were, however, beaten back, and compelled to repass the trenches, leaving the ground in front of them covered with the dead and the dying. Gustavus, after the first charge, observing a regiment of black troopers under the command of Colonel Piccolomini, said to the Colonel of his Finland cavalry that he must disperse them, or they would do to his army serious if not irreparable injury. Immediately he set spurs to his horse, which cleared the ditch at a bound; but it soon appeared that, partly on account of the rapidity of the advance and partly on account of the difficulty experienced in crossing the trench, he was supported by very few of his own men. He was at once singled out by a marksman in the imperial army, who fired a shot which broke his left arm. Immediately, as he suffered greatly from the pain inflicted by the wound, he directed one of his officers to lead him from the battle. Losing their way in the mist which soon involved all surrounding objects in deep obscurity, they suddenly encountered a body of imperial cuirassiers, one of whom, recognising him, shot him through the body. He fell on the bodies of his men who were lying slain around him. A party of imperial cavalry soon passed near the spot, one of whom, seeing him still alive, asked who he was. The answer immediately given was, ' I am the King of Sweden, and thus I seal with my blood the religion and liberties of Germany.' Immediately a pistol-shot through the head and a sword-thrust through the body released him from his agonies.

18

The sight of his steed running without a rider through the field of battle soon caused all to be aware of the death of their heroic leader.   The Duke of Saxe-Weimar at once led them on, burning with the desire of avenging his fall, to another attack on the entrenchments of the enemy.   They were again successful; but just at this moment victory was again, for the present, snatched from them by the arrival of Pappenheim with a large body of cavalry on the field of battle.   Immediately wheeling them into line, he charged the Swedish infantry, and drove them back from their entrenchments on the main body.   Pappenheim directly afterwards hurried to the right wing in search of his former antagonist.   When he had arrived he was informed of his death.   He had scarcely expressed his joy at the intelligence, when he was himself mortally wounded.   His death was a serious loss to the Imperialists.

Meanwhile the Duke of Saxe-Weimar again formed his men, and led them over the trenches; at the same time the whole left wing advanced to the charge.   They were supported by a well-directed fire of musketry and artillery. The result was that the Imperialists were driven in confusion from the field of battle.   The highroad was soon covered with ammunition-waggons, artillery, and soldiers, all hurrying from the scene of action.

The death of Gustavus cast a gloom over Germany and Europe.   Even his enemies mourned his untimely death.   His subjects, and all those who looked to him to deliver them from the power of the oppressor, were overwhelmed with sorrow.   The glory of Sweden, the prosperity of the Protestant cause, seemed buried in the grave of the hero.   But it was soon found that the work had been so well done that his early death could not interrupt it.   The Edict of Restitution was dead, and Protestant administrators were ruling in the northern bishoprics.   The empire was dead also.

Two-thirds of Germany were now in the occupation of the allies. Gustavus had left seven armies in the field; but, above all, other generals, trained in the school and animated by the spirit of Gustavus, were determined to fight the battle of Protestantism, and to secure for the Germans their civil and religious liberty. Assisted vigorously by the French, the Swedes generally came off victorious during the sixteen remaining years of the Thirty Years' War, which was terminated in 1648 by the celebrated Peace of Westphalia.

This treaty was a very remarkable event in the world's history. It increased the political disunion of Germany, for the Princes gained by it the formal recognition of their territorial independence ; but it established the freedom and security of Protestantism in that country, and drew a final line of demarcation between the two religions which divided Europe. The Roman Catholics also were compelled by it to renounce their gigantic schemes of Counter-Reformation. The struggle between the Church of Rome and the Reformation, which had now lasted for ninety years, which had been the mainspring of so many political combinations, had caused so many nations to heave and swell like the waves of the stormy ocean, had shaken to their foundation the mightiest monarchies, had led to the perpetration of crimes from the contemplation of which we recoil with horror, so far as it consisted in the mustering of armies for the battle, or aroused the savage passions of those who delighted in war, now existed only in the memory of days gone by. The Princes of Europe were no longer arrayed against one another as Roman Catholic and Protestant. They engaged in war from the lust of conquest or to preserve the balance of power in Europe. The prolonged agony of the Thirty Years' War had altogether extinguished the burning passion for proselytism. The Papacy had indeed been to some extent successful in this warfare. The tide of Protestantism had receded.   Rome had recovered her supremacy in France, and had imposed her yoke on the Southern Netherlands, Poland, Austria, Bohemia, Bavaria, and Transylvania, in which in the middle of the sixteenth century Protestantism was, with some probability of success, struggling for the mastery.   But the latter still reigned supreme in the North of Germany, England, Scotland, the Northern Netherlands, Sweden, Denmark, and Norway.   The Treaty of Westphalia has been anathematized by Innocent X., who succeeded Urban VIII. in 1644, and by his successors, because it prevented them from extending the power of their see, for it established a boundary-line between the Roman Catholic and the Reformed Churches which exists, nearly unchanged, in the age in which we live.   Rome was, in fact, obliged to abandon that dream of universal empire which might have become a reality if Gustavus Adolphus had not flung himself into the battle between the two Churches, and arrested by his victories the progress of a fanatical oppressor.

INDEX.

THE END.

Elliot Stock, Paternoster Row, London

www.ingramcontent.com/pod-product-compliance
Lightning Source LLC
Chambersburg PA
CBHW020847020726
47497CB00005B/1291